|||||| ||||||||||||||||||||||||||||||||||||||||||||||||||||
◁ **W9-BRH-009**

*All he could do was stay numb to the
terrible task of dispatching the dead . . .*

There is war coming, Dain thought as he dragged another body into position. *A terrible, costly war.* For the
first time, he understood the importance of politics, the
arrangement of treaties and the preservation of alliances.
Gant was absorbing Nether, the great and once-powerful
ally of Mandria. When it finished feeding on that kingdom, then it would turn its jaws on Klad or Nold or even
Mandria—not to nibble with these increasingly bold raids,
but to devour.

Tipping his head to the cold stars above, Dain prayed,
*Let us be strong enough to defeat them, O Thod. Give
each of us the strength of ten men. Empower our swords
against the darkness. Let us drive them back.*

Ace Books by Deborah Chester

THE SWORD
THE RING
REIGN OF SHADOWS
SHADOW WAR

Lucasfilm's Alien Chronicles™

THE GOLDEN ONE
THE CRIMSON CLAW
THE CRYSTAL EYE

The Sword, the Ring, and the Chalice

―――BOOK 2―――
THE RING

DEBORAH CHESTER

ACE BOOKS, NEW YORK

If you purchased this book without a cover, you should be aware that this book is stolen property. It was reported as "unsold and destroyed" to the publisher and neither the author nor the publisher has received any payment for this "stripped book."

This is a work of fiction. Names, characters, places, and incidents are either the product of the author's imagination or are used fictitiously, and any resemblance to actual persons, living or dead, business establishments, events, or locales is entirely coincidental.

THE RING

An Ace Book / published by arrangement with
the author

PRINTING HISTORY
Ace mass-market edition / August 2000

All rights reserved.
Copyright © 2000 by Deborah Chester.
Cover art by Jean Pierre Targete.

This book may not be reproduced in whole or in part,
by mimeograph or any other means, without permission.
For information address: The Berkley Publishing Group,
a division of Penguin Putnam Inc.,
375 Hudson Street, New York, New York 10014.

The Penguin Putnam Inc. World Wide Web site address is
http://www.penguinputnam.com

Check out the ACE Science Fiction & Fantasy newsletter
and much more on the Internet at Club PPI!

ISBN: 0-441-00757-0

ACE®
Ace Books are published
by The Berkley Publishing Group,
a division of Penguin Putnam Inc.,
375 Hudson Street, New York, New York 10014.
ACE and the "A" design are trademarks
belonging to Penguin Putnam Inc.

PRINTED IN THE UNITED STATES OF AMERICA

10 9 8 7 6 5 4 3 2 1

THE RING

PART ONE

1

THE CHAPEL AT Thirst Hold smelled of incense, dust, and candle wax. Kneeling beside Lord Odfrey and listening to the slow intonations of mass, Dain kept his head bowed respectfully, despite his impatience. Someone was snoring faintly in counterpoint to the priest's voice. Dain grinned a little to himself, and from the corner of his eye watched the dust motes dancing in the sunlight that streamed down through the oculus window overhead.

Although sunlight fell on the altar, transforming the cloth into dazzling whiteness and glinting off the plain silver and brass accoutrements, the rest of the small chapel lay in gloom. Tricks of light and shadow played along the religious paintings on the walls, making the elongated, large-eyed faces of the saints appear to be alive and watching the worshipers.

The twelve knights of Thirst selected to compete in the king's tourney knelt today in a group directly behind Lord Odfrey and Dain. No doubt each man was praying that he would be the one to win the tourney and come home covered in glory. Eight and forty additional Thirst knights crowded behind them, with the squires of all jammed into the back of the chapel.

Church soldiers filled the rest of the space, overflowing the benches and crowding into the central aisle. Cloaked and spurred, jammed elbow to elbow, these strangers had not hesitated to wear their weapons to chapel. Kneeling with creaks of their chain mail, their war helmets planted on the floor in front of each man, they listened attentively to the nervous priest's stumbling service.

Dain shifted his head slightly to glance at them. He had never seen church soldiers before, and he found them a strange breed, with their white surcoats displaying a large black circle on the front and back. Their fierce, weather-burned faces looked more impatient than tranquil, and when a response was called for, their voices roared out the words in loud unison.

They had arrived last night in the midst of the banquet feast. Their leader, a hawkish, tawny-haired man named the Reverend Sir Damiend, presented Lord Odfrey with a warrant signed by Cardinal Noncire ordering Sir Damiend and his men to assist Lord Odfrey in escorting Prince Gavril safely home. The implication, both in the wording of the warrant and in the contempt in Sir Damiend's stony green eyes, was that Lord Odfrey had erred greatly a few weeks past in letting the prince be almost killed, and was no longer trusted to protect his highness.

Furious on his adoptive father's behalf, Dain wished that Lord Odfrey would release Gavril to the church soldiers and wash his hands entirely of the spoiled prince.

Ah, but Lord Odfrey would do his duty with gritted teeth, no matter how difficult he found it. "I've received nothing from the king to confirm Cardinal Noncire's warrant," he had said privately to Dain last night. Of late they'd developed the habit of meeting in the chevard's wardroom every evening for a few minutes' chat before Lord Odfrey retired. Dain valued those talks; some days they were the only time he even got to speak to Lord Odfrey. But last night, the chevard had been sorely troubled and irritable. Pacing about his cluttered room, with its stacks of clothes, armor, bedrolls, and spare boots, Lord Odfrey had said, "What if this is some church-planned coup and they mean to kidnap the prince? Do you think my head would be safe from the king's sword were I to hand off Gavril to these men? Nay, I'll see him to the very foot of his father's throne before I call this duty done."

Sighing to himself now in the chapel, Dain wished the church *would* abscond with Gavril and take him to some far-off citadel to make a monk of him.

"Your highness will come forward," the priest said.

The prince, resplendent in a doublet of vivid blue silk, went up to kneel at the altar for his special benediction. The sunlight glowed on his golden head. With his eyes closed in prayer, and his handsome young face radiating piety, Gavril looked kind and good.

Dain shifted his gaze away. In reality, Gavril was fanatical, bigoted, and cruel. Less than an hour ago, he had been protesting Dain's presence at mass, saying it was an affront for a pagan to attend.

Impatient, eager to start on their journey, and tired of kneeling on this hard stone floor, Dain shifted slightly and received a quick jab from Lord Odfrey's elbow. Glancing up, Dain caught the chevard's censorious frown.

Heat rose into Dain's face. He bowed his head quickly, resolved not to wiggle again. But Gavril's prayer was going on far too long, undoubtedly meant to impress the church soldiers with its sheer length and content. It was good to pray and seek blessing for their journey, but they did not have to spend all day in here. Dain doubted that almighty Thod or any of the lesser gods cared how long a man could pray, once the offerings had been made. Thod saw the hearts of men. What more was needed once the worship rituals were finished? Impatience grew inside Dain, becoming a worm that consumed his entrails. He wanted to go, go, go!

Outside in the keep, final preparations for the journey were being made. It was a radiant late-summer morning, with a sky like a pale blue pearl and the air fragrant with freshly scythed hay. Furling and unfurling in the light breeze, the banners were bright with new dye.

Inside the chapel, however, the air hung stale and thick. A trickle of sweat beaded on Dain's temple. Just as he opened his mouth to draw in a deeper breath, everyone around him stood up and began to chant a prayer. Startled, Dain mouthed the words, muffling his voice among the others, because he did not know the prayer. He'd been through a hasty series of lessons, now that he was no longer to be a pagan, but little of it had stuck. With all his heart, he hoped Lord Odfrey would not suspect how little he'd learned thus far.

Suddenly the mass ended. At the rear of the chapel, someone thrust open the door, and light streamed inside. The squires, Dain's friend Thum among them, burst outdoors to freedom and yelled in excitement. Grinning, Dain longed to go running outside with them, but his new status required him to remain at Lord Odfrey's heels.

He did not mind. After all, he was still getting used to the staggering idea of being the chevard's son, and someone important. The servants who used to kick him now had to bow when he walked by. He was no longer an orphan, an eld pagan from the Dark Forest, with neither home nor family. Now he wore fine clothes, and had servants of his own, and was permitted to sit at Lord Odfrey's feet among his dogs at evening gatherings. He was even called "lord" now by the servants, and it made him feel odd inside sometimes, as though he had lost himself, his real self, and knew no longer where to find him.

"Lord Odfrey, about that route through Ebel Forest," said Sir Damiend. Tucking his helmet beneath his arm, he turned to Lord Odfrey and beckoned imperiously.

The chevard obeyed this summons, and Dain followed, seething on behalf of his father.

Sir Damiend spoke with the rolling cadence of lower Mandria. His close-cropped hair and skin were both the color of wild honey; his eyes were hued an intense stony green. He'd been born a lord, but he'd surrendered his rank when he became a church knight. Still, his aristocratic origins were plain in the haughty expression on his face and the way he conducted himself. "It would be quicker," he said, "to ride straight south to the Charva, then take barges along the river to Nuveron Point, then disembark and ride on from there. Safer, too, I think."

Lord Odfrey's face went tight and expressionless. Dain knew the chevard had spent many hours with his maps and reports, plotting the safest, swiftest route to Savroix. "I disagree, sir," he said, keeping his voice even and courteous. "Here's why."

As they talked, Dain's attention wandered. He saw Gavril already exiting the chapel, with Sir Nynth, his temporary protector, following stolidly at his heels. Dain liked and respected Sir Nynth. He was sorry the man had drawn such disagreeable duty, although for Sir Nynth it was a rise in rank.

Earlier this week, the other two fosters, Kaltienne and Mierre, had departed for their parental homes, leaving Gavril without his usual entourage.

Dain spared the prince no more than a glance, for he and Gavril stayed away from each other as much as possible. A cold little truce existed between them right now, but Dain did not believe it would last. Since the arrival of the church soldiers last night, Gavril had resumed his former arrogance and haughtiness.

Dain was counting the days until they reached Savroix and Gavril passed out of his life forever.

"Dain," Lord Odfrey said, startling him from his thoughts.

"Yes, lord?"

"This will take a moment. See that Sir Bosquecel has everyone organized, will you?"

Dain bowed and strode outside. With every step, his spirits rose, his excitement making his heart hammer inside his chest.

After the gloomy little chapel, the bright sunlit outdoors made him squint. The sun was advancing into the sky, and

it was already hot. They'd lost much precious time dawdling
about in the chapel.

Thirst Hold was a sprawling complex of unadorned stone
buildings constructed in concentric rings. The innermost
courtyard was paved with cobbles and held the chapel, the
walled gardens, and the ancient Hall. Three stories tall and
flanked by wings supporting towers, the Hall contained the
great feasting room plus the living quarters for Lord Odfrey
and the other members of his household. Beyond it stood
the stableyard, including barns and fodder sheds. The guardhouse and barracks, smithy, smokehouse, communal ovens,
and other mundane buildings were located in the outermost
keep.

Dain hurried through the milling chaos of the stableyard.
Grooms were struggling with fretting horses that were tired
of waiting. A saddled war charger lashed out with a hind
foot and sent a stableboy flying through the air.

Panicky chickens clucked and squawked foolishly ahead
of a trio of horses being led by another boy to be watered.

In the outer keep, the confusion grew worse. Loaded supply wagons were being maneuvered into a line. Yoked kine
bawled in confusion and were whipped all the harder by
their sweating, frustrated drivers. Dain blinked in amazement
at how many wagons there were. He and Thum had wandered around them last night, but they seemed to have doubled in number since then. Of course, more than half of
them belonged to Gavril, for the prince brought many luxurious possessions for his year's stay. But besides Gavril's
wagons, all of which were painted with gaudy colors, there
was one for the bedrolls and clothes chests, one for all the
armor and jousting weapons, and one for extra saddles and
tack. Lord Odfrey's crest marked his individual wagon. Dain
saw that Lord Odfrey's manservant Lyias was already
perched there, with his feet propped up on Dain's clothes
chest.

Sulein the physician, his red conical hat exchanged for a
strange, flat square tied atop his head, was trying to per-

suade Lyias to let him put his collection of bags and chests
in the chevard's wagon.

Dain swung away hurriedly before the physician could
see him and threaded his way through the church soldiers,
who were collecting their mounts with quick efficiency.

Across the way, Sir Bosquecel was busy bawling orders
at his men. A groom passed Dain, leading a saddled charger
at a rapid trot. The sixty knights who were going were considered Thirst's best, and although not all would be com-
peting in the tourney, they preened and swaggered equally.
Wearing polished mail that glinted and shone in the hot sunlight, they endured a barrage of heckling from the envious
knights staying home.

Dain delivered Lord Odfrey's message to Sir Bosquecel,
who nodded tersely. Free now to find Thum, Dain grinned
and started to look for his friend, but a muscular arm snaked
out through the chaos and gripped him around the middle.

Hauled backward so fast he nearly lost his footing, Dain
stumbled and managed to twist free. He found himself con-
fronting Lander, the Netheran smith who had gotten him into
major trouble only a few weeks before. Slab-shouldered and
clad in a soot-streaked leather apron, the smith was looking
about nervously with darting, pale eyes. Wisps of his thin
red hair stood on end.

"You!" Dain said angrily. He turned away, but Lander
gripped his arm and held him fast.

"Not so fast, boy," he said. "Come with me."

Dain pulled free and smoothed the wrinkles in his sleeve.
"I have things to do."

"This is important. You were in on the beginning. You'll
see it finished."

"What are you talking about?" Dain asked impatiently.

"The sword, boy. The sword!" Lander glanced about and
raised his finger to his lips. "Come."

"I saw your entry for the sword contest. It's not worth
carting all the way to Savroix. Lord Odfrey accepted it out
of kindness, nothing more."

Lander's pale eyes blinked. "Harsh words you say to me, boy. And after all we've been through together. Harsh words."

Dain recalled the man's boasting of the magnificent sword he would make from magicked metal. Together they'd ventured into the Dark Forest of Nold to buy the steel from a half-crazed dwarf. Lander had sworn that he possessed the skill of a master swordmaker, but he'd produced only that sword of plain steel, utilitarian and well-balanced, but with no artistry other than its simple rosettes at the guard. When Lander had presented it to Lord Odfrey last night as his entry in the contest for the king's new sword, Dain had seen the faint line that creased Lord Odfrey's brow. But the chevard had promised to enter the weapon in the contest.

Dain had felt it was an embarrassment to Thirst Hold and shouldn't be entered. Lord Odfrey had silenced Dain's protests, saying he'd given his word to Lander.

"But it's not worthy!" Dain had said.

"A man's best effort is always worthy," Lord Odfrey had told him. "It is a plain weapon, unsuitable for a king, but the blade is good and serviceable. It will not win, of course, but the smith's reward will come from having his work seen by his majesty."

Dain had not understood that at all, and right now he wished Lander would go away and leave him alone.

"Now, boy, listen close," Lander said, leaning over. "The real sword is for *you* to take, see? Not Lord Odfrey. You."

"What?"

Lander muttered something in Netheran and gripped Dain by the front of his doublet. He hurried Dain over to his smithy, and they stepped inside. Today, the circular hearth held only cold ashes instead of its usual fire. The tools were neatly put away. The shutters that were usually propped wide open on all sides of the small structure remained closed. Lander did not open them now.

Dain frowned. The scents of ash and metal were as familiar to him as the rhythmic ping-ping-ping of a smithy's hammer. He had been raised by Jorb, master armorer among the dwarves. The forge felt like home, and although in the past year Dain had come here for comfort and reminders of a childhood spent among hammers and tools, that part of his life was now closed forever. It was better to stay away and let his memories lie.

While Dain hesitated in the doorway, tempted to escape, Lander started rummaging inside a wooden cupboard.

Dain watched him with a frown. "You mean you actually made the sword you said you would? A magicked one?"

Lander jerked upright and made wild gestures. "Hush! Not so loud. Of course I made it. Every night, after my usual work was done, I worked on it. This blade was forged in darkness, where no one but myself could see it."

"Lander—"

"I told you I could do it, boy, and I have!" Lander laughed gleefully, and he did not sound quite sane. "I have the craft, the art. Now I will prove it to the world. Behold this."

With a flourish, he pulled a long scabbard out of the cupboard and held it up. His pallid face shone with pride and madness.

Dain felt pity for him. Only dwarves could create the kind of legendary weapon Lander wanted to make. The man's ambitions had undone him.

"Look at it, boy!" Lander whispered insistently. "Besides mine, your hand will be the first to draw it."

Dain could not resist that. He stepped closer and saw a magnificent hilt protruding from the end of the plain leather scabbard. The guard was a swirl of ivy, wrought incredibly from the metal. Each leaf was finely detailed, almost lifelike. The hilt itself was wrapped with gold wire. It shone and glittered in the muted light that filtered in through the shutters.

"Draw it!" Lander insisted. "Put your hand on it."

Dain stretched out his hand, and heard the sword hum in response. He hesitated, a little afraid to touch it.

"Does it sing to you?" Lander asked, his pale eyes boring into Dain. "Can you hear its voice?"

Dain could, and he did not like it. He remembered how uncomfortable it had been to ride home with the magicked metal in the cart, how it had hummed and resonated inside him until he thought it might drive him mad. All the great swords had their individual songs. Truthseeker—Lord Odfrey's own ancestral sword, made of god-steel—was a blade that Dain could listen to for all eternity. But there was nothing clear and pure about this sword that Lander had wrought. It sang of darkness and yearning and lust and fury.

Lander pressed closer. "Touch it!" he growled. "Take it, boy. Now!"

Frowning, Dain let his fingers curl around the hilt. The sword came to life with such violence he almost believed light had flashed inside him. Dazed and half-blinded, he pulled out the shining blade. Through him the sword hummed and roared for war.

"Tanengard!" he said aloud, and swung the sword aloft.

It fit his hand perfectly. Power shone off its blade, and he craved this sword with such fierceness he thought he would die if he could not own it.

Lander reached up and plucked the sword from his hand. Dain growled in anger, but quick as thought Lander sheathed the weapon.

Dain blinked and swayed. His head was still buzzing. He felt tired and lost without the sword, yet he knew it was an evil thing, or could be, in the wrong hands. Dain found it a relief to hold it no longer.

Lander wrapped it up in a cloth, chuckling and muttering to himself.

"You have crafted a war sword," Dain said.

"Of course I did, boy!" Lander said proudly. "It's made for a king, and kings must be strong. When Verence puts his hand on my creation, he won't be able to let go. And I will win the contest, and all in the land will know the name of Lander the Smith."

"It's a fearsome weapon," Dain told him.

Lander laughed. "Thank you, boy. Thank you."

"Too fearsome. It's not easy to handle."

"You're a boy," Lander said, brushing off his advice. "The king is a man. He'll handle it."

Dain frowned, hurt by that. He gave up what he was trying to say. Clearly Lander had no intention of listening to him.

"Tanengard," Lander crooned, stroking the weapon through its cloth wrapping. "I wondered what your name was. I cannot hear your song. It took this eld boy to hear what you had to say."

"Is that the only reason you brought me in here?" Dain asked, suddenly angry. "Just to get its name?"

"How else?" Lander replied.

Dain spun on his heel and started for the door. "You treat me like a dancing beyar that does tricks."

"Wait, boy! Wait! You must take this."

Lander hurried after him and thrust the wrapped sword in his arms.

Dain held it awkwardly. "What am I to do with it?"

"Are you daft? I can't give my prize into Lord Odfrey's keeping," Lander said. "One look at it and he would condemn me for sorcery."

"Rightly so," Dain muttered, wondering how Lander had managed to invoke the spells now crawling inside the blade.

Lander scowled at him but went on as though he had not spoken. "You will take it to Savroix for me. At the last minute before the sword contest, you will switch swords. Put Tanengard before the king and keep the plain one for yourself." He beamed. "That's your reward. I haven't forgotten your help, see? And you want a sword of your own, don't you? One made by me will soon be worth a great deal. You will be the envy of your friends."

"But I—"

"Go now. Go! I depend on you."

Dain's uneasiness grew. This whole business seemed dishonest and sneaky. And Tanengard's spell included a lure that would make it next to impossible for the king to choose any other weapon once he'd touched this one. It was not right to enspell a king. Dain had the horrible suspicion that consorting with Lander would get him into terrible trouble again, far worse than the last time.

"I don't want to," he said, trying to hand the sword back to Lander. "Take it to Lord Odfrey. Tell him you gave him the wrong sword by mistake. He doesn't have to see it."

"Are you mad?" Lander asked, staring at him. "Of course he'll see it. And as soon as he does, he'll want it for himself. No, boy. You're to guard it. Only you can resist it and keep it safe."

"You have a high opinion of my resistance," Dain muttered, fearing he, too, might surrender to the madness he now held in his arms.

"You're eld. Of course you can resist."

"It's too strong," Dain said. "I wonder that you can even bring yourself to give it to me."

"You know that as its maker I am immune," Lander said, but his darting eyes and red face gave away his lie.

"A magicked sword is one thing, but there are too many spells in this one. What if you drive the king mad?"

"No true warrior could fail with Tanengard," Lander said. "King Verence has a mighty heart. Yes, it is a brutal sword. But he needs it now to defend us against the darkness. Tell me true, boy: Would you want this sword in any other man's hand save his?"

"No."

"Then it's settled. Good journey to you."

"But—"

From outside came a shout. "Dain!"

There was no more time to protest. Dain was pushed outside the smithy, with Tanengard still in his arms. He glanced around, saw the Thirst knights mounted and the church soldiers climbing into their saddles. The air was bright and clear, the sunlight hot, the shouts and merriment loud. Out here, Tanengard did not seem as dark and strong as it had before. Dain realized that sometimes swords of this kind

mirrored the souls of their makers. It could be some darkness inside Lander that was tainting this weapon, Dain mused;
perhaps separation and distance would diminish that link,
making it eventually fade. Dain hoped so, for it seemed that
he was now committed to getting the sword into the hands
of the king, come what may.

"Dain!" Sir Terent shouted, riding by on his horse. "Quit
dawdling, if you intend to go. Lord Odfrey has been asking for you."

Dain gulped, realizing he was about to be left behind.
Tucking the sword under his arm, he ran to the baggage
wagons.

Lyias, of course, saw him. "What is that, Lord Dain? May
I help you?"

"No," Dain said gruffly. "It's nothing." He stuffed it hastily
out of sight among the bedrolls.

"Is that Dain?" called out an accented voice. Sulein came
riding his donkey from around the other side of the wagon.
"Ah, yes," he said with one of his intense smiles. His dark,
wiry beard was combed today, and his eyes glowed with excitement. "There is something I wish to discuss with you."

Dain's heart sank. Sulein's discussions ranged from simple questions to entire lectures on philosophy and mathematics. "Forgive me," he said as fast as he could. "I must
attend Lord Odfrey."

"But, Dain—"

"I must go."

Mounting his horse, he kicked it hard to catch up with
Lord Odfrey at the head of the line.

The chevard had reined up at the gates. Sitting tall in his
saddle, with the sunlight sparking no glints from his dark
hair, he adjusted his gloves impatiently and frowned as Dain
came trotting alongside, disorderly and out of breath. On his
other side, Gavril shot Dain a faint, disdainful sneer. Sir
Damiend did not look at Dain at all.

"Forgive me, lord," Dain said, a little out of breath. "I
was—"

"No excuses," the chevard said sternly. "You have delayed his highness. Ask his pardon before you seek mine."

Anger shot through Dain. He would sooner have his finger chopped off than apologize to Gavril. The prince was smiling openly now, staring at Dain with his brows lifted.

For a moment Dain refused to do it. But then he recalled some wise advice he'd received from Sir Terent only a few days ago.

"The prince is leaving us," the ruddy-faced knight had said. "And you're staying. The world's been laid at your feet, lad. Be patient and bide a little longer. Soon enough he'll be gone, to trouble you no more."

With those words in mind, Dain forced himself to meet Gavril's vivid blue gaze. "Forgive me, your highness," he said in as courteous a voice as he could muster. He let no sullenness be heard in his tone, for Lord Odfrey was watching him closely. "Truly I did not intend to delay your departure. I am sorry and ask your pardon."

"Prettily said," Gavril replied, begrudgingly. "But must this eld ride here in front as my equal?"

Lord Odfrey frowned. "I thought your highness might enjoy a companion on the road."

"No, thank you," Gavril said loftily, sneering at Dain. "I prefer to converse with Sir Damiend."

The commander of the church forces smiled and bowed over his saddle. "Your highness does me honor."

With his face burning, Dain looked at Lord Odfrey. "With your permission, lord, I will ride with the others from Thirst."

"An excellent suggestion," Gavril said quickly before Lord Odfrey could respond.

"My son is not going to ride at the rear like a servant," Lord Odfrey told him.

Gavril's eyes met his with wide innocence. "But, my lord, he is not officially your son yet. Until then, he has no rank and need not be set higher than his proper place."

A muscle jumped in Lord Odfrey's clamped jaw. Behind him, Sir Roye's weathered face grew watchful and alert for trouble. Sir Damiend's black cloak blew in the hot wind, and his green eyes never left Lord Odfrey.

Dain could smell a trap around Lord Odfrey. Anxiously he said, "Lord, have you any message that I may convey to Sir Terent?"

After a moment, Lord Odfrey's dark eyes stopped burning holes into Gavril. He shifted his gaze to Dain and nodded. "Yes, give him this map."

He handed the roll of parchment to Dain. His face was like stone, but Dain sensed his anger and blazing humiliation. *It does not matter,* Dain wanted to tell him. *The insult is small at best.*

"Ride behind his highness until we reach the road," Lord Odfrey commanded Dain. "Then you will give the map to Sir Terent."

"Yes, lord," Dain said.

Gavril smirked in seeming satisfaction with his little victory. "You may give the orders to depart, my lord."

Lord Odfrey bowed and passed the command along.

Then they were riding out, saluted by Sir Bosquecel, who'd been left in command of the hold. There rose a fanfare of horns and cheering serfs. Little boys ran beside them, brandishing sticks in mock swordplay and yelling. Dogs barked in their wake. Women called out from windows and the ramparts, waving ribbons and kerchiefs.

Lord Odfrey and Sir Roye took the lead, with Sir Damiend and Sir Nynth flanking Prince Gavril. Dain rode behind the prince like his squire, taking care not to let his restive horse crowd Gavril's mount. The company of fifty church soldiers, in their black cloaks and white surcoats, came thereafter, leaving the Thirst knights to guard the slow-moving wagons and donkey-mounted servants at the rear.

As soon as they left the hold, trotted over the practice field, and clattered onto the great road that led south, Dain dropped back. In a few minutes he reached the rear of the column. There, he joined up with Thum, who rode with eyes shining like stars and a big, silly grin on his freckled face.

"We're really going," he said. "Can you believe it? I've pinched myself twice already to make sure I do not dream this."

Dain grinned back. His excitement beat inside his chest, and it was all he could do to keep from spurring his horse to gallop wildly down the road. At that moment life seemed just about perfect . . . except for Tanengard, hidden back there in the chevard's wagon. He could hear its presence, like an incessant whisper in the back of his mind. Dain regretted ever knowing Lander. He wished, with all his heart, that he'd left the smith's accursed sword behind. Already it was burdening his heart, like a shameful secret he had to carry.

"Why are you scowling so?" Thum asked. "What's wrong?"

"Nothing," Dain replied. He glanced over his shoulder and saw Sulein riding on his donkey beside the chevard's wagon. Dain wondered if the physician could sense the sword's presence too.

Worried, Dain felt tempted to sling the sword into the bushes and abandon it, but he knew that would be an unwise thing to do. Its powers were too potent and might corrupt anyone who found it.

"Something *is* amiss," Thum insisted. "You look like you've eaten green berries."

Dain shrugged. "It's just something I have to tell Lord Odfrey. Tonight."

"What have you done now?"

Dain met his friend's dismayed eyes. "Nothing. I've done nothing."

"If you confess tonight when we camp," Thum said gloomily, "you aren't too far from Thirst to be sent back."

Dain had not thought of that. His eyes widened as he considered the horrible possibility of being sent back to Thirst with the sword. "Then I'd better wait," he decided.

"Dain—"

"Hush!" Dain said impatiently. "It's nothing, I tell you."

"But—"

"When we get to Savroix," Dain said, "what do you intend to see first? The Bridge of Foretelling or the sword swallowers at the town fair?"

Thus distracted, Thum began to chatter about the coming attractions. Dain let him talk, but in the back of his mind his uneasiness grew. Now the secret had forced him to lie to his best friend. And if he waited until they reached the banks of the Charva or even crossed the famous river before he mentioned the sword to Lord Odfrey, then he would be faced with the disagreeable task of explaining why he'd waited so long. Perhaps it would be better to say nothing at all, and just drop Tanengard quietly into the deep waters, to be concealed there for all time.

As for what Lander would ask him later when he got home . . . well, that was too far away to worry about now. He supposed he would have to lie to the smith as well. Dain frowned to himself, realizing with shame that already he was failing to measure up to his new father's high standards. But once he got rid of Tanengard, he would be honest and truthful. Never again would he let anything stain his honor.

Thus did Dain close his mind to the problem.

2

THAT NIGHT, CAMPED in Ebel Forest, Dain was awakened by his own shouting. He sat up wildly, fighting his blankets, and found himself gripped by a pair of strong hands that shook him hard.

"Dain, Dain, easy now," Lord Odfrey's voice said in the darkness. "It's only a dream, lad. It's only a dream."

Blinking awake, Dain shuddered in his father's grip, then drew up his knees and rested his face against them. Lord Odfrey held his shoulder a moment longer, gave him an awkward pat, and released him.

The campfires had burned down to muted embers. Sleeping forms lay rolled in blankets. Along the edges of the camp, the sentries kept watch in the darkness.

Dain rubbed the clammy sweat from his face. He felt breathless and very tired, as though he'd run a long distance. His mouth burned with thirst.

"I'm sorry," he whispered.

Lord Odfrey filled his own cup from the waterskin and pressed it into Dain's hands. The cold silver felt good against his hot palms. He drank the water in gulps, and sighed.

"Thank you, lord," he whispered. "I did not mean to wake you."

"You didn't," Lord Odfrey murmured. "I'll sleep little until we are safe across the Charva and in the lowlands."

Dain understood the reason for his unease. The Mandrians believed the Nonkind could not cross the Charva's swift waters. There had never been a Nonkind raid in lower Mandria, so perhaps it was true. But even on this side of the river, Dain had sensed no danger. He sensed no danger now. The only monsters here were those in his dreams.

"Was your nightmare very bad?" Lord Odfrey asked with sympathy.

Dain shrugged. Already the distorted shapes and images that had filled his mind were fading. He started to hand back the chevard's cup, then held it up a moment, frowning at it.

"There was a cup like this, long ago," he said slowly. "Not as large, but silver. Eldin silver."

"Yes?" Lord Odfrey said in encouragement.

Dain's frown deepened. "I don't know how I know that. I never saw such a cup while I lived with Jorb. Perhaps my sister used to talk about it. She told me many tales."

"Was your dream about something that happened to you long ago?"

"I don't think so," Dain said, rubbing his eyes. They ached and were wet, as though he had been crying in his sleep. He was glad that the night concealed him, for it was unmanly to weep the tears of a child. "It was all bright colors, brighter than anything I've ever seen before. I was in a room like the sun, all yellow and gold, but there was darkness in it, a black mist that was searching for me, coming for me." He drew in a ragged breath, feeling the cold, sick fear grip him again. "I couldn't run from it. I couldn't get away."

Lord Odfrey gripped his arm. "You're safe now, lad. It isn't here."

Absorbing his comfort, Dain tried to control his foolish emotions. He realized he'd probably awakened the others sleeping nearby, although if so, they were kindly pretending to sleep on.

"I'm sorry," he said again, and straightened his shoulders. He handed back the chevard's cup. "Thank you. I'm well now."

In silence, Lord Odfrey gave him another pat and returned to his own blankets. Dain sat a while, feeling the night breeze cool his hot face. He absorbed the sounds of the forest around him—the faint rustlings, the gliding sweep of a predator's wings, the soft sighings of the tree canopies overhead. The air smelled of wood ash, horses, and men, but beyond the camp smells lay the scents of wood bark, moss, damp soil, and leaf mold. Reaching inside his tunic, Dain curled his fingers around his pendant of bard crystal for comfort and sat there in the darkness a long while. He wished he could go off by himself into the forest, but he knew Lord Odfrey was not yet asleep. The man had enough worries already troubling his mind. Dain would give him no more by slipping away.

By late afternoon the next day, they neared the river. There was an air of anticipation in everyone. Even the church soldiers, although they did not relax their tight vigilance, occasionally spoke to each other and could be seen to smile.

Many of the Thirst knights rode slouched in their saddles, laughing and talking idly to each other. Lord Odfrey no longer looked as tense and cautious as when they'd first set out. The Thirst knights had a bet laid—much to the disapproval of the church soldiers—as to who would be the first to see the Charva, Lord Odfrey or Prince Gavril.

"A stupid wager," Dain muttered to Thum. "Even if Lord Odfrey does see it first, he will let the prince claim the win."

Thum's freckled face looked serious as he nodded agreement. "I fear our knights would bet on anything, even a race between dung beetles across the stableyard."

"They should save their betting money for who will win the tournament."

Thum's green eyes shone. "I cannot wait to get there. I wish we could gallop our horses the whole way."

Dain shifted in the saddle and winced at the ache in his hips. "And arrive with gall sores."

Thum's laughter rang out, echoing through the treetops. Birds flew through the canopy, squawking in affront. Dain leaned over and broke off a twig, sniffed the torn bark, then tasted it.

The twig had a clean, minty flavor. He chewed on it, marveling at this gentle forest, with its springy carpet of golden-green moss underfoot and large, well-spaced trees of ancient size. Dappled sunlight shifted in patterns across the riders' faces, glinting here and there off a bridle chain or spur rowel. The air was warm and humid, almost sultry beneath the trees, and fragrant with varieties of shrubs and saplings Dain did not always recognize.

He couldn't help but compare these woods with the Dark Forest where he had grown up. That was a place of constant danger, with such a tangle of undergrowth, thicket, briers, and close-set trees no decent road such as this could be built through its heart.

Now and then, a faint breeze sprang up. When it shifted, Dain's keen nostrils caught a whiff of the river. Its smell was clean, telling him the water ran swiftly in its course. He had heard much of the legendary Charva, but until today he had never seen it. Indeed, he had never traveled so far from Nold in his life. He felt his mind and heart expanding in all directions, as though something small and tight inside him was unfurling. The world was much larger than he'd ever supposed. Now he was becoming a part of it. In only a short year, his life had changed completely, and it was still changing. At times he could hardly believe it.

"Are you listening to me?" Thum asked, breaking his thoughts.

Dain blinked and looked at him with a shy grin. "No."

"I thought not. I said the first thing we're going to do when we get there is—"

Someone ahead shouted, and the column slowed down.

"It's the river!" Dain said in excitement.

He and Thum kicked their horses forward, leaving the road to race ahead of the column up to where Lord Odfrey and Sir Damiend had reined up. The forest ended at the edge of a bluff overlooking the swift, gray-green waters below.

Such a river. Dain's mouth fell open at the size of it. Wide and clean, it coursed along a straight route here beside this rocky bluff, but to the west Dain could see where the land flattened and the river began to meander. Across it, far on the horizon, lay strips of rolling meadowland bordered by trees and hedgerows. A distant curl of smoke showed him the location of a village, too far away to be seen.

The road curved away from the edge of the bluff, winding along a gentle decline to the cleared land on either side of the river's banks.

"Where's the ferry point?" Thum asked. "We can't be far."

Dain stood up in his stirrups and shaded his eyes against the afternoon sun. "That way," he said, pointing.

A short distance away, Lord Odfrey and Sir Damiend sat in their saddles, poring over the map and talking in low, serious voices.

The excitement in Thum's face faded. He looked almost pensive. "All my life I've wanted to see this river," he said. "Now I have."

"Aye."

"When we cross at the ferry point, we'll be in upper Mandria no longer," Thum said. His voice had gone quiet, and held a strange tone of wistfulness and regret.

Dain looked at him in puzzlement. "Don't you want to go on?"

"Of course! That's not it," Thum said at once. He glanced past Dain at someone else, and his face turned red. "Never mind."

"He means, pagan," Gavril said, riding up, "that he's an uplander with old treachery in his heart."

Dain frowned and Thum's face turned even redder.

Wearing a fawn-colored surcoat which had been sent to him as a journey gift by Cardinal Noncire, and sporting his new light brown mustache, Gavril twisted his handsome face into mocking contempt for them both.

"I am no traitor, your highness," Thum said stiffly, his hands clenched white on his reins.

"You would like to see upper Mandria independent again," Gavril said coldly. "All you uplanders want that, but it will never happen." His dark blue gaze shifted to Dain. "It is an old combat. We vanquished them long ago, and civilized them, but they refuse to be satisfied."

Dain made no reply. Gavril was always seeking to provoke a quarrel, and in politics he usually managed to prod a sore spot in Thum. Although it angered Dain on his friend's behalf, he kept silent. Every day, one or another of the Thirst knights cautioned Dain against offending the prince, and he intended to follow those orders.

Thum said nothing either.

The column was moving on, starting down the slope, and Gavril gave them a pitying smile before riding away.

As soon as he was out of earshot, Thum slapped the pommel of his saddle with his gloved hand. "Morde!" he said under his breath, his freckles still aflame. "Why won't he let me be?"

"He has no one to bully except us," Dain said with a shrug. "We'll be rid of him soon enough. Think on that."

"Aye," Thum said grimly. "I think on it every day. I pray for it every night. You take his needles well. Better than you used to."

Dain wheeled his horse around to follow the others. "I have no fear of him now," he said simply. "I have protection."

As he spoke, he glanced ahead at Lord Odfrey's back, and once again he felt a surge of gratitude for the man's kindness. He was Odfrey's son now. All that remained was the king's signature of permission on the warrant of adoption, and it would be official. Knowledge that he belonged somewhere, that he had friends and a new family, gave him renewed confidence. The world was sweet and full of promise. Even Gavril's sour contempt could not spoil Dain's mood.

Thum ducked a low-hanging branch and kicked his horse to move alongside Dain. "It's getting late. Think you we'll reach the ferry point before we have to make camp? It's best if we cross the river before nightfall."

"Aye," Dain replied. "I heard Lord Odfrey say he would have us across ere we see another dawn."

"Gods," Thum muttered with a sigh. "Let's hope we don't have to get these horses and wagons ferried in the dark."

Dain frowned. He'd never been in a boat before. The idea of floating on the surface of the water seemed fantastic to him, and a little daunting. He'd heard tales of merchants and peddlers who floated up and down the rivers with their wares, but it sounded unlikely. He did not believe the heavily laden wagons, especially those piled with Gavril's belongings, could stay afloat. Yet everyone else expressed no doubt, and looked at him strangely when he asked questions.

Besides that, he had the task of somehow dropping Lander's sword into the water without anyone noticing. That wasn't going to be easy, if it was even possible. Dain told himself he'd better prepare an explanation in case he was seen and questioned, but his mind remained blank. He was too angry with Lander for getting him into this mess to be clever.

A braying donkey interrupted his thoughts. Looking around, Dain saw Sulein approaching.

The physician had exchanged his customary long brown robes of learning for a tunic and leggings. Instead of his tall, conical hat, he once again wore his peculiar flat square tied to his head with a broad ribbon. His beard and frizzy hair were all atangle, and he carried a large book balanced on the front of his saddle.

As he came even with Dain and Thum, his dark, intense eyes were snapping with excitement. "Young Dain," he said with a slight inclination of his head, "I was disappointed when you did not join me last night to resume your lessons."

Dain stifled a groan. "No one said I had to do lessons in Savroix. We're supposed to have fun."

"Your attitude should be shameful to you," Sulein rebuked him mildly. "And we are not in Savroix yet. There is no need to waste the time at our disposal on this journey."

"But I have other duties," Dain began, floundering in his attempt to think up any excuse possible. How, he wondered, was he going to be able to get the sword if Sulein stayed in his way? "Tonight perhaps, I'll remember to—"

"Why not now?" Sulein asked, opening the book. "The journey is pleasant. We will have much time at our disposal while we wait for everyone to be ferried."

Dain's face was turning hot. He glanced at Thum, who was carefully looking away. Dain frowned, so embarrassed he wanted to wheel his horse around and gallop in the opposite direction. Why did Sulein have to make an issue of his ignorance before the whole company? It didn't occur to Dain that many of the knights could not themselves read or write; all he knew was that Sulein made him feel a fool by exposing his ignorance like this. He didn't want to plod along, reading faltering words aloud from some musty old book, not when the day was fine and bright and full of adventure.

Gavril's laughter made his face burn even hotter. The prince came back to him, looking curious, like a cat that's found a mouse too far from its hole.

"What have we here?" Gavril demanded while Sulein bowed low over his donkey's neck. "What pagan book of spells do you carry, physician?"

"It is a harmless book of astrology, your highness," Sulein said in a voice of oily respect. "Thus can young Dain learn twofold from a single effort—both the exercise of reading and the absorption of content."

Gavril's dark blue eyes slid over Dain, and he raised his brows. "It is a waste of your time, physician," he said in cold disapproval. "What need has an eld to learn how to read? Trying to educate someone who lacks true lineage and position is a waste. You might as well try to teach a keeback to read."

Dain's jaw clenched. He glared at Gavril. "You—"

"Your highness!" called Sir Nynth, riding up. The ugly, keen-eyed knight shot Dain a look of warning.

Fuming, Dain bowed his head and glared instead at his fists.

"Begone with you," Gavril said without looking at Sir Nynth. "I do not require you now."

"Maybe not, but my duty is my duty," Sir Nynth said heavily. He kept his voice respectful, but his brown eyes had narrowed at the prince. "I am sworn to keep you safe until you reach the king. Now how can I do that if you keep dashing off?"

Gavril flashed him a look of exasperation. "You need not recite the responsibilities of a protector to me, sir. Nor is it your place to tell me where I may and may not go. Be silent and do not interrupt me again."

A tide of red rose from Sir Nynth's collar to darken his

ugly face. His muscular jaw twitched, but he never changed his wooden expression. "Sir Damiend has requested your highness's advice," he said in a flat voice.

Gavril tilted his golden head to one side. "A clever ruse to part us, sir," he said. "But it will not work. I am not yet finished speaking to the pagan."

"Dain saved your highness's life," Sir Nynth reminded him crisply. "You might have the grace to refer to him by name. After all, he'll be Lord Dain soon enough."

Red flushed Gavril's cheeks. He shot Dain a furious look of resentment. "It is ill-mannered to constantly remind someone of an obligation. You'd better work harder on your lessons, boy, so that you can learn to imitate your betters."

"I do these lessons to serve Lord Odfrey," Dain said through his teeth. He hated how Gavril always managed to twist what was said. "By criticizing me, you criticize him."

Silence fell over the small group. Gavril's eyes widened, and he looked momentarily taken aback.

"Well, well," he said softly, and gave Dain a little mock salute. "You *are* learning, aren't you?"

He galloped away, his horse's hooves kicking up clods and spattering Dain and Thum. Sir Nynth followed the prince, but by then Thum was grinning.

He slapped Dain on the back. "Well said! Very well said! He didn't expect that, did he? Oh, it was masterful, Dain. Did you see the look on his face?" Thum went into peals of laughter.

Dain grinned back, pleased with his success, but Sulein frowned at them both.

"Take care, young Dain," he said in warning. "It is unwise to reveal your cleverness to his highness. He will enlist every defeat you give him into a sour army of grievances, and then he will attack."

Dain nodded, remembering how Gavril had ordered the other fosters, Kaltienne and Mierre, to corner and kill him only a few short weeks ago. Dain's shoulder carried the scars of that attempt. Yes, he knew well how twisted and devious Gavril could be in repaying a grudge.

"I wish he would leave us alone," Dain muttered.

"Aye," Thum said with feeling.

"In life, young sirs, there is always someone who will not leave you alone. If you want peace and tranquillity— which is a strange wish for boys as full of vim as you two— then you must go to the Beyond."

Dain rolled his eyes at this pontification, and Thum's mouth twitched as he struggled to hold back a grin.

"Now, young Dain," Sulein said in satisfaction, handing the book to him. "It is time for your lessons."

"No," Dain protested. "Maybe later. Please. I want to watch the ferrying."

The physician's dark, glowing eyes stared deep into his. "But you have assured the prince of your eagerness to obey Lord Odfrey's wish. Was that mere idle boasting, or do you intend to keep your word?"

Dain had no answer to make.

Thum laughed at him. "You are boxed in now," he said. "I'd better go attend the chevard for a while. The quicker you learn all that Sulein wants to teach you, the quicker you'll be done."

"There's no end to it," Dain grumbled, but he opened the book.

A great cloud of mustiness and old spells gusted into his face, and he sneezed. As the cramped writing swam momentarily before his eyes, he wished with all his heart that he could be free of such obligations.

But he'd been free once, free to starve and live in the forest burrows like a wild animal. Now he had a home, a father, and safety—good things all. But it seemed good things carried a price.

On the riverbank, the company halted at a wooden landing that jutted out into the swift current. The ferryman could be seen on the opposite side of the river. He waved and hallooed, then launched his craft toward them.

Several of the men dismounted, and the wagons halted in line. Dain could see that this was going to take a very long time indeed. Perhaps it was best to do his lessons now, although he wanted to be with Thum, watching every part of the proceedings.

Sighing, he began: "The constellation called The Maiden is—"

In that moment, his nostrils caught an unexpected whiff of something foul and tainted, something dead and corrupted. It made the hair on the back of his neck stand up. His heart leaped inside his chest.

He glanced around wildly, then stood up in his stirrups with a yell. Dropping the book, he clawed for the dagger at his side.

"My lord!" he shouted with all his might. "Nonkind!"

Sir Alard and Sir Terent heard his warning, and raised shouts of their own. The dismounted church soldiers stood there, staring, taking no heed.

A shriek no human throat could make rent the air, drowning out Dain's shouts, and in that instant a horde of Nonkind riders and hurlhounds came galloping from the forest. They swarmed over the crest of the bluff and charged down the hill.

It was the perfect place for ambush. Caught on the bank between river and bluff, the Mandrians had little maneuvering room. The parked wagons were in the way as the knights hastily mounted up, then reached for weapons and rode forth in disorder to meet their foes.

Everything became milling confusion. The spare horses reared in fright, whinnying and lashing out in terror. Several broke free, running amok in all directions.

Lord Odfrey's voice rose above the noise like thunder. He issued orders, but if they were obeyed, Dain could not tell.

Crying out curses and wondering why he had not sensed the Nonkind sooner, Dain spurred his horse toward the fighting.

"Dain, no!" Sulein shouted after him. "Stay with me by the water, boy! Stay with me!"

Dain paid him no heed whatsoever. The fearsome clash of swords and the screams of dying men mingled with the shrieks and howls of the monsters. He saw the pack of hurlhounds divide itself. Black-coated and thin, their vicious jaws slavering venom, the creatures attacked riders in pairs, leaping up to pull men from their saddles. Fierce barking broke out, and Gavril's prized hunting dogs escaped their handler and came charging. Although ferocious and bloody, the fighting lasted only moments. The pack of handsome red dogs lay slain, and hurlhounds ripped their bodies apart to feast before being whistled back into battle by their masters.

"No!" Gavril shouted in horror.

Dain saw him ride toward his dogs, only to have Sir Nynth race after him and grip him by his cloak to hold him back. Gavril was nearly yanked from his saddle. Snarling, he turned on his protector and swung at Sir Nynth with his dagger.

Grimly the protector blocked the blow with his arm. His surcoat sleeve was gashed, revealing the bright burnished links of his chain mail beneath. By then two church soldiers reached them and helped Sir Nynth hold Gavril back from the fighting. More church soldiers encircled the prince, moving him farther up the bank away from the main brunt of fighting.

Only then did Dain realize the Thirst knights were fighting alone. The church soldiers retreated a second time, and sat in formation, doing nothing.

Unable to believe their cowardice, Dain found himself knocked sideways by something he did not even see. Grunting under the impact, he caught himself on the neck of his horse and managed to keep from tumbling from his saddle. Above him swooped a shadow that he glimpsed from the corner of his eye. He twisted his head and saw a Believer in black armor and helmet looming over him on a darsteed that dwarfed his own mount. The darsteed was a huge, rangy beast from a nightmare. Breathing fire and smoke, it whipped its snakelike head around and sank poisonous fangs into the shoulder of Dain's horse.

The animal reared, screaming in pain, and Dain clung to the reins with all his might, spurring it forward and ducking just as his attacker's sword whistled over his head.

The Believer swore in fiendish Gantese, and pulled back on his darsteed to swing it around. Dain's heart was hammering violently in his chest. He spurred his horse again, and the animal lunged forward in a wild gallop, almost careening into two horsemen who were fighting with swords and shields.

Dain's horse veered around them, then stumbled. Nearly catapulted from his saddle, Dain felt dizzy and hot. His vision was all wrong, for the world had grown tilted and slightly out of focus. He thought he must be cut somewhere from the Believer's sword, but as yet he could not feel his wound. No blood streamed from him, but there was no time to look. He saw servants running and dodging in all directions, easy targets in their green tabards. None of them were armed, and the attackers mowed them down mercilessly. The hurlhounds snarled and bit and savaged, tearing off arms and spilling entrails. The ground grew slippery with blood. The air rang with shouts and clashing swords. And still the church soldiers took no action, save against those monsters that attacked them directly.

Seeing a hurlhound corner Lyias, Dain screamed dwarf curses and rode to his rescue. The servant, both arms bloodied, cowered back against the side of a wagon. He was weeping and pleading for mercy. Just as the hurlhound gathered itself to leap, Dain leaned down from his saddle and struck his dagger hard at the base of the monster's neck.

Black stinking blood splattered across Dain's hand, burning it. The hurlhound fell in its tracks, and Dain's dagger was wrenched from his hand as it stayed caught in its neck. He looked at Lyias, who was still cringing and screaming.

"Lyias! Are you all right?" he shouted. "Lyias! Be silent and run for the river. You'll be safe in the water."

The servant opened his eyes and stared with a gaping mouth behind Dain. He pointed, and Dain whirled around just as another black-armored Believer charged straight at him with brandished sword.

Weaponless, Dain steeled himself for death, but from his left Sir Alard intercepted the Believer and cleaved him from the top of his helmet down.

"Thank—," Dain tried to say, but the knight rode on as though he hadn't seen Dain there.

Catching his breath, Dain realized that he had to arm himself or risk being slaughtered. Certainly he wasn't going to cower in safety with Prince Gavril. Because he wasn't knighted, he could not by law bear a sword, but right now the rules meant nothing. He could have taken a weapon from one of the dead knights, but there was only one sword he wanted.

Hurrying to the wagon, Dain dismounted and searched out his bedroll. Casting everything else aside, he unrolled it, and drew forth Tanengard.

Power jolted through him so forcefully that he cried out in pain. The sword blade flashed white and hummed all the way through the hilt. Listening to its gruff war song, Dain was filled with raging ferocity.

Jumping back into the saddle, he wheeled his horse around and charged straight into the thick of action, shouting dwarf war cries and brandishing the weapon.

He had no armor or shield, but he cared not. Tanengard's battle madness seized him, and all he wanted to do was fight.

The first Believer he met parried his attack with a black sword that shattered beneath Tanengard's blade. The Believer tried to pull back, but Dain skewered him with a mighty thrust, wrenched Tanengard free with a spurt of blood, and raced toward the next enemy. His rigorous training stood him well, for Dain had ceased to think at all. His mind was filled with the drumming cry of the sword in his hand. All he wanted was blood and more blood. Fearlessly he attacked anything, his senses so heightened that he could turn to face a leaping hurlhound even as it first jumped into the air.

Tanengard sliced through the hounds until at last they fell back and fled from him. Another Believer attacked Dain, and when his blade clanged against Tanengard, smoke filled the air. Choking and squinting, Dain let the sword guide his next blow. Unerringly it found the Believer in the billows of smoke. The Believer parried, but this time his blade shattered and Dain cut off his head.

Then the battle was over. He realized it only because a sudden quiet fell over the scene, and no more Believers came at him. In the distance he heard the echoing hoofbeats of the few fleeing darsteeds. Dazed and breathless, Dain sat his horse in the middle of dead men and Believers alike, sprawled in all directions.

There were other noises, too muffled for him to distinguish. From the corner of his eye he glimpsed movement, a blur of color. His head snapped in that direction, and he focused on a shape approaching him.

"Dain," it said. "Dain!"

He did not recognize the name. All he knew was that there was still fighting to be done. Tanengard sang inside him, chanting of death and attack. He raised the sword, and someone shouted.

His wrist was gripped, then another shape came at him. Suddenly he was surrounded, and Tanengard was wrested from him. As soon as it left his fingers, they began to tingle and burn. Dain's vision cleared so suddenly he cried out. His hearing returned, and he found himself assaulted by shouts and curses and moans from all sides.

A blood-splattered Sir Terent had an arm around him, pinning him fast, and Sir Alard blocked his path.

"Dain," Sir Alard was saying with sharp insistence. "Dain! Do you know us not at all?"

"Morde!" Sir Terent swore and threw Tanengard on the trampled ground. "What in Thod's name is this weapon?"

"Some piece of magic or sorcery," Sir Alard said. He swung his gaze back to Dain. "Now, lad, can you hear me?"

"Aye," Dain said dully. His ribs hurt. His throat felt raw and sore from shouting. His muscles were trembling from exertion.

"Do you know who I am?"

"Alard." Dain frowned and swallowed with difficulty. "Sir Alard."

The knight smiled and exchanged a quick glance with Sir Terent. "That's right. He's himself again."

"Tomias be praised," Sir Terent said. He released Dain with a quick pat on his shoulder. "Let's ride away from here and see if you're hurt."

Dain looked down at Tanengard lying on the ground where Sir Terent had thrown it. Even splattered with gore, it shone brightly in the fading sunlight. Its beauty drew him, and mesmerized him again.

"I cannot leave the sword," he said thickly. "Do not dishonor it by leaving it on the ground like that."

"Better to dishonor it than to see it possess you again," Sir Terent said gruffly. "Come away now."

"No!"

Dain tried to climb out of his saddle and swayed, nearly losing his balance. Sir Terent grappled with him awkwardly, keeping him where he was.

"I'll get it," Sir Alard said, dismounting.

"Take care," Sir Terent said.

"You need give me no warning." Sir Alard approached Tanengard warily, as though afraid it might rise in the air on its own and attack him. As he bent to pick it up, a voice rang out imperiously:

"Hold there! Touch it not, by my command!"

It was Gavril who spoke, Gavril who rode up with a guard of ten wary church soldiers. The prince had lost his cap, and dirt was streaked across his finery, but although pale he was unharmed.

Of Sir Nynth there was no sign. Dain wondered if Sir

Nynth had fallen in battle, protecting this spoiled prince, and felt grief spear his chest. Hearing the moans of fallen men, he wondered who else had fallen.

He looked around in sudden consternation, seeing too many bodies, too few men still standing, except for the church soldiers. In sudden rage, he stood up in his stirrups. "Cowards!" he shouted hoarsely, his voice choked with tears. "May Olas rot your bones for what you've done this day."

Several of the men with Gavril reached for their weapons, but the prince flung up his hand. "There are no cowards here, and you will curb your tongue, pagan. They guarded me well. I will not let you insult them."

"They have insulted the brave men of Thirst with their—"

"Silence!" Gavril shouted. "I am in command now. You will hold your tongue or have it cut out."

"Lord Odfrey is in command here," Dain retorted, glancing around for the chevard, but not seeing him. "And after him, Sir Damiend."

Gavril's chin lifted haughtily. "The Reverend Sir Damiend is leading his men in prayers for the dead. As for the chevard, I saw him fall."

A rock seemed to land on Dain's chest, and he could not breathe. "Lord Odfrey is not dead," he said fiercely. "He is not!"

"Easy, lad," Sir Terent said quietly at his side. "His lordship's hurt. He wants you."

Dain looked at the knight wildly. Grief filled him, and his eyes burned. "No," he whispered. "Oh, no!"

He wheeled his horse around, forgetting Tanengard, forgetting Gavril, who turned red-faced and shouted at him: "You have not my leave to go!"

Ignoring him, Dain galloped away. Sir Terent rode with him, leading him to the landing. Lord Odfrey lay there, propped up against one of the pilings. Two Thirst knights stood nearby, watching with grief-stricken faces while Sulein worked to stanch the chevard's bleeding.

Jumping off his horse, Dain ran to Lord Odfrey and knelt beside him. "Father," he said brokenly.

Lord Odfrey's dark eyes dragged themselves open at the sound of Dain's voice. He lay there white-faced and rigid with pain. The scar on his cheek was bright pink against his pallor. His dark green surcoat was soaked with blood.

Dain could smell death on him. He reached out and gripped one of Lord Odfrey's clenched fists. "Lord, I am here," he said.

"Dain," Lord Odfrey whispered.

"You must not talk," Sulein said fiercely. He bundled up another cloth and pressed it to Lord Odfrey's wound. "Keep your strength while you lie at the mercy of your gods."

"I'm sorry," Dain said, feeling tears prick his eyes. He tightened his mouth, trying to hold back his emotions. "I didn't sense them in time. I would have given the warning sooner if I'd known—"

"Not . . . your . . . fault," Lord Odfrey said. His voice was faint and airless.

Dain could hear the chevard's breath rasping in his throat. Bowing his head, Dain struggled with his grief. "Do not die," he said. "Please, please, do not die."

"Let there be no talk of dying," Sulein said grimly, tossing a bloody cloth into the river. It swirled there and floated away, with Lord Odfrey's blood trailing in the water after it. "You," he said to Sir Terent, "take a cup from my bag. Empty this vial into it and mix it with water. Quickly!"

Sir Terent hesitated, then clumsily did as he was told. When he returned with a brimming cup, it was Dain who sniffed it and detected only a sedative. Dain held the cup to Lord Odfrey's pale lips and coaxed him into drinking some of its contents.

The chevard swallowed a few times, then shuddered and sank into deep unconsciousness. Dain pressed his hand to his father's face, trying to give him strength. Inside, he felt wild and unhinged. Part of him wanted to run away, screaming in denial. Another part of him wanted to curse the gods and be struck dead for his blasphemy. This man did not deserve to die. Lord Odfrey was good, hardworking, and kind. Cautiously, unwillingly, Dain had learned to admire and respect this man, then to love him. Lord Odfrey had become his family, replacing those Dain had already lost. It was not fair that Lord Odfrey should also be taken away.

"Ah," Sulein said, and shifted back on his heels in satisfaction. Sweat beaded the physician's face, and he wiped his brow with the back of his bloody hand. "The bleeding is stopped at last. We will not move him now, although it is a damp place this close to the water. The evil humors in the air make it unwise to leave him here long. Before nightfall, if he sleeps well still, then we shall risk moving him. But not until then."

Lyias came blundering up, dripping wet, his eyes still wide with horror. When he saw them kneeling around the unconscious chevard, he began to wail with loud, ugly sobs.

Dain rose to his feet and shook the man. "Stop that," he said sternly. "You'll wake him. Go to the wagon and get him blankets, plenty of them. Do it now, and be quick."

Wringing his hands, Lyias stumbled off to do as he was bid.

Sir Terent also stood up. His ruddy face looked grim indeed. "I'll work a detail to count the dead. As for the wounded . . ." Letting his voice trail off, he looked down at Sulein.

The physician gestured absently. "I will come soon. Gather them all in one place, and I will do what I can."

Worry seemed to be dragging Dain's wits into a knot. With great effort, he cleared his mind and tried to think of practical things. "The provision wagons," he said. "We'll need all the salt available."

Sir Terent opened his mouth as though to protest, then turned very red and stayed silent.

"Please," Dain said. "I know this is not your belief, but it must be done. Every wounded man, his lordship included, must be salted. The dead must be thrown into the water or staked through the throats to release their souls."

"Nay!" Sir Alard said in disgust. He stared at Dain as though he'd lost his wits. "'Tis blasphemy to do that. They'll have a proper burial in the ground, with service said over them."

"Then the soultakers will get them tonight," Dain said brutally, "and the rest of us as well."

"No!" Gavril's voice rang out.

All turned as the prince and his entourage of guards approached. Gavril was carrying the sheathed Tanengard in his hand, and Dain eyed it warily.

"We'll not descend to the superstitions of this pagan infidel," Gavril said arrogantly.

"Superstition has nothing to do with it," Dain said. "For our safety and—"

"We'll ferry the dead across the Charva and bury them, as is decent and right," Gavril broke across what he was saying.

Dain saw relief flash across everyone's face, and he made no more protests. In his heart, however, he vowed to see Lord Odfrey protected with salt, no matter what anyone said.

"How many are dead, your highness?" Sir Terent asked quietly.

"The count has been made," Gavril replied, and glanced at one of his guards.

The man cleared his throat. "Of our combined forces of one hundred fifteen, perhaps half lie dead. Another ten are injured, Lord Odfrey included. Of the servants, only five survived."

"And the squires?" Dain asked, thinking of Thum.

The church soldier looked disconcerted. "I know not. I saw none to count. Perhaps they ran away."

"Or perhaps they were carried off," Sir Terent muttered grimly.

Silence fell over them all. Dain closed his eyes a moment, grieving for Thum too now. His friend had not run away; of that he was sure. The only cowards today had been the church soldiers.

While he frowned, deep in his own thoughts and grief, he heard Sir Alard praying beneath his breath. Several men made signs of the Circle.

Dain stared along the bank, where the dead lay sprawled in all directions. He saw no white surcoats among them, and his anger blazed hotter than ever. It felt somehow unreal, like a bad dream or a vision that would soon end. Then these men would stand up, laughing, and call out jests. But this was no dream. The Nonkind had known to strike while they were scattered and disorganized. Dain realized they had been watched, by what means he was not sure, and a chill ran through his bones.

The few survivors looked at each other in varying degrees of shock.

Then Sir Terent set his callused hand heavily on Dain's shoulder. "If not for this valiant lad, we'd all be dead. It was he who drove them off, there at the last."

"Aye," Sir Alard agreed.

Dain dropped his gaze with embarrassment. It hadn't been him, he knew. Tanengard had made the difference.

Gavril's face grew pinched and hostile. He held up the sheathed sword. "Yes, Dain drove them off with this weapon of sorcery. I witnessed it all."

Dain met Gavril's dark blue eyes with disgust. Although he knew the prince had not been allowed to fight, Dain's emotions were too fraught to be fair. How many men, Dain wondered, besides Sir Nynth had died to protect the prince today? How many more, through the years, would lose their lives in such duty? It was a useless question, Dain realized. He might as well ask how many clouds rode the sky. Gavril would one day be king. No matter how long he lived, he would always expect men to die for his protection. Dain thought of how rudely Gavril had snapped at Sir Nynth just minutes before the attack. Did Gavril feel any remorse for that now? Dain very much doubted it.

"Where did you get this sword?" Gavril asked, looking straight at Dain. "You are not a knight. You are not permitted to own weapons."

Sir Terent intervened before Dain could answer. "Forgive me, your highness, but shouldn't this wait until we're safely across the river?"

"I will have an answer now," Gavril said angrily. "And, Dain, be warned that these church knights will judge you. On the honor of the dead around us, you must speak the truth."

It was a fine warning, coming from a liar like Gavril. Dain shot the prince a smoky glance. "It is not my property," he said. "It was to be entered in the contest for the king's new sword. Our smith Lander made it for that purpose."

Sir Terent forgot himself and swore aloud. Sir Alard stared. The church soldiers stared.

Gavril raised his brows. "You lie. I saw the entry which Lander gave to Lord Odfrey. A sorry sword indeed."

"And this one is beautiful," Dain replied. "Made from magicked steel."

They flinched at that, all except Gavril. His grip, Dain noticed, tightened on Tanengard's scabbard.

"Think of it," Dain continued. "If you were Lander, and you got the misbegotten notion in your head to make such an unlawful sword, would you not keep its existence a secret? Aye, you would. He intended that this sword be switched with the plain one at the last moment before the contest."

Again, they all exchanged glances. Gavril glared at the unconscious Lord Odfrey. "Fine behavior from a man known to be honorable. What was he thinking, to agree to such a—"

"Lord Odfrey knew nothing of it," Dain said in sharp defense. "Had he seen it, he would have ordered it broken on Lander's anvil."

"Aye, he would have," Sir Terent said loyally.

"Then who was helping Lander in this foul plot?" Gavril asked.

Dain lifted his chin, knowing the time for lies was past. "Lander gave it into my keeping."

"I knew it!" Gavril shouted, ignoring Sulein's gestures for quiet. "I knew this pagan would bring us ill luck."

"This pagan, as your highness calls him," Sir Terent said angrily, "saved us all. Had he drawn it sooner, more lives would have been spared. Thirst men fought and died alone today. Let us not forget that. If we could not have church swords drawn beside us, then we'll not denounce what did fight in our defense."

"You speak out of turn, sir," Gavril said coldly.

Sir Terent turned red, but he didn't back down. "And your highness judges too quickly. Let us hear it all."

"I've heard enough," Gavril said, but the men of Thirst shook their heads.

"Tell the rest of it, Dain," Sir Terent said, giving him a nod of encouragement.

Humiliation made Dain feel raw inside. He knew he should have refused Lander, should have thrown the sword away as soon as he was given it. He'd shown no courage at all.

"Lander wanted me to switch the swords, but I thought this unfair."

"You mean it was despicable and a dirty cheat," Gavril said.

Dain met his gaze with a flick of anger. "Aye."

"Go on, Dain," Sir Terent said. "Why didn't you come to one of us, or tell Lord Odfrey?"

A knot closed Dain's throat. He struggled a moment before he could swallow and force himself on. "I was afraid I'd be punished and sent back to Thirst with the sword. I decided to keep it hidden, and I was going to drop it in the river tonight after dark."

"Oh, a fine tale," Gavril said with a sneer. "And such a fine intention. You could have thrown it in the ditch yesterday if you really meant to be rid of it."

"And have who find it?" Dain retorted. "In whose hands

would you have it pass? A serf's? A Nonkind? Who? I may have been foolish to take it, but I'm not stupid enough to throw it away for just anyone to find. That's why I thought the river the safest place for its disposal."

Gavril's cheeks turned pink, and he said nothing.

One of the church soldiers nodded at Dain. "Well thought, lad. But the best thing for it is that it be broken and its spell released."

"By an expert!" Gavril said shrilly. His dark blue eyes glared at them all. "I shall take this to Cardinal Noncire. He has men who know the best way to dispose of such an object of the darkness."

No one protested, but Dain saw a momentary flicker of doubt cross the faces of the church soldiers. He also saw how tightly Gavril was holding that scabbard. Obviously Tanengard's spell was working on the prince. Dain hoped the prince would discover that he wasn't as immune to temptation as he believed.

"As for those who wield such unlawful weapons—"

"Hold there, your highness," Sir Terent said sharply.

"Aye," Sir Alard echoed. "Unlawful or not, the use of this sword saved us. Dain does not claim ownership, nor is he trying to keep the sword for himself. He used it to save the lives of others. What wrong lies there?"

Dain was grateful for their defense, but he did not think it would sway Gavril. At that moment, however, Sir Damiend came striding up, stone-faced. He and the church soldiers agreed with the Thirst knights, and in the end Gavril had to defer to their judgment.

"Very well," he said short-temperedly. "It's settled. Let us get on with our journey."

"But your highness," Sir Terent said. "What of—"

"I grow weary of your protests to everything I utter, sir," Gavril said.

Sir Terent straightened his heavy shoulders and didn't back down. "What of our dead and wounded? Should we not turn back to Thirst and—"

"Ah, yes, Lord Odfrey is too ill to travel onward, isn't he?"

"He is," Sulein said firmly. "It is out of the question."

"Then you people from Thirst will remain with your chevard," Gavril said. "I will continue on."

"How?" Sir Terent asked. "Your highness must have guards and provisions—"

"I have the church soldiers to protect me," Gavril said. "Once I cross the Charva, my danger is little enough. As for provisions, I will leave you a wagon for your return to Thirst."

"It's better if your highness returns with us, if we all stick together—"

"Nonsense!" Gavril said sharply. "My life has already been risked today. My dogs are dead, my servants killed. I could have been slaughtered with them. I will run no more risks by returning with you."

Sir Terent looked at him with open disillusionment. "And what of us, your highness?" he asked softly. "What of our protection as we carry back the wounded?" His gaze swung to Sir Damiend before Gavril could reply. "Reverend knight, do you not agree that we must all turn back?"

Anger sparked in Gavril's eyes, and he gestured for Sir Damiend to be silent. "I am giving the orders now," he declared. "Not Sir Damiend, and certainly not you. I will hear no more of your insubordination."

The veins stood out prominently in Sir Terent's neck. Dain laid his hand swiftly on the knight's arm in warning, and Sir Terent said nothing else.

"The ferryman is here, your highness," Dain said, pointing at the barge floating now at the end of the jetty. "Take what you will, and good journey to you."

Gavril's vivid blue eyes met Dain's pale gray ones for a long moment. Then the prince jerked a little nod to him and turned away to issue his orders.

3

IT DID NOT take Gavril and the church soldiers long to abandon them. The few remaining servants, most weeping or silent with shock, were loaded onto the wagons, as many as there were still drivers for. A few provisions were left behind; the rest were taken. By the time the sun began to set and dusk crept down over the scene of carnage, Gavril, the church soldiers, and all but two wagons had been ferried across the river and were gone.

Despite the refusal to let Dain safeguard the corpses, Sir Damiend spared no time for burying the dead. Instead, he left the task to the Thirst contingent, saying the prince must be taken home without delay.

For half the night, working by torchlight, Dain, Sir Alard, and Sir Terent collected the bodies, ferrying them across while Sir Bowin and Sir Polquin dug the graves on the far bank. This grim task was made even worse because it was their friends and comrades they buried. Just when Dain thought himself too numb to grieve anymore, he would find a friend or surrogate uncle and memories would flood him with overwhelming emotions. Finding Sir Roye, Lord Odfrey's fierce old protector, among the dead had been particularly heart-wrenching. Dain and Sir Roye had never gotten along, and yet they were not enemies. Sir Roye had disapproved of Dain and distrusted him because he was eldin, but he had also saved Dain's skin more than once. He had even been occasionally kind. Now he lay dead, his body mutilated and torn from terrible bite wounds. Dain bound his limbs tightly to his body with rope, as they lacked shroud cloth for the task, and gently laid the old protector to his rest. Tears ran down Dain's dirt-streaked face, and he was not ashamed to weep for such a valiant warrior.

Sulein sat watch over Lord Odfrey, who lay on his blan-

kets as white and still as death. "No change," Sulein said
each time Dain stopped to check on the chevard.

Thum turned up alive after all, his head bloody from
where he'd been knocked unconscious. Dazed and not sure
of who he was, he sat like a ghost in the firelight while
Lyias tried to coax him into eating meal cakes.

Dain was too weary to be glad his friend had survived.
He knew that on the morrow he would rejoice, but right then
all he could do was stay numb in order to perform the terrible task of dispatching the dead.

There is war coming, he thought as he dragged another
body into position. *A terrible, costly war.* For the first time,
he understood the importance of politics, the arrangement
of treaties and the preservation of alliances. Gant was absorbing Nether, the great and once-powerful ally of Mandria. When it finished feeding on that kingdom, then it would
turn its jaws on Klad or Nold or even Mandria—not to nibble with these increasingly bold raids, but to devour.

Tipping back his head to the cold stars above, Dain prayed,
*Let us be strong enough to defeat them, O Thod. Give each
of us the strength of ten men. Empower our swords against
the darkness. Let us drive them back.*

In the past year, he had striven to become a warrior. He'd
trained hard, afterward listening to stories of fighting glory
in the guardhouse. He'd seen the scars and limps. He'd
dreamed of battle, yearning to be in the thick of it.

Well, now he had been. As he grimly helped dig the soft,
crumbling soil, he understood at last that all the glory, honors, banquet feasts, and songs sung by the guardhouse fire
were just ways to forget the screams of the dying. Battle
was fast, dirty, and terrifying. Battle was feeling your own
entrails melt with fear. And sometimes, instead of victory
and songs, there were defeat, death, and a sick, shaky af-
termath.

Sir Polquin, sweating and slowed by his own injuries,
mumbled the words of ritual over the corpses. Dain knelt
and touched them one by one, secretly leaving a little sprin-

kling of salt in each man's mouth. If the others guessed
what he was doing under cover of darkness, they did not
stop him.

Then they all worked to fill in the long, shallow grave.
By the time they finished, the moon had risen to shine among
her court of stars, glittering cold, pale light within the rushing waters of the Charva. The breeze blew sweetly against
Dain's sweating face. He found himself reeling with exhaustion, and when the silent ferryman took them back across
the water for the last time, Dain lay slumped against the side
with his fingers trailing in the cool waters.

The river had many voices—some fast, some slow—all
murmuring a deep, low song of mountain ice, and hot plain,
and endless sea. *Onward, onward,* the voices sang. *Onward
to the sea. To be, to be. To be onward to the sea.*

The song was elemental, primitive, ancient. It was all rush
and instinct, with nothing soothing about it, nothing calming. Dain sighed and closed it from his mind.

When the ferry touched shore, Dain staggered up the bank
to where Sulein sat tending the crackling fire and looking
haggardly up at the woods on the hill above them.

"How does he?" Dain asked with a gesture at the sleeping Lord Odfrey.

"He lives," Sulein said flatly. He handed Dain a cup of
something, and for once Dain drank it without even a single sniff of suspicion.

The liquid was warm and tasted of spices and something
fermented. Dain felt a tingling sensation spread through his
limbs. Before he knew it, he was sitting down. "Have to
spread salt," he said thickly. "Have to keep watch."

Someone near him groaned and the others sank to the
ground. Sir Bowin flung himself flat on his back. Sir Alard
knelt as though his knees had given under him. Sir Terent
dropped like a stone and began to snore immediately.

"Can't move camp to other side," Dain said, struggling
to fit his tongue to his thoughts. "Safe there, but—"

"The chevard must not be moved," Sulein said sternly.

Dain nodded. "Not safe here. Got to watch."

"Aye," Sir Alard said in a voice that dragged with exhaustion. "We know they'll come back before dawn. They always do."

Sulein had removed his odd hat. His thick, wiry hair spread around his head in a frizzy corona as he shook his head. "Trouble yourselves about it no longer, my friends. I will see that they don't return for the dead tonight."

Dain smelled something burning and knew Sulein was casting spells. He prayed they worked, then fell over into a deep, dreamless sleep.

In the morning, Dain awakened with his head very clear and only a horrid, metallic taste in his mouth to remind him that he'd taken one of Sulein's potions. He was young enough for his body to have recovered from the previous day's exertions. But his heart remained troubled and sore.

He went at once to Lord Odfrey's side. The chevard looked terrible. His face had turned the color of wet ashes. His closed eyes were sunken in his skull. Flies buzzed around his blood-encrusted surcoat. He smelled of death, yet as long as he continued to breathe Dain vowed to keep hope.

He gripped Lord Odfrey's cold, slack hand in his and sent Sulein a look of determination. "If he lived through the night, that is a good sign. He is strong."

Sulein's dark eyes held compassion but nothing else. In silence he bowed and went away, leaving Dain to sit with his father. Sir Terent stood nearby, watching sadly.

Beyond the little canopy that had been erected to shelter the chevard, the morning sunlight blazed down on the scuffed and torn ground of the campsite. The kine had not yet been yoked to the wagons. They lowed from the hillside, where Lyias had taken them to graze, and one of the horses nickered back in answer.

Everything seemed faintly unreal, as though time had slowed down. One of the banners still lay torn and bloodied on the ground. A dead horse nearby was starting to swell. Soon it would stink. They had to leave before long, as soon as Lord Odfrey improved enough to travel. The other injured men had all died in the night.

Dain bowed his head, closing away his worries and concentrating on Lord Odfrey. The chevard's life force was ebbing far too low, but Dain refused to give up hope. "You are my father now," he said aloud, "and you *will* live. You will not be taken from me. You are strong, lord. You will recover, and we'll ride home together."

Lord Odfrey opened his eyes. They were nearly black with a pain so terrible that Dain wanted to look away. But he forced himself to meet Lord Odfrey's gaze. He smiled, and Lord Odfrey's lips quivered in an effort to smile back.

"Dain," he said, his voice a mere husk of sound.

"Gently, lord," Dain replied. "You must not waste your strength in talk."

"Listen. You are my . . . son. Must go on . . . go to king."

"We'll go later," Dain told him. "When you are well, then we will go."

Lord Odfrey tried to shake his head, but the effort clearly was beyond his strength. His face turned even paler, leaving his dark eyes burning like two coals.

"My son," he insisted.

Dain tightened his grip on Lord Odfrey's hand in an effort to quiet him. "Yes, I am your son," he said. "Now you must rest."

"My blessing . . . on you," Lord Odfrey said, struggling. "Take the warrant. Have . . . king sign. You *must*, Dain. Promise . . . promise me."

Tears filled Dain's eyes. He looked up frantically and saw Sulein a short distance away. The physician was watching, and when he saw Dain's expression of panic, he came hurrying over. The other knights and Thum followed, all of them gathering around.

"I promise," Dain said to Lord Odfrey, his voice shaking with grief. "But please live, lord. I want *you* to take me before the king. I don't want to go alone. It's not worth anything alone."

His tears choked up his voice, and he sobbed in silence, unable to say more.

Lord Odfrey's fingers moved a little within the harsh grip of Dain's hand. "My son," he said, and released a great moaning sigh.

He was dead.

Dain wept over him. In the hot sunshine, the others knelt and drew their Circles in silence. Finally someone began to say a prayer aloud. It was Thum, his wits having returned. His soft, clear voice wavered and choked, and his freckled face looked pale and weary beneath the bandage swathing his head, but he grimly went through the whole prayer.

For Lord Odfrey's sake, Dain said the responses with the others. But in his heart, he knew he remained a pagan still, for the prayer gave him no comfort. He was too full of loss, so sharp it stabbed him inside. He had known this man not yet a full year, but Lord Odfrey had been all he'd ever yearned for in a father, a man of worth and valor, a man he'd wanted to emulate with all his heart. Lord Odfrey, while no true kin of his, had taken Dain in, shown him kindness, given him a home, and eventually offered him everything. To Dain, the offer of adoption wasn't about wealth or property or position. The acceptance, the trusting affection which Lord Odfrey had shown him had meant the most of all.

And now this stern man with the tender heart would never ride home to his beloved Thirst again. He would never stride the ramparts of his hold, his angular profile turned to the marshlands while he surveyed the fields. He would never again bellow in anger, or allow the corners of his mouth to soften in amusement. He had outlived his lady wife, whose marriage ring he still wore. He had outlived the frail son of his loins. He had carried his grief and his disappointments through life without complaint. Valiant and courageous, he had been brave and true to the last.

He should have died old and safe in front of his own fire, with his dogs at his feet, Dain thought ruefully, but instead here he was lying cold on a blanket on the ground,

mourned by a handful, forgotten already by the prince he
had sworn to protect.

Dain did not know how long he sat there, numb and lost,
with Lord Odfrey's hand still gripped in his, but at last he
was roused by a gentle shaking of his shoulder.

Slowly Dain glanced up, and saw Sir Terent standing over
him, silhouetted against the midday sun. "It's time to go,
lad," he said in a soft, kind voice. "Time to take our poor
lord home."

Dain nodded, although his throat choked up again so
much he could not speak. He got to his feet and stood out
of the way as Sir Terent tenderly pulled the ends of the
blanket over Lord Odfrey and bound it around him with
cords. Then Sir Terent carried him away to place him in
one of the wagons.

In silence Thum came to stand beside Dain, offering mute
comfort with his presence.

Quietly he said, "It's time to go, Dain. Everyone is ready."

Dain was staring sightlessly at the river.

"Dain?"

"No."

"What?"

"I'm not going back," Dain said.

The words came out without thought. He'd made no conscious decision. But he felt right about what he was saying.
He knew what he had to do.

"What do you mean you're not going back?" Thum asked
in bewilderment. "Of course you are. Thirst is yours now."

"Is it?" Dain asked sharply.

"You aren't going to throw it away. Dain, it's a tremendous inheritance. Don't be a fool—"

"I'm not. I gave him my promise."

"Then let's take him home," Thum said sadly.

"I can't go there. I have to go to Savroix."

"It will wait."

"No, nothing is legal. I dare not wait." Dain turned his
head to frown at Thum. "That's what he was trying to tell

me. He made me promise I would go straight to the king. Without his majesty's seal, the adoption is not legal, no matter what Lord Odfrey wished."

"Oh," Thum said, blinking. "Then as soon as he's buried in the chapel, you'll have to set out."

"No, I'm going now. Delay will only cause me trouble."

Thum looked shocked, and Dain frowned at him. "How long would you have me wait?"

"Long enough to see him respectfully laid to rest and his soul sent to the Beyond," Thum said. "It's any son's duty to his father."

"And what happens if I see him settled under the rites, and lose the king's goodwill?" Dain asked. "I'm almost halfway to Savroix now. Gavril journeys ahead of me. He will have plenty of time to turn the king's mind against my petition, unless I follow closely."

"Do you think Gavril will care?" Thum asked. "He has much awaiting him. There's his investiture and his betrothal and—"

"I think Gavril will not forget to do me whatever ill he can," Dain said. "Perhaps not in the next few days—you're right in saying he will be busy. But if I go home to mourn, I am only giving him time to remember. He hates me, Thum."

"Aye, that's true."

"I have to do this for Lord Odfrey. He made me promise." Dain shot Thum a wild look. "I can't go back on my promise. Not to him!"

"Easy. We all witnessed it. We know what you have to do." Thum squared his thin shoulders. "I'll go with you."

"You don't have to. Your duties are over."

"Then I'll swear myself to your service," Thum said fiercely. "Only don't send me away!"

"All right," Dain said with a blink. He was grateful for Thum's loyalty and glad of his friendship. He did not know how to say either of those things, however, so he just nodded awkwardly and went back to frowning at the river. "Of course you may go with me, but not as a servant."

"You'll need a squire."

"I'm not a knight yet," Dain said. "All I need is a friend at my back."

"Then I'm with you," Thum said with a smile.

Sir Polquin came limping over to them. He looked cross, hot, and ravaged with grief. "It's time to go."

"I'm taking Lord Odfrey's petition to the king," Dain said.

"Aye, lad. We'll send you there in finery and fanfare, with half our knights at your back, and the banners flying," Sir Polquin said. "But first we take Lord Odfrey home and put him to his rest."

"You must do it," Dain said. "You and Sir Terent and Sir Alard. He wanted me to go straight to the king. He knew what will happen if I do not."

"There's political maneuvering, and then there's moral duty," Sir Polquin began stiffly. "You must—"

By then, however, Sir Terent had joined them. "What's the delay?" he demanded, handing Lord Odfrey's document pouch to Dain. "Your horse is saddled, m'lord. I've seen you supplied with food and a waterskin. If you're careful, you should have enough to last you all the way to Savroix."

Dain took the document pouch in his hands, feeling a new lump choke his throat. The pouch was made of sturdy leather, much worn from years of use. Lord Odfrey's hands had knotted it shut only yesterday morning.

After a slight hesitation, Dain unknotted the flap and dug through the papers until he found the one bearing Lord Odfrey's seal at the top and the petition carefully penned below it. Dain frowned at it, recognizing it only because Lord Odfrey had shown it to him. And although he could even read some of it now, he bit his lip and thrust it at Thum.

"Is this the petition?" he asked, while his face flamed with embarrassment.

"Aye," Thum said quietly.

Dain folded it up and tucked it inside his doublet for safekeeping. He closed the pouch and started to hand it to Sir Terent. "If you will take this to Thirst for—"

"Nay!" Sir Terent said, raising both meaty hands in rejection. "The chevard goes nowhere without that close by. Copies of all the warrants, land grants, and deeds are in it. It's too important to leave about."

"Oh." Dain tucked it under his arm, wanting to die from mortification. He realized how hopelessly ignorant he was, how ill-prepared and unworthy of the position that had been given to him. Lord Odfrey had been responsible for a tremendous number of people and lands. He read dispatches daily and wrote letters and reports, kept accounts, judged disputes, and accorded settlements. Dain himself could barely read and had only just learned to scratch out his name. He could be no leader of men, for he himself was not yet a man.

"This unbearded sprout wants to abandon his lordship and ride straight to Savroix," Sir Polquin growled. "Thinks only of the petition."

"And rightly so," Sir Terent said. As Sir Polquin's jaw dropped open, Sir Terent dropped to one knee before Dain. "My oath of service and loyalty is given to you, Lord Dain. Whether the king grants your petition or not, I know what Lord Odfrey wished. That do I follow, with all my heart."

Bowing his head, he drew his sword and lifted it, hilt-first, to Dain.

Astonished and touched, Dain could only stand there a moment with his throat choked up. Then he gathered his wits and touched Sir Terent's sword hilt lightly. "Thank you," he said, his voice mangled by his effort to control it. "I do accept your oath."

"Wait there!" Sir Alard called out. He came hurrying over and was there by the time Sir Terent had regained his feet. "What are you doing, Terent? Swearing fealty with Lord Odfrey not yet in his grave?"

"We're far from Thirst," Sir Terent said flatly. "What would you have me do? I heard Lord Odfrey's dying words, heard him bless Dain as his son and heir. I will serve Thirst all my days, to my last breath. And with Thirst, I serve its chevard, new or old."

Sir Alard's frown deepened, and he said nothing else.

Red came surging up Sir Polquin's stout neck into his jowls. He squinted at Sir Terent and muttered beneath his breath. Dain expected him to swear and stride away, but instead he lowered himself to his knees and raised the hilt of his sword.

"So do I swear my oath to Dain, chevard of Thirst," he said gruffly, then glared at Sir Alard. "Well?"

The tall, slim knight hesitated only a moment longer, then also knelt. Before he could speak, Sir Terent turned and bellowed, "Sir Bowin! Come here at once!"

As the last knight came hurrying over, Sir Polquin and Sir Alard remained kneeling. Dain barely knew Sir Bowin, who was taciturn to the point of unfriendliness. Without hesitation, the knight gave Dain a curt nod and knelt beside Sir Alard.

"Has to be done," he said, as though to himself, and drew his sword.

The oaths were given. Dain touched each of their sword hilts, feeling once again as though he was moving in a dream. He was incredibly grateful to them. And although he understood that their loyalty was given more to Lord Odfrey and the hold than to him personally, Dain did not care. He felt humbled by their devotion, and he told himself he must work hard to live up to what was expected of him.

And his first task, he knew, must be to secure his inheritance.

Squaring his shoulders, he faced the knights and Thum, who stood quietly nearby. "Thank you," he said, keeping his words simple. "I value your loyalty more than I can say. I will strive to keep myself worthy of it."

Sir Polquin looked at him fiercely. The master of arms was not an unkind man, but his standards were always high.

"Lord Odfrey saw the potential in you. See that you live up to it."

"I will," Dain promised, and cleared his throat. "Sir Terent?"

"M'lord?"

It felt strange, having Sir Terent address him with such respect. Dain frowned. "You and the others will escort the chevard's body home, while—"

"Nay," Sir Terent said crisply.

Flustered by this refusal to follow his first order as their new master, Dain scowled at him. "What do you—"

"For the past six years I've been the knight champion of Thirst Hold," Sir Terent said. His ruddy face looked as stern and determined as Dain had ever seen it. "For six years I've entered the king's tourney, and never have I won."

Sir Alard stared at him with his mouth agape. "How can you think of the tourney at a time like—"

Sir Polquin elbowed him in the ribs and growled something to keep him quiet.

Sir Terent ignored the interruptions and went on looking squarely at Dain. "I haven't won, but neither have I ever come in last," he went on. "I'm seasoned in countless campaigns. I've been fighting since I was seventeen. I've still got my eyes, and I'm quick on my feet. If you'll have me, m'lord, I'd be honored to serve as your knight protector."

Dain's mouth fell open.

Sir Alard's mouth grew pinched. "So you'll jump for promotion in spite of—"

"Hush that," Sir Polquin said gruffly. "This is no time for jealousy, man. Think on it! Who else among us can serve the lad better?"

"It isn't being done properly," Sir Alard insisted. "There should be a contest among all the Thirst knights above—"

"Bah!" Sir Polquin said. "We've no time for that. If Lord Dain is to ride straight to Savroix, he must be protected."

Dain tried to intervene in the argument. "But I—"

"You what?" Sir Polquin snapped impatiently. "If you

have romantic notions of riding off alone, put them aside. You're a chevard now, damne! No lord of consequence in this realm goes anywhere without a protector at his back, and so you should know it."

"If I'm not pleasing to your lordship," Sir Terent said stiffly, beginning to look hurt, "then choose another. Alard here, if you must, but choose one of us."

Dain realized he was mishandling everything, standing before them gape-mouthed like a serf. He met Sir Terent's eyes. "I'm honored to have your service as my protector, sir. There's no one else I would choose."

"Then it's settled," Sir Polquin said.

Sir Alard shut his mouth with a snap.

Sir Terent grinned broadly enough to reveal his missing teeth. He bowed to Dain. "I'll see to your horse, m'lord."

"I'm going as well," Sir Polquin announced. He glowered at Dain as though to forbid him any protest.

"Thank you, sir," Dain said mildly.

With a stiff nod and a harrumph, Sir Polquin turned on his heel and stalked off.

Sir Alard and Thum still stood there. The knight's aristocratic face was drawn tight with anger and disapproval. Dain did not understand what had offended him, but he knew he must do something to smooth over the problem. He wanted to make no new enemies this sad day.

"Sir Alard," he said carefully. "You are—"

"It's too soon, too hasty," Sir Alard muttered. "So much haste is unseemly and disrespectful. Forgive me, but I must say it."

Now Dain understood. He paused a moment, trying to consider his words. "Yes, it is," he agreed, and thus gained Sir Alard's complete attention. "If this matter were already settled, I would journey home at my new father's side, to grieve and mourn him as is the custom in Mandria."

"You are Mandrian now," Sir Alard said sharply, "if you are to inherit Thirst Hold."

"Aye," Dain agreed. "I must hold to the customs, as is

proper. But I must also fulfill the promise I made to him. Would you have me break it, Sir Alard?"

"Nay, I would not."

Inspiration came to Dain. He valued this man's intelligence and knew Sir Alard could be an invaluable ally. "Since I cannot do a son's duty until I return, will you escort my father home, sir? Will you see that the mass is said over him? Will you see him interred next to his lady wife and Hilard, his firstborn? Will you see that the serfs are allowed to pass him as he lies in state in the courtyard, and that each man bows to him in respect? Will you see that a mass is said also, later, for Sir Roye, who died to save him? And for these other valiant men who fell here? Will you take responsibility in my absence, making sure all is done correctly? I must trust Sir Bosquecel to retain command until I return, at which time all the knights of Thirst may choose whether to continue in my service or to hire themselves elsewhere. But Lord Odfrey himself I would entrust to no better man than you."

Sir Alard's face stiffened, and his eyes grew red-rimmed with emotion. He said nothing for a long moment, while his mouth compressed to a narrow line. Then he blinked and bowed his head to Dain.

"This commission will I take from you, Lord Dain. I swear I will perform these duties faithfully."

"Thank you," Dain said. "Let Sir Bowin ride with you to guard him homeward."

Sir Alard gave Dain a small nod and a parting look of respect before he strode away.

"Well done, Dain," Thum said quietly.

Dain sighed and lifted the heels of his hands to his eyes. "Gods," he muttered. "How am I to do this?"

"One decision at a time," Thum told him. "I ask you again, may I serve you as squire?"

Dain shook his head. "Nay, I tread too dangerously already. When my inheritance is secured, then will I seek investiture among the Thirst knights. If you still wish to serve me then, I will grant your request. But for now——"

"In Thod's name, do not send me back to Thirst!" Thum cried.

"For now, as I said before, come with me as my friend," Dain told him.

Red-faced, Thum looked ashamed at his outburst. "Forgive me. Of course I'll come."

Dain gave him a good-natured punch on the shoulder. "Do you really think I would leave you behind?"

Thum grinned back in relief.

Together they hurried to mount their horses. But beside Sir Terent and Sir Polquin waited Sulein as well, mounted on his ragged donkey with his flat, square-shaped hat tied firmly to his head.

Dismay filled Dain. "No," he said, with less tact than he meant to. "Physician, your place is with——"

"Lord Odfrey has no need of me now," Sulein said in his accented voice. His dark eyes bored into Dain as though to compel him. "You have much need of all the help you can attach to your personage."

"No."

"M'lord," Sir Terent said, leaning down from his saddle, "forgive me for speaking in a blunt way, but with you about to take on legal arrangements, so to speak, it'll be wise to have someone to read those documents for you."

Dain started to say that Thum could do the reading for him, but from the corner of his eye he saw Thum shaking his head in warning. Frustrated, Dain paid heed and thought it over. He realized they were right. He couldn't let his dislike of the physician blind him to how useful Sulein could be.

"Very well." The words came out grudgingly, and Sulein's eyes flashed in annoyance. Dain knew he should take care not to make an enemy of the man, but it was hard to be tactful when he wanted to send Sulein as far away from him

as he could. Biting off a sigh, Dain tried again. "Your assistance will be most appreciated, Master Sulein."

The physician's expression stayed cool, but he bowed and
in an oily voice said, "I shall cast your horoscope tonight,
Lord Dain. It might be well to begin by knowing the aus-
pices which lie over you."

Dain had no answer to this remark. He turned away and
bade farewell to Sir Alard, who was riding alongside the
wagon bearing Lord Odfrey's body. Sir Bowin had agreed
to drive it, and his horse was tied behind.

The servant Lyias climbed aboard the wagon to accompany Dain's little party, and they loaded themselves onto the
ferry. The river smelled fresh and clean, its waves lapping
against the sides of the boat as they were carried along.
When they reached the opposite shore and climbed out, Dain
glanced back, but Sir Alard and the wagon carrying Lord
Odfrey had already vanished from sight, swallowed within
Ebel Forest.

Dain shivered, and he had the sudden feeling that he
might never again return to upper Mandria or Thirst.

"What's amiss?" Thum asked him.

Dain shook his premonition away. "Nothing," he said,
and busied himself with pulling the saddle girth tight.

Under the blazing sun, they turned their faces toward the
south and rode for Savroix.

4

ALEXEIKA FLUNG BACK her long thick braid and grinned at
the three young boys helping her. "That's the last," she said

with satisfaction, and picked up a rag to wipe the blood from her hands.

It was hot today on the mountainside. The sun burned her shoulders through her coarse-woven tunic as she tossed down the rag and straightened her aching back with a sigh of relief.

They were high above the tree line, with a view that reached across the world to the mysterious Sea of Vvord. Beyond it lay the Land of the Gods, where no living man could venture. Forested valleys plunged below them, with crystalline fjords nestled like jewels at the bottom. To her right rose the jagged promontory called the Bald Giant. Its bare rock peak sported a dusting of snow today, and Alexeika knew that this late-summer weather would soon turn into the biting sting of autumn. In the back of her mind she was counting the days, thinking of all that she and the camp still had to do before taking refuge from the winter storms.

"Do you think we have enough?" Willem asked her.

She smiled at him. He was the youngest of her trio. Since the terrible massacre earlier this summer which had wiped out all the men in their camp of prime fighting age, Kexis, Vlad, and Willem had attached themselves to her like faithful burrs. Alexeika's Guard, they were called. In exchange for their help with the myriad tasks she had to do, she taught them swordplay and battle strategy and history, all that her father had taught her.

Stair-stepped in age from twelve to fourteen, they were the oldest boys in the camp. They were also the future of the rebellion, and although the rest of the camp had voted to abandon the fight, Alexeika refused to give up her dream of freedom from the tyrant King Muncel. Someday, boys like these across Nether would grow up into young men. There would be more battles. The war would never stop until Muncel was ousted from his throne. That, she vowed on her dear father's memory.

But for now, there were no battles to be fought. There was only survival to think of.

"Enough?" she echoed, running her gaze over the stack of pelts they had just finished skinning. "Let's tally them again."

The boys hurried to cut themselves new tally sticks with their knives. Separately, they counted the pelts, frowning with concentration as they cut notches in their sticks. When they finished, they came hurrying to Alexeika.

She'd already counted the pelts herself, but she carefully examined their tally sticks and was pleased to see that their count matched her own.

"Exactly right," she said. "Good!"

Willem and Vlad grinned with pleasure, but Kexis's face turned red. He swung away from her quickly. "I'll load them on the donkey," he said, trying to make his voice sound deep and gruff. "The younglings can clean the traps."

Vlad bristled at that. Sticking out his narrow chest, he raised his fists. "Younglings, are we? And you think you're so much older now that this is your birthing day? Hah!"

"I *am* older," Kexis told him repressively. "I don't have to think it. No longer am I a child."

"You—"

"Clean the traps," Kexis ordered him. "Alexeika is ready to go. You're only delaying us by arguing."

Vlad's face knotted with fury, and Alexeika judged it time to step in.

"We shall all clean the traps," she announced. "Divide them among us equally, and the task will go quickly."

Vlad and Willem accepted this and happily started stacking the traps in four piles.

Kexis scowled and kicked dirt with his toe before turning to her. "This is no task for your hands, Alexeika. You're tired, I can tell. Why don't you rest in the shade, and I'll see that everything gets finished."

She appreciated his offer of help. But of late there had been too much mooning in his brown eyes when he looked at her. He was all tongue-tied and suddenly awkward. He turned red whenever he had to speak to her. She was becoming his first love, and although she supposed it was a compliment, it was also going to be tiresome. Already he was trying to drive a wedge between her and the other boys, like an overprotective dog. She did not want to hurt him, this boy-man who had yet to grow his first beard, but she did not want matters to go too far.

"Thank you, Kexis," she said briskly. She raised her braid to let air cool the back of her neck, then headed for the traps. "I've no time for resting in the shade. We'll get these traps cleaned and the pelts loaded before we rest. I want to bring down the cached furs as well today, so there is much to do."

Kexis scowled, but he had little choice but to follow her and start the disagreeable chore of scraping off bits of fur and gore. They'd been trapping isleans—large, slim rodents with stringy, tasteless meat unfit for eating. The summer pelts of isleans came in a variety of colors and patterns, with the fawn and gray stripes being the most prized by the furriers of Karstok. Summer pelts were thin and difficult to work with, for they tore easily. But Alexeika and her helpers had become quite adept at skinning them. These short-napped furs would make gloves and trimming, and would earn them enough money pieces to buy such necessities as cloth, sugar, cooking pots, and medicines.

Come winter, Alexeika and the boys would set their traps along the banks of the fjords for vixlets, hares, and ermines. Those pelts would command high prices, unless court fashion turned in a different direction.

"Should I reset these?" Willem asked her when he finished scraping his traps. "I think up that way. There's a little canyon where I saw plenty of islean holes."

For a moment, as she paused to wipe perspiration from her brow, she was tempted. But they were high up in Grethori country, and that was always a risk. Besides, the snow on Bald Giant was a warning she could not ignore.

"Nay, don't," she said. "We're through with our summer trapping."

Their faces brightened, and even Kexis forgot to sulk. She could tell what they were thinking.

"Are we going to market them at the fair?" Vlad asked.

"They have to be sold," Alexeika said casually.

"Do you dare go yourself?" Kexis asked. "Or will Draysinko take them, like he did last year?"

She frowned. Draysinko was the only man of fighting age left in their camp. His crooked leg made him unfit as a warrior, and as a result he had not been in the battle that killed the other men. He was a weakling, a perpetual complainer who never did his full share of work. Yet he always had an opinion and sought to be in charge. Last year, he'd been given the responsibility of selling the furs, for he kept boasting of his bargaining skills. Alexeika's father had entrusted him with the task, but Draysinko had come home with far less money than he should have. Whether he'd simply sold the furs to the first merchant who offered a bid, or whether he'd kept part of the money for himself, no one knew. But Alexeika had her suspicions.

"No, not Draysinko," she said, keeping her voice calm and even. She might dislike and suspect the man, but he was a part of their camp and she knew the value of everyone's sticking together. "I may send Lady Selentya and her sister."

"But, Alexeika—"

"Or," she said, watching their disappointed faces with a smile, "I may go and do the bargaining myself."

Willem jumped to her side. "You'll need our help for that!" he said with excitement.

"Aye," she agreed, grinning back. "I will."

"Hurray!" he shouted, jumping up and down. "The Karstok fair! I can't wait to see everything there. May I load the pelts?"

"I'll help!" Vlad said eagerly.

Kexis stood up and swatted them aside. "I'll do the tying. You bring these traps."

Alexeika did not like the way he had begun to give the

younger ones orders, especially when those orders always
delegated the worst tasks to everyone but himself. "Kexis,"
she said sharply. "Come here."

He turned to her obediently, and Vlad and Willem grinned
at each other and began tying the pelts on the donkey the
way they wanted to.

"Kexis, you and I will get the caches," she said.

He went with her happily, obviously pleased to be alone
in her company. They opened the storage caves and brought
out the entire summer's worth of work, then rolled up the
pelts and tied them to their backs.

By the time she and Kexis returned, the old donkey was
loaded and their work area tidied so thoroughly no trace of
their presence remained.

Alexeika nodded in satisfaction. "Well done," she praised
them. "Not even the Grethori's best trackers will suspect
we've been here. The doubters in the camp said we
couldn't trap the summer furs, but with your help I have
proved them wrong. I am proud of each of you. You've
worked like men, and I could not have had better helpers."

Grinning, Willem and Vlad puffed out their chests. Kexis
turned bright red and gazed at her with open worship.

They headed down the mountain, going slowly because
the trail was steep and the pelts heavy. Willem offered to
divide her load between him and Vlad so she wouldn't have
to carry anything, but Alexeika declined. Her muscles were
tired, but she was strong and surefooted. She let Vlad lead
the donkey, and she dispatched Willem to scout ahead for
berries. Although he frowned a little at what he considered
children's work, it kept him occupied and useful. Alexeika
never missed an opportunity to glean all the food they could.

By the time they reached the valley floor, shadows were
sloping through the mountain ravines. Looking ahead through
the trees, Alexeika could see the ghostly outlines of the tents.
She loved coming home at twilight, when the cooking fires
were burning small and bright like glittering jewels and a
peaceful hush had descended over the camp. If she squinted

her eyes, she could look down the hill and almost imagine that the tents were maidens in white ball gowns, gathered shyly at the edge of the dancing floor. Humming an old court tune lightly to herself, she pretended the lords and ladies were about to commence the *grande glissade,* a stately court dance her father used to describe to her.

Alexeika had never been to court, had never seen a ball, had never worn a gown of exquisite silk sewn with jewels, had never veiled her hair according to fashion. Her father had taught her the steps of the formal dances, humming the tunes as they turned and skipped in a private forest clearing. But she was a princess in exile, a foreigner to the way of life that should have been her inheritance.

She could not miss something she had never known, but it pleased her now and then to wonder and pretend.

As she drew closer, she could smell the fragrant smoke of the cooking fires and mouthwatering scents of baking fish and spiced quanda roots. The ghostly court maidens became tattered and much-mended tents of sun-bleached crosscloth. A pair of unseen children bickered sharply, and their mother's voice reprimanded them. On the far side of camp, the faint strains of zithren music could be heard, strumming a ballad of love and loss.

Hearing the song made Alexeika think of her own grief, which was always a stone in her heart. It also annoyed her. She knew the tragic past would haunt them forever, but it was important to keep her hope focused on the future.

As she descended the final incline toward the camp, Alexeika checked the sentry points as always. She saw no one on the flat rock that jutted out from the steep hillside. She saw no one in the forked larch. She saw no one on the enormous log of an Ancestor—ancient trees so massive they must have been seeded by the gods. All three checkpoints had no one in position, despite the fact that it was nearly dusk.

Alexeika stopped in her tracks and stared at the positions

again to make sure there was no mistake. There wasn't. The sentries were not on duty.

She could not imagine what was wrong. Swiftly she looked toward Uzfan's tent. A puff of purple smoke was rising from the fire vent, and the sight of it eased her sense of alarm. If he was busy creating spells to ease his old joints tonight, then no crisis had happened.

But where were the sentries? This was just like the first few days after the massacre, when no one wanted to take responsibility for any task and Alexeika had to cajole, plead, and threaten to get the surviving camp members to work. Scowling, she tried to remember who was assigned tonight's watch duty. It was supposed to be Tleska, Vynyan, and . . .

"Draysinko," she said aloud.

Willem crowded up against her on the trail. "Alexeika, what's wrong?" he asked. "Why have you stopped?"

Their donkey brayed loudly, making her jump. Furiously she whirled around and glared at Kexis. "Keep that brute quiet!" she ordered.

His eyes widened, but he hastily seized the animal's nostrils and pinched hard to keep it from sounding off again. "Is something amiss?" he whispered.

All three boys were staring at her with wide, frightened eyes. Her forehead knotted and she swung her gaze back toward the camp. Everything looked well. She could see individuals moving among the tents. Someone, probably Marta, was walking toward the fjord with a wooden pail for water.

"Alexeika?" Willem dared whisper.

She tried to overcome her tight-lipped anger, tried to ignore the furious pounding of her heart. "Look yon, boys. What do you see amiss?"

They crowded around her and peered down at the camp while she fumed and kicked pebbles. "Well?" she demanded. "Do you see? Or has my training been a waste of time?"

Thus chastened, they straightened their shoulders. Turning bright red, Kexis said, "No one has fished today. It's time to start smoking extra lakecaps for winter storage."

Her gaze flicked away from him. "Vlad?"

But it was Willem who answered, "There are no sentries."

Kexis blinked and Vlad's mouth fell open.

"Impossible!" Kexis said, giving Willem a push. "You're inventing fables."

"I'm not!"

"Cease," Alexeika snapped, and they hushed immediately. She glared at the camp and started down the trail so that the boys and donkey had no choice but to follow. "The fools," she muttered under her breath.

Her stomach had been growling insistently, but now she forgot how hungry and tired she was as she lengthened her stride. With every step, her annoyance grew, destroying her previous satisfaction at a day's work well done.

She despaired of her camp folk. How could they be so careless? Must she remind them of basic safety measures endlessly? Why could they not take some responsibility for themselves?

Leadership was a heavy burden to carry. She entered camp with her fists clenched and her jaw set tight. While she always worried when she left camp for an entire day, she had also tried to convince herself that her people were sensible.

Now, they'd proven that assumption wrong.

"Alexeika, look!" Vlad said to her.

She glanced forward to where he pointed and saw two figures emerging from the cluster of tents to meet her. She recognized Uzfan and Draysinko immediately, and scowled. Uzfan, his wrinkled face looking worried above his gray beard, tried to reach her first, but she quickened her stride to confront Draysinko.

"Have your wits gone begging?" she demanded.

He came to an abrupt halt and stared at her with his mouth open. He had a narrow face with a wispy dark beard and eyes that were bright, beady, and dissatisfied.

Glaring, she gave him no chance to speak. "Why aren't you on duty?"

"Duty? But—"

"Yes, duty," she snapped. "You and Tleska and—"

"Oh, sentry work." He waved his hand in dismissal. "It's unimportant. We—"

"How dare you say so!" she shouted, not caring who heard her.

Uzfan frowned and made shushing motions at her, but she ignored him.

"Thod's bones, man!" she snapped at Draysinko. "I just came down the mountain with a donkey and three blundering boys in my wake, and none of you knew it."

"I've been watching for your return," Draysinko said. "There is something we must discuss."

"We'll discuss your dereliction of—"

His face turned red. "You cannot order me. You are but a woman, and you are not in charge."

His arrogance so infuriated her that she could not speak for a moment. It was like having boiling water thrown over her.

Uzfan stepped between them, raising his hands placatingly. "Please, please, do not quarrel. It is not seemly."

"What is not seemly is for this fool to refuse to stand watch," she said, and had the satisfaction of seeing Draysinko's dark eyes narrow. "Gods! We could have been a Grethori raiding party, on you before you knew it."

Uzfan looked troubled. "Have you seen Grethori?"

"There are no bandits," Draysinko said with a sneer before she could answer. "They would have bothered us by now if they meant to. Alexeika has the weak mind of a woman. She must invent something to worry about if there is nothing there."

"It's no good accusing me," she told him furiously. "I'm no shirker. You're too lazy to—"

"Hold your tongue!" he shouted, his face bright red behind its beard. "You should be veiled and silent, like a proper woman."

Kexis jumped between Draysinko and Alexeika and swung wildly at Draysinko. He missed, but the weaver

ducked back just the same. "You will not insult her!" Kexis
shouted.

"Kexis, no!" Alexeika said.

They ignored her. Draysinko narrowed his eyes and back-
handed the boy. Kexis went reeling to the ground. At once
he jumped up, clenching his fists, and tried to charge, but
Alexeika gripped him by the back of his tunic and held him.

"No," she said sharply.

He struggled in her hold. "That dirty—"

"Cease!" she snapped in her training voice.

He froze in place, red to the tips of his ears, and she
shook him by his shoulder.

"No," she repeated.

Kexis's brown eyes, full of indignation, met hers. "He
should not speak to you like that."

"Thank you for your defense," she said, "but there will
be no violence in the camp. That is our rule, Kexis. Go tend
to the pelts."

The boy ducked his head, nodding obediently, then shot
Draysinko a hateful glare before he walked away.

An awkward silence descended over them. Vlad and
Willem stood round-eyed, and several other women and small
children had appeared to goggle at them.

"Draysinko, you will speak to the princess with respect,"
Uzfan said, breaking the silence.

The weaver was glaring at Alexeika. "You have a retinue
of savage puppies."

She glared back. "Did it give you satisfaction to knock
down a boy?"

He turned red. "Kexis started it—"

"Please," Uzfan said, raising his hands. "Desist this bick-
ering. There are other matters before us. These fine pelts,
for instance. Draysinko, you should examine them for an estimate of their worth."

"Yes, I am the expert in such matters," Draysinko boasted,
puffing out his narrow chest. The weaver bowed jerkily to
the priest and went over to the donkey. By then, Kexis had

unloaded the animal. He stepped back at Draysinko's approach, casting a look of appeal at Alexeika. She shook her head and gestured for him to go home. Reluctantly, Kexis obeyed her.

"Uzfan," she said, but the old priest gave her a swift look of warning. Fuming, she held her tongue. Draysinko's words ran through her mind, rasping her like rough stone. She wanted to flay him for his impertinence, but his insults to her were insignificant compared with his actions. Shirking his duty. Undoubtedly persuading the others to abandon their duty as well. And then striking Kexis like that. He was a coward, braggart, and troublemaker whom she wished she could drive from the camp.

"It is late. Alexeika, you are no doubt tired from your hard work," Uzfan said. His gaze traveled past her to the silent boys and the wealth of pelts spread across the ground.

Some of the women crept closer, murmuring in admiration.

"This shows hard work indeed," Uzfan said, and the women clapped. He smiled at Alexeika. "Your traps have yielded well."

"Aye," she said, tossing her head with pride. "They have."

Draysinko knelt to examine the pelts. His beady eyes brightened, and his face shone with excited avarice.

Watching him, Alexeika felt her suspicions return. Did he think she was going to entrust him with the furs at this year's market? Her father had been more tolerant of Draysinko's shortcomings than Alexeika was prepared to be.

"I did not expect so many pelts," Draysinko said, stroking the furs with his hands. "Very good. Very, very good."

Alexeika ignored him and met Uzfan's gaze. The old, defrocked priest looked more troubled than ever.

"We must talk," he said in a low voice.

"Aye," she agreed grimly. Her anger remained with her, steaming and simmering. Wearily she shrugged off her burden of pelts, and when Vlad added them to the pile,

Draysinko caressed them and made little noises of admiration.

He disgusted her, and she turned her back on him.

"Uzfan, as soon as I deal with these—"

"Nay," the priest said, laying his hand lightly on her arm. "Rest yourself, child. Have your supper, and then I will come."

She bowed her head in agreement.

"My mother said you're to share our supper tonight," Willem spoke up. "It's our turn."

"Yes, of course I will come," Alexeika said. Since her father's death, she had assumed many of the leadership responsibilities for the camp. She also did most of the hunting. Accordingly, the women of the camp took on the task of inviting her to their fires for supper. She accepted their invitations gladly, for it was a way to keep on good terms with everyone, as well as to know their complaints. Often she could soothe disagreements before they grew into quarrels. She settled disputes, dispensed encouragement, and worked at keeping her people's spirits strong.

Hunting and trapping furs were men's jobs, nothing for a woman, but Alexeika had never been raised to sit about with her hands folded. A lady born, and a princess by rank, she wore a tunic and leggings like a man. Destiny had gone a crooked path when it made her, for although born a maid, she'd been forced to fill the shoes of a son to her famous general father. Accordingly, she carried twin pearl-handled daggers, and in her rare private moments she slipped away into the forest to work at strengthening her body and arms so that she could better wield her father's sword. Since the massacre, the camp had kept far from towns and settlements, risking no contact with the king's soldiers. But Alexeika knew that they could not hide forever. There would come a day when they would have to fight again. She took no chances in letting her skills grow rusty. Maid or not, she intended to carry on the rebellion her father had died for.

Leaving Vlad in charge of the pelts, Alexeika sent Willem

home with his tunic tail full of berries and promised to follow in a few minutes. Uzfan lingered, the smell of his spellcasting pungent on his clothes, and shot her another look of warning before he returned to his tent. Draysinko was still examining the pelts, making little cooing sounds of greed and approval.

She frowned at the man, wanting to punish him for putting the camp in danger, but she was all too painfully aware that her authority here was not the same as her father had held. The general had been the undisputed leader. His orders were law. Alexeika had to lead by suggestion and cajoling. When she snapped out direct orders, the women looked hurt. If she criticized the old men, they acted insulted. Sometimes Alexeika felt on fire with frustration. Had she been a man, they would have obeyed her without question. As it was, they held their council meetings weekly and discussed actions for the camp to take, then dithered and deferred the matter to her judgment.

Jerking her fingers through her wind-knotted hair, Alexeika abandoned the pelts and took the chance to escape to her tent.

It was large enough for two people, and all her life she had known no other abode. Until a few weeks ago, it had held two cots, and at eventide Alexeika was always there when her father came home. She made sure there was a pot boiling on the cooking fire, the lamp was lit on the small folding campaign table of exquisite inlaid wood, and a pail of oiled sand was waiting to clean her father's weapons. Now, there was only one cot. Her father's possessions and clothing had all been folded away in the chest. She seldom took the time now to adorn her little home with freshly picked flowers. Instead, she usually came in wearily, unbuckling her daggers and glad to lower the tent flap on all the problems of her day.

Tonight, however, the tent felt different inside. Something was awry. She stopped in her tracks, her nostrils flaring as she looked about. A faint, elusive scent lingered here that did not belong. It was not magic, but it made her wary.

The tent was full of shadows and gloom. She moved forward cautiously, certain that nothing lurked in here. Yet something, or someone, had been here earlier. Intrusion was unthinkable. No one entered another's tent without permission. It was the inviolate rule of the camp. Yet that rule had been broken while she was gone today.

She shuddered, there in the darkness, and drew her dagger.

5

AFTER A FEW minutes' hesitation, she crossed the tent in the darkness and lit the lamp. Its flaring wick cast a glow of golden light that drove back the shadows. Swiftly she glanced around, but saw no one.

She sniffed, but there was no stench of Nonkind, no whiff of magic. Slowly, she sheathed her dagger.

All seemed as it should be. Her clothes chest was strapped shut. The little map cabinet's door was closed. Her cot blanket was smooth and tight, just as she'd left it.

No, it was not. She frowned, seeing one corner of the blanket that had been pulled out and retucked hastily, sloppily.

A chill ran through her, and Alexeika stiffened. She stood frozen, certain now that someone had been in her tent today, prowling or searching for something to steal. A sense of violation overwhelmed her.

Suddenly she could not bear to be inside. Her own home disgusted and repelled her. Yet anger made her stay.

Swiftly she conducted a search, checking first to be sure that Severgard, her father's sword, was safe. She found it in her father's chest, lying secure in its scabbard. But the clothes beneath it had been rifled. Drawing in her breath sharply, she dug to the bottom of the chest, her fingers searching for the leather money pouch.

It was gone.

Withdrawing her hand, she curled it into a fist of rage. A thief, a petty weasyn of a thief, had dared come in here and steal from her.

The money pouch itself contained only a few coppers, nothing of much value. It was a decoy to thwart petty thievery such as this, but she was infuriated just the same.

Slamming the chest shut, she shifted it around on the rug of brightly woven colors and checked the false compartment cleverly fitted into the back. There she found the real money pouch, with its fifteen precious gold dreits still safe. The jewel pouch containing her father's marriage ring and Alexeika's own emerald necklace and ear bobs were also there.

Breathing out a sigh of relief, she replaced these treasures and resumed her search.

In the end, she discovered that the thief had fingered everything she owned, including her father's maps and her spare set of clothing. A lace-trimmed handkerchief, dainty and exquisitely embroidered, was missing.

Alexeika sat back on her heels and slowly lowered the lid of her chest. Her eyes brimmed with sudden tears, although she told herself not to be silly. The coppers and a handkerchief were minor things, unimportant things, especially when there were far more vital treasures at risk.

But the handkerchief had been her mother's. Sometimes, Alexeika would take it out and press the exquisite linen against her face, closing her eyes and pretending she smelled the lingering scent of her mother's perfume. King Muncel had ordered her mother killed when Alexeika had been an infant. She had grown up motherless, forever conscious of a void inside her that evoked intense longings. There had been many things, womanly things, that she could not ask her father. At eighteen, Alexeika often felt herself to be more boy than maid. She liked it that way. She valued her freedom and loved her independence. But when she sometimes felt soft and feminine, she enjoyed holding the dainty handkerchief in her hands and fluttering it the way court ladies did.

Now it was gone, the least yet most precious of her possessions. She wept for it, furious and hurt. Who could have taken it? Why? Who had broken her trust like this?

A faint scratching on the tent flap made her lift her head. Realizing someone was outside, she swiped her tears hastily away and bent over the water pail to wash her face.

"Yes?" Her voice came out wavery.

"Alexeika?" It was Willem. "Are you coming for supper?"

She stood up with a jerk, dripping water down the front of her tunic, and realized she'd forgotten all about eating supper with Willem and his family. Her appetite had deserted her, but although she wanted to remain hidden in her tent, she refused to let the thief see how upset she was.

Extinguishing the lamp and emerging from the tent, Alexeika paused a moment with her head held high and imperious. She swept the camp with an angry glare. But folks were busy eating at their own fires. No one save Willem was paying her any attention.

The mundane scene made her even angrier. She shoved aside the temptation to rouse the entire camp and start hurling accusations. A cool head was needed for any successful strategy. She could not think right now, while she was so upset. Later tonight, she would decide what to do.

"I'm sorry, Alexeika," Willem said. His eyes gazed up at her as though he could sense her wrathful mood. "Mama made me come because we don't want to eat without you, and Katrina gets—"

"Of course I'm coming," Alexeika said, forcing herself to be courteous to the boy. "It was wrong of me to keep your mother waiting like this."

"Oh, no," Willem said, falling into step with her. "She doesn't mind, really. It's just—"

"I understand," Alexeika said, and rested her hand on his shoulder to halt his apologies.

She walked at a rapid stride, her gaze flicking sharply to lamplit faces as she passed the various tents. And each person she saw made her wonder. She hated her suspicions, yet someone here deserved them.

The meal she shared with Willem, his mother, and his little sister Katrina was a modest but tasty stew served with flat cakebread sizzling hot from the stone griddle. Alexeika was too preoccupied for conversation, and as soon as she could thank the woman for her hospitality and leave she did so.

She started for her tent, but suddenly veered away and headed out through the trees to the steep bank of the fjord. The black surface of the water glimmered here and there, reflecting starlight. As of yet there was no moon. The breeze blowing off the water felt tangy and cool against her cheeks.

She loved and drew comfort from the deep, still waters. In the first days after her father's death, she would row out as far as she could and just sit in the quiet solitude, letting it heal her wounds. Tonight, seeking to settle her troubled heart, she inhaled deeply of the pine fragrance coming from the opposite shore.

"Alexeika."

Startled, she whirled around and reached instinctively for her daggers before recognizing Draysinko limping toward her from the shadows. She had not heard his approach, and she did not like that.

"The night air is sweet, is it not?" he said.

His thin voice grated on her nerves. She moved restlessly away from him and said nothing. He was the last person she wanted to deal with right now.

He followed her as though she had invited his company. "The pelts are handsome. I did not expect you to bring in so many."

"I told the camp I would match last year's tally," she said curtly. "I did."

"Aye, and more," he said. His voice was warm for once with approval. "Excellent work indeed. They will bring much money."

She cast him a sharp look, but said nothing.

He smiled. "You never fail to amaze me with all you can do."

She did not want his praise. It seemed as false as his smile. "We'll need a good price to help us through the winter," she answered, trying to keep their conversation away from anything personal.

Draysinko stepped even closer to her, and his voice dropped to an oily, intimate level. "I admire you a great deal."

"Keep your admiration," she replied briskly. "I need it not."

"Alexeika, are you never soft?" he asked. "Are you never womanly?"

Her cheeks felt suddenly warm. Her anger deserted her, leaving her confused and disconcerted. She kept her gaze locked firmly on the dark waters of the fjord. A sliver of moon was rising above the far mountains. She looked for its reflection in the water. "I must go," she said uneasily. "The day has been long."

"Wait." He reached out and gripped her arm lightly. "Please. I would speak to you."

She sighed. "You have spoken enough. Let us close the matter, unless you intend to apologize for your mischief in trying to rid the camp of night sentries."

"I'm not interested in the Grethori," he said. "And standing watch at night is tiresome and boring."

"Only to someone who is lazy," she retorted. "Someone who refuses to care about the good of the camp."

He tightened his grip on her arm. She tried to pull free, but when she could not, her temper flared. "Release me!"

But he pulled her into his arms and clumsily tried to kiss

her. His breath was hot and avid. He stank of the rancid beyar grease he used on his hair. "Alexeika, you're such a beauty," he murmured, trying to capture her mouth with his. "Do you know how you captivate me? I burn for you—"

She twisted furiously in his hold and punched him deep in his soft stomach with her free fist.

With a grunt he doubled over, and she backed away from him. She was breathing a little fast; she held her lithe young body taut and ready to give him worse harm. She was intensely angry with him.

"You drunken fool!" she said. "How dare you fondle me like you would some town harlot? I am not for your handling."

Still doubled over and moaning, he mumbled something inaudible. Knowing she hadn't hit him that hard, Alexeika felt her scorn intensifying.

But when she swung around and ducked a low-hanging tree branch to head for her tent, he came hurrying after her. "Wait, please," he said. "Listen to me! Do you know how magnificent you are when you're angry?"

She had never heard anything so ridiculous. "Are you mad? Leave me!"

"I won't. I can't. All I do is think about you. I would have you for mine, Alexeika."

She scowled and quickened her pace.

His fingers grazed the top of her shoulder. She ducked away from his grasp and spun about to face him, her dagger drawn in repudiation.

"Touch me not again, sirrah," she said, "or I'll cut off that hand. See how you weave then."

He dropped his outstretched hand to his side. It was too dark to see his expression, but she could tell he was growing angry.

"Is my affection such an insult?" he asked. "Don't pull your great rank here, princess, for you have no lands and no real title to claim as your own."

"I wouldn't let you near me if you were thrice a lord."

"Careful, Alexeika," he said. "I am the only eligible man in our camp now. I can have my pick of all the young women, but I prefer you."

"Am I supposed to be honored by this declaration?"

"Who else besides me can you choose?"

Her outrage increased. "I am in mourning," she said, forcing herself to explain the protocol he should have known were he anything less than an ill-educated lout. "I choose no one until that is over."

"Your father is dead," he said. "You are living. Will you waste your life following rules of a court that no longer exists? Come away with me, Alexeika. Now. Tonight. I will—"

"Go cool your ardor in the fjord," she said harshly, striding away from him. "It is not, and never will be, welcome."

That should have quelled him, but to her disgust he stayed on her heels, quickening his stride to draw even with her. "Alexeika, must I force you to love me?"

She whirled around and swiped him with her dagger. Its needle-sharp point sliced through his tunic sleeve, and he yelped shrilly.

"Gods, woman!" he said in fury. "You're mad!"

"I warned you," she replied, knowing she had but scratched him, if her weapon had drawn blood at all. "You have no right to touch me. Had I a protector, he would gut you where you stand for your impertinence. But I am capable of doing it myself. Get away from me, and stay away from me. I will not warn you again."

He was still staggering about, clutching his arm and swearing terrible curses under his breath. "I seek to do you a good turn, and you attack me!" he said, his voice shrill. "I offer you everything—"

"You?" She laughed in scorn, tossing her head. "You offer me nothing but insult."

"You'll regret this," he muttered. "Prancing about in your leggings, tempting decent men, flaunting yourself."

"What?" she gasped.

"You'll see," he told her, and now his voice was spiteful

and vicious. "You think you're as clever as a man, but you're nothing but a fool of a woman. And not even a real woman at that!"

The insult stung her so harshly she turned and swiftly hurried to her tent. Her heart was racing, and she found herself almost sobbing for air. Her fist was still clenched around the hilt of her dagger, and as she walked she struck the air with it several times, wishing she had driven it into Draysinko's chest.

By the time she reached the refuge of her tent, she was shaking. Swiftly she lit her lamp and paced back and forth, back and forth. He was a worm, a weasyn, a belly-crawler coward of a man. He was not worth her anger, but his arrogance and sudden boldness had both astonished and appalled her. How could he possibly think she would be flattered by his declaration? After she had rebuked him for his stupidity and laziness before supper, how could he yet come to her and expect her to fall into his embrace?

She shuddered, and ran her hands up and down her arms to take the shivering away. That last thing he'd said had been hateful and cruel. She had no doubt that someday she would find a man right for her, a man who could accept her opinions as those of a helpmeet with a mind of her own. There must be a man, she told herself, who would take pride in her intelligence, education, and skill in wielding a weapon. Her father had never forced her to act like a boy; he had never tried to drive her maidenly side from her. He had insisted she know what was expected of a lady, but he had also insisted she use her wits and not expect a man to think and act for her.

When she wed, she would give herself to a warrior lord who had proven himself on the battlefield. Her man would have honor and courage. He would be no sniveling coward too lazy to work. In fact, in her dreams at night this man of her future often wore the face and thews of Faldain, whose image she had once summoned by parting the veils of seeing. He would be dark-haired and keen of eye. His shoul-

ders would be powerful and straight. He would be handsome, young, and virile. But he would also be tender in
heart, just, and true. This was whom she dreamed of. Not a
sniveling weaver with a crooked leg who let his ambitions
run away with him.

Alexeika did not live formally, but she'd been raised by
an old-fashioned father. Draysinko was not only repulsive,
but a weaver, a guildsman as far beneath her rank as an ant
was beneath an eagle. She found herself shocked that
Draysinko had dared approach her this boldly. Had she any
male relatives, he would be horsewhipped and driven immediately from the camp. She wished she could drive him
out herself.

But if she did that, there would have to be an explanation to the others. She lifted her chin, refusing to tell
anyone how he'd insulted her.

Fuming, she paced yet longer, wishing she could be outdoors instead of trapped within the stuffy confines of her
tent. It was often her custom, when the weather was warm,
to loop back the tent flap to let the evening breeze come in.
Tonight she kept the flap lowered. She felt unsettled, jumpy,
and restless. And now that her tent had been violated, she
felt no security at all.

She could not even bear to sit down, and kept pacing
back and forth despite her growing fatigue. She longed for
a refreshing swim in the icy waters of the fjord, but Draysinko
might yet be lurking there on the bank.

Someone coughed politely outside her tent flap. She
jumped and whirled around, her heart thumping before she
recognized Uzfan's voice.

"Alexeika, it is I. May I enter?"

Unexpected tears sprang to her eyes. Suddenly, although
she loved the old man as an uncle, she lacked enough composure to face him. He would instantly know something was
wrong. She could not hope to conceal her agitation, and she
was not completely certain why she should want to. But she
felt ashamed and unsure of herself. She wondered if she had

given Draysinko encouragement without meaning to. Even Kexis followed her about like a lovesick puppy. Was she doing something wrong?

The priest was her mentor and confidant, but he was also a man. She needed a woman to talk to, desperately. But who had taken things from her tent? Whom could she trust?

"Alexeika," Uzfan called again. "Forgive me. Do I disturb you?"

"No!" she replied. "A moment please."

Hastily she went outside, letting the flap fall shut behind her to keep the lamplight from revealing her face.

Feeling cloaked by the darkness, she glanced around and saw that most of the fires had been put out. The camp was settling down for the night. A woman was shooing home two children, both whining to be allowed to play a while longer. Alexeika had managed to shame Tleska into sentry duty, but one sentry was not enough.

She had no desire to be consulted about whatever problem was troubling Uzfan tonight, but in courtesy she could not refuse him.

"What's amiss?" she asked. "What troubles you?"

Leaning on his staff, the old priest glanced about uneasily. "This, I fear, is not private enough."

"Then let us walk," she said.

"Alexeika—"

"Let us walk," she said firmly, and strode off into the darkness so that he was forced to hobble after her.

In a few minutes, when they were well-concealed among the trees and the darkness, she relented and came to a halt.

Uzfan came puffing up to her, and she felt sorry for taking her anger out on him.

"Surely this is private enough," she said, listening to the quiet rustle of the tree canopies, the furtive rustle and scurry of night creatures. Tomorrow night it would be Alexeika's turn to stand watch. The job was hard, of course, but what of it? Her father had taught her the warrior tricks for staying awake and alert. Dismissing that from her thoughts, she faced the old priest. "What is it you wish to say?"

"I dislike making accusations, and I have no proof other than my word," Uzfan began.

Weariness made her impatient. "Your word has ever been enough for me. What is it?"

"I saw Draysinko in your tent today. He thought no one was looking, but I saw him. I wanted to warn you when you returned, but he was in the way." The priest paused a moment, then lowered his voice even more. "I fear he means to do some mischief, child."

She could say nothing at first. Her anger was like a vine, strangling her. *He* had been in her tent, her home. *He* had been fingering her clothing, her personal possessions. *He* had stolen from her. And she had sensed no guilt in him tonight as he capered about like a knave, thinking himself lordly enough to kiss her. Draysinko, the coward and shirker, and now thief. He must indeed be mad.

"Alexeika—"

"What did you see him take?" Her voice came out flat and very calm, calmer than she expected, given how she raged inside.

"Nothing, but he was in there a long while. I sense no good in him, child. Of late, he seems always dissatisfied and scheming. And ever since we refused the king's amnesty—"

"The usurper's amnesty!" she corrected hotly.

Uzfan bowed. "Yes, child, Muncel the Usurper. Since we refused, Draysinko has been brooding all summer."

"It was false and a lie, a trick to pull all the rebels of Nether into slavery. He—"

"Yes, child," Uzfan said, lifting his hand wearily. "But let us keep our attention on this weaver and what he might do. I want you to beware of him."

Uzfan's warning was so earnest, so well-intentioned, and yet it came far too late. She nearly laughed at the irony, but it wasn't a good kind of laughter. Instead, she took the old man's hand and kissed it. "Thank you, my friend," she murmured. "You are always good to me."

"I worry, child. I worry."

Alexeika released his hand, then drew her daggers and held one in each hand. Her heart was aflame, yet she felt cold and purposeful inside. "You are right to worry," she said harshly. "The man has lost his senses. Papa's money purse is missing. Everything of mine has been handled and disturbed. He even took something of my mother's."

Her voice quavered as she said the last, and she had to swallow a moment before she could command herself again.

"Child," Uzfan said in sympathy.

Alexeika lifted her chin. "There is more to this sorry tale. Tonight, he waylaid me on the bank and tried to persuade me to elope with him."

"This is infamy!" Uzfan said in outrage. "Why did you not come to me at once? Has he hurt you in any way?"

"Nay. 'Twas he who suffered the hurt," she said with grim satisfaction. "He must be driven from the camp. At once. I'm going to rouse everyone and ask for—"

"Wait," Uzfan said, gripping her arm to keep her from charging off. "Not in haste, child. Put up those daggers, and give yourself time to think calmly."

"Do you condone his actions?" she asked, shocked.

"Nay, but we must think—"

"I need no time to think," she said. "We have rules, and he has broken them. He must go."

Uzfan was silent for a moment. "There is more you have not told me."

Her face filled with fire. Although he could not see her in the darkness, she turned away just the same. Her fingers pulled the leaves off a branch, then she rolled and crushed them so that a pungent aroma scented the air. "Surely there are enough accusations already."

"What else has he done?" Uzfan asked.

Her shame was growing, keeping her silent when she wanted to speak. She hated Draysinko, hated herself. "He said . . ." She stopped, unable to continue. "Let us not discuss it."

"Has he forced you?" Uzfan asked in a soft, deadly voice.

"No. He took a kiss only. What else he meant to do, I gave him no chance to try. He—I cut his arm with my dagger. It was not hard to drive him away." She drew a sharp breath. "Am I wrong to wear leggings? Do I flaunt myself? He said I am no decent maid—"

"Nay, child! Nay! This is not your fault," Uzfan said angrily. "If that is what he said to you, then he lied."

Tears stung her eyes. "But there is Kexis, growing so silly too. I thought—I was afraid Draysinko might be right."

Uzfan gripped her arms. "Dear child, put this unhappiness from your heart at once. You should never feel that the brutality of men is your fault. You are as sweet and comely a maid as your mother ever was. Your father raised you to be a lady, and that is what you are. Draysinko must blame his own evil for his lust, not you."

"But the boy—"

"The boy is driven by what lies inside himself. You were born a comely maid. You shine above the others in looks, in deeds, in abilities. You are a princess, child. Your lineage stretches back three hundred years. Foolish boys and men will always be drawn to you, but you are not responsible for them. Were this ungodly blight not upon our land, you would be home, safe within your father's protection. No one would dare assault you, and respect toward you would be strictly enforced."

"But I do not live within my father's castle," she said.

He sighed. "No, you do not."

"Draysinko must go," she said. "He must be driven out. But first I am going to force him to return my property. I want everyone in camp to know he is a despicable thief."

"Take care, child."

She frowned. "But why?"

"If you call council, accuse him, and run him out of camp, you will make a grievous enemy."

She snorted scornfully. "I do not fear him."

"Perhaps you should."

"What can he do?" she said scornfully. "He is nothing!"

"You know better," Uzfan rebuked her. "Because he is not a warrior does not mean he cannot do harm."

"Do I let him stay, then?" she asked. "Thod knows, I'd prefer to gut him in the woods."

"A natural sentiment. But I advise you to consider the matter with a cool head. Your own father would tell you the same."

"My father would have him flayed."

Uzfan snorted. "There are ways to shame him and see him gone without bringing harm to the camp."

"Are you saying he will betray us to the soldiers?"

"I think he would."

"Aye," she said bitterly, "and especially if he could collect a reward."

"This is why I wanted no one to overhear. Draysinko can become a dangerous man if mishandled. Right now he is merely sly and venal."

She drew in several breaths, trying to master her anger. "What would you have me do?"

"The solution will come to you."

"No, Uzfan!" she said angrily, slapping at a nearby bush. "I can't wait for solutions. This has to be dealt with now. Firmly and decisively. If I am to be a good leader—"

"Alexeika," he said in soft rebuke, stopping her tirade in mid-sentence.

She hung her head, her eyes stinging with angry tears. "I will not let him get away with this."

"You cannot prove it."

"I have you to testify."

Uzfan said nothing.

"Will you not—"

"A priest cannot testify. You know the law."

Frustration filled her. "This is *our* law, camp law. We will—"

"No, Alexeika," he said firmly. "Find another way."

Angrily she shook her head in the dark. "He will grow worse," she said. "He must go *now*."

Uzfan patted her arm. "You will think of the right solution. I will pray that your thoughts are clear."

"What are you trying to tell me?" she asked, weary of evasion and hints. "If there is something more I should know—"

"Alas, child, if I could tell you, I would."

"Uzfan—"

"I have uneasy feelings. When Draysinko crosses my thoughts, I know that something is wrong. Yet I do not know what."

"I do," she said grimly. "He is a thief and a trouble-maker."

"Look beyond your petty complaints, child," Uzfan rebuked her sharply. "Do you think my gifts would warn me so strongly if mere thievery were all?"

Abashed, Alexeika stood there with her hand curled tight around a branch. She said nothing.

The silence stretched out, and Uzfan sighed heavily. "Go now and get your rest. You're tired, and it grows late."

"Uzfan—"

"Very well!" he said in annoyance. "On the morrow we will part the veils of seeing together and determine the course of action you should take."

She blinked, surprised by his promise. Since the night she'd summoned the vision of the exiled King Faldain, parting the veils of seeing had been forbidden to her. Uzfan had been very angry with her for a long time. But now, fresh hope came to life inside her. Perhaps at last Uzfan was going to relent and resume her training.

But even the prospect of seeing visions held less appeal right now than did quick action. She still wanted to banish Draysinko tonight.

"Have you grown cruel?" Uzfan asked her softly, as though he could read her thoughts. "Would you turn him out into the darkness, alone, without even the safety of the camp to shelter him through the night hours?"

"And what protection do we offer?" she retorted, softened not at all by this appeal. Her anger came rushing back, and she stiffened her spine. "He has endangered us all. I will have to stand sentry duty tonight in his—"

"Nay, child. You have worked enough this day."

She set her jaw stubbornly. "I will do what needs to be done."

"You are only one person, Alexeika. You cannot do everything for these people."

"Father could make them stick together," she said, long weeks of frustration welling up past her control. "He could keep them at their duties. He convinced them to cooperate with each other. Why can't I? They scatter like cats at the first opportunity, and are all too eager to forget half the things that need doing."

"Alexeika, you must give them time."

"We've had half the summer, and nothing improves. Nothing!"

"These women have not had your training, child. They do not understand all that's at stake."

Alexeika curbed the temptation to spill out her grievances and complaints. She knew it was her fatigue that had brought her to the verge of tears. This was no time for such softness. "I will stand watch," she said grimly. "Perhaps my actions will shame the others into—"

"The women won't hunt, so you do it," Uzfan broke in. "They won't trap furs, so you do it. You are too impatient. You cannot do everything for them."

"If I don't, disaster will come to us," she replied.

"Perhaps it must, to teach them how to be stronger and less dependent."

She frowned, thinking his reply a strange one. "This is a dark saying indeed."

Uzfan rested his hand kindly on her shoulder for a mo-

ment. "Go and get your sleep, child. I will set a protection
spell around the camp to guard us tonight."

The offer pleased her, but at the same time she knew she
could not accept it. "Thank you, but it will be too much
strain for you."

"Nonsense," he said sharply. "I may be an old man, but
there are still plenty of powers in my sleeve. Worry no more
about us this night, at least."

"Uzfan—"

"Go," he said. "I must be alone for this conjuring."

Frustrated, she started to protest again, but she had been
reared to obey her elders. She surrendered to Uzfan's wishes,
but inside she was still seething. Most of the time Uzfan
seemed spry enough, but he was very old. Conjuring had
grown difficult for him, and she knew enough of the secret
ways to understand that a protection spell strong enough to
surround the camp all night would put a tremendous strain
on the old priest. It worried her, and that gave her something else to blame on Draysinko.

Scowling, she trudged reluctantly back to her tent by the
light of the dying fire embers. Already she could smell the
faint, acrid scents of magic from behind her. A gust of wind
blew her hair back from her face, then was gone as suddenly as it came. She could feel the tingle in her skin in its
wake. Something wild and untamed stirred inside her. She
wanted to throw back her head and run up into the mountains to the highest peak and balance there with her arms
stretched up to the moonlit sky.

Quickly, she ducked inside her tent instead and closed
the flap firmly. She was breathing hard, and without hesitation she leaned over the water pail and splashed water on
her hot face, again and again, until she grew calmer.

That was why Uzfan did not want her practicing the magic
arts, especially not on her own. Whatever gift she possessed
was wild and strong, and perhaps untrainable.

The lamp was burning low. She moved about restlessly,
then forced herself to prepare for bed.

Outside, the magic swirled through the trees, coiling around the camp protectively. Once the spell was woven about everyone like a chain, she felt more settled and no longer had to force herself to sit still.

She took out her carved wooden comb and worked the snarls from her long dark hair. The lamp's light continued to burn down, and the camp lay quiet and peaceful.

Alexeika combed her long tresses until they were smooth and shining, then she put out her lamp and lay there on the blankets Draysinko had touched.

Despite Uzfan's advice, she chafed at having to wait. It seemed to her that leaving Draysinko unpunished would only encourage him to commit worse deeds. Well, tomorrow would decide the matter, when she joined Uzfan in determining what the future held for the despicable weaver. After that, no matter what the seeing showed them, she would make Draysinko go.

6

THE WILD SCREE and wail of pipes came through Alexeika's dream and awakened her. She opened her eyes, hearing the harsh, bizarre sounds without comprehension. It was a dreadful noise, barbarous and unnatural. She had never heard anything so awful in her life. Then someone screamed, and shouts rose above the thunder of hoofbeats.

Alexeika sat bolt upright in the gray dawn. Thunder swept past her tent, causing it to shake and sway. She heard a sharp rip, and saw the tip of a sword zigzagging its way through the cloth side of her tent.

"Thod's mercy!" she shouted, and jumped off her cot. Her clothes were always ready. She yanked them on, reached for her pearl-handled daggers, and slung the belt of Severgard over her shoulder. With two deft twists, she looped her long hair in a knot to keep it out of her way.

Her worst fears had been realized: They were under attack by Grethori raiders. Tleska, their lone sentry, had failed to warn the camp. Uzfan's protection spell had obviously failed as well. Alexeika swore long and hard, telling herself she should have insisted on proper sentries, should have stood guard herself, should have lined up everyone in the camp last night and chastised them all for their laziness.

But she hadn't. Instead, she'd surrendered to her own fatigue. She'd listened to Uzfan's advice. She'd tried to be gentle and accommodating to the others, despite her own instincts. What a fool she'd been.

But there was no time for thinking about what she should have done. She had to take action now.

"Papa, keep my arms strong and my courage high. May the gods themselves protect me," she prayed, then launched herself outside.

As soon as she went through the tent flap, she heard a whistling sound overhead. She ducked instinctively, and a curved scimitar missed beheading her by inches.

Crying out in fear, Alexeika dropped to the ground and rolled away from the trampling hooves of the Grethori war pony. Its rider, a terrifying figure with shoulder-length braids, a long mustache woven with rows of fingerbones, and a sleeveless fur jerkin, shouted at her in his clacking heathen language and kicked his horse toward her.

She scrambled desperately, unable to get to her feet, unable to draw Severgard or her daggers. Before she realized it, she was trying to burrow beneath the bottom of the tent, as though that flimsy structure offered any safety.

Laughing and screaming words she did not understand, the rider plunged his mount straight into the side of her tent, knocking it awry. Alexeika heard a snapping twang of the ropes. The cloth billowed and folded down around her while she tried to roll in the opposite direction. She heard a thud and the crunch of broken furniture. The Grethori's horse neighed and kicked wildly while its rider tried to spin it around.

Certain she was going to be trampled to death, Alexeika fought her way clear and scrambled to her feet. The rider shouted at her, and without looking back, Alexeika ran.

But there was nowhere to go. The raiders were everywhere, galloping back and forth as they ripped open tents with their scimitars and forced out the screaming inhabitants. One of the tents was now on fire, and the blaze shot up toward the trees with a whoosh of sparks. The air smelled of smoke and cold dew and death.

Beyond the trees, she could see a melon-gold slice of sun rimming the horizon. The fjord's calm surface reflected the sunrise, looking like a sheet of hammered copper at the snow-dusted feet of the mountains. The air held a sharp bite that surprised her after last night's sultriness. She had misjudged the change of season this far north. In her greed to get as many pelts as possible, she'd lingered too long. The Grethori bands moved about in autumn. She should have broken camp more than a week ago.

More "should haves," Alexeika realized. A waste of time now, when everything was happening too fast and more and more bodies were sprawled on the ground. She wanted to see if Uzfan was among them, for she hadn't spied the old priest anywhere, but there was no chance.

More tents were burning. The camp's few precious pack animals had been set free and were dashing back and forth in panic. A woman ran by, screaming. It was Larisa, Willem's mother, and she was trying to save Katrina from the barbarian who was chasing the little girl.

Alexeika couldn't help them. Running and dodging her own pursuer among the trees, she tried to look for the boys, but didn't see them.

"Willem!" she shouted. "Kexis! Vlad! To arms!"

No one answered. She doubted she could be heard over the din and chaos. Out in the woods, she saw an outlandish figure clad in furs, busy puffing into an unwieldy contraption of pipes that wailed loud and eerie. The noise grated on her nerves, and she had to force herself not to be distracted by it.

She also saw Draysinko, a furtive shadow slipping away with a fur-laden donkey in tow, but there was no time to go after him.

Alexeika leaped into a thicket of undergrowth, scratching her face and hands in the process. But her pursuer was too close behind for her to hide. His mount plunged right into the bushes after her, the same way it had knocked down her tent. Alexeika realized she couldn't defend herself hemmed in against the brush like this.

Again she broke away and ran. Another horse and rider brushed past her from the opposite direction, almost knocking her down. She dodged away, stumbling, and heard harsh laughter.

That angered her, and some of her fear faded. She realized she was reacting in panic. Her father had often told her that in battle the panicky fools who lost their heads were the first to die.

A shrill scream caught her attention, and she looked around in time to see an old woman with long gray braids falling in a flurry of long skirts. The rider who'd knocked the woman down with his sword then rode over her at full gallop, charging toward his next victim.

There was no time to see if it was Lady Natelitya or someone else, no time to react. Alexeika drew Severgard and swung around just as her own pursuer reached her. She kept her shoulders level and her feet braced, exactly as her father had taught her. In that moment, as time slowed down, she seemed to hear the general's calm voice coaching her through the moves.

"Be one with the sword, Alexeika. The sword is a part of you. Let it live in your hands."

She felt strangely calm as she faced the oncoming rider. His teeth flashed as he laughed at her, and his scimitar flashed up in an arc that caught the copper light of the newly risen sun. She gauged his swing, ducked it, and lifted her own weapon.

Severgard sliced off the man's leg below his knee.

Blood gushed in a mighty spurt. The Grethori screamed, a high, piercing sound of agony. Sawing at his horse and swinging it around so that Alexeika was nearly knocked off her feet by the animal, the raider reeled in his saddle and fell off. His severed foot remained in the stirrup on the side next to Alexeika. It flipped upside down and dangled like that as the horse shied away.

Meanwhile, the man was writhing on the ground, screaming curses at her. He still held his sword, and beckoned to her with scorn and fury.

"Woman!" he said in a guttural voice. His face was nearly purple above its beard. "Fight!"

Alexeika knew she had to finish him. She didn't let herself look at the blood still gushing from his stump, didn't let herself hesitate.

Gripping Severgard more tightly, she ran toward him as he brandished his scimitar in defiance. Alexeika stamped her foot down hard on his stump and swung Severgard with all her might.

The Grethori screamed, arching back helplessly. His bearded face turned gray, and Alexeika knocked his scimitar spinning from his hand. He choked out a curse, floundering in a futile effort to reach his sword. She plunged her weapon tip through his throat.

It took her a moment to realize it was over. The Grethori lay there, no longer a terrifying barbarian with long braids and fingerbones, but just a body covered with blood. It was her first kill. Drawing Severgard free, Alexeika felt suddenly weak, as though her knees could not support her. Breathing hard and shaking, she stumbled back.

A child's scream roused her, and she knew she must help the others.

Swiftly she grabbed the dangling reins of the Grethori's war pony and knocked the man's severed leg from the stirrup. She did not know if the animal would let her ride it, but she had to try. On foot, she stood little chance of survival.

The horse snapped at her, but she struck its muzzle with her hand before it could bite. Alexeika pulled herself into the saddle, smelling the rancid stink of beyar grease used to oil it. A braided rope of skulls was tied to the pommel, clacking with every step of the nervous pony. She cut off the rope and saw the skulls go bouncing on the ground behind her.

Her mount was iron-mouthed and mountain-bred, as savage as its dead owner. It shook its head, resisting her, but Alexeika shouted at it and struck it on the rump with the flat of her sword.

Snorting, the pony bucked and plunged toward the center of the camp, where the confusion was the worst. Smoke stung her eyes from the burning tents, but she could see that a few women and children were being rounded up and herded together. A handful of people had reached the safety of the fjord and were swimming in the cold waters where the superstitious Grethori would not follow. They should have all headed for the fjord, Alexeika thought grimly. At the first inkling of trouble, they were supposed to flee to the water. The plan had been discussed often during council meetings. Why had they not remembered it?

The fighting still going on was sporadic and pitiful. Of the handful of elderly men, she saw only Ulinvo and Tomk trying to fight. Vlad was nowhere in sight, but she saw young Willem—his head bleeding from a wound—staggering about pathetically as he tried to wield a sword too big for him. His opponent was circling him on horseback, laughing and toying with him cruelly. Kexis—red-faced and determined—faced a pair of raiders with a spear in his hand. Both of the barbarians were advancing on him with great gusts of scornful laughter.

Alexeika headed in his direction, but just then the boy's nerve failed him. Throwing down his spear, he turned and ran for the woods.

A chase seemed to be what the raiders wanted. With whoops of excitement, they loped after him.

Swearing under her breath, Alexeika kicked her horse forward to rescue Willem. He was crying, but despite the tears and blood running down his face, he tried to stand as she had taught him. His small fists gripped the long hilt of the broadsword, and with all his might he swung it up to meet the blade of his opponent.

The gleaming curved scimitar crashed down against Willem's weak parry, and knocked the sword from his hands. Defenseless, the boy staggered back and lifted his palms in an involuntary entreaty for mercy.

Horror filled her. "Willem!" she shouted.

The boy didn't hear her, and she was still too far away to help. She kicked her pony harder, but it bucked and fought her.

Then another rider crossed her path and blocked it.

Alexeika drew rein so hard the pony reared with her.

"Demon!" shouted the man in front of her. "Woman-man demon you are."

Alexeika gulped in air, but before she could do anything, the Grethori charged her, his horse plunging and darting from side to side. He held two scimitars, one in each hand. His mustache was so long it flowed back over his shoulders, and instead of bones woven through its length, tiny skulls bobbed on the ends. His long, multiple-braided hair was burnished dark red, his skin weather-beaten bronze. He rode a black pony with white spots, and a large disk of hammered gold adorned the breastplate of his mount.

She supposed this was the chieftain. That meant he would be the best fighter, for the Grethori leaders ruled by ability, not inheritance. The air left her lungs. She had beaten one fighter by luck, but she could not depend on luck this time. Already Severgard's weight was making her arms weary. She was not strong enough to wield it much longer.

The chieftain yelled at the top of his lungs, a queer rising sound that made goose bumps break out on her skin. Alexeika mastered her fear and screamed out a war cry of her own.

"Ilymir Volvn!" she shouted at the top of her lungs. It was her father's name, proud and illustrious, a name which had once led men into battle.

From the corner of her eye, she saw old Boral suddenly pop into sight from hiding. "Ilymir Volvn!" he shouted, his voice quavering.

From among the prisoners, a woman's voice took up the cry. "Ilymir Volvn!"

Alexeika took heart. There was still courage here. They weren't defeated yet.

The chieftain stopped grinning, but he didn't slow his charge. He came at her, brandishing his scimitars so that their blades flashed gold and copper in the sun.

Holding her heavy black sword, Alexeika shortened the reins in her other hand and forced her restless mount to stand where it was. She let the chieftain come to her.

"Woman-man demon!" he shouted with contempt when she did nothing. "Fight me!"

She knew she would lose this battle. If she lifted Severgard against him, she would be lost.

Another corner of her mind was screaming at her to move, to brace her feet in the stirrups, to raise the sword. But she curbed her instincts and stayed motionless and watchful. Her heart started to beat very fast, and she felt breathless, but she waited, refusing to move.

When he was close enough, when she could see his dark eyes narrow as he leaned forward in the saddle, she dropped the reins on her mount's shaggy neck, pulled a dagger from its sheath, and threw it with a deft, economical snap of her wrist.

He dodged by twisting his upper body. The blade missed his throat and sank instead into his shoulder.

Alexeika barely bothered to see if it hit its mark. Already she was moving to attack, taking advantage of this one tiny moment that was hers. Kicking her startled pony forward, she swung Severgard, hoping to cut the raider in twain at the waist. Despite the dagger in his shoulder, he parried with a scimitar. Their swords struck with a resounding clash.

The impact jolted into her wrists, and as strong as she was for a maid, she nearly dropped Severgard. Gritting her teeth, she disengaged and swung it again.

Too slow, she was thinking.

The chieftain's blade was quicker. He parried with her again while his face twisted with strain and anger, growing pale about the cruel mouth. Shifting her next swing, she stabbed Severgard deep into the neck of his horse.

The animal reared, screaming and flailing with its front hooves. She swung again at its rider. This time her blade touched him. It was a weak blow, badly delivered, and it cut him only a little.

He snarled something at her she did not understand, and she laughed back in reckless scorn. Her blood was up, and she knew no fear now. She would fight him to the death, her own if need be, but she would never give up.

At that moment, however, two other riders swooped at her from either side. Surrounded and cut off, she was driven back from the chieftain. Severgard was pinned against the top of her horse's neck by one man's scimitar, and the other man gripped her by her hair, yanking her halfway out of the saddle.

Tears of pain filled her eyes. She twisted and fought, but they were too much for her. It was the chieftain himself, bleeding from his wounds, who leaned over to wrest Severgard from her hands.

"No!" she screamed, hanging on to the hilt with all her strength. "No!"

But he was stronger, and he pulled it away. Lifting the

sword so that the sunlight caught the large sapphire in the pommel and made it flash, the chieftain examined her sword with admiration and ran his fingertips along the runes carved on the blade.

Fury consumed Alexeika. She couldn't bear for her father's sword to fall into the hands of this barbarian. For generation after generation it had passed down through her family. Revered for what it was and stood for, it had been carried always with honor. She herself had saved it from the Gantese looters after the battle in which her father had died. It was hers now, and one day it would belong to her son. This Grethori dog could not have it.

"That is not for you!" she shouted, glaring at him. Her voice was steel, and from inside her came a great force of anger so hot and terrible it was like a blazing ball of fire. *Heat and fire!* she thought, and her anger seemed to explode from her.

There was a flash of light, momentarily blinding her and making her mount rear in fright. The chieftain swore and dropped the sword. It landed on the ground with a thud, and lay there glowing faintly.

Dazed and half-blinded by the power which had escaped her, Alexeika belatedly realized that her hair was no longer being pulled. She twisted free, barely aware of the men's stunned faces and the white-eyed panic of their horses. She dismounted, ran to the sword, and picked it up.

The hilt felt hot enough to burn her, but she didn't care. She held it up in a mocking salute, and said, "Get gone from here."

The chieftain's expression grew stony. Without a word, he pulled her dagger from his shoulder and held up the bloody weapon in a silent salute of his own.

She relaxed slightly, thinking she'd won. "Leave our camp," she ordered them, her voice gruff and powerful. "Get out!"

The chieftain threw her dagger. It came at her so fast it was a blur. She couldn't duck in time. Her fear rushed back, filling her with such intensity she thought she would be sick. This, she realized, was death. She was not ready for it. Her whole life still stretched before her. She had dreams and ambitions and plans that should not be cut down by this dirty savage in his furs and braids. She realized she must lay her heart before the gods, but there wasn't time even for that.

No! she thought.

Pain exploded in her temple, and she knew nothing else.

PART TWO

7

SOUTH OF THE Charva River, the land of Mandria grew soft and tame. Rolling meadows held fat, sleek livestock. Crops grew tall and straight in their rows, showing the plentiful harvests to come. Villages were sometimes small, but seldom were they as grubby or as poor as those in upper Mandria. More often, Dain and his companions came to towns with public squares and houses built of stone or brick. Sometimes, even the streets were paved with cobblestones, and there was not a pig to be seen rooting at doorsteps.

The roads between towns became smoother and wider as Dain traveled south. Tall, lush grass grew on either side of the road, filled with fluttering red-winged birds, bustling rodents, and humming insects. Nonkind had never come to this land. To feel free of the constant need to watch and fear . . . It was marvelous to find no taint anywhere in this land of plenty where occasional road bandits caused the only problems. Twice bandits started to ambush them on the road, and both times they galloped away as soon as they saw who they were attacking.

"Guess we got nothing they want, eh?" Sir Terent asked.

"Naught but a sword down their gullet," Sir Polquin

growled. The master of arms was still pained by the wound
in his leg, and grouchier than usual as a result. Sweat running down his round face, he glanced over at Dain. "Your
pardon, m'lord. Have you a waterskin to spare?"

Dain handed over his waterskin without hesitation.

Sir Polquin looked embarrassed, but thanked him. "It's
this fever in my leg. I'm sorry."

"Apology is not needed," Dain told him kindly. "There
is water enough for all."

Sulein edged closer on his donkey. "If you would allow
me to lance the wound tonight, it would ease you greatly."

"Nay," Sir Polquin said hastily, handing the waterskin
back to Dain. "I'm well enough. There'll be no hot knives
stuck in my leg, thank you, no."

He wheeled his horse over to the other side of the creak-
ing, swaying wagon. One of the kine pulling it lowed at
him.

Sulein, wearing his strange flat hat and sweating in the
heat, tilted his head to peer up at Dain. "The man's leg is
infected. It needs attending."

"He fears you," Dain said, keeping his gaze on the dusty
horizon. A town lay ahead. Dain could see its spires, their
banners fluttering brightly in the sunshine. "He will heal well
enough, in time."

"Time," Sulein muttered. "I could save him time. I could
save him pain, and that limp he is likely to keep. He is a
stubborn fool."

"He does not believe in your methods," Dain said sharply.
"Leave him be."

"You could order him to accept my treatment," Sulein
said.

Dain swung his gray eyes around to lock with Sulein's
dark ones. "But I will not."

Silence hung between them a moment. Frustration narrowed Sulein's eyes, but he dropped the argument.

The physician had given way to Dain most of the time
since they'd resumed their grim journey. Dain could tell him-

self it was because of his new rank, but he did not believe it. Sulein would never be someone he could entirely trust. An ulterior purpose lay always behind the physician's actions. For now, he clearly wanted to remain close to Dain. Therefore, he acquiesced to Dain's decisions, but Dain wondered how long such compliance would last. He knew that the physician still believed him the lost heir to Nether's throne. There was no way to prove such a claim, even if Dain intended to try—which he did not. Perhaps eventually Sulein would realize how futile restoration would be. Perhaps then he would go to someone else's court, and leave Dain in peace.

In the meantime, the physician remained with them. And despite Dain's dislike of the man, he had many uses and talents to offer.

Now, as Sulein started to rein his donkey aside, Dain frowned. "When we are past this town, physician, perhaps you would give me another lesson."

Sulein's face brightened as though he'd been handed a gift. He bowed low over the neck of his donkey. "I would be honored."

Only a few days ago, Dain had been busy avoiding lessons whenever he could. It seemed strange now to be the one insisting that he keep up his studies. But Dain's life had changed with the death of Lord Odfrey. He knew he had much to learn, and that he had only a short amount of time in which to learn it in order to avoid acting like a totally ignorant bumpkin if and when he gained an audience with the king.

That night, they camped on the bank of a clear, rushing stream, beneath the swaying fronds of graceful water trees. A crimson flower grew on the bank near the water's edge, and its fragrance was heady in the long hours of dusk.

Dain lay near the water, his long body sprawled on the grass, while he listened to the song of insects and the swaying rustle of the trees. The night air was sultry. He'd removed his tunic to be cooler, and intended to wash himself in the stream later to ease his aching muscles.

Sir Terent had put him through a rigorous weapons drill shortly before supper. Sir Polquin, perched on a fallen log with his wounded leg stuck out stiffly in front of him, had rapped out corrections and instructions until Dain was dripping with sweat and reeling with fatigue.

"Getting better, m'lord," Sir Terent said with an encouraging slap on Dain's shoulder. "That last exchange was worthy of any knight."

Dain grinned at the praise, but in truth he was too tired to much care. As soon as he choked down his ration of cold meat and dry bread, he forced himself to stay awake through another reading lesson with Sulein. The physician also praised him for his improvement, but Dain did not want to admit that he was peering through the physician's mind for some of the words and their meanings. It was cheating, in a way, but Dain was desperate to acquire knowledge as fast as he could.

Now, reclining on his elbow in the grass, he toyed idly with a scroll of mathematics. He intended to study the figures by firelight, after he'd rested a short time longer. Sometimes Sulein told him he'd studied enough for one day and would give him no scrolls. But Dain always had the contents of Lord Odfrey's document case to pore over while the others slept. He had read through nearly everything the case contained. He did not understand it all yet, especially the legal matters. The phrasings were often archaic and confusing, but he had learned that Thirst lands had been granted to Lord Odfrey's ancestor by the Sterescials, half-mortal representatives of the gods in the ancient days. This same ancestor had been given Truthseeker, the sword of god-steel now locked away in the secrecy of the Thirst vaults. Centuries later, when upper Mandria was joined to lower under one king, the rulers of Thirst became chevards and swore loyalty to the sovereign, but it was more an alliance than fealty. This explained why Thirst, so remote from court, received more requests than orders from the king.

Presently Dain was studying mathematics so he could master the complex finances of Thirst Hold. Dain had always thought lords were men who lived at their ease and did what they wanted, but that was far from true. Sometimes he wished himself back in the Dark Forest of Nold, apprenticed to Jorb the swordmaker. Then, his only worry had been how to keep the dwarf from yelling at him for shoddy work. Now, he felt that he must measure up to Lord Odfrey's even higher expectations. Guilt often rode on his shoulder, and he told himself he should have studied harder while the chevard was alive.

"More study?" Sir Terent asked him.

Startled from his thoughts, Dain sat up with a jerk. His sore muscles gave him a twinge, and he winced slightly.

The knight gave him a gap-toothed grin. "Stay at your ease, m'lord. It's only a moment of your time that I crave."

Dain gestured, and Sir Terent squatted on the ground near him.

"What is it?" Dain asked him.

The burly knight began to draw aimlessly on the ground with a stick. "Orders for tomorrow, m'lord."

Dain's brows pulled together. "What makes tomorrow different from today or yesterday?"

Sir Terent looked at him strangely. "Well . . ."

"Are we low on rations or—"

"We'll be in Savroix-en-Charva on the morrow."

"Oh." Dain's face flamed. He felt a fool. "I didn't realize we were that close."

"Didn't you?" Sir Terent looked surprised. "With all the people on the road, and the towns as big as they are?"

Dain didn't want to admit he'd hardly paid attention. He said nothing.

The knight coughed into his hand. "Well, now. 'Tis no surprise, considering this land is strange to you. But we're maybe a half-day's journey short now, maybe less if the road ain't too crowded. I was wondering if we should—"

A shout in the distance interrupted him.

Dain rose to his feet, his keen ears hearing the faraway babble of distraught voices. A donkey brayed out of sight in the trees, and he put his hand on his dagger.

Their camp was well off the road, but they had fires lit and had taken no special care to be concealed.

"Help!" shouted the voice. "Help us please!"

Dain started forward, but Sir Terent put a meaty hand on his shoulder to hold him back.

"Let me deal with this, m'lord."

He hurried away, but Sir Polquin limped up to block his path. "Terent, you fool!" he said sharply, brandishing his drawn sword. "Stay with his lordship, as is your place."

It was Sir Terent's turn to grow red-faced. Growling to himself, he wheeled about and came back to Dain.

By this time, Lyias and Thum were standing, round-eyed with curiosity. Sulein even appeared, hatless and garbed in his linen subrobe.

"What is this?" he asked, his accent thick in astonishment. "What comes upon us?"

No one answered him. Dain saw a figure stumbling into the clearing from the trees. Frowning, Dain went to him, Sir Terent close on his heels.

Already Dain could see that this was no enemy, but instead a man in servant attire. With bleeding head and torn sleeves, he carried a stout club in his hand. At the sight of Sir Polquin and Dain closing in on him, he dropped to his knees in supplication.

"Please, help us!" he cried, and doubled over as though in pain.

Sir Polquin reached him first, then Dain came up and pushed the gruff master of arms aside.

As soon as he touched the servant's torn and dirty shoulder, Dain felt a jolt of memories and recollections, including raw terror, sunlight flashing on weapons, and the shouts of violent men.

Flinching back, Dain took his hand away and did not touch the man again. "Be easy within yourself," he said in compassion. "You have found friends."

"Help," the man said, moaning. "Help us."

"Aye, we will. What has happened to you? What battle were you in?"

Gasping for breath, the man tried to straighten and pointed behind him. "My master follows. He's hurt. Robbers!"

Dain turned to Sir Polquin. "Give him water and let Sulein attend him. Sir Terent, Thum, let us go give what help we can."

"Wait," Sir Terent said in protest. "It could be a trap, to lure us into the forest."

His caution was well-meant, but Dain shook his head. "It's no trap." He strode off, leaving the others to follow.

At the edge of the clearing, he plunged into darkness. The moon overhead was a useless sliver. The woods themselves were not thick, but the light of the campfires did not penetrate far. Dain drew on his keen hearing and sense of smell to guide him.

But Sir Terent blundered into a bush behind Dain and cursed. "Damne! I can't see a thing. Dain lad—uh, m'lord! Slow down."

Dain grinned to himself, but by then his ears had picked up voices ahead. They hushed, but by their scent he knew at once that they were Mandrians all, including some women wearing costly perfumes.

Dain hesitated long enough to let Sir Terent catch up with him, then pushed ahead through a stand of gnarly scrub and came to the travelers he sought. They were huddled together against a stand of hackberries, barely seen shapes and shadows in the night. Dain smelled two donkeys and a fear-lathered horse. Someone wept softly in the darkness. Someone else moaned in pain. The scent of blood was no longer fresh, but it was pungent enough in Dain's nostrils to make him frown. They were afraid still, these folk, although time had passed since their ambush. They had traveled perhaps half a league since then, judging by the amount of road dust he could smell in their clothing.

"Good folk, fear no longer," he said.

"Hark!" a voice cried out. "We are set upon again!"

With sounds of panic, they rose from their hiding place, but before they could run, he stepped forward.

"Calm yourselves," he said in Mandrian, his voice sounding clear and crisp in the night. "We are friends. We mean you no harm."

"Thod be thanked," replied a man. His shadowy shape pushed itself forward, hampered by a female who clung, weeping, to his arm. "Elnine, hush now."

Divesting himself of her, he walked over to Dain. Close up, he smelled of herbs and sweaty cloth and leather. "We were attacked by bandits on the road. My men at arms are dead or badly wounded. Have three women to protect, plus the servants who have not deserted me. Saw your fire and would seek refuge with you, sir."

"Of course," Dain said. "My companions and I are traveling with a physician of considerable skill. Come now, and let us help you. Are these bandits still in pursuit?"

"No," the man replied with scorn. "Took our horses and wagons—"

"My new gowns!" wailed one of the women, a young one with a lilting voice.

"My jewels!" sobbed another.

"Hush, both of you," scolded a third, much older woman. "Vanity has no place in these circumstances."

"But, Selia, there can be no vanity in *any* circumstances if our things are stolen from us."

Despite his sympathy for their situation, Dain couldn't help but grin in the darkness. Quickly, he, Sir Terent, and Thum pitched in to shoulder the scant boxes and possessions, assist the wounded, and herd the entire group back to their camp by the stream.

In the firelight, the newcomers looked bedraggled indeed. The old man's clothing was torn and coated liberally with dirt and bits of leaves. He wore a broad-brimmed traveling hat of woven straw. Part of the brim had been broken. His neatly trimmed gray beard was streaked with blood from a now-dried cut on his face. Despite his dishevelment, it was apparent he was no commoner. His bearing and stance were that of a lord, and he carried a finely made thin-sword and a matched pair of daggers. Dain took care to show him respect.

"Would you care to sit down here, sir, and rest yourself?"

"No," the old man said sharply. His eyes snapped bright and angry within the seams of his aged face. He might have been an old man, but he was far from infirm. That he had been set upon by common thieves clearly enraged him, but that his own men had failed to protect him and his possessions angered him even more.

"Infamy," he muttered over and over. He paced about with his hands clasped at his back. "Morde a day, the raw impertinence of these blackguards! Should have ridden forth with a full company of knights at my back instead of these fools. Shall write to my steward at once—the pompous fool—and discharge him for his stupid suggestions of economy."

"In the morning we'll help bury your dead," Dain offered, but the old man brushed this aside with a gesture.

"No need, thank you," he said gruffly. "Left two men behind to clear our dead off the road. They'll come on when they've finished. Blast and damne, if that isn't woe enough, but there's more. My champion is dead. Legre was the best—"

"Legre!" Sir Terent blurted out before he could stop himself.

Dain glanced up at his protector, who turned red and bowed in apology at the interruption.

The old man was looking at Sir Terent with plain disapproval. "As I was saying, Legre was the best of all the knights in this realm. A true champion. Now he is felled by the freakish arrow of a heathen bandit come down from the north. Don't know what that fool Muncel of Nether is doing, but he should at least be able to manage his own affairs of state. In my day we beheaded any bandits that were caught plaguing travelers. Kept them in a state of mortal terror, and they soon found other roads to lurk on than the ones running across my land."

He went on at considerable length, complaining about bandits and many other things. Sir Terent stood there goggle-eyed and kept mouthing "Legre" as though struck with wonder. Dain knew nothing about this so-called champion, but no doubt Legre's absence from the tourney would change the odds in favor of the other contenders, Sir Terent included.

In the end, it was the women who distracted the old man from his tirade. They fussed and exclaimed and wailed over the contents of their few small boxes. They proved to be the old man's two daughters, Elnine and Roxina, both heavily veiled to their eyes and introduced perfunctorily by their father. Selia, their stout, grim duenna, was not veiled, but her face was so ugly and fierce that Dain wished she were.

Thum turned his back to them and shuddered. "She has a face that would sour milk," he whispered.

Dain's mouth twitched, and he barely restrained a laugh. Mirth was not suitable when these folk were in such dire straits. He gave quiet orders to Lyias to serve them what food there was to spare. One of the servants, looking pale and shaken to his core, stumbled off to the stream and came back with two pails of water.

"We can offer you nothing stronger," Dain said when the water pail was offered round. "We have no ale or mead ourselves."

By now, the old man had taken time to look over Dain's small camp, his single wagon pulled by the pair of strong kine, Sulein's humble donkey, and the plain mail of the two knights themselves. As the women were persuaded to sit on a blanket spread across the ground near the wagon and Sulein bent over the pair of wounded guards, the old man swept his gaze back to Dain.

"You command these two knights?" he asked Dain bluntly.

Dain met his gaze. "Aye, I do."

The old man's gaze raked over Thum without much interest and came back to Dain. "Well, the three of you will be useful to us. Three trained knights plus my guardsmen who remain unwounded should be adequate to protect us the rest of the way. With my own protector dead, I cannot rest easy without better men about me than I have now."

Dain frowned, displeased by this old fellow's assumption that he was some hirelance. "I am not a knight," he said sharply.

The old man's perceptive eyes looked him over. "You're big enough. By Thod, you'll soon be old enough, if you aren't already. You walk like a swordsman. And the muscles in those shoulders of yours are impressive enough. Aren't you in training?"

"Aye," Dain said, embarrassed at being evaluated like a piece of horseflesh. "I am."

"Well, then. You'll do."

"Will I?" Dain retorted. Behind him, Sir Terent coughed in warning, but Dain paid him no heed. "I am not for hire, sir. Nor are these knights."

"Look as though you are. Oh, yes, I know the ploy. You protest in hopes of getting better wages from me. Think because I've lost my horse and most of my men that I'm desperate and will pay any price. Well, I won't and that's an end to it. Ten—"

"We are not hirelances!" Dain broke in sharply to silence him.

The old man sniffed. "The lot of you make a pathetic ragtag. Can be nothing else."

"You are mistaken."

"Am I?" The old man looked haughty and annoyed now. Probably he wasn't used to being challenged by anyone,

Dain thought. "If you're aught else, then what name do you go by?"

"I am Dain of Thirst."

The old man blinked. "Thirst! That's Odfrey's hold."

"No longer," Dain said with an involuntary catch in his throat. He gestured at the black cloth which had replaced the banner flying from their wagon. "Lord Odfrey is dead."

The old man's eyes flared wide in shock. He stood stiff and still for a moment, then frowned and drew a Circle on his breast. "Thod's mercy! How? When?"

"Nonkind attacked us at the Charva," Dain said. His terse explanation seemed to be enough, for the old man nodded.

"And this is all that remains of your company?" he asked. "Wasn't he supposed to be escorting the prince—"

"Prince Gavril is safe," Dain broke in flatly.

"Tomias be thanked."

Dain frowned but held his tongue. Tomias had shown no mercy to Lord Odfrey, Sir Roye, or the other dead men. They'd been true believers, for all the good it had done them. Dain could not bring himself to feel thankful to the saint for saving Gavril at their expense.

"I'm Clune," the old man announced in a more civil tone. "Thank you for your kindness and hospitality, Dain of Thirst."

Dain inclined his head graciously. "It is my honor to give it, Lord Clune."

One of the maidens tittered behind her veil and whispered to her sister. The old man frowned slightly, and Dain wondered what he'd done wrong.

Beside him, Thum hissed in warning, but it was Sir Terent who bent to Dain's ear and murmured, "Clune is a duc, m'lord. Call him yer grace, and bow. He outranks you."

Dain's face grew hot with embarrassment. Still, he knew his mistake was an honest one. He forced himself to meet the old man's keen eyes. "I ask your grace's pardon." He was suddenly aware of his accent as he spoke Mandrian, and self-conscious about his bare chest and torn leggings.

"You journey with sad business," the old duc said grimly. "Of course, you're traveling to Savroix to inform the king of what's happened to his former protector."

Dain blinked, impressed in spite of himself. He hadn't known Lord Odfrey had once been the king's protector. That was a high honor indeed. No wonder Odfrey had been so favored by the king. Yet, while thinking of the many things he had never learned about his adoptive father, and of all the things they would never discuss together, Dain felt his grief freshen. He struggled to return his mind to the conversation at hand. Bowing to Clune, he said, "I intend to seek audience with the king immediately."

The duc nodded. "That's as it should be. Well, sorry for your circumstances. Appear to be as dreadful as my own. Sad state of the world when we meet trouble while traveling within our own realm. Damne, but I'm weary."

Clune took off his straw hat and rubbed his brow. His face had turned pale. Dain escorted the old man over to his daughters, but they were interrupted by the sound of something large crackling and crashing through the brush. Dain put his hand on his dagger, and Sir Terent drew his sword, but it proved to be Clune's two surviving guardsmen, struggling to pull an unwieldy wagon through the forest into the clearing.

Elnine and Roxina jumped to their feet and clapped in delight. "Oh, Father, look!" Elnine of the dark blue veil exclaimed. "They have saved some of our things after all."

"Stalwart fellows, both of them," said Roxina. She was more buxom than her sister, and wore a plain gown with crimson lining in its sleeves. "Let us reward them well."

To their credit, the guards ignored this foolish prattle and faced their master respectfully. "It be the provisions wagon, yer grace. Looted, but there be still a few sacks of food so we won't starve ere we get there."

Dain stepped forward and gestured toward the parked wagon from Thirst. "Over yon is the flattest part of the bank. Take your wagon there, next to ours. Your donkeys and horse can be hobbled among the trees with our animals. The duc and his family will stay here in the center of camp. You men can sleep over that way, between the camp and the road. It is a terrible business, burying the dead in the darkness of night. Go that way to the stream and refresh yourselves, then come to our fire and share our food."

The guardsmen bowed to Dain in thanks and hurried to do as he ordered.

Clune's tight mouth twitched into what was almost a smile. "You set us here and there in a clever defense strategy, young Dain of Thirst. Do you expect attack in the dead of night?"

The gibe was a gentle one, but under the circumstances Dain found it offensive. "It's my habit," he said shortly. "Considering that you've survived one attack today, you might appreciate whatever protection we can offer."

Clune's brows rose, and Thum gripped Dain's elbow. "Dain!" he whispered in horror. "Take care."

But Dain refused to back down. He bowed to the old man and started to turn away, but Clune was not yet finished with him.

"Odfrey trained you well," the duke said in gruff compliment. "It is exactly what he himself would have said to me. Are you his bastard son?"

Dain stiffened, and his head lifted proudly. "No, your grace. I am not."

Clune looked very surprised. "Forgive me. I meant you no disrespect, young Dain."

"I take none," Dain replied, but his voice was stiff. "I am his adopted heir."

Clune put his withered lips together as though he might whistle, but he made no sound. "Well, well," he said under his breath. "So that's the lay of it, eh? Odfrey, what have you set in motion?"

It did not seem to be a question he wanted answered. Dain moved restlessly, ready to go, but Clune gripped him without warning. With a sharp tug that hurt, he lifted a hank of the black hair that concealed Dain's ears. "Thought so!" he said in triumph. "You have eldin blood, all right!"

Annoyance swept Dain. It was all he could do not to knock the old man's hand aside. But standing there rigidly, he kept his dignity. "Aye, your grace. I am eld and would have said so, had you asked."

"Not fully blooded, but those eyes give you away." Clune released him and stepped back, nodding to himself. "Must have enspelled Odfrey, to make him take such a risk. These are different times we live in today. The Odfrey of old would have done such a reckless thing, but not the Odfrey of late." Clune's fierce old eyes bored into Dain. "What do the eld folk want with a Mandrian hold? Tell me that! What spell did you put on Odfrey to addle his wits this way? You'll have the uplands in rebellion next."

Dain's face was burning. By now, he regretted ever showing this old man hospitality. "No," he said fiercely. "I am no spellcaster."

"Easy to say now, when the man is dead and cannot speak for himself. You've no claim, boy. No claim at all. The king won't grant *you* audience."

Dain opened his mouth to hotly contest this pronouncement, then realized he needn't waste his breath arguing with the duc. None of this was Clune's business.

"The king will see me," Dain said with confidence.

Snorting, the duc glanced at Sir Terent. "You there. Have you any knowledge of court to share with this young knave?"

Sir Terent bowed, looking very red-faced. "I am no courtier, your grace."

"Obviously." The duc glanced around the camp while his daughters looked on, tittering behind their hands. "Fools, all."

His voice was cutting. Dain's hands curled into fists at his side, but he said nothing.

"You won't see the king," the duc said, returning his gaze to Dain. "Because you bring news of poor Odfrey, it's likely you'll see the chamberlain or perhaps even a minister of state. But the king won't give you more than one minute of his time."

"A minute is long enough," Dain said through his teeth. "More than long enough. I have a petition of adoption—"

"The king won't grant it."

"Why not?"

But Dain already knew before the answer flickered in Clune's eyes. A trace of the old humiliation passed through Dain, but he ignored it. He was no longer the starving, frightened boy who had crouched in the marshland reeds, fearing humans and their cruelties. Standing tall, conscious of the others looking on and listening to this confrontation, he faced Clune squarely. "I carry no shame for what I am," he said in a quiet voice.

The duc's mouth curled downward in disapproval. "You'll find Verence's court no friendly place for your kind," he said harshly. "Oh, you'll be a novelty at first. They prate of tolerance there within the palace walls. But try to claim Thirst for your own, and you'll find a number of new enemies ready to stop you. If you don't know why, I'm not going to enlighten you."

Dain frowned. "Thank you for your advice," he said with cold sarcasm. "But I need no counsel."

"Dain!" Sir Terent whispered in warning.

Dain ignored him. He was tired of this arrogant old man and his criticism.

"If you're too stupid to accept good advice when it's offered to you, then you're hardly worth Odfrey's trust in you. Plainly you've the judgment of a gnat."

Dain glared at him, but the duc gave him no chance to reply.

"Aware that you've been hospitable and helpful," Clune said. "Grateful for it, and so I offer you the truth. Whatever old ways of tolerance are still practiced in the uplands, you won't find them down here. Might as well go home now. Aye, go home, boy, before Cardinal Noncire calls you a heretic."

"Dain is *not* a heretic!" Thum said hotly in Dain's defense. "Your grace has no right to say so."

Clune stared at Thum in a way that made the youth turn bright red beneath his freckles and stammer to a halt.

Looking aghast over his outburst, Thum bowed. "I beg your grace's pardon."

"So you should," Clune said coldly. "No doubt grief clouds your mind and makes your tongue unruly. Otherwise, you would not dare speak to me in such a way."

Thum's face grew pale. He bowed again and would have perhaps apologized further, but Dain gripped his arm to silence him.

"Your grace is injured and tired," Dain said with more courtesy than he felt. "Our provisions are yours to share."

Clune's men were coming back from the stream. He looked away from Dain with an absent nod. "With food of our own, no need to avail ourselves of your provisions," he said. "Go back to your own business. No further need of you."

The abrupt dismissal annoyed Dain, but it was a relief as well. Bowing stiffly, Dain remembered enough of his manners to say, "May Thod guard your grace's rest this night."

The duc nodded in bare acknowledgment and did not return the courtesy.

Seething, Dain spun on his heel and strode away. Thum and Sir Terent hurried after him, but Dain was barely conscious of their presence. He was angry and humiliated. It did no good to tell himself that the Duc du Clune was a shallow-minded, prejudiced old goat. In his heart Dain knew the man's warning was sound, whether he wanted to hear it or not.

No, Dain realized with dread, it was not going to be easy to enter the court of Savroix. Not for someone like himself, no matter how many warrants and petitions he carried.

8

ALEXEIKA AWAKENED SLOWLY, painfully. She first became
aware of the throbbing agony in her back, something terrible she didn't want to awaken to. But the pain pulled her
forward, and then her mind cleared so suddenly there was
no way to flee back into oblivion. She opened her eyes and
found herself lying on the dirt. Her face was just inches
from the wooden bars of her cage.

Tears blurred her vision momentarily, but she blinked
them away. Since her captivity by the Grethori three weeks
ago, she had refused to let herself cry. Tears were for the
weak. Tears were for those who didn't survive.

Alexeika had every intention of surviving.

She pulled her hands beneath her to push herself up, but
the cuts on her back opened and pain flared so intensely she
gave a little cry and closed her eyes. She lay there, still and
frozen, waiting for the fire raging in her back to subside.

When at last it did, she opened her eyes again. She felt
weak and sick to her stomach, but she intended to get up.
She had to, not only to defy her cruel captors who had
whipped her yet again last night for trying to escape, but
also to show them how strong she was. The Grethori lived
by a savage code that despised weakness. Only the strong
survived in their roving bands. Anyone injured or sickly
was eventually killed rather than nursed back to health.

Gasping for breath, she reached out and curled her left
hand around a wooden bar. Gripping it with all her might,
she strained until she managed to push herself onto her
knees. The pain was relentless, and flies swarmed around
her, but she held on and refused to faint.

Finally she shifted her weight and sat on the ground. For
a long while she could do nothing except draw in shallow,

hissing breaths to keep from screaming. But at last the pain faded again, and she was able to look around.

It was early morning. The sun shone brightly on the top of the mountain where this Grethori tribe had pitched its tents. Woven in garish hues of crimson, purple, yellow, and cerise, some with geometric stripes and designs creating eye-crossing patterns, the tents were simple structures consisting of a pole frame over which tent cloths were thrown and then lashed in place with leather cords.

Despite the sunshine, Alexeika found herself shivering. The air felt cold on her naked skin. Her fingers looked almost blue, and the sun did not reach her cage where it had been wedged beneath an outcropping of glade-stone.

When she'd been captured many days ago and brought unconscious into the Grethori camp, her clothes had been the first thing taken from her. She'd awakened, her head pounding horribly from the blow she'd taken in battle, and found herself spread-eagled on the ground with a circle of men surrounding her in silence. Her heart had nearly stopped in fear.

But they had not touched her. Holoc, the chieftain with the tiny skulls tied to the ends of his red hair braids, had claimed her for his battle prize and displayed her like this to all in the camp before letting the slaves garb her in a striped robe and stake her by a tether in front of his tent.

The other women prisoners were not as lucky. Stripped naked and confined to a pen of wooden stakes, their cries and pleas for mercy went ignored.

All day, Alexeika hunkered on the ground in a small knot, averting her gaze from those who came to stare, until a pair of scarred leather boots planted themselves before her.

"Woman-man demon," the voice said.

Slowly, trying to hide her fear, she forced herself to look up. It was Holoc the chieftain. He wore a sleeveless jerkin of vixlet fur, its russet tips glinting in the sunlight. His bare muscular arms were bronzed and smooth. His dark red hair, plaited in dozens of long, tiny braids, hung thick and full to his shoulders. His face was young and cruel, with a thin gash of a mouth and a nose that jutted out beneath stony, merciless eyes. Around his waist was belted Severgard, her father's sword.

She wished her dagger had found his heart instead of his shoulder. Infuriated by his very presence, she rose to her feet, standing as tall as the tether would let her, and faced him. Her dark hair hung in a wild, dust-streaked tangle down her back. The robe she wore stank of horse sweat and fire smoke. Its coarse weaving scratched her skin. The stony ground hurt her bare feet. But she let none of her fear or discomfort show as she faced him as a general's daughter should. Her chin lifted and she squared her shoulders. She had fought him in battle once. She vowed she would do it again if she ever got the chance.

His dark eyes stared back at her, implacable and unreadable.

One of the tribesmen took a prisoner from the pen and pushed her out of sight behind the tents. When she began screaming, Alexeika flinched. "Have you no mercy?" she demanded, unable to keep quiet. Although she hated to beg this savage for anything, she knew she must try to spare her friends. "Stop your men. Stop them! In the name of the gods, have some pity."

He frowned slightly, but said nothing. Either he didn't understand her or he didn't care.

Frustrated, she tried to take a step toward him, but quick as thought he moved, striking her in the chest with the heel of his hand.

The blow hurt so much it stunned her. Before she knew it, she had toppled backward and found herself sitting on the ground. She couldn't get her breath at first and wheezed for several moments before she finally recovered.

"Quiet tongue," he told her, his voice gruff and harsh. "Slave now. No speak."

Alexeika scrambled to her feet. "I am not your slave!" she shouted. "These are my people, not yours—"

He whipped out his dagger and pressed the point to her throat. Alexeika stopped her protest abruptly and froze in place. All she could feel was that sharp point at her throat, and her own vulnerability. She could not breathe, and her heart thudded heavily inside her chest.

He glared at her. "No speak. You slave now. I keep."

Her gaze shifted involuntarily to where his people stood gathered around, watching impassively. The woman who'd been taken away screamed again and began to weep with harsh, choking sobs. Hatred swelled inside Alexeika. Forgetting all caution, she swatted aside Holoc's dagger.

"Where are the children?" she asked. "What have you done with them?"

Holoc looked puzzled.

"The children!" she shouted. "The little ones!"

"Sold," he said with satisfaction.

She stared at him with horror. "All of them?"

He grinned, showing teeth filed to points.

Shuddering, she asked, "And the men? Uzfan and Boral and—"

"Men no use," he said with a shrug. "Dead now."

"Dead."

She whispered it, feeling as though a stone had fallen inside her. Her knees lost their strength, and she sank to the ground at Holoc's feet. He planted one of them on her shoulder, pushing her down.

Her fear came back, and she tried to shove his foot away, but he only stamped it harder against her shoulder. She cursed him, desperate not to let him see her fear.

Holoc laughed then, and a look of pride flashed in his dark eyes. "My woman-man demon. Good fighter. Maker of power. You are mine."

"Never!" she yelled, panting.

He moved his foot, releasing her, and walked away.

That had been the first day. That night, she remained tethered outside his tent like a dog and was given no food or water. Across the camp, the other women huddled together in their pen. Alexeika's heart went out to them, but there was nothing she could do except worry the leather rope which held her captive. By dawn, she managed to free herself. She went straight to the other prisoners to free them, but an elderly woman with bare arms and leathery skin rose from the shadows with a screech and beat Alexeika back with a stick.

The noise the old crone made brought the entire camp awake. Alexeika fought and flailed, but she was quickly surrounded and dragged away by several men, then flung at Holoc's feet.

He stood there in the shadowy gloom, silent and implacable. Alexeika lay at his feet, afraid yet filled with defiance, longing for a weapon.

Holoc gestured silently, and the Grethori women came to strip off her robe. Torches were lit, and Alexeika cringed in an effort to hide her nakedness. She had never felt so humiliated. Then the women twisted her arms behind her back and forced her over to a tree. There in the torchlight, she was lashed to the trunk so tightly she could move nothing except her head. The bark scratched her skin, and from the corner of her eye she saw Holoc shake out a whip.

"No," she whispered in horror.

A toothless, wrinkled, hideous old woman sprang at her from the other side, shouting words she did not understand and shaking yellow, evil-smelling dust over her.

Sneezing, Alexeika did not even know the first lash was coming until it cracked across her back. The pain went beyond her comprehension. She heard herself screaming, and could not stop until the second lash struck her. Then her breath seemed to vanish. She choked, and by the time she'd managed to suck in air, the third lash came.

It went on and on, each blow seeming to last an eternity. She thought she would die, but she did not. At the tenth, Holoc coiled his whip and returned to his tent. The women cut her down. She could not walk. Half-conscious and whimpering from the pain, she was half-dragged, half-carried to the cage under the outcropping of rock and put inside it.

That was her first whipping.

When she recovered enough to walk, and then to run, she escaped again. This time she did not try to release her fellow prisoners. She went instead to the horses, where one of the camp sentries caught her.

Her second whipping was short, for two lashes were all it took to have her sobbing and pleading for Holoc to stop.

Much to her surprise, he did. Again, the women put her in the cage. This time they starved her for three days, not even giving her water. She sat there, her stomach aching and her thirst ravaging her almost to the point of madness. She watched the men saddle their shaggy, half-wild ponies and ride away. She watched the women weaving cloth and tanning hides. The slaves, silent and rail-thin, worked to chop wood and fetch kettles of water. They prepared the food, cleaned, fetched, and carried. Now and then a few children, as leathery-dark and savage as their elders, came by Alexeika's cage to stare at her. Sometimes they threw stones at her bars to see if she'd flinch.

She sat there in silence, ignoring them, staying deep inside her mind to keep from crumbling. She was in agony. Her pain, thirst, and hunger made her so weak and hopeless she did not know how to go on.

Had anyone come to her cage at that time, she would have groveled on her belly for a bark cup of water. She would have done anything they asked. Her weakness horrified her, and she prayed to Thod and her father both for the strength to go on.

Later that day, the ancient women, the *mamsas,* untied the other captive women and led them to the center of the camp. Alexeika barely recognized them now. Their bare skin was burned by the sun. Their hair hung in filthy tangles over their eyes. Apathy slackened their faces as they were forced to sit in a circle. The *mamsas,* toothless and fierce, surrounded them, and then the *sheda* came out of her tent.

This was the hideous creature who had thrown yellow dust over Alexeika during her first whipping. Today, the *sheda* hobbled slowly across the camp on crippled feet. Her spine hunched low, bending her nearly double. Her long, snow-white hair was plaited like a man's, and her eyes shone black and alert in her withered face. Leaning on a carved staff tied with tiny skulls and bells that tinkled softly, she shuffled over to the captives.

Her cracked old voice gave an order, and the first captive was forced to lie on the ground.

The *sheda* bent over her with a bronze knife in her palsied fist. Alexeika held her breath, but the knife was only to cut a hank of hair from the captive's head. Holding the blonde tresses aloft in the wind, the *sheda* chanted while a firebrand was brought to her. She set the hair on fire and dropped it into a bowl. Peering intently over the ashes, she prodded them with her finger, then nodded.

The captive was allowed up, and another brought to her place.

Again and again the ritual was performed over all of them. In the end, three were separated from the others, Larisa among them. The rest were given shabby robes and food, then led away out of sight. Larisa and the other two were tied together and forced to kneel before the *sheda*.

She glared at them, spitting out something that sounded like a curse. Then she shook her staff bells at them, and three *mamsas* stepped behind them and cut their throats in unison.

Alexeika screamed, gripping the bars of her cage in horror.

But it was done, and the *mamsas* squatted next to their victims, draining their blood into bowls. Later the slaves dragged the bodies away and threw them into a ravine. The *mamsas* mixed the blood with horse's milk and curdled the concoction with mysterious herbs and spices before feeding it to the survivors. Alexeika suspected that the women al-

lowed to live were pregnant; those who had just been killed
were not.

She had heard stories all her life about the atrocities of
the Grethori savages. They were said to eat their own children, to drink the blood of their vanquished enemies, and
to steal babies by the use of dark magic. When Alexeika
was a young child, before the days of exile, her old nurse
used to frighten her with threats, saying she would be stolen
and eaten by the Grethori if she did not behave.

Now, as an adult, Alexeika was witnessing the truth about
the Grethori ways. They did indeed drink blood; that was
true enough. They did not eat their children, but apparently
their women bore few. And from the few understandable
comments she overheard, it seemed that they kept some
slaves as broodmares, their only purpose to bear infants that
were then kept to be raised in the camp or traded away for
goods.

Joyska, one of the surviving women and Vlad's mother,
glared at Alexeika, who sat crouched in her cage. "This is
your fault!" Joyska screamed. Her hatred came at Alexeika
like a blow. "We could have been pardoned and *safe,* but
for you!"

A *mamsa* tried to silence her, but Joyska shook off the
old crone and went on glaring at Alexeika. "Your father led
my husband to slaughter. Then my boy died for you. And
now I come to this. A thousand curses of my heart on you,
Alexeika Volvn!"

They beat Joyska then and hustled her away with the
others. Her words, however, seemed to go on hanging in
the air.

Alexeika leaned forward, gripping the bars of her cage,
and closed her burning eyes.

No one had told her why she'd escaped the others' fate,
unless it had something to do with the fact that she'd fought
Holoc like a man, and that she'd used her unreliable powers in the battle. She had no other theory to explain it.

Now, although she rubbed her face again and again with

shaking hands, she could not wipe away the horror of this latest Grethori ritual. Over and over, she saw the sharp knife drawn across Larisa's throat. Over and over, she saw the bodies fall to the dust. Over and over, Alexeika heard Joyska's curse.

Her spirits were devastated. She thought back over this difficult, tragic summer that had begun with such high hopes of defeating King Muncel and seeing freedom restored to Nether. Instead of victory, there had been defeat after defeat, tragedy after tragedy. Yes, she had argued long and hard against accepting Muncel's amnesty. The cost for such a pardon to all rebels was to become slaves in Gant. She thought she was keeping the camp strong. She thought they were all of one mind with her. It seemed she was wrong.

But the Grethori were not her fault. The deaths of Uzfan, Vlad, Larisa, and so many others were not her fault. No matter how low her spirits plummeted, she would not accept false blame. Draysinko the coward had betrayed them. He had left the sentry posts vacant, and at the first attack he'd fled with their supply of furs and the money he'd stolen from Alexeika's tent. She realized that he'd known what was going to happen. Perhaps he'd even arranged it, leading the Grethori to them in exchange for his miserable life. She'd never know the entire truth, but she knew enough to hate him for his betrayal. No wonder he'd urged her run away with him there on the bank of the fjord that last night.

And now, she could not imagine what fate awaited her and these few other prisoners. Alexeika's eyes burned, but she did not weep. She could not. Her tears were locked away somewhere inside her, where she could not reach them.

"Demon," said the cracked, wheezing voice of the *sheda*.

Startled, Alexeika looked up and saw the ancient crone standing hunched over before her cage. Alexeika had not heard or seen her coming, but suddenly she was there.

Her black, malevolent eyes peered at Alexeika through the wooden bars of the cage. "Demon," she said again.

Alexeika's faltering spirits steadied. She lifted her chin in fresh defiance. "Do you fear my powers?" she asked.

The *sheda* glared at her and struck the cage with her staff.

Alexeika flinched in spite of herself, and the *sheda* grinned toothlessly at her.

"Your turn will come soon," she said. "His lust grows hot in the spell I make. When the moon turns, he will no longer be able to control it. Then will he take you. He is strong, our chieftain. Strong and brave, but he is only a man, and he fears you."

"Good," Alexeika said defiantly, although her heart had frozen inside her. "He should fear me."

"You cannot harm him," the *sheda* said. "My protection spell keeps him safe, as it did the day your dagger missed his heart."

Alexeika frowned and drew in her breath with a hiss.

The *sheda* smiled. "My powers are stronger than yours, demon. You do not like to hear that, but it is true. Holoc knows not whether you are woman or man, for you look like one and fight like the other. But I know."

She laughed again in a gasping cackle that made the hair rise on the back of Alexeika's neck. "A son you will bear him, demon. Your powers will make a strong son whose name will ride the heavens. My hands will make your food, and I will feed you with many spells to make your child so thick of hide he will not need a shield. Claws will he have for fingers, that he can rend his enemies without dagger or sword. Flame will be his eyes, that he can destroy all who stand before him. Death will live in his mouth, that he has only to breathe forth in order to slay."

Alexeika found herself half-mesmerized by the old woman. Her mind seemed gripped by a force she could not resist, and she understood every word clearly. Somehow, she found the last scraps of her defiance. "I will bear no such monster."

The *sheda*'s black eyes narrowed and she hissed in displeasure. "Fool! I have seen a vision of the coming days.

We will have this leader. Like a dragon will he be, son of demon and Holoc the Brave. He will lead our people against the pale-eyes. Like the locusts of the steppes will we ride. Fire will flash from our spear tips. Lightning will smite our enemies. Then there will be no more pale-eyes. Then there will be only Grethori."

Alexeika tried to draw back from her, but the *sheda* thrust her staff inside the cage and prodded Alexeika's stomach with the end of it. "Your womb, demon, is mine. I have seen the visions."

"Thod smite your visions," Alexeika said. Her mouth was dry and her voice shook, but she faced the old crone with all the spirit she had left. "The Grethori can only fight helpless women and children. They run from armed knights, and even if you made a monster to lead your people, the Grethori would still run."

Glaring, the *sheda* shrieked in outrage.

"I'll be no part of this," Alexeika declared.

The *sheda* moved her staff up and down Alexeika's belly and thighs. "Beauty and fire," she mumbled. "Fire and beauty. He burns for you. You are flame to him. Let the blood mingle. Seed and soil. Grethori and demon will unite, bound into one being." She paused in the chanting of her spell and tapped Alexeika's stomach with the end of her staff. "When the moon turns, you become his forever."

Snarling, Alexeika grabbed the staff with both hands and yanked it away. The *sheda* screeched with anger, and the *mamsas* came running to surround her.

Alexeika ignored their shouts as she knelt and tried to break the staff. It was made of a smooth, dark wood as strong as iron. She could not snap it, so she tore the bells off and flung them at the *mamsas,* who screamed in rage and beat the bars of her cage with sticks. Alexeika pounded the small skulls on the ground, letting her pent-up anger and horror free as she tried to smash them. One of the little skulls cracked, and the *sheda* screamed as though in agony.

Grinning to herself, Alexeika smashed the little skull

again. But the *mamsas* wrenched open her cage and swarmed inside it. The staff was wrested from her hands and she was dragged outside. She tried to get up, but she was too weak from lack of food and water to struggle much. They kicked and beat her until she lay there, spent and half-conscious, in the dirt.

She felt something tug at her thick hair. Lifting her head, she saw the glint of the *sheda*'s bronze knife. That fast, it was done, and the *sheda* held up a lock of her hair.

"This he will eat," she said triumphantly. "What is lust now will grow into his madness. Beneath the stars will he take you. Before us all will he take you. And the *mamsas* will sing chants of our war-songs while you bleed to make this son. Demon, dragon, and Grethori will this child be. So do I say."

She hobbled away, Alexeika's hair fluttering in her hand like something alive and captured. Alexeika lay there helplessly and clenched her hands on the dirt. "Not while I live," she muttered. "Never!"

But she knew that if she didn't escape, this fate would indeed be hers. Determined neither to be mated to Holoc nor to bear some monstrous babe of witchery, Alexeika made her plans.

Every night while her body mended, she watched the rising of the moon. Every night its fullness waned a little more. Her time was running out. Holoc seldom came near her, but when he rode out of camp in the mornings his gaze went to her cage. When he rode in at eventide, he looked for her. She knew whenever his eyes watched her. She had a special sense for it, as though all her instincts had been attuned and sharpened. His sun-bronzed face remained impassive, but his dark eyes burned with a fever that intensified daily. She feared it with all her mind and soul.

It was no good trying to summon her powers—they never came when she wanted. She knew her fears made them even less reliable than usual. If only she could draw forth Faldain, the true king of Nether, and turn vision into reality.

He lived, somewhere in this world. Lost and exiled from Nether, he delayed his coming for reasons she did not understand. If only she could reach out to him as she had once before. If only she could send her plea for help to him. He was strong, manly, and handsome. His heart was good, and he had the blood of eld in his veins. If he were here, he would fight for her. He would save her.

But such thoughts were only the foolish imaginings of a lovestruck girl. She had glimpsed him once, and endangered him in the very process of parting the veils of seeing. How Uzfan had scolded her for it.

If the old priest were here, he could counteract the *sheda*'s spells.

But there was no one here who could save her except herself.

Faldain, even if he knew of her plight, even if he chose to care enough to rescue her, could not come in time. Such thoughts were pure fantasy. And Alexeika knew no fantasy could save her. She had only her own determination and wits to rely on.

Twice before, she'd broken free only to fail. This time, she knew she must succeed. The stakes were far too high for failure.

Although they now fed her well, Alexeika picked out only the berries and meat. She feared the spells and seasonings in everything else. Sometimes she was not successful, because her dreams would be wild and lustful. She would find herself heavy-eyed the next day, staring at Holoc despite herself.

She hated such manipulation and was tempted to quit eating completely. But she needed her strength for her coming escape. This time, she would not try to take a horse; they were too well-guarded. She would head instead straight down into the ravine. It would be dangerous at night, because the footing was so treacherous. But her trail would be hidden there and hard to follow. She would rather take the risk than lose all by being too cautious and careful.

During the day, she was allowed occasional exercise. She walked around camp, followed by the *mamsa* who guarded her. At night, however, she was caged and guarded by a different *mamsa*. As the camp bedded down under the stars on the mountaintop, Holoc walked past Alexeika's cage like a silent shadow. Sometimes he stopped and stood there, unmoving for perhaps an hour, before he walked on.

These silent nightly visits unnerved her more than anything else. She felt the nets of the *sheda*'s spell closing around her. As time dwindled, her fear continued to grow. And with fear came a sense of paralysis and defeat, until sometimes in the darkness she lay there on the cold ground, shivering and wretched, and believed that nothing she did or tried would be successful.

But she always fought off such bouts of self-pity. She refused to give up or surrender to fate the way the others had. They never spoke to her now. Whenever Joyska or Shelena or any of the others walked past her, they averted their eyes. She watched them change, becoming anxious to please, to fit in, to do well. They all looked the same, with the same fearful apathy in their eyes, the same mendicant smiles, the same semi-cringing posture as they learned their new slave duties.

I am a princess, not a serf, Alexeika reminded herself to keep her courage going. *It is better to die in defiance than to live crouched at the feet of a master.*

She prayed to Thod for protection. She spent time envisioning her father in her mind. His proud, upright figure, princely stance, and uncompromising values always gave her comfort. She told herself again and again that she must be a worthy daughter of such a man. He had died for his principles. She could do no less.

Meanwhile, the days passed. One morning, when the men left the camp at a dead gallop, whooping and shouting more than usual, the *mamsas* ordered the slaves to roll an enormous stone with a flattened top into the center of camp. Other stones were placed in a circle around it. A robe of yellow and vivid blue stripes was draped over the center stone, like a garish cloth over an altar.

Generous platters of food, heavily spiced, were brought to Alexeika. She ate nothing.

In the afternoon, two of the *mamsas* slipped her robe off her shoulders to her waist. One rubbed her back and arms with unguents. The other painted her breasts with intricate patterns that were themselves a spell of desire. Alexeika's skin felt on fire, as though it had come to life itself. She tried to pull away, tried to resist, but she was slapped until her head rang and forced to sit quietly for these ministrations.

"Tomorrow," one of the *mamsas* muttered as she began to paint Alexeika's back. "The stars align as the *sheda* has said. Tonight, your body will begin the dance alone. You will burn with fire, igniting his. But there must be the waiting and the burning and the waiting. Tomorrow night will you lie on the stone of Adauri, mother of all Grethori. The *ini* stones will surround you with their power, controlling you, demon. And the spell will be completed. Then will he come. Then will we watch our future begin."

Alexeika tried to push them away, but they took leather ropes and tied her up. All day in the bright sunshine they painted her body with fantastic coils and flowers and serpents. Her heart thundered inside her chest, and she told herself over and over, *Tonight I must escape.*

The young women of the camp pretended to ignore these proceedings. They were supposed to be weaving, but Alexeika could hear them talking over the clack of their looms.

One slender maiden, very bronzed of skin and black-eyed, glared at Alexeika more than the others. Today, she finally threw down her shuttle and came to Alexeika with a face of fury and hatred. Shouting a curse, she picked up a stone and hurled it. It skimmed past Alexeika's ear, barely missing her. Furious, Alexeika cursed her in return, and strained against her bonds to pull free.

Both *mamsas* dropped their paints and unguents to turn on the girl.

"He is mine!" the girl shouted. "I am promised to him!"

"No longer, Vika," one *mamsa* said. "The *sheda* has spoken."

"This creature put a spell on him. He is not—"

"Hush, or you will be beaten for your defiance," the *mamsa* said sternly. "The promising is broken."

"But I would have been first wife of the camp," Vika protested. "I was to be over all the women and one day *sheda*—"

The *mamsa* gripped her by her thin shoulders and shook her hard. "Must I cut out your tongue to silence you? That is over."

"But I love him!"

"He is yours no longer. You will be given to Mudlic in—"

"No!" Vika wailed. She ran at Alexeika, only to be dragged back, slapped, and taken away.

Alexeika listened to Vika's sobbing for a long time. Then there was silence, and Vika came no more to torment her. For a while, Alexeika sat there, deserted and still tied, while the paints dried on her body and the cool breeze made her shiver despite the sunlight. Finally the *mamsas* returned, looking flustered, and resumed their work. But their attention had been affected. They painted more rapidly, with less care now. Alexeika's skin crawled, but she could tell the spellcasting was less potent than it had been at first.

She smiled in her heart, hoping Vika caused even more trouble.

In the evening, as one by one the campfires were extinguished, Alexeika bided her time. She had been working on loosening the bars of her cage ever since learning what was to be her fate. Each night, as soon as the camp bedded down and the last sounds faded and grew quiet, the *mamsa* on duty would fall asleep. Alexeika would go to work, turning the bar back and forth. Tonight it was very loose, loose enough to pull free. She knew she could wriggle out through the narrow space.

Her heart beat with feverish impatience. She wanted to go now, to flee. But she forced herself to wait. This was her only chance. She must not ruin it with haste.

She waited, her skin itching beneath her robe, knowing that Holoc would steal forth in the darkness to stand at her cage as he always did. What a fool he was, wanting her but afraid of her. She was no demon, but she had no intention of letting anyone in camp know that. In her heart, she made herself despise him, telling herself he was no man if he needed his grandmother to make a lust spell for him.

For half the night, she waited, agonized by fear, caution, and impatience.

Holoc did not come.

She saw a light burning in his tent for a long time, but he never emerged. Alexeika knew the spell must be nearly overwhelming him. Perhaps he did not trust himself to come near her tonight. Perhaps the *sheda* did not allow it.

In the quiet, she listened to the distant buzz of insects in the brush. She saw the stars come out, cold and twinkling in the black sky. She listened to the soft moans of a man and woman together, and frowned in resistance. There was no burn in her skin tonight, as the *mamsa* had said there would be. She was too afraid.

Finally, silence lay over the camp like a blanket. Her guard slept. Holoc's light went out.

It was time.

The air felt bitterly cold, blowing off the snowy peak of the Bald Giant. Alexeika blew on her half-frozen fingers, then reached out and pulled the loose bar away. Laying it down carefully on the dusty ground, she held her breath and slithered out of the cage.

Crouching low, she paused to listen. The *mamsa*'s breathing remained hoarse and steady.

Alexeika knew where the other sentries were posted. The horses moved about sleepily, and she froze anew.

Nothing else stirred.

She crept away from the stone outcropping. The best way to avoid the sentries was to cut straight through the center of camp. Though her heart lifted to her throat, she took that route. Her feet wanted to fly, but she knew better than to run.

She forced herself to go slowly, silently. Barely did she breathe, that the air might not be disturbed around her. Her foot stumbled against a stone, and she looked down in the darkness, realizing she had disturbed the ini circle around the large Adauri stone.

Satisfaction touched her heart. She hesitated, then crouched down and swiftly pulled the other stones out of place. She took the robe of yellow and blue stripes from atop the Adauri stone, crumpled it in her hands, dropped it on the ground, and walked over it.

Across the camp, she edged between two tents, skirted the silent looms where the cloth in progress popped and billowed softly on its frame. She listened to a man's snoring and crept onward.

When she was clear of the tents, she hesitated yet again, still resisting the urge to plunge recklessly into the ravine.

She had to go slowly. She had to make sure she knew where all the sentries were.

So she waited. No sound or whiff of rancid beyar grease came to her. She knew she must be upwind of them, but she heard them, one by one, as they shifted position and stamped their feet against the cold.

Now.

Crouching low, she moved to the top of the ravine. A whiff of decay came to her nostrils. This was where the Grethori threw their trash, offal, and the bodies of their dead victims. She would have to climb down through that.

It did not matter. The stink would help hide her trail.

Carefully she lowered herself over the edge. Down she climbed into the thicket and briers. In the darkness, it was impossible to see where she was going. She moved by feel and stealth, trying to make as little noise as possible.

And all the while, she was so tense her muscles ached. She expected the outcry of discovery at any moment, with the chase to follow, and then capture.

But the *mamsa* on guard did not awaken and find her gone. The sentries did not hear her cautious progress through the brush and undergrowth that choked the ravine. She clambered over one of the corpses, nearly gagging on the stench, and refused to imagine what she touched.

A stone dislodged beneath her foot and went rolling down the hillside ahead of her. It clattered and tumbled loudly, and Alexeika froze there. Suddenly she was breathing hard. Her hands were sweaty, and she could not think or move.

She stayed crouched there in the brush, her hair snagging on twigs, and moaned softly in the back of her throat.

No shout came from the top of the ravine, however. After a few moments, the night sounds of insects came back. A little creature rustled in the leaves. The breeze sighed through the trees.

She managed to stop shaking and forced herself to continue.

Near the bottom of the ravine a small stream gurgled over the stones. The scent and sound of the water refreshed her. Quickly she knelt at its edge and cupped her hands in the icy liquid to drink.

She would walk down the stream the rest of the way to the bottom of the mountain. By morning, she would be well away from here, and almost impossible to track. She swore to not let them find her.

Karstok was where she meant to go. If she kept up her strength and managed to keep herself fed, she thought she could reach the town before snows blanketed these mountains. Down in the lower lands, she would have little trouble finding a place for herself. Even if she had to work as a serf, she would do it until her fortunes turned again.

For the first time, she allowed herself to feel a tiny sliver of hope. She'd escaped, against the odds. She was free, and soon she would be safe.

Suddenly something wet and slippery touched the back of her neck.

She jumped and floundered into the stream, nearly falling as she did so, and struggled to whirl around. Her involuntary scream stayed trapped in her throat, for the thing that grabbed her snaked a wet arm around her throat and squeezed hard.

"Now you will never be his," Vika's voice whispered in her ear. "I will make sure of that tonight, when I slit your throat and drink your blood."

Alexeika shuddered as Vika's arm tightened across her throat. She couldn't breathe. Her senses were spinning, and her struggles only made it worse.

"We are promised, Holoc and I," Vika whispered, squeezing even harder so that Alexeika's ears roared. "With your demon blood in me, the *sheda*'s spell can still be made. I will bear the dragon-child, not you!"

Alexeika tugged at Vika's arm with both hands, but the Grethori girl was stronger than her slenderness would have indicated. When she pressed the merciless cold metal of a dagger blade against Alexeika's throat, Alexeika stood horrified and frozen in Vika's arms, certain she'd drawn her final breath.

9

FAR AWAY AT Savroix, Lady Pheresa du Lindier was perched on a cushion at the rear of the Countess Lalieux's sitting room. Just last week, the countess had become the king's sole mistress. Her older rival had left the palace in a huff and flurry, trailing mountains of baggage and, it was whispered, half the furnishings in her wing of the palace. Consequently, Lalieux's position at court had grown very powerful. Although as a member of the royal family Pheresa was not supposed to recognize the king's mistresses, she no longer had a choice. It was poor strategy to make enemies among those in power.

Today, Pheresa had accepted the countess's invitation. She had come reluctantly, hoping she would not land herself in some wanton orgy.

But it was only a staid gathering of ladies listening to a concert of lute players.

Trying to stifle her yawns, Pheresa turned her gaze away from the trio of female musicians. One of them was Sofia, newly married and now the Baroness de Briard. Pheresa could not help but remember Sofia as the wanton, mischievous girl she'd seen cavorting in the gardens on many occasions; it was hard to watch her now attempting to be a grand lady of married status without thinking of all her previous exploits. Still, at this court respectability could be established in a day if fashion decreed it. Pheresa still believed in honor and proper behavior, though perhaps her presence here in Lalieux's company, she realized, indicated otherwise.

Turning hot-faced, she wished she hadn't come.

Plinking on their lutes, the ladies sang in sweet harmony, making the audience of court women coo with admiration behind their fans. Pheresa's mind, however, could not stay on the melodies. It was far too preoccupied with her troubles.

She wore her finest gown today, one of mushroom-colored silk embroidered with silver threads and tiny pearls. A cap sewn all over with pearls and crystal beads was fitted atop her thick reddish-gold tresses. Her fan was made of dyed ivory, and intricately carved. It was very old and valuable, having belonged to Pheresa's grandmother. She was dressed this way because Prince Gavril had returned three days ago, to much fanfare and pomp, and she believed—nay, hoped—that today at last he would send for her.

Yesterday evening, she had seen him at the dancing following the nightly banquet. The festivities were merry indeed, enlivened by the prince's presence. How gracefully he moved, how quickly he learned the new dance steps which had become fashionable while he was away. When he threw back his head and laughed, the tenor sound of his voice rang through her like a bell.

He had grown into a stunningly handsome young man, broad of shoulder and tall. He wore a thin mustache now, making him look even older. His hair shone in the candlelight like gilt, and his dark blue eyes flashed with wit and high spirits. They had passed over her without recognition, however, as she'd sat grouped with other young maidens of the court.

Her disappointment haunted her still. She had joined in the dancing when given the opportunity, but by then Prince Gavril had gone to chat with other young men his age. His back was to the dancing the whole time she and Lord Fantil were on the floor. Gavril never saw how gracefully she could execute the *spinnade* or the *gliande* in the hands of her partner.

Fantil, of course, understood everything. His cynical eyes gleamed at her as she pivoted before him. "He doesn't remember you at all, does he, little dove?"

Her eyes flashed to hide her disappointment. "Why should he? I have not seen him in years."

But her bravado was all a facade, and Fantil only laughed at her.

Since this morning, everyone had been gossiping about how Gavril had ignored her. Humiliation almost kept Pheresa locked in her room, but she came forth at last, dressed in her best, and determined to let no one see how hurt she was.

Life was perilous at court for someone like herself, with high hopes and higher ambitions, but no real position of

power. There were factions who supported her as the future
queen, but others sought to trip her into making some fatal
mistake that would force the king to banish her from court.
Thus far, she'd avoided most of the pitfalls. But her nerves
were stretched to the breaking point, and this afternoon as
she sat at the concert, pretending to enjoy the music, her
mind was racing and her emotions were chaotic. She'd been
here for months—niece of the king, yet a nobody who was
by turns laughed at, ignored, or pitied. Thus far, she'd endured the waiting by telling herself that once Gavril returned
everything would change.

It hadn't. He didn't even know her.

In the back of her mind she could hear her mother's furious voice, castigating her for failure. In her mind's eye she
could see her father's cynical look of disappointment. Rank,
position, and achievement meant everything to her parents.
They did not permit failure. The idea of returning home to
their country estate unchosen and humiliated filled Pheresa
with distress. She curled her slender hands into tight fists in
her lap and vowed, as she had sworn last night in her prayers,
that she would make the prince notice her.

That was why she had dressed so resplendently today.
Pretend a thing was, and sometimes you could bring it to
pass. Or so she had been taught by old Nyswan, her childhood tutor. She dressed as though Gavril had already spoken to her of betrothal. Emulating her mother's regal carriage,
she held her head erect and made her eyes look proud.

And if perhaps there was more anger and simmering disappointment flashing in the depths of her gaze than happiness, it hardly mattered. She did *not* look defeated. By
midday, her ploy had begun to bear fruit with some of the
courtiers. Already a rumor had been started, and while this
pleased Pheresa, it also worried her. From what she knew
of Gavril, he did not like to have his hand forced. He might
reject her now out of sheer stubbornness.

But better to be rejected than simply ignored. That was
what mortified her so deeply. She was not some nameless

country maid of indifferent lineage with unfounded hopes. She had been brought here to become his bride, if he would have her. The least he could do was speak to her for a few minutes. If they did not suit each other, well and good, and no blame to anyone. But his indifference wounded her feminine vanity and undermined what self-confidence she possessed. He was acting discourteous and cruel by subjecting her to the mockery of the courtiers.

She wished he could be more like his father. Despite his many faults, King Verence was a kind and courteous man. Because he was so pressed by the demands of state, he was inclined to be self-indulgent and forgetful of others. He abhorred unpleasantness and went out of his way to avoid confrontations and quarrels. It was said by some, quietly, that Verence was a better man than he was a king. His heart was too generous and forgiving. He overlooked too many faults in too many men, his own son among them.

But however rude he might be, Gavril was so very handsome. When she thought of him, her anger melted. All her life she'd heard what a fine-looking boy he was. But she had not expected to find him grown and manly and this magnificent. Seeing him last night had filled her breast with inner tumult. She'd hardly been able to tear her gaze away from him. Pheresa always kept a cool head, but since last night she'd been awash with dreams and fantasies. If only his eyes would turn to her. If only he would actually look at her and *see* her.

Now, at the concert in the countess's chambers, Pheresa's emotions overtook her. Suddenly breathless, she dropped her gaze to where her hands trembled in her lap. Did she love him already? How could she? She felt ill inside, but that was only nerves. Or perhaps she was simply exhausted from so many festivities. She must steady herself, must not grow sickly. She knew the importance of keeping her courage here under the scrutiny of so many. For even at this moment, Lady Esteline—her court chaperone, but no friend—was staring at her.

The woman's mouth curved in a small, malicious smile, and Pheresa felt herself blush.

The music stopped at that moment, mercifully, and she applauded with the others. Her back was aching from sitting so erect on the uncomfortable cushion, but Pheresa did not slouch, ever.

A rustle came from the rear of the room. A servant in the king's livery had entered. He crept quietly forward through the throng of seated ladies, carrying his cap in his hand.

Pheresa's heart leaped wildly in her chest. A king's footman. Surely it was a message at last.

But she forced herself to sit still, to pretend indifference. After all, how many times had she watched a footman pass her on his way to summon someone else? She no longer allowed herself to hope for anything. But just the same, as she lowered her eyes and pretended to pick at the carving on her fan, her heart was pounding hard and fast.

Let this be my summons at last, she prayed.

A touch on her shoulder made her look up.

The footman was bending over her. She met his eyes; he bowed low to her.

"My lady," he murmured softly, "your presence is requested at once."

There was silence in the room. They all heard him say it. Everyone now turned to stare at her.

Tremendous relief, hope, and joy poured over Pheresa in a wave. This was one of the king's footmen, not Gavril's, but surely the king would not send for her today if it were not significant. The eyes of the women around her held bold speculation and envy, and Pheresa let herself believe the moment had finally come.

She wanted to jump to her feet, but instead she rose in a fluid motion and followed the servant out with no expression on her face.

She had been taught how to walk gracefully and with exquisite poise. Only the iciness in her veins and the pulse pounding madly in her throat belied the outer calm she exhibited. After all, she was long skilled at maintaining her composure. As a child, she had been poked daily at dinner with a meat skewer. Her mother, Princess Dianthelle, would lean toward her, poking even harder while she whispered, "Show nothing of what you feel, Pheresa. Show nothing!"

Such training had been harsh, but it served her well during these difficult days at court. She relied on it now as she walked past Lady Esteline and went out the door.

She was glad she'd worn her best dress today. Her instincts for survival had not failed her after all. Today her life was changing forever. She sensed it, and her steps quickened until she was almost crowding the footman's heels.

As she walked down the long galleries and corridors of the palace and neared the chambers of state, more courtiers thronged the passageways. Some of them stopped talking among themselves to stare as she walked past them regally, her head held high. A few of them bowed to her.

Pheresa's eyes flicked right and left to these few individuals. Her quick and intelligent mind made note of their faces so that she would remember them later. They wanted to be her allies, and she needed as many as she could get.

In her wake arose a buzz of speculative conversation, and her heart sang with pride and anticipation.

Then the footman turned aside and led her down a lesser passageway. He stopped before a door and tapped three times.

A muffled voice responded, and the door swung inward. The footman bowed to Pheresa.

Frowning a little, for this was unexpected, she walked past him. On the other side of the threshold, she saw a man in church livery. He handed the king's footman a purse of money. She heard the coins clink inside it as the footman tucked it away.

Before Pheresa could turn back, he was gone and the door was being shut behind her.

Alarm touched her. The exchange had been so deft and quick it was over almost before she knew what had happened. Now she found herself inside a small, sumptuously appointed antechamber. There were many such rooms off the main galleries, rooms where important personages waited in private for audiences with the king.

Pheresa looked at the man in church livery. He had the closed, secretive face of a servant. His eyes held infinite knowledge, but indifference to it all. His expression told her nothing. In silence he gestured for her to advance into the room. Fearing abduction, Pheresa wanted to flee, but the man was between her and the door. She had no choice but to go in the direction he bade her.

Smelling of incense, the air was sultry and too warm. Heavy draperies shrouded the windows, closing out all sunlight and requiring candles to be lit. They burned in generous groups in each corner of the room, casting forth clear, yellow light.

At first she thought no one else was there, but then a movement caught her darting gaze and she realized a man was standing in the shadows near the draperies. Her breath caught. She thought it might be Gavril, using subterfuge to gain them privacy, and her fright left her. He turned and walked toward her, his feet soundless on the thick carpets.

As he came into the light, he was revealed to be not Gavril at all, but instead a short man, immensely fat, with a neck that bulged and rolled above his tunic collar. His vestments reached to the floor and were snowy white, except for the embroidered sash of yellow binding his ample girth. He wore heavy rings, one of which had a seal. A Circle set with immense round diamonds hung on a gold chain around his neck, flashing and glittering on his chest. His face was broad and fleshy, his lips thick and red. He wore a small, gray goatee on his chin which ill-suited him. His dark eyes, almost buried in layers of fat, held rapier intelligence.

She had never been introduced to this man, but she knew instantly who he was. With a gasp, she curtsied low. "Cardinal Noncire," she whispered.

Halting before her, he briefly placed his hand atop her beaded cap in benevolence. "Lady Pheresa," he murmured.

His voice was incredibly rich of timbre, deep and warm and vibrant. It amazed her that a man of such physical ugliness could have been blessed with such a voice. Could she have closed her eyes and imagined him, he would have been tall, fit, young, and manly, a knight of valor and fighting prowess, a man to follow to the ends of the earth.

Her fancies startled her, and she dismissed them in swift shame. This was a cardinal. It was improper to indulge in such frivolous thoughts about him. In her mind, she begged pardon from Saint Tomias, and rose from her curtsy with her face aflame and her thoughts chaotic.

"Thank you for coming to see me," Noncire said.

She frowned slightly. "I thought I was obeying a summons from the king."

"Ah." Noncire's fleshy lips twitched in what might have been a smile. "Discretion is useful, my dear."

She did not like for him to call her that. Cardinal or not, he was a prince of the church only. He had been born the younger son of a chevard, and was not her equal. But she curbed her annoyance, reminding herself that his power was great, perhaps greater than she knew.

"What do you wish from me?" she asked.

"Such impatience!" He held up his thick hand. "Please seat yourself, Lady Pheresa, that we may talk in comfort."

She did not like his mannerisms. His deep voice was almost hypnotic, inducing within her the desire to obey him. Frowning, she steeled herself against his influence and chose a chair different from the one he'd selected for her.

The cardinal's expression did not change. Once she was seated, he lowered his bulk ponderously onto a chair, which creaked beneath his weight.

"Better," he said with a sigh of relief, and fixed his tiny eyes on her. "You are young and impatient. We will not parry with each other. For what purpose have you joined Lalieux's set?"

Pheresa blinked, surprised by such a direct attack. "I . . ."

"Come, my dear, do not attempt to dissemble with me. I am far more clever than you."

"Then you must already know my reasons," she retorted angrily, "and I need not waste your time by repeating them."

Anger flashed in his small eyes, and for a moment she was frightened by her own temerity. He could destroy her, she knew. All he had to do was lay accusations against her, and she would be banished from court immediately.

"That reply was unwise, Lady Pheresa," he said after a long moment of silence. "I am not your enemy. You do not want to make me into one."

"Forgive me," she said with a gasp, trying to rein in her temper. When she was queen, he could do less against her. But right now, she was nothing. She must remember that. She must govern herself more carefully.

"Lalieux is pretty and extends considerable influence over the king in private," the cardinal said. "She has no influence politically. Why, after all this time, have you suddenly joined forces with her?"

"I haven't," Pheresa said, wondering if her simple attendance at a concert had caused all this concern. "I wanted to hear the music. I had no other invitation for the day."

He sat back in his chair, making it creak again, and Pheresa felt new shame steal through her heart. She resented having to make such an admission to anyone. It revealed how pathetically lonely she was here at Savroix, how isolated she really was.

"But you will now accept her other invitations," he said.

"I don't know."

"You will. To refuse is to snub her and perhaps annoy the king."

Pheresa opened her mouth to defend herself, but shut it again in silence. She had been raised not to offer excuses. She realized how foolish her little act of rebellion had been. Every action at court carried ramifications. Intrigue was rampant here. Interpretations of behavior and words grew complex far beyond their original intention.

"Thank you for advising me," she said at last, her voice tight and small. "I didn't think—"

"I am not advising you," he broke in curtly. "I advise the prince."

Her eyes flashed up to meet his. With sudden insight, she said, "Have you instructed him to avoid me?"

A tinge of red appeared in the cardinal's face. "You are either a very brave young woman or a complete fool," he said softly.

Pheresa gripped her hands together to hide their trembling and forced herself to meet his gaze steadily. "You have chosen against me, and told him so," she said after a moment. "I see."

For a moment she was intensely angry, but she also realized the futility of trying to combat Noncire's powerful influence.

"My efforts are for naught, then," she said.

"He has gone hunting for the day," Noncire said. "Tomorrow he will be allowed to compete in the final rounds of jousting. Then will he go to his investiture into knighthood. He has no time to stand about and gaze at you. Your finery is a bold but wasted effort. The rumor it's caused is like a summer weed. It will be gone by tomorrow when no announcement of betrothal is made. You will wish you'd never started anything so foolish."

Anger and embarrassment mingled inside her. She hated being so transparent to him.

The cardinal pulled himself ponderously to his feet and stood over her, dominating her with his bulk and disdain. "My momentary concern was for naught," he announced. "You are no intriguer, no meddler. You are simply a vapid girl, with little brain and no character. Your show of spirit is foolish indeed, and reveals how insubstantial you are. Trying to catch Gavril's eye with this gown is a trick we might expect of some little servant girl. You are not worthy to become Princess of the Realm. You are not worthy of *him*."

Noncire turned from her and waddled away. Clearly the interview was over.

Humiliated and furious, Pheresa rose to her feet. She glared at Noncire's back, wanting to hurl invective at him. But there was nothing she could say to refute his cruel words. He'd spoken lies, of course. He was not as clever a man as he thought he was, for she was neither foolish, nor characterless, nor stupid, nor a trickster. But she would not dignify his insults with denials.

Drawing in a sharp breath, she said softly, "I threaten you somehow. How is that, lord cardinal? Is it that you fear I might supersede you in the prince's affections? That he might grow to listen more to his betrothed than to his tutor? That he might become a man, and be no longer a boy under your instruction?"

The cardinal's shoulders stiffened. He turned around to confront her, his face dark with arrested anger.

She looked at him with her head high and her eyes bright with defiance, and said, "We could have been allies, you and I. Instead, you choose to make us enemies."

He snorted. "Your words are empty, girl. You will never win him."

"Nay, sir. 'Tis *I* who am to be won," she replied. Her voice shook, angering her. She wanted to it be strong in this argument. "Here at court, I am not popular, for all the maidens at Savroix see themselves as my competitors. But the people want me at Gavril's side—"

"The people!" Noncire said with scorn.

"As does the king."

His beady eyes flashed, but he said nothing.

Ah, she thought, *so you do not quite speak in the same tone about his majesty.* "If I go unchosen by Gavril," she said, keeping her voice as brave as she could, "then my father will wed me to a suitor from another realm, forging an alliance that may be to Mandria's cost."

Noncire stared at her. "Is that a threat, Lady Pheresa?"

She had made an enemy of him, she realized. But there'd never been any real chance of his becoming anything else. "I would not presume to threaten you, lord cardinal," she replied demurely, but with steel in her voice. "I am not that foolish."

"What would you call it, then?" he asked furiously. "If not a threat, what?"

"A statement of speculation," she replied.

"You cannot win Gavril's love," he told her. "That is a woman's ploy, to entrap a man through his senses, but it will not work."

"I do not seek Gavril's love," she said. "I prefer his respect and his courtesy. Do you judge me cheap, lord cardinal? This is a matter of state, of creating a union deemed best for the realm and its future. I can see that, even if you do think me vapid and lacking in character. I had supposed you, as a man of such intellect and power, would also understand something so basically political."

"Lady Pheresa—"

She abruptly curtsied to him and whirled away with a swish of her long skirts. The implacable servant in church livery waited at the door, but did not open it for her.

She was forced to halt, trembling and feeling sick to her stomach. Her open defiance both amazed and frightened her. So much for telling herself to take care. She realized she had let her emotions sweep all caution away. She'd said things she had no business saying, for none of it could she back up, least of all the threat of her father's marrying her to the sovereign of another realm. Thod forbid that she should end up bound to King Muncel's sickly little boy or to some ignorant Klad chieftain for the rest of her life.

"Lady Pheresa," Cardinal Noncire said from behind her.

The servant would not open the door, and she could not flee. Unwillingly, Pheresa turned back to Noncire.

He stood there in the candlelight, the Circle of diamonds

flashing against his white clothing. "Thank you," he said softly.

She frowned. "I don't understand."

He stretched his fleshy lips in a smile that never reached his tiny eyes. "A little provocation was all I needed to force you to reveal exactly what lies behind your placid facade. You are indeed your mother's daughter, as I have suspected all along."

Pheresa's frown deepened. She found herself annoyed and confused, for she did not wish to be likened to her mother at all. "Was this conversation a sham, then?"

"Not at all. Consider it a lesson, however. You cannot and will not force Gavril's hand. Should he decide to wed you one day, it will be at a time of his own convenience. You and the king are far too optimistic in having you reside here at court with all your expectations aired before the world."

She flushed at that. She hadn't wanted to come here until things were settled. Her father hadn't listened. Her mother had told her to be quiet and do as she was told.

The cardinal tilted his blocky head to one side. "I do not think Gavril will desire a bride as opinionated and defiant as you. But I will discuss this with him later."

Pheresa felt as though she'd been poleaxed. Her mouth opened, but there was a moment of struggle before she could get out any words. "You mean you . . . he sent you to judge me?"

Noncire bowed his head.

Flames consumed her. She wanted to stamp her feet and hurl things, the way she had when she was a child. "He couldn't be bothered to speak to me in person, to grow acquainted with me. Instead he sent you!"

Noncire's chuckle infuriated her even more. "Of course. The Prince of the Realm is far too busy to waste his time with idle dalliance."

"But—"

"And as you said, Lady Pheresa, this is a matter of state, not of love. Hmm?"

The scorn and mockery in his voice as he turned her own words back against her was too much for her to bear. She raged with embarrassment and mortification. If this had all been Gavril's idea, then he was crueler than she'd imagined. Perhaps he was hiding behind the draperies right now, laughing at her discomfiture.

Tears sprang to her eyes, but she refused to let them fall. "This—this was beastly!" she said in a muffled voice.

"On the contrary, dear child. It was practical. Don't worry. His highness will have my full report by eventide. Go now and change your gown. There's no need to soil such lovely magnificence when the prince isn't at court today to see it."

The servant opened the door.

Blinded by rage and tears, Pheresa swept through it. Noncire chuckled behind her until the closing door cut off the sound. Still, his amusement echoed in her ears as she fled.

She couldn't go back through the galleries, to be stared at by everyone. Muffling her sobs, Pheresa picked up her skirts and ran for a hiding place, where she could stay unseen and unheard for the rest of the day.

10

As A TOWN, Savroix-en-Charva sprawled larger than any other settlement Dain had ever seen. Buildings made either of stone or wood towered as high as five stories and were crammed so closely together a person could lean out of an upstairs window and touch the wall of the adjoining structure. The streets were paved with stone, and the clatter of horses' hooves and cart wheels made an awful din and racket that went on day and night. To the south side of the city, the mouth of the Charva River spread nearly half a league wide as it joined the sea. Rich black farmland bordered it, lush with crops nearly ready for harvesting.

To Dain, there had never been such sights or smells or sounds. He found it disorienting at first, for the city was so large he felt closed off from trees, and the soil, and growing things. All he could sense was a bewildering flicker of men-minds and the constant bustle and hurry of movement. It took him time to adjust and block out the worst of it.

Then he discovered the sea, and stood for nearly an hour, mouth open, just gazing at its vast expanse. It stretched so far that on the horizon it blended with the sky. And within it, deep beneath the heaving waters, swam such a bounty of life. His mind reached out to new creatures—the fish, and the little spiny urchins that grew on rocks, and the weeds swaying in their own dim fluid world. More than that, he felt the sea itself as an entity, vast and powerful, like the mountains or the Dark Forest.

And to Riva, goddess-consort of Thod, who ruled the moon and held power over the sea, Dain knelt and worshiped.

Sir Terent's meaty hand gripped his shoulder and squeezed it hard. "Dain!" he said in a strangled voice. "What're you doing?"

Dain ignored him until he finished, then he rose to his feet and looked into the red face of his protector. Beyond Sir Terent's burly shoulders, a crowd of people came and went on their business. "I was praying," Dain said.

"Aye, 'tis what I thought. Take care, now. A pagan you no longer are, and you aren't to be praying to whatever it was that you were praying to."

Dain frowned. "But Riva is part of the—"

"Hsst!" Sir Terent uttered in warning. He glanced over his shoulder as though worried they'd be overheard in the din and commotion. The wharf, however, was a busy place. Sailors in short cloaks and bare legs were arguing loudly over the unloading of their cargo. Merchants were inspecting wares. From all sides could be heard haggling and argument and laughter.

"But, Sir Terent—"

"Enough now," the protector said.

Dain planted his feet stubbornly, ready to argue.

"*Enough,*" Sir Terent said firmly. "She whom you named has no more place in the Reformed Church. You know that."

"I feel her presence," Dain said in protest, gesturing toward the ocean.

Sir Terent's eyes bulged in shock. He shook his large head. "Unwise, m'lord. Very unwise. Only Thod and Tomias are we permitted to worship. Do you want to be thrown into prison for heresy *now*?"

"No, of course not." Dain relented, and let himself be drawn away from the wharves.

It was nearly sunset, and the streets were jammed with people out for revelry. Streaming ribbons of every imaginable color fluttered from open windows and doorways. The banners of lords and knights flew from lodgings and inns. Horses, too numerous to be stabled in the mews, were tied up in groups in the smaller streets and guarded by zealous grooms.

Music was playing, mostly enthusiastic pounding on drums accompanied by tambourines and rattles. The clear voice of a huckster rose over the hubbub: "This way, good people! This way to see the sword swallower. . . ."

Dain swung in that direction, but Sir Terent grabbed his arm and herded him onward.

"Got to be fresh for tomorrow, m'lord."

With increasing difficulty they pushed their way through the throngs. Pickpockets abounded, and Dain kept one hand on his dagger and the other on his purse. Sir Terent crowded even closer on his heels, gripping their food pouch and grumbling curses beneath his breath all the while.

Dain pretended to ignore his complaints, but he knew it was his fault they were out so late. He and Sir Terent had gone to the food shops to collect dinner for everyone, but Dain wanted to look at the sea, and he'd lingered there too long. It was unfair to the others, cooped up at their miserable lodgings with armor to polish and the horses to tend in readiness for tomorrow's jousting. Now Dain tried to hurry back, but it was impossible to do anything other than elbow and shove his way through the crowd.

"Have your fortune read, handsome!" called out a woman.

"Sweetmeats, nice 'n hot!" roared a man.

"See the two-headed donkey!"

"Three coppers for a dance with the Siren of the Sea!"

A woman with only one eye leaped into Dain's path and flung a handful of ribbons in his face. "Buy these for your sweetheart, m'lad!"

"No." He shoved past her, and felt her nimble fingers dance along his purse.

He had a firm hold on it, however, and heard her curse him as he elbowed on by.

"Gods!" Sir Terent swore, treading on his heels.

A clanging bell warned them, and they jumped back from a street just as a ponderous carriage rumbled by. A dog snapping at the wheels got his paw run over. Yelping, he dodged back and limped away.

Dain and Sir Terent ran across the street and turned down a narrow passage between buildings. It smelled foul and was so dark only Dain could see where he was going.

At the other end, they emerged into a tiny square, where three inns stood in fearsome competition with each other. Theirs was the smallest and filthiest, although its prices were a king's ransom. They were lucky to be lodged even there, although Dain, Sir Terent, Sir Polquin, Sulein, and Thum had to share a single room and bed, with Lyias on the floor. The food was bad, the service worse, and the ale unspeakable. That was why Dain and Sir Terent had sought out one of the food shops, where they could get plentiful, tasty provisions at more reasonable prices. The landlord knew what they were doing, but he'd made no protest as yet. His ale-room was now filled with other customers camping on the floor and sleeping beneath the tables. He and his staff were so run off their feet trying to supply food and drink to these latecomers that he had no time to demand board from Dain's party.

Dain ran up the wooden steps and rapped three times on their door.

"Aye?" Sir Polquin asked cautiously from within.

"It's Dain."

The door opened, and Dain and Sir Terent shouldered their way inside the cramped chamber. The whitewashed ceiling was fly-specked and stained from old leaks. It was so low Dain had to duck to keep from bumping his head.

Thum, who was kneeling on the floor and polishing Sir Terent's helmet, dropped his cloth and rose to his feet. "About time," he said gruffly. "Our backbones are rubbing our—"

"Never you mind that," Sir Polquin said, silencing him. "Clear your work away now so there's room."

Sulein was already sitting cross-legged on the wide bed, which stretched nearly from wall to wall. The physician's dark frizzy hair billowed about his head, and his eyes were snapping with excitement.

"Come, come," he said, gesturing with his long slender fingers. "Did you get the delicacies from Markeesh? The cakes made from the flower petals of Khalei, the little puffs of *cunishe* wrapped in slivers of sweetened ham?"

"A good joint of roast would serve us better," Sir Polquin said, sniffing the air.

With great ceremony, Sir Terent opened the food pouch and Dain removed two enormous meat pies in pastry, a roast, little packets of peas and miniature vegetables that smelled delectable, a loaf of bread that was still faintly warm, sweets, and a small package wrapped in linen that he handed to Sulein.

"I couldn't get the cakes," he said. "They were sold out. But the proprietor said these things called—"

"—*disals*!" Sulein shouted, already opening the packet and sniffing. He threw back his head in ecstasy. "What blessings have befallen me this day. *Disals* with poppy seeds. Great thanks to you, Lord Dain, for your kindness."

"All your heathen food cost twice as much as the rest," Sir Terent grumbled with a frown.

The physician ignored him. He was too busy fingering the little morsels of food and smacking his lips over each bite.

Muttering something about ungrateful foreigners, Sir Terent helped divide the food into the wooden trenchers that Lyias unstacked and held for him. Soon they were all eating, and there was no sound except solid chewing and the faint shouts and whoops downstairs in the ale-room.

Not until they were nearly finished did Thum break the silence by looking at Dain. "Any luck?" he asked.

Dain swallowed his mouthful and shook his head.

Disappointment clouded Thum's thin, freckled face. "Damne, I was sure you'd gain audience with the king today."

Sir Polquin gave him a nudge. "Don't be daft, boy. The king won't be giving audiences until the festivities are over. Told all of you so a dozen times already. You, Terent, did you take him to the palace again?"

Sir Terent's face turned a deep shade of red. "We went to inspect the jousting field."

"Aye, but on the way you stopped to petition the palace." Sir Polquin pointed a thick finger at his fellow knight. "You'll not fool me into thinking otherwise."

"What harm in it?" Sir Terent asked, glancing sideways at Dain. "No audiences were being given today, but we had to ask. It's Lord Dain's duty to inform the king about our dear chevard. No point in shirking that."

Sir Polquin scowled and grumbled in his mustache.

"If only Dain were knighted," Thum said wistfully. "Then

he could compete with you, Sir Terent, and we'd have two chances of someone from Thirst winning the day."

The protector licked meat grease off his fingers and nodded. "Aye, we would at that." He cast Dain a speculative glance.

Dain frowned and put down the last crumbs of his pie. "Nay!" he said sharply.

"We could do it," Sir Terent said, looking between him and Sir Polquin. "Have our own ceremony of investiture."

Sir Polquin scowled, but Thum jumped to his feet.

"Oh, do it!" he said in excitement. "For Dain's sake if not—"

"No!" Dain said, cutting him off.

The color leached from Thum's face, and they all stared at Dain.

He stood up, hunched awkwardly against the ceiling. "Don't do it."

"We have the right," Sir Terent told him. "Our rank permits us to invest new knights if the need arises—"

"On the battlefield," Sir Polquin put in.

"I don't want it," Dain said. "Not this way." He met their eyes and struggled to find words to express his meaning. "I mean I do want it, more than anything. But it must be done properly, and in correct order. There's been enough jumping over the rules already. You, Sir Terent, calling me 'lord,' when my petition has not yet been heard by the king. Us, having to come here now when we needed also to go home and bury Lord Odfrey."

"The king won't refuse your request," Sir Terent said. "He was near to granting it already when Lord Odfrey asked him. Once he gives you audience, he won't say no."

"But I can't assume that he will and proceed as though it's already done," Dain said.

"Quite right," Sir Polquin agreed brusquely. "Best to be proper. Best to do it right."

Sir Terent frowned. "We will do it in the correct way—"

"But if you and I invest him, then his rank as knight will be below us. Is a sentry knight the best you want for him?" Sir Polquin chewed on his mustache and glared at everyone.

Sir Terent drew in an unhappy breath and clenched his big hands helplessly. "I want to give the boy every chance."

"Nay, sir," Sir Polquin said sharply, "you want to win tomorrow's contest. You want it like a fever in your blood, never mind your other duties. And if you can't win, then you want Dain to take the victory. It's as Thum said—victory for Thirst, no matter what."

Sir Terent turned red, but he didn't deny the accusation.

Sir Polquin shook a finger at him. "Dain's right about this. If he's knighted later, with the rank of chevard already bestowed on him, then he has full standing as a knight and lord of the realm. Lord Odfrey would want nothing less. We won't cheat Dain by doing this in haste."

Sir Terent, looking redder than ever, cast Dain a look of apology. "Forgive me, m'lord. I didn't mean to cheat you. I wasn't thinking of that at all—"

"You weren't thinking, period," Sir Polquin said.

"No need to apologize," Dain said. "I wish I *could* fight tomorrow."

"There'll be other years, better years," Sir Polquin told him. "Now enough of this nonsense. Let's turn in and see that we're all properly rested for tomorrow."

Dain looked at Sir Terent. "Will you let me squire you tomorrow?"

His protector blinked, but Sir Polquin spoke before he could: "Nay! Thum will do the job. You, Lord Dain, will come away and sit in the stands with the rest of us, as is proper."

"But, Sir Polquin—"

"Damne, boy!" the master of arms cried in exasperation. "If you're to be a lord, you must learn to act like one! That means you watch from the stands, with your entourage with you. We ain't much, by Thod, but we're men of Thirst and have our honor. Enough and have done."

Dain bowed his head meekly and protested no more. But inside, he chafed at all the restrictions they put on him.

"Have patience, Dain," Sulein said to him later, while they were all pulling off their boots and piling into the bed together like dogs, snarling and pushing to make space. Lyias, as the servant, slept curled on the floor. Privately Dain thought he had the best spot in the room. Sulein tugged at Dain's arm to regain his attention. "All will come in its good time. Your name will resound across the land one day."

Dain glanced at him impatiently. "Have you finished casting my horoscope?"

"Not all of it. You were born under very complex conjunctions, but I have seen enough to know that much greatness lies ahead of you."

Dain did not entirely believe him. He knew the ambitions Sulein harbored. He knew also that he had made his choice to take Lord Odfrey's rank, instead of pursuing the identity that the vision king had given him.

"All I want is to see King Verence," Dain said.

"Patience," Sulein advised him, patting his shoulder. "Patience is necessary for all things."

The light was put out, and they settled down. Soon snoring filled the room and shook the bed like thunder.

Lying awake, Dain frowned in the darkness. He felt both uneasy and excited about tomorrow. Most of all, he felt eaten alive with impatience to make things happen. He'd never imagined it was so difficult to reach the king's attention. He knew that King Verence would want to know the news about Lord Odfrey's death. But there were too many men—these servants and chamberlains—in the way. They chose whom King Verence saw. They decided when and where. It was frustrating, and being told to have patience did not help at all.

I must make something happen, Dain decided as he closed his eyes. *Even if I have to climb into the king's box tomorrow, I must find a way to reach him.*

• • •

Later that night, Dain dreamed he was walking in the moonlight. The ocean rushed and ebbed nearby, crashing on the shoreline, only to recede with bubbles of foam that glowed eerie white on the dark sand. The salty air smelled sharp and damp in his nostrils, and he was cold enough to shiver as he plodded along.

Then another, far less pleasant odor came to him. Dain halted, his head lifting in alarm. He stared into the darkness and listened hard for what came. His ears picked up no sound but the restless crash and stir of the water.

The smell grew more pungent, and then he saw the creature coming from a distance. Although it was far off, and the moonlight dim, Dain could see every detail of the beast.

Taller than a horse, it pranced forward on black, razor-sharp hooves. Its long, sinuous neck whipped back and forth with suspicion as it came, and fire blazed within its nostrils. Its eyes were an unholy red, glowing in the darkness. He could hear the hiss of acid dripping from its fangs, burning the sand into little droplets of glass. When it rumbled deep in its throat, he felt the violent wash of its hatred against his mind.

The Nonkind could not come to lower Mandria, Dain reminded himself, but the hold of his dream was strong. When he tried to back away from the creature, his bare feet stuck in the sand and he could not move.

He reached for his dagger, but found himself clad only in his leggings for sleeping. He had no weapons.

Fear curled in the back of his throat. His heart began to pound. Swiftly he grasped the pendant of bard crystal which hung about his neck and held it tight for courage.

"Faldain," said a voice.

It was deep, commanding, and somehow familiar.

Dain turned his head, trying to see from whence it came. The shore was empty, however, except for him and the approaching darsteed. When Dain looked back at the beast, to his surprise he found it now carried a rider.

The man astride the evil creature was broad-shouldered

THE RING 161

and erect. He rode his mount like a god, his stern visage
keen-eyed and beautiful, his long black hair blowing back
in the wind. A gold breastplate and the circlet around his
brow told of his kingly rank. His muscular arms bulged as
he drew back on the reins, halting the darsteed before Dain.
The darsteed hissed and snapped its poisonous jaws, glaring
red-eyed at Dain, while its mind beat against his:
Eat/eat/eat/eat.

Dain paid it no more attention, however. His fear had
faded when he saw who rode the animal. For it was the king
of his previous vision, the king who had warned him in
Thirst Hall just before the shapeshifter attacked.

"Faldain," the vision said now. His deep voice sent a
shiver through Dain. "Long have I waited for you."

"I am here, Great One," Dain replied. "What do you want
of me?"

"Far are you from the quest," the vision replied. "Go back
to it."

Dain frowned. He did not understand what this ghostly
king wanted him to do. "What quest?" he asked, spreading
wide his hands. "I know not what you mean."

"The Chalice of Eternal Life is lost from its people, Faldain. They suffer because of its absence. Find the Chalice
and restore it to Nether. This is your kingly duty."

Dain gulped and hastily gripped his bard crystal again.
Only royalty may wear king's glass, whispered a voice in
the back of his mind. It was the only possession he had from
his lost past, the only possible proof for an impossible claim.

"King?" he echoed, his voice thin there on the moonlit
beach. The surf roared and thundered around them. Stepping closer to the darsteed, which hissed in warning, Dain
stared up through the gloom into the vision's pale eyes. "Do
you t-tell me, Great One, that I am the m-missing k-king of
Nether?"

He could barely say the words. His mouth was so dry he
was stammering and nearly choking.

The vision bowed his head and pointed at Dain. "You are king by blood and divine right."

"Thod's mercy!" Dain said, gulping again. He stared, his mouth agape. "But I am a nameless bastard, raised by—"

"You are Prince Faldain, son of King Tobeszijian and Queen Nereisse, princess of the eld folk. You are brother to Princess Thiatereika, now a spirit of light in the third world with her beloved mother."

Dain drank in the words, barely able to believe them, yet it was as though years of shame fell from his spirit. His head lifted, and his heart expanded in wonder and amazement. He was not a bastard. He had a family, lineage, a history. And this . . .

"Years ago did I conceal you in the Dark Forest with Jorb the swordmaker," the vision said to him. "It was the only way to save your life."

"Are you my father?" Dain whispered.

"Return to Nether," the vision told him. "The hearts of your subjects call out pleas for help. You alone can save them from Muncel the Oppressor."

Dain's mind was spinning. The enormity of all this had stunned him, yet he knew he could not go about proclaiming his newfound identity. "I need proof of who I am," he said aloud. "No one here will believe me."

"You fear that which is no danger, Faldain," the vision told him sternly, "and fail to prepare for that which is a true threat. Find the Chalice of Eternal Life and return it to Nether. That will prove you to all men."

"But the Chalice is only a myth," Dain protested. He thought of how Gavril had searched the Dark Forest for it and failed. He thought of the entwined legends and tales told about the mysterious missing Chalice. No one alive knew where the sacred vessel was hidden. But if this ghost told him and he could indeed find it . . . A shiver of anticipation ran through Dain.

"How can I find a myth?" Dain asked. "Where do I go?"

The ghost's pale eyes seemed to be all swirling mist and

shadow. They stared into Dain, and he felt cold to his very marrow. "You know how to find it. Look within your memories."

"But—"

"The Chalice is the responsibility of the true king of Nether. *Your* responsibility, Faldain. Turn not from your destiny."

Dain thought of Lord Odfrey's petition to King Verence that would make him legal chevard of Thirst Hold. He thought of his friends in Mandria and the new life he had forged for himself. Was he to toss everything aside and chase after something told to him in a dream?

Frowning and troubled, he looked up to ask another question, but the darsteed and its mysterious rider were gone. Dain stood alone on the beach, the surf foaming white atop the black waters.

When he awakened the next morning, he felt stiff and far from rested. His eyes were swollen and gritty. Yawning, he sat up in the shaft of sunlight streaming in through the narrow window.

A rolled-up tunic hit him in the head. " 'Bout time you woke up, lazybones," Thum's voice said impatiently. "We're all waiting on you, but if you lie abed much longer, we'll miss the whole thing."

Dain pulled his tunic over his head and stretched until his joints popped. "I was dreaming all night. I feel I hardly slept."

"Well, don't prattle about it," Thum said. He tossed a boot at Dain, who ducked barely in time. "Get dressed, will you?"

It was only a dream, Dain assured himself, thinking of the moonlit beach and the ghostly king who had urged him to leave everything here and set off on a quest to find the Chalice. In the brightness of daylight, the dream seemed less vivid, less compelling.

Yawning again, he flung back his blanket and swung his

legs off the bed, only to stop and stare, bemused, at his sandy feet.

It could not be, and yet . . .

With a sense of wonder, he bent over and ran a finger-tip along the top of his right foot. Tiny grains of dried sand trickled to the floor.

Impossible, Dain thought, his puzzlement changing to alarm. He'd gone to no beach last night. He did no walk-ing in his sleep. It was a dream, not reality. Yet his feet were crusted with sand and dried salt, and the bottoms of his leg-gings were damp.

He could have asked Sir Terent if he'd gone walking in his sleep, for his knight protector was bound to have ac-companied him for his safety. Lifting his head, he glanced around the empty room. "Where is everyone?"

"They're without," Thum said impatiently. "The horses are saddled, no doubt, and Sir Terent will miss the jousting if you do not hurry."

"Why doesn't he ride on?" Dain said, but even as the words left his mouth he knew the answer and was ashamed of himself.

"He's waiting for you. He's still in your service, Lord Lout!" Thum said. "Of all days for you to laze in. No one could rouse you, though we all tried until Sulein made us stop. Sir Polquin was able to get Sir Terent down to the sta-bles at last, but he's sworn he will not go to the contest without you."

"Nonsense," Dain snapped, finally regaining his wits. "He is not my protector today; I released him from that service last night. He must go and fight. Run and tell him so."

"He won't believe me," Thum said. "If you'll get dressed, you can tell him yourself."

Dain hastily pulled on his clothes, then grabbed a crumbly hunk of leftover cheese for his breakfast as they hurried out. Clattering down the steep, narrow stairs of the inn, he found the place deserted, and only a serving girl sweeping the floor. Outside, the sun was well up, and already the day felt hot.

Horrified that he should make Sir Terent miss the jousting, Dain quickened his step. He found the Thirst contingent mounted in the yard, talking idly among themselves while they waited.

"Sir Terent!" Dain said loudly, causing the knight's head to snap around to face him. "What are you doing here? Get yourself to the lists, right away."

"M'lord, I wanted to—"

"That's an order," Dain snapped. He glared up at Sir Terent until the knight bowed his head obediently. "I have released you for the day. Get to your business."

"Your safety must come first."

"I am well-guarded by these others," Dain replied, although he had no intention of spending the day in the stands like a chaperoned girl. "Now go. I'll be there as soon as I can. I want to watch you take the victory."

Sir Terent's ruddy face darkened. He said something in a choked, eager voice, then spurred his horse away. Sir Polquin followed after him.

Sulein, perched on his donkey, grinned at Dain. "Good morning blessings shine on you this day, Lord Dain. You have walked in the land of Between, and the spirit world still glows in your face."

Thum's freckled face knotted in bewilderment. He shot Dain a strange look, and Dain scowled at the physician.

"You should go with Sir Terent, in case he takes some harm today," Dain said sternly. He had no intention of discussing his encounter with the ghost king with Sulein. *Faldain, rightful king of Nether,* whispered a voice in the back of his mind. Dain shoved the thought away. This tourney had been long anticipated. He wanted to see the jousting, to eat at the fair, to catch a distant glimpse of the king, and to enjoy himself. And neither Lord Odfrey's death nor the ghost king's quest were going to rob him of these pleasures. There would be time enough to decide what to do later, when the merrymaking was over.

The physician's dark eyes were knowing. He nodded.

"Yes, your concern for the health of Sir Terent is good to see, Lord Dain. But with you will I stay, for the conjunctions today are most unsettled around you. Most unsettled. I feel something has happened that you need to explain to us."

"What's that?" Thum asked, suddenly alert. "Is something amiss?"

"Nay," Dain said impatiently. He went to get his horse.

Thum followed him. "What does he mean by conjunctions? What has happened? And what was all that talk about the land of the spirits? Is it magic he speaks?"

Inside the mews, Dain saddled his horse and gave a last, tightening yank on the girth. Coiling the reins in his hand, he turned his horse around. "Sulein's mysteries need not concern you," Dain said to Thum. "The physician speaks much puffery, that's all."

"But—"

"Come on," Dain said impatiently. "And be quiet. We're going to sneak out through the side door and leave him behind."

Thum's thin, freckled face grew alight with mischief. "Think you that we can?"

Dain nodded. "I have no intention of spending my day with him on our heels. Come!"

But Thum hesitated. "You have no protector with you. If aught—"

"You're protection enough," Dain said shortly. "No one in all this great throng knows who I am. There is no danger. Now stop swooning like a maiden and hurry!"

11

THE KING'S TOURNEY proved to be a shifting, colorful mass of cheering crowds and brutal fighting. The enclosure itself was small, barely long enough to hold the jousting lists and as wide again. The muddy ground was much trampled. Stone risers filled the central section of the stands, with an arched wall at its very top. The king's pennants flew from this point, and garlands of entwined flowers festooned his box. Guardsmen in the palace colors stood watch in the aisles of the stands. Beyond the king's box, the stands were filled with courtiers, visiting diplomats, and lords and ladies of the realm. At the west end, wooden stands for the common folk towered on rickety supports. And more spectators thronged the gates, jostling and craning for a look inside.

By the time Dain and Thum arrived, there were no places left. Guards turned them away from the seats reserved for those of title.

"Get away with you, young rascals!" one of the guards said gruffly. "Passing yourself off as lords. That's a serious offense, that is. Count yourselves lucky I don't haul you before the town jailer for such shenanigans."

Smarting with embarrassment, Dain swung away. Thum's freckled face turned as bright as his hair. He drew in a deep breath to argue with the man, but Dain snagged him by his sleeve and pulled him along.

"It's no good arguing," Dain muttered. "We'll think of something else."

"But you *are* chevard of—"

"Never mind," Dain said.

"I mind a great deal!" Thum said hotly. "My father is—"

"We'll sit in the west stands," Dain said. "Anything to get a quick seat and miss no more than we already have."

"And whose fault was that, Lord Lazybones?"

Dain ignored the gibe and started into the cheapest section of the wooden stands, only to find his way blocked by a burly guard who was sweating in the heat.

"Nay, you two. There's no more bodies what can be let onto this. It'll fall from the weight and crush all a-perched on it."

Dain frowned up at the tall structure. It was indeed swaying visibly as the spectators on it shifted about. Women screamed and men shouted in excitement. None of them seemed afraid. "We'll take our chances," Dain said, but the guard shook his head.

"Falls most every year, and a sad business it is, sorting out the dead from the living afterward. There's always someone who talks his way onto it and becomes the one too many for it to hold. The lords in the palace lay bets on it, see? But it ain't happening on my watch. I've sworn to that."

"But—"

"Off with you both," the guard said, and made a lazy swipe at them with his spiked club.

Fuming, Dain went back down the ramp, pushing his way past others who were rushing in the opposite direction.

On the other side of the enclosure fence, hoofbeats thundered in the lists, followed by a tremendous crash and then a deafening cheer. Dain craned his neck and jumped in an effort to see, but the fence was too high and there were too many people crammed too close together. Behind him, Thum swore with impatience.

"We can't see any of it like this," Dain said.

"Try going closer to the fence."

As he spoke, Thum shoved Dain from behind. The men in front of Dain were tall and stalwart. They didn't budge, and Dain elbowed Thum to get him to stop shoving. "Give way!" he said. "I can't go forward, Thum. There's no room ahead."

The air smelled of sweat and excitement. The scent of roasting meat wafted over the breeze, but it had no power to entice Dain away. He heard another crash. The crowd roared, many of them jumping to their feet, and through the din of the cheering, Dain could hear the steady clang of swordplay.

He groaned in frustration and retreated, shoving past Thum in the process.

"Where are you going?" Thum demanded, turning with him. "We'll get no closer than this. If those men in front step aside—"

Dain gripped him by the shoulder of his tunic and hustled him back to the wooden stands. It was a rickety contraption, clearly built in haste for the tourney. The rough-sawn wood smelled fresh cut, and when the crowd jumped to their feet, the entire structure swayed again. Ducking underneath it, Dain looked up at the crosspieces that formed a ladderwork beneath the benches.

"Come out from under there!" Thum yelled at him. "The guard said this thing is bound to fall. Do you want it to come crashing down atop your head?"

"Nay," Dain replied absently, still looking at the structure in hopes that he could climb it to the top. "Do you think we could climb up there? Nay, it's no good," he answered his own question. "Not enough bracing."

"No, indeed there is not," Thum said. He retreated another step and gestured to Dain. "Come out of there. You're tempting fate."

It was cool and shady under the stands. Dain glanced around. All kinds of trash and litter had been thrown under here. A pig and several dogs were rooting about for scraps of food. Dain ducked beneath a brace board and scattered the dogs. A ragged child burst from their midst and ran away, cursing.

Thum jumped back. "Morde a day! What was that?"

"Someone starving," Dain replied. "Come."

"Why? It's not safe under there."

"Shortcut," Dain said, and headed on without Thum.

In seconds, however, his friend was by his side. Thum

kept glancing apprehensively at the thumping feet overhead. He spent no time in dawdling and muttered beneath his breath.

At the other end of the stands, they emerged back into the sunlight and stood blinking. Here, they found themselves in one of the ready pens. It had become an impromptu infirmary. A double handful of men were either lying on their shields or sitting on the ground. A pair of physicians in long robes and their assistants were binding wounds and mixing potions, amid much moaning and swearing.

"Thod's mercy!" Thum exclaimed.

Dain pushed him onward. This time they had to skirt a long section of stonework, hearing all the while the cheering going on constantly over the noise of hard-fought battle. The crowd rose to its feet with a moan, then sank down again.

Dain and Thum exchanged impatient looks and came to another ready pen. This one was more interesting, for knights were busy fitting on their armor and checking their weapons. Grooms and squires scurried in all directions. Warhorses, restless and excited, champed their bits and pawed the ground.

"Look!" Thum said, pinching Dain's arm to get his attention. He pointed at an immense knight in a hauberk of black mail worn beneath a fine white-and-black-striped surcoat. The knight bowed his head for one of his servants to fit a steel cap to his head atop his mail coif. Another servant stood by, holding a visored helmet much ornamented in black steel and gold. The squire waited patiently with a lance painted in black and white spirals down its entire length. A vivid banner hung from the tip, flapping lazily in the hot breeze.

Thum's elbow jabbed Dain in the ribs. "That's Roberd of Minceau Hold. I know the colors. My older brothers have talked of seeing him fight. I wonder if they were ever this close to him. Look at his sword!"

Dain stared, too transfixed to speak. He watched a sec-

ond squire hand a long broadsword to the knight. The blade
flashed in the sunlight as Lord Roberd swung it aloft and
brought it down. He grunted an order to his servants, and
sheathed the weapon.

Dain eased out his breath, and Thum's elbow jabbed him
again. "Look at his horse. What a brute it is."

Another knight rode by just then, calling out greeting to
Lord Roberd. The newcomer flipped up the visor to his helmet, revealing a nose that had been broken in the past and
a pair of twinkling brown eyes.

"Good job unseating the Thirst knight in the early rounds,
Roberd!" the mounted knight called out.

Lord Roberd lifted his hand with an easy laugh while
Dain winced and Thum moaned.

"Sir Terent is defeated already," Thum said. "And we
missed it. Damne, what a shame."

Dain frowned, feeling sorry for Sir Terent, who'd come
here with such high hopes, only to be eliminated early. "We
should have been here to cheer for him."

"Aye," Thum said gloomily.

"I'm sorry, Thum. I don't know why I couldn't wake."

Thum gave him a lopsided smile and shrugged a little.
"It's past. Can't be helped now. We'd better find Sir Terent
and Sir Polquin in the crowd and—"

"What, and be smothered the rest of the day by their protection?" Dain said in protest. "Not me!"

The mounted knight was still talking to Lord Roberd.
"When do you go in again? Without Legre to meet, it hardly
seems worthwhile."

Both knights solemnly drew the sign of the Circle. Lord
Roberd sighed. "Legre of Clune was a true opponent. Pity
we shall never fight him again."

"You'll be champion today, Roberd. You have no other
true competition."

"Perhaps," Lord Roberd said with a shrug. "I'm to face
the last man today, then whoever wins that—"

"You will. You know it."

"Aye, but 'tis bad luck to say so."

The mounted knight laughed merrily. "Thod willing, it will be me you meet today."

Lord Roberd grinned back at him. "I'll spike your gullet, Gilon."

"Or my lance will break your ribs," Sir Gilon replied. "I've done it once. I can do it again."

"Perhaps," Lord Roberd agreed, although he did not look worried. "Whoever takes the championship is slotted to face the prince."

Sir Gilon tightened his reins enough to make his horse toss its head. He shouted with laughter. "Then I withdraw and name you winner! Take that task, my friend, for I don't want to meet his highness on the field."

Lord Roberd shrugged his massive shoulders. "Has to be done. I'll be honored to do it, of course."

"Of course," agreed his friend with so much sarcasm Dain had to hide a grin. He and Thum edged closer to listen. "But he ought to be invested before he enters the tourney."

"Aye," Lord Roberd agreed quietly, with a glance around. "That's the proper way, but I hear the lad insisted against all reason and his majesty has consented. Against that, I will not argue."

"No, indeed. It's said the prince has a way of thinking the rules do not apply to him, and I see that it is true. You'll let him win, of course."

"I will not," Lord Roberd said with spirit. "Damne, I'm no pudding-heart to give way to an untried boy, whatever his rank."

Dain and Thum grinned at each other, and Dain whispered, "I must see this contest, if only to watch Gavril eat a mouthful of dust."

"Aye," Thum agreed fervently.

"Go you back to Minceau on the morrow?" Sir Gilon asked. "Or will you be joining the king's hunt?"

Lord Roberd looked stunned. "What? Does his majesty depart that soon? What of the—"

"Everything's to finish today and tonight. As soon as his highness is invested in the morning, the king rides out." Sir Gilon shrugged and plucked at his horse's mane. "So I heard from the chamberlain—"

"Damne, I'll be sore and much galled by morning."

Sir Gilon laughed. "So will we all! I hope you go, for I'm asked to accompany his majesty to the south for that journey. It would be good to have your company."

"Aye," Lord Roberd said dourly. "I've been asked."

"His majesty hopes to catch the last of the marlet herds before they migrate."

"Poor coursing, that," Lord Roberd said.

"Aye, but it's the last chance before the seasons turn. You know how the king is."

Their conversation went on, but Dain felt as though a knife had been plunged through his chest. He turned to Thum and gripped his arm hard.

Thum winced. "What—"

"The king is leaving Savroix!" Dain whispered. A shout warned him, and he jumped back just in time to avoid being trampled by a feisty warhorse. A groom dangled at the end of the animal's tether, swearing and trying to calm his charge.

Dain retreated, pushing Thum ahead of him. "You heard them. Tomorrow!"

"When will you have your audience?" Thum asked.

"Thod knows. The chamberlain promised me as soon as the festivities were ended." Dain scowled. "He lied to me, and I didn't even realize it."

"How could you?" Thum said.

Frowning and bitterly disappointed, Dain held his tongue before he betrayed the fact that he could read truth and lies inside men-minds.

"After all," Thum said, "the king is known for acting impulsively. Perhaps he only decided to go this morning."

Dain grimaced. "It does not matter. What's important is that he's *going*. And I must talk to him first."

"You can't."

"I must." Dain set his jaw in determination. "And I will."

"Don't be rash," Thum said worriedly. "Every minute of his majesty's day is planned. As soon as the tourney ends this afternoon, there is to be the choosing of the king's new sword. And then the banquet feast, and Prince Gavril's investiture. You can't even hope to get close to his majesty. You'll just have to wait until he comes back."

Dain felt despair. "And how long will that be? Kings spend weeks hunting, do they not?"

"They can," Thum said unhappily. "I'm sorry, Dain. There's nothing you can do but wait here."

"I could spend the winter, 'waiting here.' That's what the old duc was trying to warn me. I thought him unkind, but now I see his advice was true."

"You can only do—"

"No!" Dain said angrily, slamming his fist into his palm. "I will not wait here until my money runs out and I starve, until I lose the hold, until my petition is completely forgotten. I promised Lord Odfrey, and I must keep my word."

"His lordship would understand the difficulties and delays."

"Would he?" Dain asked grimly. "I think he would not."

"Dain—"

"No, Thum. I must see the king. I must speak to him today."

"Well, you can't," Thum said flatly. "No matter how much you want to, it's impossible. Only the champion of the tourney will speak to his majesty—"

"That's it!" Dain said.

"What?"

"I know what I'll do."

Thum's freckled face knotted in a frown. "This is ill-advised, Dain."

"You haven't even heard my plan yet."

"Nor do I want to."

Dain stared at him a moment, then spun on his heel and

set off. Thum darted after him, catching up in a few strides
and gripping him by the back of his tunic.

"Dain!"

"Let go," Dain said, pushing off his hand.

They stood in the midst of the bustle and chaos, glaring
at each other.

"This isn't Thirst," Thum said. "You can't pull some prank
and hope to get away with it."

"Either you are with me," Dain said grimly, "or you are
not. Help me, or let me go about this as I must."

Thum's hazel-green eyes darkened with anger. He glared
at Dain, saying nothing, until Dain started to turn away.

"Damne!" Thum swore. "Of course I am with you.
Though it probably means my head. What mean you to do?"

Dain grinned at him in relief. "I knew you were a true
friend. Come, for there isn't much time."

He set off again, dodging his way through the squires
and horses. Thum stuck close at his heels.

"But, Dain," he said, "what mean you to do?"

Dain ducked behind one of the tents. Close by, he could
hear the steady plink-plink-plink rhythm of a smithy's hammer. He gripped Thum's arm and pulled him close.

"Well?" Thum demanded impatiently. He looked pale with
apprehension. "What—"

"Hush," Dain said softly, keeping a wary eye out to make
sure they weren't overheard. "I mean to take Sir Terent's
armor and enter the tourney."

Thum's mouth fell open. "You can't!"

Dain growled at him and gave him a little shake. "You
said you were with me."

"Aye, but not to help you be a total fool!" Thum said
with brutal frankness. "Gods, Dain, have you lost your wits?"

"I have not," Dain said with stronger determination than
ever. "I'm near enough his size—"

"You can't take his armor!"

Dain reddened. "I do not intend to steal it," he said stiffly.
"If I ask him, he will lend it to me."

"Think you so?" Thum said sternly. "If you command him to surrender his armor, you might as well command him to cut out his heart. It is not done."

"Morde a day, these rules you all live by!" Dain cried, throwing up his hands in exasperation. "Can nothing be altered? Do circumstances never matter? I am not seeking to destroy the man. I only want to wear his mail for an hour."

"You are not a knight, and therefore you are not eligible to enter the contest. Unlike Gavril, you cannot insist the rules be waived for you."

"All right then," Dain said. "I won't—"

"And even if you broke the rules and entered the joust, what makes you think you could win? You are very good, Dain, but you—"

"All right! I won't fight," Dain said in a huff. "I'll just wear the armor and—"

"And what?" Thum broke in.

"With the helmet on, I can approach the king."

"The guards won't let you within a stone's throw of his majesty."

"I can ride up to his box and speak to him."

"They won't let you," Thum insisted.

Dain set his jaw and glowered off across the enclosure toward the far stands. Purple and gold banners—the king's colors—flew merrily in the hot wind, marking his majesty's box in the stands. The man was so close, and yet he might as well have been on the other side of the realm. And what good was Thum, if he meant to raise objections to everything Dain suggested? Frustration spread through Dain. He released an angry breath and dug in the dirt with his boot toe.

"You had better wait for a proper audience, Dain," Thum said softly.

There was kindness in his voice, but pity also. Hearing that, Dain stiffened. All his instincts urged him to seize whatever chance he could, while opportunity remained. He glared at his friend. "Waiting is for fools. I won't give up."

"Dain—"

"No. Something inside me knows that if the king leaves on the morrow without having heard my petition, he will never hear it."

"How can you know that?"

"Call it my eld blood. I just know." Dain looked at Thum earnestly. "I must do this. I must take my chances now."

"But it's madness to try."

Dain frowned. "What risk lies in wandering about among the other knights?"

"What risk?" Thum's voice cracked, and he coughed. "Damne, how can you ask that? If you're caught, you risk your entire investiture. Some of the knights might forgive you for wearing armor out of rank, but others will not. Do you want to be denied your knighthood just because you cannot hold your impatience?"

"Have you ever known me to be wrong?"

A thoughtful look entered Thum's green eyes. He met Dain's stare without flinching. "No, not when it mattered."

"Then trust me now. I cannot wait. I will not wait, not until I have tried everything I can. The king will talk to me, Thum, if only I can reach him. He was Lord Odfrey's friend. He will want to know about . . . about all that happened."

"Aye," Thum said gloomily. "Perhaps you are right."

"Come, then. Let's go to Sir Terent quickly."

"He won't agree to this. Or even if he does, Sir Polquin won't."

Dain gnawed on his lip. "Then you must lure them away, and Lyias too, if he's guarding their gear. I will take the armor."

"Dain—"

"Hush, Thum. We've been through all that."

"But what if Sir Terent has not removed his mail?"

"He must. By the rules of the joust, no man not in competition may wear—"

"You're right," Thum agreed. He sighed, looking much troubled.

Dain waited only a moment, his impatience growing. "Well?" he demanded.

Thum held out his thin hand. "I am with you, to the last. Win or fail."

"Win or fail," Dain repeated, making it an oath, and gripped Thum's hand hard.

"Hurry," Prince Gavril snapped to his servant, twisting impatiently beneath the man's fingers. "Can't you finish the buckles? What is wrong with you today?"

"Sorry, your highness," the man whispered, intent on his work. "Just . . . finishing . . . now." He stepped back and gestured in triumph. "Most handsome indeed."

Even through the stone walls of the guardhouse, Gavril could hear the cheers and shouts of the crowd. He tilted his golden head, listening to the noise and wishing the cheers were for him. Well, he told himself, they would be soon enough.

He turned around and looked at his reflection. His new chain mail gleamed brightly even in the muted light in here in this semi-underground room. In the sunshine, it would dazzle everyone. Smiling to himself, Gavril ran his hands down the front of his hauberk and glanced past the Reverend Sir Damiend toward another figure standing in the shadows.

"Well?" he asked.

Cardinal Noncire waddled slowly forward into the light. His spotless robes gleamed white. His yellow sash of office girded his broad middle. His small, dark eyes regarded Gavril solemnly.

"Turn about," he commanded softly.

Gavril obeyed him, feeling almost giddy with excitement. His emotions were rushing about inside him nearly beyond his control. In a few minutes he would be out there, acknowledged a man at last by his father's subjects. The king had expected him to sit in the royal box until it was time for his part in the tourney, but Gavril had long planned this surprise.

"Yes," Noncire said at last. "It will do."

Faint praise, but Gavril grinned at the cardinal in satisfaction. "Isn't it fine? I wanted a breastplate, but that fool armorer said he could not finish the work by today."

Sir Damiend cleared his throat, but it was Noncire who said, "The breastplate is perhaps more appropriate for later, your highness."

"What, after my investiture?" Gavril asked, turning around again to look at his reflection. He shifted his shoulders beneath the weight of the double-linked mail, pleased by how heavy it was. "But that's merely a formality—"

"Do not say so, your highness," Noncire corrected him. His voice was, as always, soft, gentle, and very precise.

However, Gavril caught a subtle tone in it that made him stop his preening and look over his shoulder. "Well, it is," he said, but with less assurance. "I can't be turned down, after all."

"Perhaps not," Noncire said while Sir Damiend frowned. "But it is not courteous to say so."

"Oh . . . courtesy." Shrugging, Gavril returned to his reflection.

"The knighthood vows are sacred," Sir Damiend said, as though he could no longer hold his tongue. "They must be uttered with reverent sincerity and a true heart."

Annoyed, Gavril shot the church knight a cool look. "I believe I know the correct attitude for the ceremony," he replied. "My spurs, please."

Sir Damiend cleared his throat, but Noncire made a slight gesture with his plump hand, and Sir Damiend retreated with a bow.

Gavril's servant scurried forward with the new spurs of gleaming gold. Kneeling, he buckled them on. Gavril stamped his feet, pleased by the sound the rowels made.

"Aren't they fine?" he asked, and snapped his fingers. "Kels, the helmet. Quickly!"

The servant handed the helmet to him. It was steel, plated with gold, and intricately carved all over, with a tall crest of hammered gold plumes on top. Gavril held it up between his two hands and stared at Noncire with shining blue eyes.

"At last!" he said, triumph in his voice.

"Very fine indeed, your highness," Noncire said.

But there was no enthusiasm in his voice. Gavril's brows pulled together, and he lowered the helmet slowly. "You don't like it," he said in disappointment. "I thought you, most of all, would be pleased by the entrance I shall make."

"It is premature, your highness," Noncire said.

Gavril's frown deepened. He hated argument, especially when his mind was made up. Noncire's criticism hurt him. To hide it, he chose defiance. "I do not see why."

"Of course you do," the cardinal replied evenly, "and you have chosen to take these actions despite convention."

"I do not wish to be conventional," Gavril said sullenly. "I am Prince of the Realm. The people must learn to take heed of me."

"They will. Have no fear of that," Noncire assured him. "However, your father stands to be disappointed by this."

"I intend to surprise him."

"You will succeed there," Noncire said. "However, this is his majesty's birthday, and his light should shine brighter today than yours."

Scowling, Gavril said nothing.

"The contest of swords is your father's way of making a grand ceremony out of a simple act of custom. When a son enters knighthood, his father passes on his sword. His majesty intends to give you his blade and his spurs and—"

"—his old mail. Yes, I know that," Gavril broke in impatiently. "What of it? I would rather have my own, everything new and made for *me,* than his castoffs."

Noncire's fat face never altered expression, but something flickered in his beady eyes. Gavril met his stare for a moment, unabashed by the silence of disapproval. He did not care what the cardinal thought. This was a day of battle, not of piety. Gavril knew what was best for himself, and he intended to prove it to everyone else. He was a boy no longer, seeking guidance and education. He was a man, able to stand by his own judgment and decisions. He had wanted to surprise his father this day by presenting him with the Chalice, found and recovered. It would have been a momentous occasion. The people would have rejoiced beyond all measure. The king would have been astonished and amazed. Everyone would have praised and honored Gavril to the highest.

Instead, he had no Chalice to offer. That meant he had to create another, different surprise in its place. His new armor was a poor substitute for the original plan, but it would do well enough.

"Only one more day, your highness," Noncire was saying. "Surely some patience—"

"No!" Gavril said rudely. He tucked the helmet beneath his arm and walked over to pick up his new sword. The moment his fingers closed about the scabbard, a tingle shot through his flesh. He felt a surge of strength and power. He straightened his shoulders, feeling invincible, and faced the cardinal arrogantly. "One would think, lord cardinal, that you dare to disapprove of my actions."

Noncire blinked and tried to mask his surprise by bowing as low as his fat body would permit. "Indeed not, your highness."

"You come very close to criticism," Gavril told him. "What passes today, tonight, and on the morrow lies between the king and myself."

Noncire spread out his plump hands. "Very well, your highness."

Belting on Tanengard, Gavril felt himself growing even stronger. Angrily, he glared at the cardinal. A few minutes from hence, he would be facing the champion, Lord Roberd. Gavril intended to defeat the man. With Tanengard he could do it. *He* would be the champion of the tourney, and the knights would respect him. All would cheer his name, and no one would doubt his prowess as a warrior. In the next few weeks, as he began urging his father and the ministers to wage a war of annexation against Klad, they would listen to him as a man and a fighter of distinction. Gavril intended to be the commander of those forces. Today's victory was simply the first small step toward achieving his goals.

"I would have your blessing for my victory to come, lord cardinal," Gavril said, and he made the statement a command.

Noncire's eyes were stony within their layers of fat, but he raised his hand and drew a Circle in the air. Softly he chanted the words of benediction, while Gavril prayed with him.

When the cardinal finished, Gavril straightened. He glanced toward the shadows, where Sir Damiend waited. The church knight had been designated Gavril's temporary protector for today. Gavril had been thrilled, for he admired Sir Damiend's fighting prowess very much. But Sir Damiend was not the same man he'd been during their journey here from upper Mandria. He'd made no secret of his disapproval of Gavril's fighting today. Of course he was a stern, conservative, pious man, but to Gavril he seemed suddenly old-fashioned and unnecessarily critical of Gavril's plans to flaunt the ancient rules of knighthood. *What did a day matter?* Gavril asked himself yet once again. *It was all a giant formality. Why not hasten the whole procedure and stop making such a mystery of it?*

"Sir Damiend," Gavril said sharply, "I am ready to proceed."

The commander of the church soldiers strode forward, exchanging a silent look with Cardinal Noncire as he fell into step behind Gavril. The prince noticed, and his annoyance grew. Until today, he had looked up to both these men. But they were not his masters, and if necessary he would teach them that lesson.

Gavril walked out of the guardhouse and up a flight of steps into the sunlight. It was so bright in the ready pen he had to squint until his eyes adjusted. A servant was waiting with his mount, a fine new warhorse beautifully trained. Armored and saddled, the horse tossed its noble head and pawed the ground impatiently. Hanging at Gavril's side, Tanengard seemed to blaze within its scabbard. It was all Gavril could do not to seize the hilt and draw it. He wanted to charge full-tilt, swinging the weapon and shouting at the top of his lungs.

Somehow, he controlled himself and kept his composure while he was assisted into the saddle. He fitted on his helmet, leaving the visor up, for it limited his vision more than he'd expected.

Sir Damiend mounted his own horse with athletic grace. The breeze caught the man's lightweight cloak and streamed it out over the hindquarters of his horse.

Gavril laughed aloud and spurred his mount. "Away!" he called, gesturing to the servants to pass the word.

By the time he reached the gates separating him from the tourney enclosure, Gavril heard his name being shouted forth by the heralds. Trumpets sounded flourishes, and the gates swung open.

Gavril rode forward, spurring his horse and reining it hard to make it leap and prance. The sun gleamed off his golden mail, turning him into a shining figure of light itself, glinting and radiant before them all.

The people gasped aloud, then surged to their feet with such enthusiasm the wooden stands swayed. "Prince Gavril!" they shouted, stamping and clapping. "Prince Gavril! Prince Gavril!"

Beaming, Gavril swung his horse around and waved to the crowd as they acclaimed him. This was the most glorious moment he had ever known. Joy and pride filled him. He no longer cared that he'd failed to bring home the Chalice. The people loved him anyway. They loved him for himself, their prince and future king.

He smiled and waved, letting his horse prance and sidle, while the trumpets blared and the people went on cheering. And when at last he rode before the king's box and bowed

over his saddle, he took little note that King Verence sat
there amidst his standing courtiers with a face like stone and
his eyes cold indeed. The Lady Pheresa sat next to the king,
wearing a gown of sky blue. Her blonde hair was coiled inside a jeweled net, and a winsome scarf fluttered from her
slender white fingers. She looked pale beside the king; her
large eyes stared at Gavril with reserve. He cared not; to
him she was an insignificant detail, someone to be dealt with
later.

"Father!" Gavril called out as the noise began to die down.
"I come to fight before you. Cheer me on, majesty, that I
may be assured of a victory!"

The king leaned forward. Although he did not smile, he
gave Gavril a jaunty wave. "Go forth, my son, and do well."

Pleased, Gavril wheeled his horse around and cantered
back and forth, while the people cheered him again. He did
not notice that the king never smiled at him, or cheered, or
clapped. Gavril had made the people love him, and that was
all—in his mind—that mattered.

Clad in Sir Terent's chain mail and battered old breastplate,
and wearing no surcoat, Dain found the helmet to be immensely heavy and hotter than the desert of Gant. Sweat
poured down his face and stung his eyes. He blinked and
swore beneath his breath, guiding his restless horse through
the milling crowd of still-mounted knights, all of whom were
both dust-stained and blood-splattered. Lord Roberd had
beaten Sir Gilon in ferocious combat that had kept the crowd
on its feet, cheering throughout. Dain had watched it all, and
he was still caught up in the drama and excitement that it
had provided. From their earlier chat, Lord Roberd and Sir
Gilon had seemed like close friends on excellent terms. But
they had fought like enemies, neither man giving quarter,
each expending his all. Not until Sir Gilon lay flat on his
back in the dust with Lord Roberd's sword tip pressed to
his gorget had the herald called a halt and proclaimed Lord
Roberd's victory.

Lord Roberd had sheathed his blade and given his friend a helping hand up. The two men had hugged each other, and Lord Roberd had supported his limping friend as they'd left the enclosure to thunderous applause.

Since then, there had been a period of rest, while serfs raked and resanded the field. Musicians played stirring tunes and men with trays of sweet pies and fruit roved about, hawking their wares. Servants set up an awning over the king's box to cast shade against the merciless sun.

Lord Roberd did not return to claim his leafy crown of victory, which was now resting on a pillow in the king's box. It was said a hefty purse of gold dreits lay beneath that crown.

When Gavril came forth, glittering like flame incarnate, Lord Roberd's absence began to make the crowd restless.

The knights surrounding Dain in the ready pen were particularly impatient. "Where's Lord Roberd?" someone called out. "Where's our champion?"

Laughter and hooting catcalls came in answer.

"Gone for a wineskin!" a merry voice shouted.

"Aye, the champion needs ale courage to face *this* opponent."

Looking back at the enclosure, Dain saw Gavril cantering back and forth before the stands, waving grandly while people cheered for him. When he came past the knights, many of them cheered too, but in mockery, not love.

Dain grinned to himself inside his helmet, glad to see that few knights admired Gavril, and hoped Lord Roberd would make a quick end of him.

"Thod's teeth, he's blinded me!" a voice said. "Did you ever see such a high polish on armor?"

More laughter broke out among the men. "I want Lord Roberd to maneuver him to that mud hole at the end of the list. That's where his highness should be unhorsed."

"What? And get his golden mail all muddy? Such a shame," said another.

A wizened old knight with knobs of gray hair and a disfiguring scar sat slumped in his saddle. His helmet was tied to his saddle and his mail coif was shoved down around his neck. He spat in disgust. "Knaves and rascals, the lot of you are. Making merry sport of his highness, who ain't got the right to be on that field, much less wearing mail. An insult to the knighthood, I call it."

"Aye," muttered the man next to Dain. He twisted about impatiently in his saddle. "Ah, damne now, where is the fellow?"

"Think you that Lord Roberd has lost his nerve?" asked a knight who was missing his front teeth.

They roared with laughter at that one.

A squire came running up, out of breath and sweating beneath his cap. "Please, sir knights, make way that I may pass. I must speak to a herald."

"Let him through!"

They reined their horses aside, while more knights, long since eliminated from the contest and no longer attired in mail, came to join the throng of onlookers.

"That's Lord Roberd's squire. Hold up, boy! Where's your master?"

"Having another horse saddled," the squire replied as he pushed past Dain's mount. "His best charger—the one he was resting for this contest—has cast a shoe."

A general groan of sympathy went up.

Out in the lists, Gavril drew rein at last to rest his lathered horse. The prince looked around impatiently as the common folk in the wooden stands began calling for action.

The squire went running across the field, and was met partway by one of the heralds in red livery. The boy delivered his message and came running back.

The herald rode over to the king and passed word to him. King Verence leaned forward to the edge of the box, listened, and nodded.

Watching him, Dain felt gnawing impatience. When the contest ended, he was going to ride up to the king's box, exactly like the herald had done, and say Lord Odfrey's name loudly. That should catch the king's attention.

"Lord Roberd is delayed!" the herald announced.

He started to say something else, but Gavril stood up in his stirrups. "Delayed!" he said in a voice of loud disbelief. Pulling off his helmet, he gazed around haughtily. "Or does he fear to meet his prince?"

A hush fell over the stands, and the knight sitting next to Dain swore beneath his breath.

"Gods," muttered someone else. "Does he mean to insult Lord Roberd?"

"I have come to fight!" Gavril announced with supreme confidence. "If the champion will not meet me, then I challenge anyone else who will! Let my opponent come forth."

Dain ignored the outraged voices around him and watched the king. His majesty was frowning and actually leaned forward as though to call out to Gavril, but then he settled back in his chair and did nothing. His face showed no expression at all. A fat man in white robes bent to speak to him. The king shook his head, and the fat man retreated.

It was bad, Dain thought, to shame one's father. How heedless Gavril was of the feelings of others. It was not Lord Roberd's fault he was delayed. Courtesy demanded that Gavril wait, but he went on boasting and calling out insults.

The knights around Dain began to mutter darkly. Dain frowned, still watching the king. He saw the pretty maid say something and gently touch the king's sleeve. His majesty smiled at her in reply, but his annoyance with his son was plain to see. Still, he did not call Gavril to order.

I would never cause my father such embarrassment, Dain thought.

"Will no one meet me?" Gavril shouted again, while a babble broke out across the stands.

"The young puppy!" said the old knight with the scar.

Dain could stand no more. Before he realized it, he was kicking his horse forward.

Laughing, the knights parted to make way for him. Their
gleeful words of encouragement rang in his ears.

"What-ho! The prince and the knight of mystery."

"Hirelance, I hope you put him in the mud."

As Dain rode into the enclosure, a delighted cheer rose
from the wooden stands. The courtiers in the stone seats fell
silent. Gavril wheeled his horse around to stare, then rode
toward the lists for a lance. Dain thought he heard Sir
Polquin's bellow rising over the noise of the crowd. He
looked up at the many faces, but saw no one he recognized.

He couldn't believe he was doing this, and yet he kept
riding forward. Gavril had issued the challenge, had opened
the contest to any opponent. Let him reap the consequences,
Dain thought.

However, another horse and rider came forth to block
Dain's path. This was Sir Damiend, attired in silk doublet
and fine cap for today's occasion. The garb looked wrong
on him. His lean aesthete's face belonged atop serviceable
mail and his church surcoat, not court fashion. But whether
he wore mail today or not, the man remained a soldier to
his marrow. Narrow-eyed with suspicion, he gestured for
Dain to stop. When Dain obeyed, Sir Damiend looked him
over from the top of his battered helmet to the tips of his
plain brass spurs. Dain's armor was old and rusted in places,
despite having been soaked in oiled sand and relacquered
before they'd set out for Savroix. It was also a poor fit. The
mail sleeves were too long and kept bunching over the tops
of Dain's gauntlets. The padded undercoat he wore beneath
the armor was too large in the chest and too narrow across
the shoulders, causing the mail to chafe Dain in places. His
gorget had been hastily laced on once he'd donned the coif,
and Dain was sure it was crooked, the sign of an amateur.
He carried Lord Odfrey's sword and rode Sir Polquin's horse,
as it was fresher than Sir Terent's, which had already been
in the contest. The horse was a sturdy, experienced old
charger, but its saddle was plain and worn and it had no
armor cloth for its protection. Still, Dain thought, not every

knight was able to afford the best equipment. Although he looked patched together, he told himself, he had no less right to be on the field than Gavril.

By now Dain was certain Sir Terent had seen him out here, if not Sir Polquin too. He wondered if Thum had found them, and what kind of explanation he was giving. They all—even Sulein—would be having a fit, but it was too late for them to stop him. He looked past Sir Damiend at the king, but his majesty was speaking to someone and paid Dain no heed at all.

"May I see your weapons, sir?"

His attention jumping back to Sir Damiend, Dain nodded and drew his sword. It was a plain but finely crafted weapon. The inscriptions were almost worn off the blade. Thinking of the man who had carried it, Dain felt a lump filling his throat. He handed it over, hilt-first, vowing anew to carry it with honor.

Sir Damiend gave the sword but a cursory glance, then examined Dain's dagger. Clearly he was checking for poison or other trickery. Dain sat quietly in his saddle, praying Sir Damiend would not ask him to remove his helmet.

He'd not intended to come out here for combat, but now that he was committed, he could feel his body quickening with excitement. The chance to meet Gavril, to put the prince down in defeat, was too tempting to resist. He could not wait to strike the first blow and dent Gavril's pretty armor.

"You wear no colors," Sir Damiend said, handing back the dagger. "Are you a hirelance?"

Dain pulled his wandering attention away from Gavril, who was shouting something to the wooden stands that was evoking a noisy response. "Nay, I am not."

"Your name, sir?" Sir Damiend demanded as the cheering grew even louder.

Dain hesitated a moment. If the herald announced his name, Gavril would know who was facing him and would insist Dain be thrown out. Dain's future as a knight would be jeopardized for passing himself off falsely as a member of the knighthood. However, the king would hear his name spoken, and that might gain his majesty's attention as nothing else could.

In any case, Dain was not going to lie. "I am D-Dain of Thirst," he stammered out.

Just as he spoke, a tremendous roar came from the crowd, nearly drowning out his words. Sir Damiend frowned as though he did not understand. The noise around them increased, and Dain turned his head to look at what was causing the commotion.

Lord Roberd was riding into the enclosure. The champion made an awesome figure indeed. His black mail seemed to absorb the sunlight. His black-and-white-striped surcoat was a clean one, dazzlingly bold. His saddle and armor cloth were black, and he rode a stout white horse, snorting and prancing as it came. He carried the lance with the black and white spirals, and his pennant fluttered from it in the hot breeze. Black and white plumes waved from the top of his helmet. He looked monstrous in size, immensely powerful, and ready for combat.

Seeing him, Dain's mouth went dry, and he knew his hopes for defeating Gavril were as the dust blowing around his horse's feet.

The herald, bright in his red livery, came galloping up. Looking flustered, he glanced from Dain to Lord Roberd, who rode up to them and lifted his visor.

Close up, the champion revealed a weathered face and eyes that looked tired and serious indeed. He stared at Dain, who kept his visor closed. Dain's heart was thumping hard. He told himself to bow out of this, while he could still escape.

"Ah, Lord Roberd," the herald said with a little bow of respect. "There seems to be some confusion."

"So I see," Lord Roberd said, still staring at Dain. Finally he shifted his gaze back to the herald. "Was my message not brought?"

"Oh, aye, sir, it was indeed," the herald replied. "But his

highness ... um, Sir Damiend? Would you be kind enough to bring the prince to us?"

The commander of the church soldiers wheeled his horse away and rode to Prince Gavril, who was already coming toward them, bearing his lance and clearly fuming with impatience.

"I am being kept waiting!" he complained as he reined up before them. His blue eyes glared at them all from within his helmet. "Am I to perish of the heat before I have an opponent?"

Lord Roberd bowed to him. "Forgive me, your highness. I was delayed by my horse, which cast a shoe."

"Then you forfeit the contest to me," Gavril said smugly. "Such are the rules, Lord Roberd."

There was a moment of stunned silence. Dull red crept into Lord Roberd's face, and the herald's mouth fell open.

Clearly Lord Roberd was not accustomed to being dismissed by young upstarts, whatever their rank.

Gavril turned his gaze on Dain. "As for you, sir. Have you been vetted by Sir Damiend?"

"I have examined his weapons," Sir Damiend replied. "He wears no colors, but he swears he is not a hirelance."

"On your honor?" Gavril asked Dain harshly.

That question was an insult to any man, of any rank, but Dain bowed to him. "On my honor," he said very quietly.

"Your highness," Sir Damiend broke in, "if the contest between you and Lord Roberd is now forfeit, then claim your victory and let this be at an end. There is no need to accept this stranger's challenge."

"Indeed not, your highness," the herald agreed eagerly.

They all stared at Gavril, whose blue eyes shifted away. He rested his hand on Tanengard's hilt, with its magnificent guard shaped in the form of gold ivy. Even at this distance Dain could feel the humming power of the tainted sword.

"I have come to fight," Gavril announced, "and fight I shall."

"Then let it be with Lord Roberd—"

"Nonsense!" Gavril snapped. "He is dismissed. You," Gavril said to Dain. "Are you ready to face me?"

Dain bowed. "Aye."

"Then let's get to it." Without waiting for anyone else to speak, Gavril wheeled his horse around and spurred it away.

The herald was sputtering, and Sir Damiend had a sour, pinched look on his face that made Dain nearly laugh inside his helmet. He curbed his mirth, however, well aware that it was inappropriate here.

Lord Roberd, of course, had all of Dain's sympathy, for he did not deserve the insult Gavril had dealt him. Still redfaced, the champion gathered his reins and gave Dain a small salute. "The field is yours, sir knight," he said with courtesy.

"Thank you," Dain replied. He knew Lord Roberd could not wish him victory against the prince, but that he clearly wanted to. Dain could feel the man's chaotic thoughts and emotions hammering wildly beneath his controlled exterior. Out of kindness, Dain added, "But of course, lord champion, this is only an exhibition and not the true jousting, which you have already won."

Lord Roberd's gaze snapped to Dain for a moment. He said nothing, but inclined his plumed head to Dain in respect before he rode out of the enclosure.

The herald and Sir Damiend both stared at Dain in approval. "Well said," the herald praised him. "Very well said, sir knight."

From the stands, a great murmur of consternation was rising. People stood and craned their necks to watch as Lord Roberd rode away in all his magnificence. In his box, the king stood up and beckoned to the herald.

The man rode to him at once and spoke earnestly. Gavril rode over to them, boasting and making large gestures. The king looked unmoved.

"Take no offense by this delay," Sir Damiend said kindly to Dain. Clearly he had not understood the name Dain gave him earlier, for he seemed not to recognize Dain at all. "The king is understandably concerned. You do realize that his highness is not yet knighted, and therefore by the rules of challenge and combat, cannot legally meet you without your consent."

Dain swallowed again, feeling himself caught in the morass of his own deceit. "Aye," he managed to say. "I understand."

"The king is summoning you," Sir Damiend said abruptly. "Come."

Dain's heart seemed to plunge, then he rallied himself, for this was the very thing he'd wanted all along.

He rode over to the king's box and bowed low over his saddle before the monarch of all Mandria.

Close up, King Verence made a splendid figure. Handsome still, despite the softening of his body and the lines of dissipation in his face, the king had barley-colored hair that grew thick and long to his shoulders. His beard was gray and closely trimmed to his jaw. He wore a long doublet of embroidered silk, with a white linen shirt beneath it. An embroidered cap perched atop his head, and he wore a jeweled thin-sword belted around his waist. A wide collar of magnificent gold, studded with rubies, encircled his neck in proclamation of his royalty. His eyes were a hazel mixture of green and blue, flecked with brown.

Meeting them, Dain felt a small shiver go through him. *Sacred eyes,* he thought, and wondered if he should dismount in obeisance. A king this man might be, but he was clearly more even than that. In that moment, Dain felt as though something momentous was happening to him, as though the field of destiny was shifting beneath his feet.

"Your name," the king demanded.

His voice was ordinary, commanding in tone but carrying no magical power. Relieved, Dain struggled to find his voice.

It was Sir Damiend who answered for him. "He said he is Danov of Tern, your majesty."

The king blinked, and a murmur of curiosity rippled

through the entourage surrounding him. Even the fat man in white church robes stepped forward.

"Your majesty, is he Netheran?" the fat man asked. "Is this tourney open to foreigners?"

"I don't care who he is," Gavril said angrily. "I have issued challenge, which he has agreed to meet. Let us fight!"

An argument broke out, but Dain felt a pressure inside himself, the pressure to be honorable, to do the right thing. This was his moment, perhaps his only moment, to speak to the king. He must not let his desire to fight Gavril in anonymity cause him to throw away this opportunity to accomplish what he had promised Lord Odfrey he would do.

He reached up and pulled off his helmet. "No, you're all wrong," he said, breaking across the voices. He looked up into the strange eyes of the king with his own of palest eldin gray. "I am Dain of Thirst, Lord Odfrey's adopted son. I have come to your majesty, as my father bade me, and I bring you sorrowful news of the chevard's untimely death."

Grief clouded the king's eyes, and he nodded. "This news have I heard. My heart has mourned the loss of a good and loyal friend."

"No!" Gavril said, his voice shrill. He glared at Dain, white-lipped with fury, and pointed a shaking finger at him. "You—you—how *dare* you come here under false pretenses. You have no right to be on this field of honor. You have no right to challenge me!"

"My son," the king said with a weary sigh, "'twas you who issued the challenge. Do not fault this young man for accepting it."

"I won't fight him," Gavril said, nearly spitting. "He has no business here at all. Trickster! You aren't even a knight—"

"Neither are you," Dain shot back, annoyed by his interruption.

There was a moment of total silence, broken by the king's snort of amusement.

"Truthfully said. This lad shows spirit."

"Your majesty," Gavril said in exasperation, "he is naught but a—"

"Have done," the king interrupted impatiently. "What is his trickery in comparison to yours?"

Gavril's face turned white. "Sire, I but wished to—"

The king raised his hand, and Gavril cut off his protest.

Impressed that there was finally someone who could command Gavril, Dain turned his attention back to the king. Verence was looking at him without much approval, but Dain knew he must not be daunted.

"I was wrong to come before your majesty in this guise," he admitted swiftly, "but I knew no other way to reach you."

"There are audiences," the fat man said reprovingly.

Sir Damiend was scowling at Dain in disgust. "Sire, this creature is indeed who he claims to be: Lord Odfrey's pagan whelp. Although why—"

"Your remarks are not desired," the king said coldly, cutting him off. "There will be no insults spoken of my dear friend Odfrey." His gaze swung about to encompass them all. "Is that clear?"

Everyone bowed to him, and Dain was left to face the king, who now looked very stern indeed.

"You have reached me," the king said, "through trickery and deceit. What would you say to me?"

Dain swallowed and struggled to keep his courage. The king's peculiar eyes bored right through him, and Dain knew that he was being given an opportunity he might never get again. Swiftly he pulled out the petition, much creased and battered now. He held it out, and Sir Damiend was swift to pluck it from his fingers.

"From Lord Odfrey, your majesty," Dain said.

Sir Damiend started to unfold it, but the king held out his hand for it.

Dain held his breath, watching the king read the words that Lord Odfrey had penned with such care. His heart was pounding so hard he almost felt dizzy. His whole future depended on the king's decision. At that moment, he could almost feel Lord Odfrey's presence beside him, waiting also.

The king finished reading and folded the parchment with no change in his expression. "I understand that Lord Odfrey died on his road here."

Puzzlement filled Dain. He struggled to keep himself as composed as the king. "Aye, your majesty," he said. His voice roughened with memory of that dark day. "We were escorting his highness, as was the chevard's duty. Nonkind attacked us on the banks of the Charva. The prince was saved, but Lord Odfrey died of his wounds."

Tears burned Dain's eyes, but he held them back as he remembered how Lord Odfrey had died there, deserted by all save a few of his most loyal companions. "With his last words he spoke of your majesty," Dain whispered. "He bade me promise to come straight to you."

The king's green and blue eyes never wavered from Dain's face. "And did you?"

"Aye, your majesty. I—I did not even take my l-lord home to be buried, but instead sent him with knights to guard his journey back to Thirst while I rode on southward. I did seek audience, but—"

"Who came with you?" the king demanded.

Dain frowned. "My knight protector, Sir Terent. The Thirst master of arms, Sir Polquin. My friend Thum, who is the younger son of—"

"Nay, boy, not an entire list," the king said impatiently. "How many knights? What numbers do you command here?"

"Two knights came with me," Dain said, not understanding his question. "Two knights did I send to convey Lord Odfrey's body home."

"And the others?"

"There are no others, save the men which were left to guard Thirst Hold in our absence."

The king blinked and stepped back. "Thod above!" he swore in consternation. "Are you saying all the rest died with Lord Odfrey?"

"Aye," Dain told him. "One-third of the standing Thirst forces set forth for Savroix to guard Prince Gavril's safety. They were slain in the ambush, though they fought as valiantly as men could. All but four knights died there."

Grave murmurs spread among the royal entourage. Verence himself drew a Circle, and the fat man began to pray beneath his breath.

"I was not told of this," the king said. His gaze flashed to Sir Damiend first, and while the knight reddened, the king looked at his son.

Gavril tossed his head. "Would you receive such grim news during your birthday festivities, sire?"

"By Thod, I would," the king replied grimly. "Especially when it affects the realm."

"Hardly that," Gavril said with a shrug. "A great pity, of course, but not—"

"Those men died for *you,* my son," the king said to him.

Gavril blinked and abandoned what he was saying. "Yes," he admitted quietly.

"And did the Nonkind take them?" the king asked.

Someone behind him—the girl, perhaps—gasped aloud. Everyone ignored her while they stared at Dain for his answer.

He shook his head. "Nay, your majesty. My companions and I ferried their bodies across the Charva to the southern bank. They were buried there, with what rites we could give them."

"Pagan rites?" Sir Damiend asked.

His hostility and contempt made Dain's eyes flash.

"Nay, sir. With the church rites they believed in." Dain returned his gaze to the king. "All save Lord Odfrey. His body was sent home, guarded by Sir Alard and Sir Bowin. I hope it reached the hold safely."

The king drew another Circle and murmured something. When he looked up again, it was not at Dain but at Sir Damiend. "None of this was in your report."

The church knight opened his mouth, but hesitated

with his answer. "I knew not these particular details, your majesty."

"Why not?"

Sir Damiend did not flinch. "Because as soon as the attack was over, I gathered the church soldiers of my command and brought Prince Gavril southward as fast as we could travel. His safety was my primary duty."

"Indeed, but could you not even tarry to protect the souls of the dead?" the king asked with acerbity. "It *is* one of your sworn duties, is it not, Reverend Sir Damiend?"

The knight's face went white. "Yes, your majesty."

"How many men did you lose in this battle?" the king persisted, although from the flicker in his eyes Dain suspected that he already knew the answer.

Sir Damiend swallowed. "Five men."

"Five. And did you bury them at the field of battle?"

"We brought them with us, sire."

"I see." The king's voice was growing colder with every word. He glared at Sir Damiend, who looked frozen before him. There was not a sound among the onlookers. Even Gavril had lost his expression of impatient arrogance. The king's eyes held Sir Damiend pinned. "Tell me, sir knight. Are the men of your command such superb fighters that only five fell to this dread enemy while—" His gaze snapped to Dain. "How many Thirst knights fell?"

"One and sixty," Dain replied.

"While one and sixty Thirst knights lost their lives?" The king glared at Sir Damiend. "Or have you taken up the Netheran custom of keeping a *sorcerel* near you in battle to counteract the magic of the Nonkind?"

Red flared in Sir Damiend's cheeks. He glared back. "Never, your majesty! We would never commit such sacrilege!"

"Then answer my question. How do you account for the men you brought back with you? How large was your force? Fifty men, was it not?"

"Yes, your majesty."

"And five and forty rode home with my son."

"His protection was our chief concern."

"Very dutiful. And what was Lord Odfrey's concern?" the king asked, his voice whip-sharp.

The fat man rose to his feet and moved closer to the king. "Sire," he said in a soft, gentle voice. "Your grief carries your heart too far into sadness. Let this be dealt with elsewhere—"

"Let us deal with it now," the king said harshly, never giving the fat man a glance. His gaze remained on Sir Damiend, who squared his shoulders.

"We surrounded the prince and did not engage in combat, except as it came to us," he replied. His voice wavered on him before he firmed it once more. "That was my duty and my decision. I gave the orders."

"And Lord Odfrey was expendable?" the king asked. "One and sixty seasoned knights under the bravest chevard in the land were expendable? Combined, you could have been a formidable force. Yet you divided and let the Thirst men fall to this horrendous foe."

"My orders committed me to the preservation of the prince's life," Sir Damiend said. "Half of our combined forces fought valiantly to engage the enemy. The rest fought to protect his highness. Clearly capture of Prince Gavril was their intent. This, we foiled. To that end, every man present was expendable."

"Yes," the king agreed, surprising Dain. "So they were." He nodded at Sir Damiend. "I wanted to hear you say it before this gathering, that all men here might know what occurred. A pity this was not stated as completely and eloquently in your report."

Sir Damiend's face reddened again. He said nothing.

"Reports can be amended," the fat man said to the king in soothing tones. King Verence stared into the distance, his face drawn with disappointment and grief. "Let today's festivities not be marred by the sad tidings this young man has brought before your majesty," the fat man added.

Gavril turned his dark blue eyes on Dain. "You have brought your message to his majesty, as you promised Lord Odfrey. Now you can go."

Dain frowned, not ready to accept dismissal yet. "My petition?" he said, gazing at the king.

"How dare you pester his majesty!" the fat man said. He gestured imperiously. "Send this boy away."

"No," the king said, rousing himself from his thoughts. He turned his gaze on his son. "You and this young man knew each other at Thirst Hold, I am sure."

"Dain was there," Gavril admitted. "He's a stray, brought in from the wilderness by Lord Odfrey's kindness. Of course, he has sought to take advantage of—"

"Is this not the young man who saved your life, Gavril?" the king asked.

Dain held his breath, feeling hope return.

Gavril scowled and reluctantly nodded. "Yes, your majesty. He did, when my protector Sir Los failed to guard me."

"Sir Los died protecting you," Dain felt compelled to say.

"I remember reading Lord Odfrey's account. There is much to consider," the king said.

Dain looked at him with hope. This man was indeed as fair-minded as Lord Odfrey had said. He was a good king, with justice in him, unlike his son, who lied, schemed, and manipulated to get his way.

Abruptly King Verence gestured. "Go to it, Gavril. Let us see what your training has wrought in you."

Gavril stared at him blankly. "Sire?"

"Do not waste this fine new armor you have commissioned for yourself. There is a challenge on the field, I believe. Herald, announce the contest."

Dain's eyes widened, and his blood began to pump faster. He stared at the king in amazement.

Gavril also stared at his father. "But, sire, do you mean to call Lord Roberd back to the field?"

"I do not," the king said with asperity. "You dismissed

him for forfeiture. This young man—Dain, is it? Dain is your challenger."

A grin spread across Dain's face.

Gavril sputtered. "But—but I cannot meet *him*! He's a pagan savage, not a knight."

"So you said before," the king replied serenely, impervious to his son's protests. "And I believe this 'pagan' answered you well. You are no more a knight than is he."

Gavril reddened in fury. "Is your majesty forcing me to fight this creature?"

"I am," the king said. "You have boasted before us all. Let us see what you can do."

The fat man bent over to whisper in the king's ear. Verence ignored him. "Well?" he asked his son.

Gavril glared at Dain. "I will trounce you like the dog you are."

Knowing better than to insult him in return, Dain satisfied himself with "I will do my best to see that you don't."

Someone among the courtiers laughed aloud.

The herald, recalled to his duties, spurred his horse to the middle of the field to make the announcement. The crowd came alive at once, clapping their approval.

Dain turned to the king. He had no answer to his petition, but at least he'd been heard. He must force himself to be patient now. As respectfully as he could, Dain bowed to his majesty. He admired the king for having treated him fairly, without regard for his ragged appearance or unorthodox method of gaining an audience.

"Thank you for your kind attention, your majesty," he said.

The king's gaze flickered to him briefly, and Dain was given a slight nod.

Aware that he could be forgotten within the hour, Dain wheeled his horse away and headed for the lists. Sir Damiend rode beside him, still red-faced from the reprimand he'd been dealt.

As Dain reined up and surveyed the lances standing in

their rack, Sir Damiend said, "Heed this, boy. You're going into a contest against his highness. Mind you give him the victory."

Dain's brows knotted. He shot Sir Damiend a sharp look.

"You heard me," the church knight said. "Think you that his majesty wants his son trounced this day before all assembled?"

"This contest will be fought with—"

"It will be fought with care," the knight said harshly. "No harm comes to his highness. For I am still sworn to his protection. And I swear to you, pagan, that if you go too far, I will be at your throat with my own sword. Do you understand me?"

Anger suffused Dain. He stared at Sir Damiend through a haze. "You want me to lose, just to satisfy the prince's ego. What dishonorable request is this?"

"Call it what you like," Sir Damiend replied. "I have given you fair warning. Go too far, and I will finish you."

12

SUN BLAZED DOWN on Alexeika's head and shoulders. Barefoot, with her ankles hobbled, she stumbled over a canyon's rock-strewn bottom in Vika's wake. Alexeika's hands were bound in front of her. Whenever she stumbled or slowed down too much, Vika yanked the noose around her throat to keep her going. Coughing and half-choking, Alexeika quickened her pace, forcing herself to ignore the rocks that cut and bruised her feet. She was still alive, she reminded herself. Still alive, although she knew not for how long.

At dawn, when Vika had captured her, Alexeika expected the Grethori maid to slit her throat then and there. "If you kill me," she said in desperation, "Holoc will hunt you down and slay you."

Vika moaned deep and low. Her well-honed knife blade pressed against Alexeika's throat. "Holoc loves me. We are promised to each other."

"The *sheda*'s spell has ruined that. I don't want your man. I—I have chosen another in my heart. Let me go, and Holoc will be yours again."

Vika had growled curses in her native tongue and began to pummel Alexeika. Her blows were harsh and painful. Alexeika twisted in her hold, evading the knife, and elbowed Vika back away from her. They fought ferociously in the semidarkness, rolling over and over on the ground for possession of the knife. Shouts from the top of the ravine stopped them both.

Vika made a little sobbing sound, and Alexeika wanted to scream. She would not let herself be captured again. Better if she died on Vika's knife than that. Together, they lay amidst the bones and offal thrown into the bottom of the ravine and listened to the shouts and angry voices of Alexeika's pursuers.

She closed her eyes to hold back her tears. Fear clawed at her throat, but she mastered it quickly. She had to think. This was her only chance to get away; she must not lose it.

Squirming, she tried to break free, but Vika clamped a hand on the back of Alexeika's skull and mashed her face into the ground to hold her.

"Let me go!" Alexeika whispered. "If they capture me, I will be given to him. Is that what you want?"

Before Vika could answer, Holoc's voice rose above the others.

"Find her!" he said savagely. "She is mine. Mine! I will slay any man who does not bring her to me."

"Vika is also missing," another said. "They have run away together."

Holoc swore terrible curses. His voice had a frantic, out-of-control quality. *The spell is still on him,* Alexeika thought with a shiver. She listened to the men crashing through the brush as they climbed down the precipitous ravine.

"If Vika has stolen my woman-man demon," Holoc said, "I will cut out her bowels and wear them for a necklace. I will drink her blood and pound her bones into meal for my bread. This I swear."

Vika's grip on Alexeika's head loosened. Feeling hope that now they could be allies, Alexeika pushed her way upright. Vika snarled something soft and vicious and scrambled to her feet.

"This way," Alexeika breathed, aware that the men would soon be close enough to hear them. She ran across the uneven ground, and Vika followed her.

Together they followed the bottom of the ravine until it grew shallow and petered out. Then it was Vika's turn to take the lead, as she guided them through the brush and trees that grew thickly on the mountain slopes. By the time the sun came up, its pink rays slanting across the slopes, they had a good head start.

Eventually, they flopped down to rest. Panting, Alexeika grinned at her new ally. "We've doubled back and forth across our trail enough times to confuse them well."

Vika grunted. In the sunrise, her skin looked drawn too tight across the prominent bones of her thin face. Her eyes were dark with hatred. She bared her filed teeth in what was not a smile. "They will come," she said, almost grunting her words. "They will come forever. Holoc will not give up."

Alexeika rose to her feet. "Then let us keep going." She had lost everyone and everything she cared about, but she had her life and her freedom. She would begin anew. "If we can make good time all day, by nightfall we should be close to—"

The blow caught her in the back of her head. The world spun around her, faded, and went dark.

Minutes later, she woke up and found herself lying on

the ground, her hands bound to a stake driven into the ground. Vika was crouched next to her, busy plaiting another rope from vines she had cut down from a nearby thicket. She knotted the end, twisted it about Alexeika's ankles, then made a longer rope that she fitted about Alexeika's throat.

"Why do you do this?" Alexeika demanded furiously. Her head was throbbing, and she fought against being sick. "We can help each other."

"You have ruined my life," Vika told her, sending her a look of loathing. "Now you will bring me a new one."

Alexeika didn't understand what she meant, but she feared that Vika meant to sacrifice her in some strange Grethori ritual. "I am not your enemy, Vika."

Vika growled something and pulled her onto her feet. "Walk," she said harshly. "You are my prisoner. I will get good price for you. When we find another tribe, I will use you to buy my way into it."

Alexeika's spirits sank. If they found another tribe, Vika might secure a new place for herself, but Alexeika would be no better off. She started to plead with Vika, but compressed her mouth instead. Volvns did not beg. If there was a way to escape from Vika, she would find it.

Vika gave her a shove. "Walk."

By nightfall, they reached the foot of the mountain. Weary and footsore, Alexeika sank down to rest. Vika prowled back and forth nervously, as though she still feared pursuit. Eventually they slept, but sometime in the dead of night, Vika sprang up with a choked cry.

Startled awake and certain they'd been discovered, Alexeika scrambled to her feet. But she heard nothing out there in the darkness, save the quiet song of insects and the cold wind's sigh.

She relaxed. "There's nothing—"

Vika rounded on her and struck her across the mouth. Reeling back, Alexeika struggled not to fall. Already Vika was yanking on the rope. "Come," she muttered. "Come fast."

Alexeika gave her no trouble. They walked until a shivering Alexeika could no longer feel her bruised, half-frozen feet. Cold, clammy air and the smell of water told Alexeika a fjord must be nearby. If only she could jump into it and swim to freedom, she told herself, knowing that the superstitious Grethori would not go near deep water if they had any choice.

Fog writhed about their ankles, thickening as they walked. Alexeika listened with all her might, straining for the sound of soft lapping that would tell her how near to the bank they were.

In the autumn, when the summer gave way to colder weather, there were frequent fogs that came off the surface of the fjords. Alexeika could feel the mist kissing her face. Tipping back her head, she inhaled deep lungfuls of air.

Ahead of her, Vika slowed down. The Grethori girl was muttering to herself, and when Alexeika crowded her, she whirled around with a snarl.

"Nothing pursues us," Alexeika said.

"You don't know that. You don't know!" Vika said raggedly.

"I am a demon," Alexeika said, playing on Vika's superstitions. "I *know.*"

Vika drew in breath with a little sob. "I dreamed of him. He is near."

"No."

Something in Alexeika's calm voice seemed to reach Vika. She turned about, twisting the end of the rope between her hands, then sank down on her haunches in the midst of damp brush.

Alexeika was glad to rest. She yawned, fighting off a crushing sense of exhaustion, and crouched beside Vika. She heard the snick of a knife being drawn.

"Not too close," Vika warned her with a growl.

Sighing, Alexeika moved as far away as the rope around her neck would permit. The ground felt damp and cold when she stretched out on her side. In the quiet darkness, she could hear water lapping against the rocks of the bank.

How far away was the water? Five strides? Six? It might as well be fifty, for she could not run in these hobbles.

Vika began a soft chant under her breath. Presumably it was to ward off evil. Ignoring her, Alexeika stealthily drew up her knees and began to worry at the knots of her hobbles. Her nimble fingers pulled and tugged, trying to loosen her bonds. If she could get her feet free, Alexeika reasoned, she would be able to outrun Vika as far as the fjord. Once she jumped into the water, Vika would not pursue her. Although at this time of year the water would be like ice itself, Alexeika counted the risk worthwhile. She would not be able to swim with her hands bound, but as long as she floated and kicked, she would manage somehow.

Night stretched on, cold and foggy. Shivering there in the darkness, Alexeika worked at the stubborn knots and at last felt one loosen. Swallowing hard, her hope growing, she renewed her efforts until the hobbles fell from her ankles.

It was all she could do not to kick out in joy. Instead, listening to Vika's soft chanting, she forced herself to lie still. She wished the girl would go to sleep, but it seemed unlikely. Whatever had disturbed her dreams kept Vika sitting bolt upright among the bushes, wary and starting at the smallest sound.

A faint whiff of something burning tickled Alexeika's nostrils, and she realized Vika was trying to cast a spell. The girl kept repeating the same incomprehensible words over and over again. Something about the rhythm and force with which Vika uttered them made Alexeika uneasy. Whatever Vika was trying to do was not working.

Alexeika wanted to make a run for it, but she thought it best to wait until daylight when she could see the fjord. She was weary and weakened from the inadequate food and water of the past few days, and knew that Vika had more stamina than she. If Vika outran her before she reached the water, she would die. So Alexeika told herself to be patient and wait until she had the best chance possible.

Vika's muttering gave her the idea to try a spell of her own.

Alexeika had worked no magic since the night when she summoned the vision of Faldain from the waters. Uzfan had been very wroth with her for taking such a risk and had forbidden her to use the magic again, lest she bring harm to herself or others.

But now, Uzfan was dead. There was only herself or Vika who could be harmed here. Alexeika did not know if she could conjure a spell, but she decided to try.

She thought of the fjord, the mist, and the darkness. She wanted to make a mist *krenjin,* a sort of imp of the snow-country legends. It didn't have to be very good; all she wanted to do was distract Vika enough for her to run.

At first, as Alexeika lay there straining to create the spell, nothing happened. Vika's chanting distracted her, and, shuddering with weariness, Alexeika felt herself perilously near to giving up.

Just one *krenjin,* she thought, and tried one last time. She reached deep into her thoughts and formed a mental image of the creature. Gray it would be, as gray as the fog or the dawn sky. Winged it would be, flying swiftly through the forests. Fanged and clawed it would be, and ferocious. When it attacked its scream would make the blood run cold.

Vika jumped to her feet and screamed.

The sound tore through Alexeika, scattering her thoughts in all directions. She stared through the gloom at Vika, who started flailing and clawing at herself, then dancing about like a person gone mad.

When she spun around, one of her shoulders looked misshapen. Alexeika jumped to her feet, wondering if Vika had somehow mutilated herself with her own spellcasting. Just then another scream came, drowning out Vika's cries.

Alexeika realized there was a creature on Vika's back.

How it got there was impossible to say, unless it had simply dropped from the sky.

Vika whirled around again and threw herself backward against a tree in an effort to dislodge the creature. Then Alexeika saw a pair of leathery wings unfurl and begin to beat at Vika's head and shoulders.

Astonished, Alexeika realized her spell had worked. This, she reasoned, must be a *krenjin*.

At last she had the diversion she needed. Pulling the noose off over her head, she threw down the rope and ran for the fjord.

When the uneven ground made her stumble, something small and gray flew harmlessly over her head. Straightening with a gasp, Alexeika saw the *krenjin* wheeling in the air overhead. It attacked her again, but she ducked in time.

Clacking its talons together, the creature screamed in fury. Alexeika dived into some bushes for cover and wondered why the thing had left Vika to attack her instead. Was it because she'd run and attracted its attention?

But, no, she saw Vika still flailing and struggling to dislodge the one on her back.

"Two!" Alexeika said aloud.

At that moment, a third one screamed and came flying through the air. Alexeika went cold inside. How many had she created?

There was no time to worry about that now. "Vika! Get in the water!" she yelled, and burst from the undergrowth to make another run toward the fjord.

The two *krenjins* after her matched her speed, then dived at her in an effort to turn her back. Alexeika dodged under a tree and snapped off a small branch. The next *krenjin* that came at her was swatted from the air.

It landed with a squawk of pain and lay still, a boneless lump in the shadows. Its companion flapped leathery wings and clacked its talons, but stopped its attack.

Shaking the stick at it, Alexeika ran once more. In the fog and darkness, she was barely aware of where she was headed when suddenly the ground dropped from beneath her feet. She realized she was falling, and her arms flailed wildly in the air before she hit the water with a loud splash.

The impact stung, and she sank under the surface like a stone. It was incredibly cold, so cold she thought her heart would stop. Down she plummeted through the black water until her feet hit bottom.

Instinctively, Alexeika flexed her knees and shoved herself back to the surface. Her head broke water, and she dragged in air with a gasp. Her body felt like it was being jabbed with knives of ice. Barely able to breathe, she began to shake convulsively.

On the bank, Vika screamed again—a long, shuddering wail that cut off abruptly. As she bobbed there in the icy water, Alexeika knew the *krenjins* had killed her. Closing her eyes, Alexeika whispered a brief prayer for her own soul. She had done this without meaning to. It would have been one thing to kill Vika in a fight, but it was a far different matter to set demons on her like this. Ashamed, Alexeika understood how right Uzfan had been to warn her against using magic.

Not wanting to be nearby when the *krenjins* finished with their victim, Alexeika turned away from shore and tried to swim. She sank a few times, then treaded water until at last she managed to untie her wrists. The water had loosened the knots, which made it easier for her to work free.

The struggle to swim kept her from freezing, although she felt cold to the marrow and her teeth wouldn't stop chattering. She wept with misery, but kept going.

Finally, as dawn broke over a new day, she emerged from the other side of the fjord, streaming water and shivering. The sunrise turned the still waters at the foot of the mountains into a shield of hammered copper, shimmering in hues of gold, bronze, and pink. The mist burned off the surface and retreated onto the bank. She staggered up beneath the trees and paused to wring water from her hair and the hem of her sodden robe.

In the new light of day, she looked at her shriveled blue fingers. The air was so cold she thought she would die. Teeth chattering, she dropped to her knees and hunched there, moaning with misery.

But she was alive, and she was free. She had escaped the Grethori, and the consequences of her own erratic spell-casting. Now her life could begin anew.

First, however, she had to build a fire and warm herself. For if she froze to death, all her efforts to escape would have been for naught.

Without a strike box, building a fire proved next to impossible. She searched in vain for rocks along the bank, but this side of the fjord presented her only with smooth dirt, hackberry brambles tipped with frost, and kindling wood. Stumbling along with her robe dripping down her bare legs, Alexeika finally found a clearing of sorts and hopped about until the sun began to warm the air.

She stripped off the robe and wrung it out thoroughly, then spread it on the ground to dry. The painted designs on her skin had run together or in some cases washed off completely. Plucking handfuls of grass, she scrubbed her skin until it hurt, making sure she eradicated every last trace of the Grethori magic. Then she gathered berries—sour, dried things clinging like knots to their brier vines. She ate them ravenously, shivering still, and winced as they hurt her stomach. It was useless to wish she'd managed to steal Vika's dagger. She would have to cope, and she had confidence in her woodcraft.

The most important thing was to finish getting dry and warm, before she went about setting traps for small game. Braiding together long pieces of grass, she constructed a lure while sitting in the sun. At last her bluish skin began to turn pink and she stopped shivering so violently. Combing through her damp hair with her fingers, she removed the worst of the tangles. Her thick, luxuriant tresses flowed down her back, curling at the ends as they dried. After she braided her hair, she put on the robe. Still somewhat damp, it made her cold

again. Its bright colors had all faded and run together into a
dreadful hue. She didn't care. As soon as she had trapped
enough small game, she would stitch the skins into new clothing, however rudimentary. Then she would burn this garment
of her enemies and say curses over the ashes.

It was very quiet and solitary in the forest. Now and then,
inhaling the pines, she glanced out over the fjord. She saw
no evidence of settlements, heard no voices. It seemed she
was the only person in the region.

Loneliness pressed her heart. While she knelt in the falling
leaves to set her lure, she found herself sobbing. Swiftly she
choked back her emotions. This was no time for tears. She
had to survive. Winter was coming, and it was a long way
to Karstok, or even Lolta. She could not survive the long
cold season on her own, not up here by the mountains. She
had no shelter built, no caches of food stored up. And she
did not want to spend the eternal months of snow and raging storms alone, with no one to even talk to.

No, she must take care of her immediate needs first, then
find her bearings and start the long walk to a settlement.
Someone among the rebels would take her in. Although she
had lost everything else, her name still counted for something.

The fetid stink of decay hit her nostrils only seconds before the hurlhound struck her in the back and knocked her
down.

She yelled in fear, and then the impact of hitting the
ground jolted the remaining air from her lungs. Wheezing
and terrified, she struggled to roll over while the beast
growled and sank its poisonous fangs into the thick cloth of
her robe. It dragged her, then shook her from side to side.
She heard cloth rip and felt the sting of pain as the monster's teeth tore her skin.

Red-eyed and powerful, the hurlhound was a dreadful
thing that stank of the grave. She screamed at it and struck
its snout with her free fist. The creature was momentarily
driven back, but then growled and lunged at her again.

She scrambled to one side, trying to dodge it, but the beast was too quick for her, and it knocked her down a second time. Alexeika's flailing hand found a branch lying on the ground. She twisted, swinging it with a yell, and hit the creature's head with all her strength.

The stick broke across the hurlhound's bony skull and made it yelp.

Scrambling free, Alexeika crouched low and began to back away from the monster. It stalked her as she brandished the jagged end of the stick. When it growled, she growled back just to keep herself from screaming in terror.

But despite her outer defiance, her heart was thudding hard enough to break through her chest. Despairing, she knew she could not defeat the creature. Everything she did only delayed her death a few seconds more. Blood was dripping down her arm from its bite, and already she felt the fire of the venom that had entered the wound. If she did not cleanse the wound soon, she would be destined to become Nonkind herself, and that was too horrible a fate to think about.

The hurlhound growled, but backed a few steps away from her. Its powerful jaws hung open, panting and dripping venom that hissed on the mossy, leaf-strewn ground.

Alexeika didn't understand why it was hesitating in finishing her. At best, her stick was a poor weapon. Perhaps the vile beast was waiting for its mate to circle behind her unprotected back. Fear melted her bowels. Every sound made her start. Her breath was sawing raggedly in her throat, and her heart still pounded so fast she thought it might burst. She dared not take her eyes off the hurlhound in front of her, for she knew that one second's inattention would encourage it to attack her again.

Desperately she prayed aloud, "Thod, have mercy on my soul."

And as though her prayer was heard, in the distance came the sound of rapidly approaching hoofbeats. Certain her ears were playing tricks on her, Alexeika lifted her head to listen. Aye, she could hear the rider crashing closer through the undergrowth. Hope shot through her.

"Hullo!" she shouted. "Help me! Please! I need help!"

The hurlhound growled, lowering its head and hunching its powerful shoulders. She froze, her shouts dying in her throat.

Another growl came from behind her. Alexeika gulped, aware that the second hurlhound had arrived, exactly as she'd expected. Her heart pounded even harder. She told herself not to look, but she couldn't stop herself.

Gripping her stick even more tightly, she risked a glance over her shoulder.

The new monster stood there, all right, black and evil. It bared its fangs and crouched low to spring.

It was a mistake to have looked. The moment she turned her attention away from the first hurlhound, it bayed a note of triumph and leaped for her. The second hurlhound sprang from the other side.

Caught between them, Alexeika swung her stick around and screamed with all her might.

13

WITHIN THE TOURNEY enclosure at Savroix, the herald rode up beside Sir Damiend, who spoke to him quietly. The herald galloped away to the center of the field. Trumpets blew for quiet, and the crowd settled down.

"Prince Gavril will meet his challenger, Dain of Thirst!" the man shouted.

A speculative murmur rippled around the stands. Dain ig-

nored it. He tried, also, to ignore Sir Damiend's threats, but
they had shaken him more than he wanted to admit. Angrily
he tried to regain his composure. Gavril had never engaged
in a fair fight with him yet, he reminded himself. Why should
today be any different?

"Let my challenger come!" Gavril called out, hoisting his
lance aloft. "I am ready!"

But Sir Damiend did not move his horse out of Dain's
way. "Mind you remember what I have told you," he said
harshly. "Do you understand me, eld?"

"Aye," Dain replied through his teeth. Glaring at Sir
Damiend, he lowered his visor with an angry clang.

"Leave him be, Sir Damiend!" Gavril called out impatiently. "I want to fight. Let us get to it."

Dain heard something rough and reckless in Gavril's
voice. When he noticed that the prince was carrying Tanengard in his scabbard, Dain understood that it was Lander's
evil sword making Gavril so heedless and wild. As soon as
he became aware of the magicked sword's presence, Dain
heard its seductive hum. He remembered fighting with it to
annihilate the Nonkind attackers. For a short time, he and
the sword had been united into a single entity. And tainted
though it was, the sword's call twisted through Dain's heart.
He felt the momentary sear of jealousy, for he'd been the
one who named the weapon and blooded it first. It should
belong to him, not Gavril. But then Dain drew a sharp,
steadying breath, and told himself that while the blade he
carried today was only ordinary steel and would not pour
fire into his soul, he was better off without a dark thing like
Tanengard. Besides, it was an insult to the magicked blade
to use it in a tourney. Tanengard was forged for war and
death, not mock combat. Gavril should not use it so.

Wheeling his horse over to the lance rack, Dain selected
one of ash wood, straight and lightweight, but strong. Painted
crimson, it looked quite battered from the jousting, but he
hoped it would serve him well.

The straps of the shield he picked out were made of old,

very soft and worn leather. The shield itself was heavy, crafted of thick linden wood that was strong yet could give. Dain hefted it, disliking its weight but hoping the shield would prove to be stout protection. He fitted his arm through the straps, struggling a little where his mail sleeve was too loose.

"Losing your courage already, pagan?" Gavril taunted him.

Anger surged into Dain's throat. Just in time, he kept himself from hurling back an insult.

"Ah, fear has robbed you of your voice," Gavril said smugly. "Very well!"

Seething, Dain trotted his horse to the far end of the list and entered the narrow wooden stall. Gavril entered on the opposite side. They faced each other, lances held ready across their saddles, and the crowd grew silent and hushed.

It was a bright, unforgettable moment. The hot sunlight baked Dain's shoulders and suffocated him inside his helmet. Gavril's armor shone like new-minted coinage beneath his bright blue surcoat. Dain could smell the leather of his saddle and the sweat of his horse as it pawed and champed the bit. It flicked its tail and stamped a fly, tossing Dain lightly up and down. He settled himself deeper into the saddle, clamping hard with his legs. Inside, he was tense and ready, his entire being focused on Gavril. No matter what Sir Damiend threatened, Dain did not intend to lose the joust on purpose. As it was, Tanengard was capable of cleaving through his mail like butter. Gavril had the advantage in what would probably have otherwise been an equal contest, but Dain shut away his fear. He would do his best, and by Thod, he would not let Gavril finish him quickly, Tanengard or no Tanengard.

The herald waited nearby on his horse, holding aloft a flag. It fluttered brightly in the sunlight, then swung down.

Gavril yelled hoarsely, spurring his horse forward. Dain's mount jumped into a gallop before Dain could give it the command. Caught off guard, Dain regrouped hastily and tightened his grip on the lance. He aimed it, resting it on the pommel of his saddle exactly as he'd been taught, taking care that the butt of the handle did not wedge itself against the inside of his thigh. Such carelessness, Sir Polquin had taught him, was why most novices ended up unhorsed.

Dain rushed straight at Gavril, who came toward him in flashes of gold and blue. The hoofbeats sounded like thunder in Dain's ears. He held the lance steady, although he could no longer see if the tip of it was aimed where he wanted it.

Don't change your aim midway down the list, Sir Polquin's voice said in his mind. *Stay steady all the way through the hit.*

Remembering the advice helped quell Dain's momentary panic. He could see Gavril shifting slightly in the saddle, and hoped the prince felt equally nervous in what was the first public joust for both of them.

Fear this! Dain thought as his lance tip struck Gavril's shield. The jolt came up the weapon into Dain's arm and numbed that entire side of his body. At almost the same instant, Gavril's lance hit Dain's shield square center and skidded.

Dain twisted his torso, and the lance point passed him harmlessly. There was no time to feel relief, for his own lance tip was skidding across Gavril's shield, marring its new paint. The tip jabbed beneath the edge of the prince's shield, and Dain twisted his forearm with all his might, using the impetus of his charging horse to lift Gavril from his saddle.

The prince actually cleared leather, and gasps rose from the onlookers. But although Gavril twisted to one side and looked as though he would fall, he managed to sling his shield off his arm and disengage Dain's lance. Then Dain was galloping past him, his lance tip veering wildly. Dain managed to swing it aloft by the time he reached the end of the list. His horse splashed through the mud hole and jolted to a halt. Snorting, it turned around and pawed the ground in readiness for the next pass.

At the opposite end, Gavril lifted his lance high and gestured to a squire, who came running to hand up his shield.

Watching near the herald, Sir Damiend glared at Dain and shook his head in warning.

Angered anew, Dain compressed his mouth. The honor of Thirst was at stake today. He thought of Lord Odfrey, who would not have backed down from either the challenge or the threat.

Turning his head in the other direction, Dain peered through his visor slits at the king's box. He saw King Verence sitting quite still and intent in the midst of chattering courtiers. The maiden at his side with the beautiful golden hair watched with her fists pressed against her mouth. Dain squinted at her, admiring her beauty, and wondered how she could fear for Gavril when all the advantages were his.

But I nearly unhorsed him, Dain thought in satisfaction.

"Round two!" the herald announced, and raised his flag.

Dain swiftly pulled his attention back to the business at hand. This time when the flag dropped, he was ready at the same time as his horse. He held his lance more efficiently, aimed it quicker and higher.

He hit his mark, but too high. Chips flew off the top edge of Gavril's shield, bouncing off the gold helmet and making the prince flinch. Gavril's lance crashed into Dain's shield with more force than the first time, rocking him back in the saddle.

As he fought to hang on, Dain also struggled to keep his lance firm against Gavril's shield. Then he heard a mortal snap of wood. Bits of wood went flying against Dain's helmet. He could hear them hit, but there was no time to duck. The end of his lance flew up, disengaging from Gavril's shield and walloping the side of the prince's helmet. Gavril reeled in the saddle and shouted something.

The prince's lance rammed its way between Dain's shield

and his side. Dain felt a tremendous blow, and suddenly found himself out of his saddle.

He went tumbling over the hindquarters of his horse before he knew what happened. He hit the ground hard enough to rattle his teeth, and the helmet rang about his ears like a gong.

Dazed and furious at his apparent defeat, Dain struggled up and pulled off his helmet. His ears were still ringing, and it took him a moment to focus his eyes.

When he did, he saw Sir Damiend and the heralds gathered around Gavril, who was lying flat on his back with his arms outstretched.

The crowd watched in absolute silence. Amazed to find it a draw instead of a defeat, Dain grinned to himself. He saw the king leaning forward, one white-knuckled hand gripping the front edge of the box.

As he dragged in a shaky breath—finding it hurt his ribs to do so—Dain glanced back at Gavril, who had not yet moved. If he'd killed the Prince of the Realm, Dain knew, his life would be worth less than the dung his horse was currently depositing.

He felt an overwhelming desire to run for the gates, then scorned his cowardice and stood his ground.

At that moment, Gavril sat up, with Sir Damiend's assistance. He staggered to his feet, holding his helmet in his hands. Applause broke out, increasing as the crowd realized he was shaken but unharmed. Glaring over at Dain, he mouthed an insult that Dain chose to ignore.

The herald climbed back on his horse. "Lances are declared a draw," he announced, "with both contestants unhorsed in the second round. Swords are next."

There was more cheering from the crowd.

"Contestants will engage!" announced the herald. "Swords only. No shields."

Dain put his helmet back on and gave his borrowed horse a pat before striding forth to meet Gavril.

"Over here, sir knight," said the herald, gesturing to an

area of freshly raked sand well away from the lists and its
mud hole. Dain smiled grimly to himself and veered over
to where he was told to go.

This fighting area happened to be directly in front of the
king's box. Conscious of the crowd, as well as the royal on-
looker, Dain did not draw his sword as he had been taught.
Instead he waited as Gavril strode up, holding a drawn Tanengard in his hands.

Dain bowed to Gavril in courtesy, and heard a murmur
of approval from the courtiers. Gavril cursed him and swung
the weapon without waiting for the herald's signal.

It was poorly done of him, and the crowd booed. Dain
had been hoping the prince would lose his temper. With
quick feet, Dain skipped out of Gavril's reach, evading the
whistling menace of Tanengard, and swiftly drew his own
weapon in a single motion that became a parry of Gavril's
next blow.

The weapons clanged against each other, and the crowd
cheered for more. Fast and furiously they fought, these two
youths who had been enemies since their first meeting. Back
and forth, parrying and attacking with too much speed and
force for long endurance. Gavril moved like a cat, springy
and light on his feet, but his preferred weapon was the thin-
sword, a light, delicate, and deadly weapon that killed by
piercing, not with its edge. He seemed ill-practiced with the
broadsword he now wielded.

Dain, on the other hand, had never been allowed to hold
a thin-sword. For him, there had instead been long hours of
drills with the broadsword, a heavy, slower weapon. Swinging it in practice, over and over and over, had built strength
in Dain's arms and shoulders. His muscles rippled smoothly
now, although he was hampered today by the ache in his
ribs and the unaccustomed weight of his mail and helmet.

Roaring a muffled curse, Gavril charged him. Dain caught
his blade high and held it. As the two youths strained against
each other, Dain heard the war-song of Tanengard humming
louder and louder. He looked through his visor into Gavril's

eyes and saw nothing in them but fury and the lust to kill. For a moment, Dain felt his courage quail before such opposition, but as he kept his weapon locked and straining against Gavril's, he felt Tanengard's strength flow into him as well.

It was as though, as a hound seeks its master, the sword's power had sought him. It began to hum more loudly than ever, resonating inside Dain with such intensity he grunted and pushed Gavril back.

Disengaging his weapon, he retreated several paces and drew in several deep breaths to clear his mind.

Misunderstanding his retreat, Gavril laughed and came at him again.

Dain pivoted on his back foot, turning to place himself well within Gavril's reach. Ignoring the swing of Tanengard with such recklessness that the crowd gasped, Dain felt the blade whistle past him. It should have cleaved him in twain. But he forced himself to sing in his mind, a clear song of battle and strength, forced himself to match his song to Tanengard's, and the blade did not strike him. It twisted in Gavril's hand to miss Dain, as he had known it would.

Disbelief flashed in Gavril's eyes, but he had no more time to react. Dain swung his weapon, lifting it high. He could have taken Gavril's head off at the neck with that blow, but at the last moment he tilted his blade and let the flat of it strike the prince's helmet.

It hit with a mighty gong, and the prince went staggering back three steps before his knees buckled and he fell. Tanengard landed in the sand and lay there, glittering brightly.

The crowd jumped to its feet, yelling so loudly Dain's own head buzzed with the noise. Dazed, he stood heaving for air. Under his armor, sweat poured off him in rivers. The helmet was suffocating him. After a moment, he regained his wits enough to pull it off.

Cool air hit his face and revived him enough to step out of the way as people rushed to Gavril's side. The prince lay where he'd fallen, unmoving. The king, looking concerned, leaned over the edge of his box.

Sir Damiend pulled Gavril's dented helmet off and cast it aside. By then, a man in physician's robes was kneeling beside the prince. Gavril's eyes opened, blinking slowly. He did not look as though he had his wits.

Dain took another step back. Still panting for air, his arms trembling with exhaustion now that the fight was over, Dain felt a surge of jubilation. He had beaten Gavril, and this moment was sweet.

"Dain!" shouted a voice he knew well.

He spun around with a big grin and waved to Thum, who was pushing his way through the crowd now spilling into the enclosure. Sir Terent and Sir Polquin were with him, but it was Sir Terent who reached Dain first.

Red-faced and round-eyed, the knight planted himself in front of Dain. "Well!" he said, as though he could find no other words. "*Well!*"

Sir Polquin came limping up and clapped Dain on the shoulder. "That was the best-delivered blow of mercy I have ever seen. A reckless attack there at the last. You took far too big a chance, but beautifully ended."

"Lord Odfrey would have been proud of you," Thum said.

The unexpected praise made Dain glow with pride. He grinned at them, still too breathless to speak.

Over on the ground, Gavril slowly sat up. The court physician rose to his feet and smiled at the king. "All is well, your majesty. He is unharmed."

Relief flashed across the king's face. "Help him to his feet."

When the guards tried to obey, Gavril shook them off. Glowering in ill temper, he kicked the squire who tried to pick up his sword. "Leave that!" he snarled.

The boy retreated hastily, and Gavril picked up Tanengard himself, wiping the blade with care before he sheathed it. As he looked up, his dark blue eyes met Dain's, and his scowl deepened.

Dain met his murderous look impassively, taking care not to smile or gloat. The people surrounding them buzzed with excitement, gesturing widely as they recounted the contest to each other.

The king called to Gavril, and he swung away without a word to Dain.

Instead, Sir Damiend, looking dangerous, stepped up to him. His green eyes were stony. "So," he said in a quiet voice of menace. "You chose to defy me. You are an impudent pagan and in need of the lesson I promised you."

Dain, unsure if Sir Damiend meant to draw on him then and there, gulped but held his ground.

Sir Terent stepped between Dain and Sir Damiend. "What's this about?" he asked sharply, glaring at Sir Damiend. "By what right do you insult Lord Dain?"

Sir Damiend frowned and shifted his attention reluctantly to the burly knight. "*Lord* Dain, is it?" he said with contempt.

"Aye, 'tis," Sir Terent said gruffly.

The church knight's gaze took in Sir Terent's size and steely determination. Sir Terent was no knight of the court, but instead a rough fighting man, as tough as they came, and utterly fearless. "You're one of the Thirst men," Sir Damiend said.

"I am. As you should remember, commander. I'm one of the 'expendable' men you watched fight your foe while you held back."

A flush spread across Sir Damiend's cheeks. Before he could answer the king's voice rang out:

"There'll be no challenges between protectors. Desist, both of you. The contests are over."

Sir Damiend bowed and backed away a few steps, but not without a parting glare at both Dain and Sir Terent.

Sir Terent sniffed in contempt. "Damned puppy."

The crowd suddenly parted to make way for the king,

who came now into the enclosure and walked up to Dain.
The hot sunlight shone on his gold collar and sparked fire
inside its enormous rubies.

"Well fought, young Dain of Thirst," he said, and held
out his hand in friendship.

People gasped. Dain, nearly overwhelmed by the tremendous honor shown to him, extended his hand. It was grasped
firmly and released.

King Verence smiled at him through his neatly trimmed
beard. His green and blue eyes twinkled in good humor. "I
can't say I cheered for you, but I like a good contest that's
well-matched." He turned his head and beamed at his sulky
son. "The next time you two joust, I daresay Gavril will be
hot for revenge. That will liven up the game, eh?"

Dain stared at him in wonder, hardly able to believe the
king was chatting to him in such a friendly way. And what
did he mean by saying there'd be another joust? Was he im-
plying that he would approve Lord Odfrey's petition of adoption? Dain's heart began to thump.

"Mind, however," the king continued, "that you do not
infect his highness with your reckless ways. You are bold
on the field, young Dain—a bit too bold. These older knights
will soon take that out of you, eh, Lord Roberd?"

The champion, attired now in a doublet of black silk and
a fine chain of gold, looked like a simple country baron of
wealthy means, except for the scars on his knuckles and a
hawkishness about his dark eyes. He bowed to the king and
shot Dain a glance of keen appraisal. "Promising," he murmured.

To Dain, that was the highest praise of all. Among the
onlookers, Sir Polquin beamed as though bursting to tell one
and all that he'd been the one who trained Dain in arms.

Laughing, the king patted Dain on the shoulder and moved
on. His guards, protector, and entourage followed him. The
courtiers, especially the ladies, stole quick looks at Dain as
they passed by. Embarrassed by all the attention, Dain was

relieved when the royal party began to wend its way across the enclosure.

"Well," Sir Terent said, heaving a huge sigh. "You've won the king's favor today, m'lord. But you're a demon and a scamp, stealing my armor this way. Victory or not, I'll see you scrubbing the rust off my mail tonight."

Dain's grin vanished. He looked at his protector and saw that Sir Terent meant what he said. "Aye," Dain said in a chastened voice. "I meant no harm in borrowing—"

"Hah! Is that what you call it?" Reaching over, Sir Terent pulled off Dain's steel cap and the mail coif beneath it, without bothering to unlace the gorget. It raked Dain's face as it was pulled off. "The king may be charmed by your rascally ways, but you look to me like a lad in serious need of chores."

He swung away from Dain and whistled to his horse, which came trotting across the field with its reins dangling. Thum caught the animal and held it by its bridle while Sir Terent put the cap and coif atop the saddle and held them in place by crossing the stirrups over them.

"You took a good hit from that lance," Sir Polquin said to Dain. His gruff voice was softer than usual, and his gaze held concern. "Any hurts?"

Dain wondered where Sulein had gone to, and shook his head.

Sir Polquin stuck his finger in the new dent made in the side of the breastplate. "And this?" he asked. "Ought to be a wondrous bruise underneath."

When Sir Terent reached for the buckles that fastened the breastplate, Dain had a vision of them shucking him out of the mail there in the enclosure in front of everyone.

"Don't fuss," he said sharply, evading Sir Terent's reach. "It's nothing."

Sir Terent gripped him. "Stand still," he commanded, and took off the two halves of the breastplate.

Being rid of its weight gave Dain immediate relief. The mail alone was heavy enough.

"I'm surprised you didn't wear my surcoat as well, while you were stealing gear and horseflesh," Sir Terent grumbled.

Dain's face flamed red. He glanced at Thum, who shrugged and looked away.

"Cease plaguing him," Sir Polquin said unexpectedly. "It's in your armor that he defeated the prince. Take pride in that and stop scolding like a fishwife. We might almost think you jealous of his victory today."

Sir Terent's jaw bulged and he turned on the master of arms with a glare. "Jealous, am I? You must be afflicted with heatstroke. I had his promise that he'd come straight here and stay out of mischief. How can I protect him when he—"

"But you *did* protect me," Dain broke in quickly. "You stood against Sir Damiend exactly when I needed you."

Sir Terent grunted, looking unappeased. "That white-livered church knight with his holy airs. I'd like to run my sword up his pious—"

"Your pardon, sirs," interrupted a young page. Dressed in the king's livery, his long brown curls reaching to his shoulders, the page bowed to Dain. "If it pleases you, my lord, the king requests your presence at the sword contest."

Dain blinked, thrilled anew by the honor extended to him.

Thum grinned. "Aye! You're in favor, right enough. Run to—"

"Nay!" Sir Terent said sharply. "No chevard of Thirst runs hither and yon like a squire."

Sir Polquin scowled at Dain. "And you not cleaned up, looking no better than a—"

"Stop fussing at him and help me strip off this mail," Sir Terent said.

Horrified, Dain backed up a step. "You won't undress me out here!"

Sir Polquin froze with an arrested look on his craggy face, then began to laugh. "Thod's bones, the lad's right."

Sir Terent laughed with him. The two men slapped each other on the back and howled with mirth.

Dain glared at them both, then exchanged a puzzled glance with Thum.

The page, meanwhile, was hopping impatiently from one foot to the other. "If you please," he said. "The king awaits."

"Of course," Dain replied, striding forward with his hand resting casually on his sword hilt. "Sir Terent," he said over his shoulder, "will you attend me please?"

Still chuckling, Sir Terent broke away and came hurrying after him. Dain tried to keep what small amount of dignity he had left as he crossed the enclosure in his ill-fitting hauberk, his brass spurs ringing softly with every step.

He was let out between the gates, passed through a ready pen, and made his way among the stream of people still emptying the stands.

"Make way!" the page shouted imperiously. His shrill, assured voice and crimson livery made up for his diminutive size.

Dain followed in his wake, conscious of people staring and pointing at him.

"He's eldin!"

"Look at those eyes—no, don't! They'll put a spell on us."

"He defeated the prince."

"Isn't he handsome?"

"Well done, boy!"

Someone whistled. A few people jeered. Others applauded him.

Embarrassed, Dain hurried along as fast as he could without stepping on the page in front of him.

Up ahead, he could see a square that had been roped off in the meadow beyond the tourney enclosure. It seemed that all the town and more now gathered out here. An impromptu fair was going on already, with merry piping of music and acrobats leaping and cavorting for the crowd's amusement. Children darted here and there among the thronging adults. Ruffians with sharp faces and sharper eyes sought the gullible for their con games. Ale-soaked laborers, flushed with merriment and the excitement of the occasion, shouted cheers for the king.

Haughty church soldiers, clad in their white tunics and black cloaks, strolled about in small groups, looking offended by much of what they saw. Foreign peddlers called out their wares, hawking them shamelessly. Beggars reached out filthy hands, pleading for alms with tremulous voices until the guards chased them away.

And through all this tumult, the king strolled with members of his court. Clearly enjoying himself at this festival in his honor, the king looked at ease among the commoners. Smiling as his subjects cheered him, he stopped occasionally to speak to men and women alike. Sometimes he threw coins, then laughed as people scurried and fought over them.

Dain smiled as he watched until a sudden prickle of unease crawled along his shoulders. Instantly alert, he looked out across the sea of faces.

"What's amiss?" Sir Terent asked quietly. "I'm learning to pay heed to that look on your face, m'lord. Are Nonkind here?"

Dain blinked at him in surprise. "What makes you think so?"

"That look you have, all wary and tense, like you're listening to something none of the rest of us can hear." Sir Terent frowned. "But then, you being part eld, I guess there be things that you alone hear and know. You've shown us that often enough now."

Dain trusted Sir Terent, but the old habits of caution had been too strongly ingrained in him for him to confide the true extent of his abilities. Instead he shrugged. "No Nonkind. I just . . . Perhaps the crowd is too large for me. Too many people are here."

Sir Terent nodded and said no more, but his eyes searched Dain's with concern as they followed the page up to the assembly of courtiers surrounding the king.

Gavril was not in sight. Nor was Sir Damiend or the fat

man in white robes or several others who had been present
before. Relieved, Dain felt himself relax.

The king stepped inside the roped-off area and walked
up to a long table. On it were displayed a row of swords,
their blades gleaming in the sun. Dain counted forty swords,
some plain, but most ornate with carving and jewels.

The chamberlain, a pudgy man with curled reddish hair
and a self-important expression, stood nearby with a sheet
of parchment in his hand. No names identified the makers
of these various swords, only numbers. It seemed the king
would choose his new blade for its looks and heft alone.

Sir Terent leaned close to Dain's ear. "Damne, but we
forgot Lander's sword," he whispered. "He'll never forgive
us for failing to include his entry."

Dain frowned. Lander's plain sword—the one sent home
in the baggage wagon with Lord Odfrey's body—had never
really been intended for this contest. Lander's true entry,
Tanengard, was now in the hands of Gavril, and it seemed
that it would remain there.

"Lord Roberd, attend me," the king commanded.

The champion joined him with a bow. "How may I assist your majesty?"

But the king was looking around impatiently. His gaze
alighted on Dain and brightened. "You!" he called out, beck-
oning. "Come to me."

Dain hesitated, but the chamberlain gestured impatiently,
and he went forward. Sir Terent followed at his heels, until
the king's protector held him back.

In all his dreams, Dain had never expected to find himself at the king's side, here in front of so many. The courtiers
nudged each other and murmured softly. The pretty maiden
with the golden hair was not here, much to his disappointment. Instead there were older ladies—wearing painted faces
and gowns so embroidered with pearls and jewels that the
skirts were stiff—who stared at him with open appraisal.
Dain felt his face growing hot. He'd never seen women who
looked or acted like this. His keen ears overheard their bold

remarks as they made fun of his borrowed mail or said he was handsome or speculated on what kind of lover he would make. Dain thought them incredibly rude and cruel, and shifted his gaze away.

Rubbing his hands together in excitement, the king glanced first at Lord Roberd, then at Dain. "You two will be my advisers today. Tell me which swords you would pick. Do not touch them, mind! Only I may do that. But tell me the ones you favor." He gestured. "You first, Lord Roberd."

The champion bowed to the king and walked slowly down the row of weapons, the king and Dain following him in silence. "Numbers one, five, seven, twenty, and twenty-two, your majesty."

The king glanced at a hovering clerk. "Are you making note of that?"

"Yes, your majesty."

The ladies sighed over Lord Roberd and applauded him. He glanced at them with a smile and bowed.

Dain frowned a little in bewilderment. This was no way to choose a weapon. They should be allowed to pick them up, heft the balance, flex the blades, examine the workmanship. The king was making a game of this, sport to entertain his courtiers. Dain, who knew how desperately at least one smith in the realm was counting on the king's choice, could only imagine how the other smiths were praying for his favor right now. The king, of course, was either oblivious or simply did not care.

He glanced at Dain. "And now, young man, I would have your choices. Which ones do you fancy?"

"May I not touch them at all, your majesty?"

The attendants looked alarmed by Dain's question. When the king's smile faded, Dain realized that he'd erred.

"No," the king said tersely. "I have given you the rules. Make your choices."

"Aye, your majesty," Dain said hastily.

As he walked down the length of the table, he cast his expert eye on the weapons and took his time while the courtiers made bets as to whether he'd choose the same ones as Lord Roberd.

The champion had chosen swords which were heavily adorned with jewels, but usable as well. Two of the weapons, however, were poorly forged. An untrained eye would not notice, but Dain sensed the stress in the metal at once. He frowned and turned away from them. Reaching the end of the table, he stood a moment in serious thought, and walked back to the head of the table once more.

"Oh, come, come," the chamberlain said in protest. "Do not dawdle all day."

"Leave him be," the king said, looking amused again. He gave Dain a nod of encouragement. "Take all the time you wish, young Dain."

One of the more outlandishly dressed lords sniffed through his long, thin nose and said loudly, "I believe it is an old custom—preform, of course—to let eld folk choose the steel for one's sword. His majesty charms us by reviving these ancient practices."

More laughter and applause followed this sally. Dain looked around, and the onlookers laughed at him.

"Take heart, boy!" shouted a rough voice from the commoner side of the crowd. "You choose what you like!"

The courtiers laughed at that, too. Frowning, Dain returned his concentration to the weapons. If everyone saw him as the rest of the afternoon's entertainment, so be it. He understood, even if they did not, that a king's sword must be finely made and carefully chosen. If he could touch them, he would know in an instant which was the best suited for his majesty. Instead, he sniffed and listened and looked, training all his senses on each of them.

Halfway down the table, he paused and stared very hard at a handsome sword with a black blade carved with rosettes and vines. It was beautiful indeed. Lord Roberd had named it as one of his choices. The craftsmanship looked superb.

"I believe you must like that one," the king remarked

over his shoulder, making Dain start. "Lord Roberd certainly did."

"Aye, your majesty," the champion agreed. "It looks to be a fine weapon."

But something about it seemed wrong to Dain. Beautiful it was, yes, but he found himself disliking it. He could not say why. There was no magic in the steel, none in any of these swords. There were no enspelling runes hidden within the carvings on the black blade. He sensed nothing to alarm him, and yet he drew back from it in sudden rejection.

"No, I do not choose it," he said.

The king's eyebrows shot up, and Lord Roberd grunted with surprise. Dain walked on to the very last sword. It was plain, lacking the ornate carvings that so many of the other weapons featured. But the craftsmanship was dwarf-trained and beautifully presented. He admired the subtle curve of the blade to its tip. The hilt was designed to fit the shape of a man's hand. He bent down to peer at the small bulges beneath the wire wrapping of the hilt that betrayed the balances. They looked to be exactly the right size. The maker had not spent his time fitting jewels into the hilt or carving the blade. Instead, he had worked to make a weapon true and strong, with plenty of give in it so that it would last a lifetime and carry the king through the fiercest battle. Most of all, Dain approved of the metal itself. He bent low and sniffed it, recognizing the slightly blue sheen that marked it as having been forged from High Mountain ore, the best of Nold.

"Thod's bones," Lord Roberd said at last with a half-laugh, "is the lad going to taste it?"

Dain straightened with a flush and faced the king. "I choose number forty," he said.

The king's brows went up a second time. "And no other?"

"No. This is the best of them."

"But it's so ugly!" a woman complained.

"Your majesty!" called out another lady. Dressed in a magnificent gown of green silk, she smiled at the king. "Do not listen to this young ruffian. What does he know of style? 'Tis a sword a hirelance might carry."

"A hirelance could not afford this weapon," Dain retorted, impatient with her ignorance. From the corner of his eye he saw Sir Terent gesturing at him to hold his tongue. Abashed, Dain frowned and dropped his gaze at once.

The king stared at him without expression, and Dain felt the weight of royal silence. Instinctively he took a step back.

A varlet gripped his sleeve from behind and pulled him aside. Some of the onlookers tittered, and Dain's face flamed again. He wanted to crawl into a burrow in the Dark Forest and never come forth. What was he doing here, in this strange land among these folk? He did not understand them at all.

"Very foolish," the varlet murmured in his ear with a savage satisfaction that bewildered Dain even more. "Rebuttals to the royal mistress are unwise, especially in front of his majesty."

Dain shot him an astonished look, and the man met his stare with a strange little smile.

"You are bolder than I shall ever be," the man whispered, and moved away from him.

Humiliated and now ignored, Dain watched the king pick up each blade in turn. With Lord Roberd still at his side, murmuring advice, the king went down the row until he came to the black sword in the center. Then, apparently just to tantalize the crowd, he smiled and walked to the other end of the table. Everyone groaned in good-natured anticipation.

He picked up the last sword, the one chosen by Dain. Hefting it carelessly, he paused and gave it another look. "It does sit well in the hand," he commented.

Some of Dain's embarrassment lessened. Although he might err with his manners, he knew his judgment was sound when it came to swords.

Lord Roberd took the weapon and stepped aside to brandish it with a couple of broad sweeps that made the ladies shriek in mock alarm. The men laughed and applauded. Bowing to them, Lord Roberd handed the sword back to the king, who held it with visible appreciation.

"It's a superb sword," he said, glancing at Dain. Then he looked at the woman whom Dain had offended. She sniffed with disapproval. "Pity it's so plain," the king said with a sigh, and put down number forty.

One by one, he picked up the others. Number thirty-nine, number thirty-eight, number twenty-two, number twenty.

Now he stood looking at the black sword in the center, the handsome one that drew the eye and seemed to stand out more than all the rest. Clearly it had captured the king's favor. When he reached for it, the crowd applauded and his mistress smiled.

Dain felt a sudden presence in the crowd, a shifting evil, elusive yet strong. It wasn't Nonkind, yet he sensed a taint of that on this individual. And in that moment, his mind touched the thoughts of whoever lurked out there in the throng.

Yelling in alarm, Dain leaped for the king. "It's poisoned!" he shouted. "Don't touch it!"

Looking startled, the king turned halfway in his direction. Lord Roberd lifted his hand, but by then Dain had tackled the king and knocked him to the ground. Together they rolled into one of the table legs. Swords flew all directions.

Clamped in Dain's arms, the king struggled and cursed him hoarsely. Then rough hands seized Dain and dragged him off. The king's protector drew his sword to run Dain through, but the king spoke sharply. Instead, the guards seized Dain, lifting him onto his feet and ramming the butt end of a pike into his midsection.

It drove all the air from his lungs. Dain doubled over in agony. Another blow across his shoulders sent him to his knees, and everyone seemed to be shouting at him.

"He attacked the king! Arrest him at once!" the chamberlain shouted.

Another man, one who looked important, stepped forward. "Letting an unknown, nameless stranger—*and* an eld to boot—into his majesty's company was folly, sheer folly!"

The noise spread. "He attacked the king. Kill him!"

Dain looked up in fear. "I did no such—"

A guard knocked him flat. "Silence!"

In sick disbelief, Dain lay sprawled on the grass while they milled and trampled around him. Now brushed off and on his feet, the king looked furious. Dain knew he was finished. No one would even listen to him. They believed what they wanted to.

"Clean this up!" someone ordered. "You there. Pick up these weapons. And you, bring the king's chosen sword to him."

"Your majesty, come away."

Solicitously they swarmed around King Verence. Dain tried to sit up, but the guard's foot stamped him flat again.

Miserable, he wondered where Sir Terent was. Had they arrested the knight as well? How could this go so wrong so quickly?

The overturned table was righted, and two of the squires began to pick up the swords and lay them on its surface.

Fresh alarm filled Dain. He tried to get the squires' attention. "Don't touch the black sword!" he shouted.

Cursing, the guard kicked him in the face.

The world went black and all the noises in it swirled together. Awash with pain and skidding on the edge of unconsciousness, Dain heard a scream.

His senses returned. Somehow he managed to open his eyes.

People were shouting and running backward, fleeing from the screaming squire, who stood frozen and contorted, his back arched, his hands curved into claws.

He screamed again and clutched his hand as the black sword fell from his fingers. Then he began to convulse, falling on the ground while he made the most terrible cries of pain. No one rushed to his aid. They stood around him, watching openmouthed while he died.

Sulein came pushing his way through the crowd until the guards stopped him. "Please!" he cried in his accented voice. "I am a physician, with much expertise in poisons. Let me examine him."

But the guards pushed him back and would not let him approach.

The commander of the palace guards, looking very stern indeed, rushed up. He bowed to the king, who was white-faced and clearly shaken.

"Your majesty must get away from here at once."

Ignoring his advice, the king instead gestured at the dead squire's cohort, who crouched in fear, staring at his dead comrade. "No one must touch the black sword with his bare hand," the king commanded.

"We will see that it's safely removed, sire," the second squire promised.

"Who made it?" the king roared. "Who brought it here?"

Dain's guard stamped yet again on his back. "This knave, of course, your majesty. It's clear he was part of the plot."

The king turned around and stared at Dain, who lay there helpless on the ground. Furious at the guard's accusation, Dain wanted to protest but dared not speak. His fists clutched the turf in anger at such injustice, and his eyes found the king's with mute appeal.

Frowning, the king hesitated a moment, then approached Dain despite the protests of his court.

"Stay back from him, majesty!"

"He has the evil eye!"

"He'll put a spell on your majesty!"

Ignoring them, the king gestured at Dain. "Let him up."

More protests broke out, but the guards grabbed Dain's arms and lifted him to his feet. The world swirled around him, and Dain felt his knees buckle. They held him upright, giving him a rough shake that made him bite back a grunt of pain.

The king came closer and stared deep into Dain's eyes. "You knew," he said quietly. "How?"

Dain struggled to keep his wits about him. There was nothing he could say but the truth. "I am eld," he replied simply. "Someone in the crowd wanted to harm you. When I learned his thoughts, I tried to warn you."

"Majesty, come away from that vile creature."

The king nodded to Dain. "We will talk more of this later. Let him go!" he commanded. His voice rang out, and the hubbub fell silent. "This young man saved my life. He is to be praised, not punished. Release him at once!"

The guards dropped their hold on Dain. He swayed and nearly fell before he managed to brace his knees.

The king flashed a furious look around at everyone. "He is to be given full hospitality of the palace. Tonight, he will feast beside me in a place of honor. Commander!"

"Sire?"

"Seek those behind this plot. I will have the name of the black sword's maker. I will have the man's head."

Saluting, the commander took the parchment enumerating the swords from the chamberlain and hurried off.

The king glared at his chamberlain, who looked both white and faint with alarm. "See to this young man's needs," the king said. "Admit his companions to him, and make all welcome. This is my command."

The man bowed low. "Yes, your majesty."

In an instant, everything changed for Dain. Instead of being beaten and reviled, he was surrounded by varlets and attendants. Enraged by their fawning hypocrisy, Dain shrugged off their helping hands.

Sir Terent, now permitted to join him, pushed some of them aside. "Get away from him!" he bellowed. "M'lord, are you much hurt?"

"I'll live," Dain said grimly.

"They held me, m'lord. I could not reach you."

His distress and alarm somehow steadied Dain. With a lopsided smile, for his face was aching, Dain reached out to his protector. "And what would you have done if you had?

Attacked the palace guards? Run the king's protector through?"

"Morde, I thought the man would kill you before my eyes," Sir Terent said in a shaken voice. But he seemed calmer now. Putting a reassuring arm around Dain's shoulders, he said, "Easy then. Let's get you away from here."

The king's entourage was already streaming away while the crowd was broken up. Guards pushed through the throng, but there was no chance of their finding the agent they sought. Dain knew he was already far away.

He started to tell Sir Terent so when suddenly the world swirled around him without warning.

"Dain?" Sir Terent said in alarm. "In Thod's name, stay with—"

His voice faded. Dain struggled against the darkness and opened his eyes as wide as he could. The last thing he saw was the face of the dead boy, now being covered with a cloth by some of the servants. Then all went blank for Dain, and he knew nothing more.

14

CAUGHT BETWEEN THE two attacking hurlhounds, Alexeika screamed and swung her stick at the closest one. As she did so, all her fear and anger suddenly coalesced inside her and channeled forth. The stick burst into flames, scorching her hands and burning the hurlhound she struck with it.

Yelping, it veered off.

Unable to hold her fiery weapon, Alexeika threw it at the

second monster and missed. Crying out, she ducked just as the hurlhound's snapping jaws closed on thin air.

"*Regsnik!*" commanded a gruff voice.

The hurlhounds snarled but retreated at once.

Breathing hard, her hair hanging in her face, Alexeika lay on the ground, unable to believe she was still alive. Her body was tense and trembling, but slowly she realized the hurlhounds were not going to tear her apart.

Another creature rumbled and snorted behind her. When Alexeika managed to pull herself up and look, she saw a rider on a darsteed at the edge of the clearing.

Tall and long-legged, with cloven hooves and a hide of black scales that glittered in the sun, the darsteed's red eyes glared balefully at her while smoke rumbled from its nostrils.

Its rider looked to be a man, but Alexeika was not sure. Clad in blood-red mail and a breastplate embossed with arcane symbols that hurt her eyes, he stared at her through his helmet visor. Much of him remained in the shade, and she could see no glimpse of his eyes.

He was either Nonkind or a Believer. Both were supremely dangerous. Her mouth went dry, and her heart pounded so hard she felt dizzy. The two hurlhounds still crouched on either side of her, menace in their eyes as they waited for permission to attack.

Shuddering, she forced herself to stand up. She faced the rider with all the courage she could.

"Let me go," she said.

He made no response. Her fear flared anew, for if he was Nonkind that meant he was nothing but an animated corpse, soulless and controlled by a Believer somewhere nearby. Alexeika had grown up on tales of entire battlefields of dead men rising forth to serve the Believers of Gant. Such gruesome creatures could fight endlessly against mortals. They could not be killed by normal means. They did not tire. They would not flee in disarray.

Yet this rider had spoken a command to the hurlhounds. Surely he was not one of the dead if he could do that.

"Let me go," she said again, more loudly this time.

The rider lifted his gloved hand and pointed at her. "*Sorcerelle,*" he said. His voice sounded like a file rasping on bone. "You are *sorcerelle* of much power."

"I am not."

He chuckled, the sound muffled and dreadful inside his helmet. "You lie, Chalice hunter. Power has been wielded. It is how I found you."

Uzfan's warning ran through her mind. He was right; her few erratic powers had drawn the Nonkind to her. Alexeika frowned. How she wished Uzfan was here to cast a spell to drive this Believer away.

"Chalice hunter, come," the Believer said. "You are mine now. Come."

Alexeika frowned in refusal. Were the gods this unkind, to let her escape the Grethori only to fall into worse hands? "No!" she said. "I will not be a Gantese slave!"

Smoke blew out through the Believer's visor. He pointed. "Obey!"

"I will not."

"Then you die."

The hurlhounds growled, edging closer. The threat in their glowing eyes and slavering jaws vanquished her defiance. She did not want to die. Not like this.

If she tried to run the hurlhounds would bring her down. Without her pearl-handled daggers she lacked even the slimmest of fighting chances. There was nothing she could do but obey her new master.

Trying to hide her despair, she crossed the clearing and went to the Believer. The hot stink of the darsteed's fetid breath sickened her. Without warning it lunged at her with a snap of its poisonous fangs.

Screaming, Alexeika dodged, and its jaws missed her by a scant inch. Shouting angrily, the Believer pulled back on the reins and cursed his mount.

In that moment, an arrow sang forth from the woods and thudded into the Believer's breastplate. It bounced off, but the Believer stood up in his stirrups with a shout of alarm. He drew his sword, and Alexeika jumped into the undergrowth, out of the way, as the darsteed galloped forward.

From the same direction as the arrow came a rough mountain pony, bursting from the thicket with Holoc on its back.

The chieftain, gaunt-eyed and fierce, rode full-tilt, with Severgard in his hands instead of his usual pair of scimitars. The magicked blade of Prince Volvn's weapon glowed white in the presence of the Believer and his Nonkind beasts. Shouting Grethori curses, his long, skull-adorned braids bouncing on his shoulders, Holoc charged the Believer fearlessly.

Black sword met white with a tremendous crash that echoed through the forest and sent a flock of keebacks flying out of the trees. The Believer's sword shattered under the first blow, and he reeled back in his saddle.

Snarling, the hurlhounds sprang toward Holoc, parting to attack him from separate sides. Knowing he could not prevail against them all, Alexeika picked up a stout branch off the ground and jumped from the bushes.

She hurled the stick with all her might, and her aim was true. It bounced off the skull of one of the hurlhounds and deflected it from sinking its fangs into Holoc's leg.

He swung Severgard at the other hurlhound, cutting the creature in half. Poisonous black blood spewed while the two halves of the monster writhed on the ground.

Shouting Gantese death curses that popped and flashed in the air, the Believer thrust the jagged end of his broken sword into Holoc's bronzed, bare arm.

Yelling, Holoc twisted in the saddle and swung Severgard around. The glowing white blade sliced through red mail, popping links, and took off the Believer's head.

Still in its helmet, the head went rolling over the ground in a trail of blood and gout, and came to rest at Alexeika's feet.

The remaining hurlhound and darsteed vanished into thin air, leaving only sparks and their evil stench behind.

Silence fell over the clearing, broken only by the sound of Holoc's panting. Alexeika stared at him for a long moment, amazed that he'd rescued her. His brown, savage face—handsome by the standards of his people—stared back at her with a combination of lust and triumph.

Her sense of relief quickly faded, and she realized Vika was right: Holoc would pursue her forever.

Fresh despair filled her. There must be some way to break the spell on him, though appeals and reason, she knew, would not work. Perhaps nothing would.

Holoc kicked his pony forward, coming straight to her, his bloody sword lying across the front of his saddle. Blood streamed down his wounded arm, but he seemed not to notice his injury.

Alexeika told herself to run, to get away, but her feet seemed frozen to the ground. She'd been through too much. Her mind had gone blank, and she knew only weariness and a clawing sense of desperation.

"Mine," Holoc said in triumph. With a gesture of bravado, he threw Severgard between them. Its point struck the ground and lodged there, quivering upright.

A corner of her heart raged at seeing that noble blade dishonored so. Holoc was a savage, too ignorant to fully appreciate the qualities of the weapon he'd stolen. None of the scimitars or daggers in the village had been cared for. A Grethori warrior never cleaned his blade. When the weapon rusted or grew too nicked to use, it was discarded. After all, a true Grethori warrior could always steal another one. But if he ruined Severgard, he would never obtain another sword like it. She supposed he did not care.

Holoc dismounted, then swaggered up to her. His dark eyes burned hot and intense.

"Mine," he grunted again, and reached for her.

With a cry, she whirled away, but he was too quick. Gripping her arms, he slammed her against a tree trunk and pinned her there with his body. He kissed her roughly, murmuring words she did not understand.

She tried to fight him, but she could not break free. His hands were everywhere, his mouth masterful and cruel. She slapped him, then tried to scratch his face, but he only laughed and ripped open the neck of her robe.

She thought of the *sheda*'s prophecy and the spell the old crone had woven over Holoc. Defiance grew inside Alexeika, burning away her terror. She would not submit to this. She would not bear this man's child or live as his slave, a cowed despicable thing to be used as he pleased and then discarded.

His rough hands finished ripping open her robe, exposing her slender body to him. For a moment he only stared at her, then he laughed low in his throat. It was an arrogant, evil, bestial sound that snapped the last of her hesitation.

As he gripped her with his cruel hands, grinding his body against her, Alexeika reached sideways for the hilt of Severgard and just managed to grab it. His mouth was hot on hers, and she bit his lip with all her might. He swore, jerking back his head, and with a shout she pulled the sword from the ground and swung it at Holoc.

At such close range, the blow was clumsy. She hit his back with the midsection of the blade, nearer the hilt than the tip.

Nevertheless, Severgard sliced through his fur jerkin and drew blood.

Spitting blood and cursing, Holoc spun around to evade the sword. Blood was running down his back, but he ignored it.

Alexeika moved quickly away from the tree where she'd been pinned. Her robe hung open, exposing her body, but she made no effort to hide herself. She gripped Severgard's hilt with both hands, brandishing the sword, and prayed to the spirit of her dead father to strengthen her.

Holoc began to laugh. His eyes burned with the madness of the spell.

"To fight is better, my woman-man demon. Fight me like man! It will make the conquering of your woman side much sweeter. Fight me, but still you are mine. The *sheda* has made it so."

Alexeika forced herself to laugh back in defiance, although the sound that issued from her throat was grim and harsh. "Your *sheda* picked the wrong maiden for you."

With all her will she focused on Severgard, mouthing the words of power that she'd once heard Uzfan say over it on her father's behalf. The weapon's blade began to glow white, and she felt power thrumming through its hilt into her hands. With a toss of her head, Alexeika's confidence came back. Uzfan was wrong. She *could* control her powers, after all. She could be trained. She could be a *sorcerelle* if she chose to be.

Holoc's eyes widened a little, and his laughter died. Sanity almost returned to his face.

Alexeika bared her teeth at him. "You forgot my demon side," she said, using his superstitions to taunt him. "Will you force me to recall my dire companions?"

His eyes widened still more. She knew she had made him believe that the hurlhounds were hers to command. Making that claim was blasphemous, but Alexeika felt reckless and wild.

"You have come alone to my forest, Grethori," she said. "You are at my mercy now."

He swayed as he stared at her, and braced his feet wider apart. He had begun to look pale, either from fear or the blood he was losing. He said nothing.

"When the hurlhounds return to feed on your flesh, I will watch and laugh at my enemy," she told him. "The one who dared think I was his to command."

"Demon," he whispered.

Alexeika smiled, thinking that if she pretended to cast a spell, he would panic and flee from her.

She reached toward the sky as if grasping something.

"Now begins *my* spell, Holoc. See if you like it better than the *sheda*'s."

Her confidence had taken her too far. He stepped back, muttering something hoarsely, but she'd forgotten that no Grethori ever fled in fear. When cornered, he would fight to the death if necessary.

Holoc bent his head so that his braids and skulls clacked together, and drew his dagger. Quicker than thought, he sprang at her.

Caught off guard, she pivoted instinctively on her back foot and swung Severgard up and toward him.

Holoc's charge ran him onto the sword. Blood spewed, and his head tipped back in a silent scream. His eyes opened wide, but he was dead already. When she drew out her sword, his body crumpled at her feet.

Alexeika uttered a soundless little cry and staggered back. Turning away, she pressed her hand against her mouth.

That's when all of it, the long ordeal that had started weeks ago with Draysinko's betrayal of their camp to the Grethori raiders, overwhelmed her. Perhaps she went mad for a little while, there in the forest. She walked around and around brandishing Severgard at the two corpses and weeping.

But at long last, when the shadows of afternoon began to slant through the trees, she stopped and lifted her face to the sky. Sinking to her knees, she prayed her gratitude for the mercy of the gods. Then she gathered up dagger and sword and stripped Holoc's clothing from his body.

Stripping off her own clothing, she pressed Severgard's blade to her bite. The steel flashed white, and the heat as its power cauterized her wound made her cry out. Gritting her teeth, she breathed hard and fast for a moment while her eyes streamed with tears of pain, but at least the hurlhound venom was gone from her.

When she felt strong enough to move, she lowered herself into the clean cold waters of the fjord and bathed until her body felt nearly frozen, but renewed. After she threw the torn Grethori robe into the bushes, she knelt at the water's edge to scrub and pound the blood from Holoc's leggings and jerkin.

Leaving the clothing draped on tree limbs to dry, she walked naked up the bank and stripped off the Believer's mail. When she finished cleaning it by dragging it through water and sand, she laid it on the ground to dry while she scrubbed and polished Severgard.

She felt conscious of weariness and hunger, but her mind remained clear and calm. As she worked, she sang one of her father's old battle songs, softly.

She was no longer the Alexeika she had been. Reborn, she felt a hundred years old, instead of eighteen. Her father used to talk of a warrior's first battle—how it was a trial by fire, how it separated those who would survive from those who would perish. Now she knew how to survive. She thought of the different life she could have lived had fate been kinder to her family. She would have worn beautiful gowns and sat decoratively at court. Or perhaps by now she would have been married, with expectations of children and a long productive life spent managing her husband's household. But such a life would never be hers. Her path was taking her along a far different journey.

By nightfall, Alexeika wore the leggings and hauberk of a man. Although she did not cut her hair, she braided it tightly up against her neck in warrior fashion. She owned two daggers again, Holoc's and the Believer's. The Believer's broken sword she had flung as far as possible into the fjord, along with his head. The bodies she did not bury. Instead, she covered them with branches and leaves that she set afire with the strike box found in Holoc's pouch. If the blaze brought Grethori or Nonkind to this place, she did not care. She was leaving.

While the flames caught and shot up, Alexeika tightened the girth on Holoc's pony and mounted. The animal snorted and fought its unfamiliar rider, but she mastered it with iron determination and sent it trotting forth into the forest.

The stars in the evening sky gave her the bearings she needed. She turned her pony's head southeast. There were still pockets of resistance among the towns of Nether, and groups of rebels that she could join. She had learned hard lessons up here in the mountains, and from now on her purpose was clear: To her last breath, she would fight to overthrow King Muncel. If she could regather the scattered rebel forces, she would. If they would listen to her and follow her, then she would lead them. If they would not, she would ride alone. But she would fight as long as it took, and never again would she be soft or defer to the stupidity of others when her judgment was right.

At Savroix, Gavril emerged from his bath and glanced at the window, where eventide shadows were gathering. His servants moved unobtrusively about his luxurious chambers, lighting candles and clearing away the remains of his light meal.

He was supposed to fast until dawn tomorrow, but Gavril believed the rituals of his investiture to be unimportant. In his mind, he had been a man *and* a knight since the Nonkind attack on the banks of the Charva, when he'd first held Tanengard in his hands and known its power.

The sword lay atop his table, its blade oiled and gleaming in the candlelight. Gavril frowned at it. Today in the combat against Dain, he had felt the sword twist in his hand in order to miss. The sword had betrayed its master to spare Dain. Instead, it had been Gavril who suffered humiliating defeat.

He should hate the sword, but one did not hate an object of beauty and perfection. The strong power within this blade was not yet tamed. Excited, Gavril knew he must somehow find a way to master Tanengard and make it truly his. He would learn how to make it serve him and him alone.

A soft tapping on the door interrupted his thoughts. Sir Damiend, wearing mail and his church surcoat, peered inside. "Is your highness ready? The cardinal has arrived to escort you."

Gavril sighed and tightened the belt of his robes. He wore long, soft garments of undyed wool to symbolize his purity. His blond hair, still wet from his bath, was sleeked back from his brow. As required, his feet remained bare.

"Yes, I am ready," he said, and left his chambers.

Cardinal Noncire waited for him in the corridor, along with a guard of men in church surcoats. Their faces looked grim in the torchlight, and Gavril raised his brows at the cardinal. He had no need to ask why they were present. The king's brush with death this afternoon had unsettled the whole palace.

"Let us go," he announced.

Noncire bowed as deeply as his girth would permit. He gestured toward the stairs, and they went down the winding stone staircase to the ground floor. There, in silence, waited a group of knights in brightly polished armor. Representatives of the various noble houses in current favor with the king, they carried shields draped with pennants of various colors and crests.

Their spokesman was Lord Roberd. Grave of mien, he stepped forward in his splendid black armor. "Who is delivered to us?" he asked, adhering to the ritual.

Sir Damiend responded, "We bring one who would be knighted."

"What is his heart?" Lord Roberd asked.

"It is pure," Sir Damiend responded.

"What is his mind?"

"It is prepared."

"What is his spirit?"

"It is willing."

Gavril listened to the ritual and sighed with boredom. Beside him, Cardinal Noncire placed a hand on his shoulder and gave it a reassuring squeeze. Astonished that the cardinal could believe him to be nervous, Gavril glanced at the cardinal's bland, expressionless face and frowned.

Lord Roberd raised his hand. "Let the suppliant come forth."

The church soldiers parted, and Gavril walked forward alone until he stood among the secular knights. His church escort remained behind, except for Noncire, who led them through a short passageway down into the lower regions beneath the palace.

These ways were ancient, with walls made of rough, crudely cut stones. Rusting iron sconces supported torches made of twisted straw soaked in pitch. Their pungent smell made Gavril recall Thirst Hold and its antiquated amenities. In the distance he could hear water dripping. Down the worn, spiraling steps they went, double-file. The air smelled musty, damp, and cold as they descended. Gavril's bare feet grew chilled.

At the bottom of the steps, they followed another passageway that opened into a vaulted chamber supported by rough-hewn timbers. Candles burned around a stone altar with a kneeling bench. From the shadowy ceiling overhead a cable supported an enormous suspended Circle. Burning candles were fitted into small metal rings affixed to its surface. The Circle appeared to be on fire as it hung there. Despite himself, Gavril was stirred by the sight, and some of his impatience faded. He realized that perhaps the ceremony was not something to be scoffed at after all, that it was grounded in ancient customs, shrouded in mystery, and centered in faith.

When Lord Roberd administered the first series of oaths, Gavril knelt and replied sincerely to each of them. Afterward, Lord Roberd pressed his hands against Gavril's shoulders in a sort of benediction.

"May you be strong," he murmured, and left.

The next knight stepped before Gavril and repeated the action. "May you be valiant."

The third knight approached him. "May you be victorious."

On and on they came, each of them touching his shoulders and pronouncing a blessing for his knighthood. Gavril knelt there on the hard stone, his golden head bowed, until the knights were finished. They bowed to him in silence and returned the way they'd come, up the winding staircase into the shadows.

Only Noncire remained, a broad, somber figure whose white robes seemed to glow in the flickering candlelight. "I shall return for you at dawn," the cardinal said. "The knights will stand vigil at the door at the top of the stairs."

Gavril nodded with impatience. He knew all this. There was no need for his mentor to repeat it.

Yet Noncire lingered, as though reluctant to leave. Gavril recognized the signs by how the cardinal drummed his thick fingers on his yellow sash of office, how he narrowed his dark, beady eyes, how he pursed his fleshy lips. He wanted to talk, but he stood there in silence.

In times past, Gavril had been eager for such private talks with his mentor. He'd admired Noncire's brilliant, intricate mind. There had been so much to learn from the cardinal, who'd showed him how to manipulate men. Now, however, Gavril felt there was little left for the cardinal to teach him. He was eager to pursue his own dreams, and they did not all coincide with Noncire's plans for him.

As the silence drew out, Gavril lifted his vivid blue eyes to the cardinal's dark ones. "My message to you was sent this morning," he said quietly while above him the candles hissed and flickered.

Noncire bowed. "I received it, your highness."

"And your answer?"

The cardinal spread out his plump hands. "Must there be an answer today, your highness? Let this ritual be finished first, and then you and I will have a long—a very long— talk indeed about the lady."

Gavril's heart closed against this man. He swung his gaze away, aware of his sense of urgency.

"There is a suitable time and place for everything," Noncire droned on. "Surely your highness understands that—"

"Yes, of course I do," Gavril snapped with fresh impatience. He had written to the cardinal asking for advice on how to escape his obligation to marry Lady Pheresa. His cousin was comely enough in face and figure, but she did not interest him. Full of plans and ambitions after his year's exile to Thirst, Gavril had many things he wanted to do. But settling down into a betrothal, with all its attendant occasions and ceremonies, was not one of them.

"The lady seems to be an excellent choice," the cardinal was saying. "Her opinions can be molded, and perhaps if your highness will—"

"Thank you," Gavril said furiously. "You make your answer quite clear."

Noncire smiled. "Be not displeased. I will find a way to satisfy all concerned."

"No doubt." Gavril understood all that Noncire left unsaid. The king favored the match. For Noncire to agree with his majesty meant a bargain had been struck between them. The very thought of it made Gavril grit his teeth. He was no longer a child. Vowing that he would not be manipulated by either of these men, he decided then and there that he absolutely would not have Pheresa. She was too intelligent, too quiet. There was something willful about the curve of her mouth. As a child, he had despised her; he saw no reason to revise his opinion now. But he refused to argue about it further with Noncire.

"There's something else I want to discuss," he announced.

"Yes, your highness?"

Gavril drew in a deep breath, gathering himself. This must be asked delicately. He did not want to alarm the cardinal enough to have himself put under scrutiny.

"I have been thinking much, since I escaped death so narrowly."

"Ah, the attack of the Nonkind in Thirst Hold." Noncire pursed his thick lips and nodded. "I have been expecting this conversation. Yes?"

"In the uplands, these creatures attack boldly. They roam

and raid at will, with increasing menace. No doubt it is due in part to how weakly Nether is ruled."

"It is true that Nether was once diligent about keeping the creatures at bay," the cardinal agreed. "We hear rumors that they have forged an alliance with Gant. The king, of course, believes this not, since he and King Muncel are presently working out the details of a new treaty."

Gavril shrugged off this political news. "The point I am making is that the danger of Nonkind attacks grows worse."

"Yes, they *seem* to be. Your highness is naturally distraught over two recent narrow escapes. However, it is our understanding here at court that the uplanders tend to exaggerate the dangers in an effort to maintain the king's support."

Anger swept Gavril, and he stared at the cardinal in surprise. Never before had he lost his temper with his old tutor, but the man's remark was as patronizing as it was stupid. "You forget, lord cardinal, that I have spent a year among these uplanders. I have seen the dangers close-hand. They are *not* exaggerated."

The cardinal bowed, clearly unconvinced. "From time to time, there are increased outbreaks of trouble. They will cease."

"What happens if my father does not forge a treaty with Nether?" Gavril asked, unwilling to argue with a stupid viewpoint.

The cardinal smiled. "Imagine the tossing of a stone into a pond of water. The ripples spread out in numerous rings. That is—"

"I did not ask for a lesson!" Gavril broke in. "Can you not supply a simple answer?"

The cardinal raised his brows, but did not look provoked. "Politics are never simple," he said in his soft voice. "Your highness has perhaps forgotten that part of his education."

The rebuke was delivered in a gentle tone, but there was steely disapproval running beneath the words.

Infuriated, Gavril replied in a voice equally soft, "I have forgotten nothing, lord cardinal."

They stared at each other, young man and old, both with formidable minds and wills of iron.

"Was the attack on my father this afternoon an attempt to prevent the treaty with Nether?" Gavril asked.

Noncire blinked, but a look of respect entered his dark eyes. "I have not discussed the incident with his majesty. In my opinion, it was."

Gavril nodded to himself. "Then he will sign the treaty with haste, simply to defy his enemies."

"Perhaps," the cardinal said in a neutral tone. "Some of its conditions do not please his majesty."

Gavril had no interest in the conditions of the treaty. "We face increasing danger from Gant and its darkness. Without a strong ally in Nether, our uplands are in jeopardy. Having been attacked personally twice by Nonkind in less than two months, I want"—he paused and drew a deep breath to steady his voice—"I want to learn the ancient arts of the priest-hood."

Noncire's eyes widened in shock.

"For my own protection," Gavril said hastily. "As well as for the good of the realm. As a priest-king, one day I will have to govern a realm less settled, less secure than it is now. The future is clear to me: My rule is not likely to be as peaceful as my father's."

Noncire said nothing, but simply blinked at Gavril, as though seeing him in a new light. At long last he spoke, and his voice was as smooth as thick cream. "Your highness must allay his fears for the future. Recent events have no doubt proven unsettling, but the realm is hardly in jeopardy. Becoming a priest-king is, perhaps, too extreme an action for our reformed beliefs."

There it was, the barbed criticism concealed like a thorn amidst the cardinal's flowery words. Gavril frowned. "You know my piety runs deep."

Noncire bowed. "I pride myself on that accomplishment."

"I will believe in Tomias forever," Gavril said. "But the ability to sense what elements of darkness lie beyond our borders is surely useful."

"Oh, indeed, it does appear so." Noncire studied Gavril so closely, the prince felt his cheeks grow hot. He ducked his gaze and frowned at the pattern of floor stones. "But the true proof of our faith," Noncire went on, "is if we—unlike those of lesser religions—can withstand the demons without using magic."

Gavril's frown deepened into a scowl. He thought with secret shame of the night he'd been attacked by the shapeshifter. He'd held up his Circle and tried to repudiate the creature. Although his father was strong, he had not prevailed against the monster. Even now, Gavril could feel its talons rip through his leg, bringing an agony so terrible the memory still made him sweat.

Noncire's hand clamped on his shoulder. Gavril jumped, his heart pounding as his memories scattered.

"Fear not the past, your highness," Noncire said in a reassuring voice. "Your future holds only brightness."

Intensely angry, Gavril ducked away from his hand. "I am *not* afraid," he said in a low voice. "I want to increase my knowledge. I want to be—"

"Yes, a worthy ambition," the cardinal agreed a shade too heartily. "Knowledge can be a useful weapon, providing it is the right kind of knowledge. As for this desire to become a priest-king, perhaps your highness should not rush into a decision. 'Tis a pious aim, but you must consider the line of succession, which lacks strength at the moment. I think you would serve Mandria better by marrying Lady Pheresa and siring a progeny of—"

"Her again!" Gavril broke in, rejecting this advice. "Have I a choice in this or is she to be forced on me?"

Noncire bowed. "Merely a suggestion, your highness. If she does not fill your eyes, then there are many other equally suitable maidens for—"

"And what of me? What of *my* plans and vision for Mandria?" Gavril interrupted.

"I am sure your highness has many wonderful objectives—"

"Oh, don't talk to me that way. You sound like Lord Minvere fawning over the king's new shoes."

Fresh silence fell over the chamber. The cardinal's face had grown stony; his black eyes were cold.

Gavril didn't care if he'd offended the man. Noncire had certainly offended *him*. How dare he refuse a reasonable request so brusquely, without even considering it? Were an ordinary subject to ask to learn the ancient ways, yes, that could be interpreted as backsliding. But Gavril was *not* ordinary. He had studied religion with Noncire himself. His mind and heart were pure. He could not be corrupted by old texts and teachings. All he wanted was enough knowledge to harness and master the power within Tanengard, to make the sword serve him and him alone.

When he was younger, he would have confided everything in the cardinal and asked for his help. But Gavril knew now that Noncire would simply quote the mindless rules of the church and insist that Tanengard be destroyed. He would not consider how its powers could be used for the good of the realm.

Still, the cardinal's refusal of Gavril's request was not entirely unexpected. Gavril was disappointed, but he had another plan in place.

"Forgive my discourtesy," the prince said, breaking the silence at last. "This has been a momentous day. I am not quite myself."

"Of course," Noncire replied, accepting the apology.

Gavril seethed at having had to say it, but he knew he could not get rid of the cardinal otherwise.

"Shall I be seated and keep your highness company?" Noncire asked. He gestured at a nearby stool. "I am prepared to stay as long as I am needed."

Exasperation filled Gavril. Had the cardinal permitted him

access to the ancient teachings, there would have been a wealth of questions to ask. They could have talked long into the night. But since the cardinal refused his cooperation, Gavril wanted him to leave at once.

"I would prefer to be alone now."

Noncire looked surprised. His small eyes dug deep into Gavril, but the prince had been taught by this man how to keep his face impassive.

He let the silence stretch out a moment, then he said, "I intend to pray and think. Tomorrow, when I emerge from this chamber, I shall find a different world before me. My responsibilities will be larger. I will no longer be a child. I have much to consider."

The cardinal's gaze flickered away. He bowed, wheezing a little as he did so. "Well said. Your highness is wise to reflect on these matters. It speaks highly of the development of your mind and character that you have determined this need on your own."

"I have grown a great deal this past year," Gavril said softly. "I am no longer the boy you sent away."

Noncire's rare smile appeared, and his dark eyes softened. "Ah, indeed. You were an apt pupil. I hope henceforth we may discuss strategy and statecraft on an entirely new level."

"We shall," Gavril promised him. Inside, he thought harshly, *If you do not stay my close ally, old man, you will be left behind.*

Noncire bowed to him. "May I leave you now?"

"Go," Gavril said, already turning away. Folding his hands, he bowed his head as though in prayer, listening while the cardinal made his slow, ponderous way up the steps.

When the door at the top creaked open, then closed, Gavril looked up and rose to his feet.

He knew he would not be disturbed until dawn. The knights would guard that door upstairs with their lives. They would permit no one in.

But there was another way out, a small servants' door

that led into the dusty back passages. As a boy, Gavril used to explore them and knew them all.

Now, tapping his way along the rear wall of the chamber, Gavril found the door he sought. It was hidden behind years of grime and cobwebs. Clearly it was long unused. As he pried it open, the hinges creaked. Gavril winced, but no one came in to check on him.

On the other side of the door lay darkness, and a dank, musty smell.

Swiftly he took off his pale robes, then folded them carefully so that they would not get dirty. He was supposed to be naked beneath them, but he'd packed clothing into a large pouch that he'd slung by a cord over his shoulder. Beneath the loose robes, it had not shown at all.

From the pouch, he extracted leggings, thin leather shoes, and a plain tunic, along with a belt and his jeweled dagger. He dressed swiftly, then eased his way into the secret passageway. Three steps inside the door, he found a torch in a wall sconce.

Gavril carried it back into the chamber and lit it, then reentered the passageway with the ruddy torchlight flaring before him. He left the door open to allow the light from the candles to spill into the dark passageway as well.

Not for a moment did he hesitate. Noncire had been given first chance to serve his prince, and had not unexpectedly refused. Consequently, Gavril would now go forth to meet a man of fewer holy scruples, a man who would teach him the forbidden rites of the old ways. In his plain clothing, Gavril would be an anonymous seeker of knowledge. No one would know his identity or importance. Once he escaped the palace, he would blend into the crowds still celebrating the festival. No spies or guards or protectors would follow him.

Gavril drew in a sharp breath of excitement, feeling the exhilaration of freedom. Tonight was going to change the course of his life. The next time he met that pagan Dain, Gavril vowed, he'd have magic fully on his side. There would

be no more public defeats, no more humiliations at the hands
of one unworthy to even lick his boots. He would be Tanengard's master, and as such, invincible.

15

THE CEILING OF the palace was painted with a mural de-
picting the parting of celestial clouds to let the radiance of
the gods shine down on some long-ago king. Craning his
neck back even more, Dain let his mouth fall open as he
drank in the scene.

"Damne, will you pay attention?" Sir Terent snapped in
exasperation.

Recalled to the here and now, Dain shut his mouth and
shot an embarrassed look at his protector. "Sorry," he muttered.

The knight protector had been scrubbed and combed ruthlessly. His big craggy face was bright red from nervousness
as he glared at Dain. "There isn't much time to get this right.
Stop gawking at all the pretties around you, *m'lord,* and pay
attention."

Dain sighed. Since saving the king's life this afternoon,
he had been at the center of a whirlwind of activity and attention. Palace minions had whisked him and his companions away, installing them in a fine suite of rooms. Their
meager belongings had been fetched from the inn, and Dain
was forced to bathe, endure having his hair trimmed, and
dressed in his best clothes. He smoothed his hand down the
front of his doublet of green silk, aware that he was growing again and that the sleeves were almost too short. Even

his new boots, given to him less than a month ago by Lord Odfrey, pinched now in the toes.

Thinking of Lord Odfrey brought a frown to his face. He knew how much the chevard had looked forward to this day when Dain would be taken before the king. The new clothes had been a gift reserved for this most special of occasions, but the chevard would never see Dain wear them. He would never see Dain here in the palace, about to walk into the king's audience hall.

Dain's throat choked up. It was all wondrous here, but somehow none of it seemed as exciting as it would have been had Lord Odfrey still been alive. As he stood on the soft, intricately knotted wool carpets, surrounded by priceless objects, costly furniture, and bowing Mandrians, Dain could not help but think of himself less than a year past, when he was just a starving, vagrant, homeless eld roaming the Dark Forest, reviled by any Mandrian whose path he crossed.

Any Mandrian save Lord Odfrey. From the first, the chevard had shown him tolerance and kindness.

"*Dain*," Sir Terent said loudly.

Blinking, Dain roused himself and realized he hadn't heard a word the protector said.

Sir Terent threw up his hands and scowled at Sir Polquin, who was pacing back and forth. "See what you can do with him. He doesn't even hear me."

"Hear what?" Dain asked.

Shaking his head, Sir Terent walked to the other side of the room. They had been left in this fine chamber while they waited for their audience. Dain did not understand why Sir Terent was so nervous. *He* didn't have to walk through a hall filled with staring Mandrian nobles.

A tap on the door brought the three of them to alertness, but it was only Thum who entered, grinning from ear to ear. Sulein followed him. For this grand occasion the physician was attired in robes of dark green cloth edged with monkey fur. He wore a conical cap of the same color, and his beard had been combed into small, oiled plaits. Unusual rings of heavy gold flashed on his long fingers, and tiny bells jingled on the toes of his shoes. He looked, and smelled, most exotic and foreign.

Thum wore his best doublet of rust-colored silk with a matching brimless cap perched jauntily atop his red hair. His green eyes were ablaze with excitement. "Good!" he said. "I feared we'd get here too late. We took a wrong turn somewhere and got lost. This palace is monstrous large."

"You've missed nothing but waiting," Dain said. "I'm famished. I wish there would be an end to these ceremonies so we could just sit down to a trencher."

Sir Polquin snorted. "Time you learned the responsibilities of title and power, m'lord. 'Tis the servants who eat first, not the lords."

"And the king last of all," Sulein said.

Certain they were making a jest, Dain frowned at them.

"Sulein," Sir Terent said, "mayhap you can get him to learn his oath. He's used to taking lessons from you."

Sulein's dark eyes gleamed. He stared at Dain as though he were a delectable morsel. "The oath of fealty? Of course, of course. Now, my young lord, do you understand tonight's occasion?"

"Aye, I do," Dain said impatiently. He wished they would stop making such a fuss. "An official explained everything to me. I am to walk up to the king and bow to him. He will make the proclamation of my legal adoption, and I shall become Chevard of Thirst. Then we'll eat."

Thum laughed, but Sulein shook his head with a little tsking noise and glanced at Sir Terent. "I see the problem."

Dain's brows knotted together. "What problem? It is a simple business."

"That, yes," Sulein explained. "But there is *your* part, young Dain."

"My part? What must I do?"

"You have to give the king your oath of fealty," Sir Terent said in exasperation. "That's what I've been trying to tell you. He will expect it, and if you just walk away, it will be a grievous insult to his majesty."

Dain blinked, understanding at last. "Oh."

"Yes, 'oh,'" Sulein said. "Now, do you understand what giving of your fealty means?" His gaze bored into Dain. He was no longer smiling. He looked very serious indeed, as though he was trying to inject another meaning into his words. "You pledge your loyalty and your service to King Verence. You become *his man,* and all that you have and own are given toward his support. If he declares war, then you must join his army with your knights. If he levies taxes, then you must pay them. The charter with Thirst stipulates that the hold and its knights are to guard the northeast boundary between Mandria and Nold. That is your primary service to the king, and in exchange his majesty supplies Thirst with additional forces as needed."

Dain thought of the papers in Lord Odfrey's document pouch that he'd struggled to read and understand. According to them, Thirst was more an ally than the possession Sulein described. Yet he recalled how frequently Lord Odfrey had sent reports and dispatches to the king on all kinds of matters, as though his duties were sometimes more that of a clerk than a warrior.

"I understand about guarding the border," Dain said.

"The oath you must make is binding," Sulein said, and the warning in his tone was now unmistakable. He stared very hard at Dain. "You must understand all to which you agree. You will be lord over many men, men of lesser rank than you, but when you give the oath of fealty you will be servant to the King of Mandria."

Dain stared back as Sulein's meaning soaked into his brain. The physician remained convinced that Dain was the rightful king of Nether. What Sulein was trying to tell him was that one king should never make an oath of fealty to another. But Dain was not willing to give up the title of chevard, so soon to be awarded, for the uncertain kingship of a land he had never seen. He had no proof of his claim, no supporters, no way to accomplish that which he had been told to do.

Yet in the back of his mind lay a thought, coiled like a sleeping serpent: *If I command Thirst Hold, I shall have an army of men loyal to me. A small army, but a start.*

Swallowing hard, Dain nodded. "I do understand. Thank you, Sulein, for explaining this matter so clearly." He shifted his gaze to Sir Terent. "What are the words of this oath I must say?"

Sulein looked dismayed, but Sir Terent shouldered forward with a nod of satisfaction. " 'I, Dain of Thirst, do hereby kneel to King Verence.' And that's what you'll do, m'lord— kneel to him as you say those words."

Dain nodded.

" 'I, Dain of Thirst, do hereby kneel to King Verence and give to him my oath of fealty, pledging my heart and sword to his service, as long as I shall live.' " Sir Terent frowned. "Now repeat that."

Dain said the words back to him, feeling a strong sense of unreality as he did so.

"Much better," Sir Terent said in approval.

"Aye," Sir Polquin said gruffly, and gave Dain a small, quick smile. "He'll do now. Stop fretting over him."

Sir Terent turned red. In his long tunic of dark Thirst green and his cloak, he looked weather-roughened and out of place in this scented, overfurnished room. But Dain saw an honest man without guile or pretense, and knew he'd rather have one Sir Terent at his back than a thousand courtiers.

"I just want our new lord to do well before these dandified court daisies," Sir Terent said. "Show them that Thirst Hold has its pride."

"Aye," Sir Polquin agreed gruffly, giving Dain a nod. "You'll stand for us now."

Drawing a deep breath, Dain now understood why they were so nervous. He regretted his earlier impatience with them, realizing that from now on he would truly be their lord and master. He knew he must conduct himself worthily so they could take pride in him. He must strive to be fair and just in dealing with them. He must never take their steadfast loyalty for granted.

A page came in and looked around with a sniff before his gaze fastened on Dain. "You are summoned."

Dain's self-confidence vanished. Dry-mouthed, he found his feet rooted to the floor. Thum's elbow jabbed his ribs, and Dain stepped forward.

Sir Terent took his position at Dain's heels. Sir Polquin followed him, with Sulein coming after, and Thum brought up the rear. By Savroix standards, it was a tiny entourage indeed, but Dain felt grateful to have such stalwart companions at his back.

He followed the page through immense galleries and countless sets of double doors opened by bowing lackeys. Finally they came to an entrance guarded by pikemen in the royal colors. Beyond, Dain glimpsed a hall of such grandeur and magnificence it took his breath away. Double rows of polished marble columns supported a vaulted ceiling high overhead. The hall was so long Dain could not see its opposite end. Swallowing hard, he walked in that direction, but before he reached the entry, the chamberlain blocked his path.

The man, wearing his hair elaborately curled and puffed up with his self-importance, bowed slightly to Dain. He was garbed in a heavy tunic of dark blue, and wore a chain indicating his rank. In his hands he held an ornately carved ebony staff of office. His skin was pale, his eyes cold and unimpressed as he ran his gaze over Dain.

Returning his stare measure for measure, Dain knew that the chamberlain was seeking fault in appearance or behavior, but that there was none to find. In his thoughts, this man deplored Dain's tailor, but Dain refused to feel shame. Lord Odfrey had given him these clothes. They were suitable, if not as fancy as what most of the courtiers were wearing.

As Dain returned the chamberlain's cold gaze, his own grew compassionate. He saw through the pomposity and hauteur to the truth. The chamberlain lived here in this palace of many treasures, yet he owned no property of his own. He worked among the most notable men of the land, yet he had no rank beyond his appointed position. He wore rich clothing, yet it came of the king's largesse. The man lived in fear—fear that he would lose his office when he grew older, fear that he might make a mistake and be laughed at as he had laughed at so many others, fear that his daughter might be carrying a married lord's child, fear of the scandal if this became public knowledge. Dain understood that this man never walked in the forest, never heard the whisper of leaves or the flow of tree sap. He knew not the songbird's warble, nor the laughter of a rushing stream. In all ways that mattered, this man was very poor, and was to be pitied.

"You understand the procedure?" the chamberlain asked him haughtily.

"I do," Dain replied.

"Have you any other title, that you may be announced to his majesty?"

Dain thought of what the ghost-king had told him, but he held that secret back. He was not ready yet to share such things. Tonight, he wanted the praise of this assembly, not their laughter.

"I have no title," he said to the chamberlain. "You may announce me as Dain."

The chamberlain frowned, looking flustered by this, but Dain was already walking forward. The chamberlain bustled ahead of him, and the courtiers gawking in the doorway moved back to let them pass. The chamberlain spoke to a herald hovering just across the threshold.

"Your majesty, my lords and ladies!" the man announced in stentorian tones that quelled the general babble of conversation. He paused, also looking a trifle flustered. "Dain, his protector, his master of arms, his physician, and his companions."

Dain walked into the vaulted audience chamber, indifferent to the fact that he had been announced by name only, without title, in the manner of monarchs. People stared, whispering. Somewhere a titter of laughter broke out, only to be swiftly muted.

He walked with his head high and his shoulders back, his gaze sweeping the magnificent room, with its enormous tapestries hanging beyond the columns, its arched windows filled with panes of expensive glass, its floor of polished stone laid in intricate triangles of color. He felt many minds pulsing around his. Some of the courtiers were amused by him; others were contemptuous. But all pretended outward respect, for he had saved the life of the king. They would not offend his majesty's latest favorite by laughing openly at a part-eldin youth with pretensions of glory, but he felt the sharp flick, flick, flick of their emotions like slaps to his face as he walked past.

At the end of the enormous hall sat the king on his throne. Tonight he looked a most impressive monarch indeed in his crown that glittered with jewels, his gold collar of royalty, and his crimson robes. A corona of fat candles blazed behind his head. Impassive men in livery stood on either side of him; one of these held a tall mace, heavily carved with symbols of power from ancient times, the other an ewer wrought of purest silver, containing water laced with something Dain had never encountered before. He faltered ever so slightly, then corrected his step at once.

"You see? You see?" whispered a man in the crowd. He spoke softly, but Dain's keen ears heard every word. "He felt the holy water's presence there. His pagan blood must be screaming for him to run."

Dain kept his gaze straight ahead, but he tightened his lips to control his uncertainty. From his brief stint of training in Mandrian religion, he knew what holy water was and what it was sometimes used for. Perhaps the old folktale about throwing an eld into water to make him melt held some truth after all. Dain had an inkling that the water in this ewer might be poured over him in a test. It was not water blessed by priests, however, not like the water in the chapel at Thirst Hold. Nay, this held lacings of strange power and magic such as Dain had never encountered before. He did not know what it was, but its presence surprised him. He thought the Mandrians were opposed to magic, yet to one side of the throne stood a trio of men in white church robes. Did they not sense the spells crisscrossing the king? Did they not object?

The priests wore white coifs that framed their faces tightly. Their eyes watched Dain without expression, but he knew they opposed him. Their minds were walls of hostility.

After one glance in their direction, he pretended to ignore them and focused his gaze on the king.

The chamberlain, who had walked ahead of Dain, now stopped and bowed low. "Your majesty," he said in a voice of the deepest reverence.

King Verence, despite his grandeur, looked like a man impatient to be done with ceremonies and off to his supper. He caught Dain's eye over the head of the bowing chamberlain and motioned him forward.

Dain glanced back at his companions and saw that they were shuffling aside, leaving him to stand before the king alone. Sir Terent looked strained and proud, as though Dain were his own son. Sir Polquin was beaming. Sulein wore no expression at all, but his hands were clenched so hard that the knuckles were white. Thum was all eyes and freckles, looking as pale as his linen.

Dain tried to remember to keep breathing. He stepped forward past the chamberlain, who was now backing out of the way. His instructions had been to halt three steps short of the throne and bow. But he thought of the king's great majesty. Verence had shown him kindness, and was allowing him to fulfill his last promise to Lord Odfrey. Overcome with a rush of emotions, Dain simply knelt at the king's feet, bowed his head to the floor, and placed his hand in gratitude on the royal foot.

A babble of voices broke out among the courtiers. The chamberlain hissed at Dain and made aimless little gestures, but Dain ignored him. The only person who mattered in this room was the king.

"Dain," the king said. His voice held amusement, surprise, and gentleness. "Rise up and stand before me. Do not prostrate yourself to me like a barbarian."

Embarrassment rushed through Dain with such force he thought his temples might burst. He rose to his feet with his face on fire and bowed as he should have done in the first place. At that moment he did not know what he was doing here in this sumptuous palace among these resplendent people of wealth and position. He expected someone to jump up—Gavril perhaps—and shout, "Throw him out! The impostor should be in rags, eating scraps with the swine. Throw him out!"

But Gavril was not present. He was gone for the evening to perform the rituals of his investiture. And no one else protested Dain's standing here, garbed in finery instead of rags, while the king smiled at him.

At the king's gesture, a clerk garbed in dark brown came shuffling forward. Lord Odfrey's much-creased and stained petition was held in the man's thin, ink-splattered hands.

"Read the petition of Odfrey, Chevard of Thirst," the king commanded.

The man cleared his throat and read the words aloud so that all might hear them. The brief document was eloquent in its simplicity. It stated how and why Lord Odfrey had wished to adopt Dain as his son and heir. It pointed out that Dain had saved Lord Odfrey's life during the battle with the dwarves. From his first days in the hold, he had exhibited nobility of character, a sound regard for the safety and well-being of those within the hold, and a kindness and honesty of spirit that made him a worthy young man. Although his origins were mysterious, Lord Odfrey had no doubt that Dain carried noble blood, as evidenced by his stature and carriage, by his keen intelligence, and by the pendant of king's glass which he had worn since infancy.

A fresh babble of conversation broke out among the courtiers, almost drowning out the clerk, who kept reading. During the journey to Savroix, Dain had read the words again

and again, seeking comfort from them, hearing Lord Odfrey's
voice speaking them in his mind. He knew them all by heart,
yet he listened enrapt as though for the first time. It was not
Lord Odfrey's praise of him that he craved, but the structure
and cadence of the words the chevard had penned. For through
those words, the way in which they had been written, the
thoughts which had arranged and selected them, Dain could
be with Lord Odfrey again.

With his eyes moist, his mind awash in memory and grief,
he barely realized the clerk had stopped reading. A silence
fell across the assembly, broken here and there by tiny rivulets
of whispering. Curious eyes bored into Dain's back.

King Verence stared at him. "Do you wear the pendant
referred to?"

The pendant was Dain's most precious and private possession. He kept it concealed beneath his clothing, wanting
no one to know about it, lest they try to take it away from
him, as Sulein had once done at Gavril's urging.

He could not lie, however, to the king. Reluctantly he nodded. "I do wear it, your majesty."

The king held out his hand. "I would see this for myself."

Refusal flew through Dain. Although his back stiffened,
he knew he could do nothing save acquiesce. Slowly, his reluctance more evident than he realized, he hooked his thumb
beneath the cord of plain leather around his neck and pulled
the pendant forth.

A gasp arose from the crowd. Dain pulled the cord over
his head, then handed it to the king. In that second, the bard
crystal caught the candlelight and glittered fire within its many
facets. Dain's hand trembled, and the crystal sang softly, its
notes pure and magical. Then it was laid across the king's
palm, and royal fingers closed over it.

Dain felt bereft and lost, as though his very heart had been
taken from him.

The king held up the pendant to the light and squinted at
it. Then Verence smiled and drew forth his own pendant. His
was a small, round disk, smooth without facets. He laid Dain's

slim, finger-sized pendant across his, then drew them apart with a quick motion of his hands.

The dual notes harmonized perfectly, ringing forth with such purity that Dain forgot his unease and let his spirit fly upon their sound.

"It is genuine," the king announced, handing the pendant back to Dain and tucking his own away. He looked at Dain rather sharply for a moment, his hazel green-and-blue eyes filled with questions. "Where did you get it?"

"I know not, majesty," Dain answered, slipping his pendant back beneath his doublet. "I have always had it."

"Strange," the king murmured. His thoughts seemed to flow away from Dain for a moment. "It was a handsome gift someone gave you."

"Aye, your majesty," Dain agreed. He told himself to say nothing else, but something about the occasion, the heat within the room, and the headiness of standing here before the king made him say more on the subject than he ever had to anyone other than Sulein and Lord Odfrey. "My sister had one as well."

Verence's brows shot up. "Your sister!" he echoed. "Damne, and where is she?"

"Dead, your majesty. Her bard crystal lies buried with her."

"Bard crystal? You call it this?"

Dain frowned a little. "Aye. You call it king's glass here in Mandria, but I—"

"Quite so. Well, as Lord Odfrey said in his document, your origins are mysterious. No doubt he questioned you thoroughly when you first came to him."

Memories, fresh and keen, flooded Dain. He smiled a little. "Aye, majesty," he said ruefully. "Lord Odfrey did."

"For my old friend to move past the memory of his lost son Hilard, to abandon his grief and be willing to look once more to the future, speaks highly of you, Dain," the king announced. "I have not forgotten the dispatch which came from Thirst nearly a year past, saying that Lord Odfrey's life was

spared in battle by the quick actions of a half-wild boy of
the eld folk." The king smiled at Dain, who felt his throat
choke up. "Nor have I forgotten a much more recent dispatch
from Thirst, saying that the life of my own son and heir,
Prince Gavril, was saved by the quick actions of a boy named
Dain, a boy whom Odfrey wished to adopt."

The king rose to his feet and faced the assembly. "And
today, not many hours past, this same boy—a stranger to my
majesty, and indeed, a stranger to Savroix—did save the royal
life of the king from a vicious attack by foreign agents and
enemies of this realm. Truly, all that Lord Odfrey wrote about
you, Dain, is fact and not mere praise. You have shown yourself to understand the responsibilities of the rank offered to
you. You have not shirked your duties. You have displayed
prowess with arms in today's contest—much to the chagrin
of his royal highness."

Polite chuckles broke out, for the king was smiling as he
spoke.

Dain smiled too, but not much. He felt frozen and weak-
kneed, unable to breathe properly. His head was buzzing,
making it hard to listen to the king's words.

"Were you anyone else, I would hasten to confer the adoption and titles which you seek."

Dain blinked, caught by this unexpected remark. His heart
fell like a stone inside him.

"But you are part eld, Dain, and a mystery to us. The rank
of chevard holds within it a sworn duty to protect the borders of this realm. And Thirst is special to us."

Dain blinked. "Aye, majesty."

The king frowned. "It has been said to me that you are
studying our religion in order to convert."

Dain's mouth was so dry he couldn't speak. Those lessons
had fallen mostly by the wayside, although Sir Terent still
made sure he practiced the few prayers he'd learned before
leaving Thirst. Dain swallowed hard. "Aye, majesty."

The king glanced at the trio of priests, and his brow knotted. Anger, possibly a trace of resentment, flashed in his eyes before he swept his gaze down and concealed it.

"There is a test before you," the king said. "Will you take it?"

Unease touched Dain as an expectant hush fell over the crowd. He glanced at the trio of priests, waiting impassively for his answer. Somewhere among the press of thoughts around him, Dain sensed a glimmer of a mind gloating at his discomfiture. He frowned, but already the sensation was gone, as elusive as smoke.

Meeting the king's gaze, Dain asked, "Do all petitioners take this test?"

The king's eyes narrowed. Among the courtiers, someone gasped, as though astonished that Dain would defy his majesty this way. Abruptly Verence threw back his head and let out a great, boisterous guffaw.

"You have spirit, lad, I'll grant you that," he said, clapping Dain on the shoulder with such force Dain nearly staggered. "No, not all petitioners take this test my priests have devised for you."

And there it was, the challenge laid forth in the cool appraising look the king gave him.

This time Dain did not hesitate. It was not fair, but he knew life seldom was. "I will take your test," he said.

The king stepped aside, and one of the priests beckoned to Dain. "Come forward."

Wary now, for this felt like a trap, Dain obeyed.

One priest stepped forward with a small box in his hands. The man's light brown, almost yellow eyes burned with a fanatic's zeal. "We shall test your eld blood and your pagan heart."

"He is not pagan!" Sir Terent said sharply from behind Dain.

The protector's alarm was plain, his denial too vehement. Someone in the crowd laughed in disbelief. Dain turned around and lifted his hand to quell Sir Terent's protest.

"Let them test me," he said with a reassuring smile he did not feel. "I won't melt."

Looking worried, Sir Terent gnawed his lip. Beside him, Sir Polquin was scowling and huffing beneath his mustache. "Superstitious lot, these lowlanders," he muttered loud enough to be overheard.

"Is there refusal?" the priest with the box asked.

Dain heard hope in the question and turned back to him quickly. "No refusal," he said.

"Your ambition burns hot," the priest said. "Now we will see what else burns inside you."

As he spoke, he opened the lid of the box.

Dain smelled the heat of the coals within as the priest tipped the box to show him embers glowing red atop ashes.

"Purity fire," the priest announced. His yellow eyes blazed. "Put your hand inside and bring forth one coal."

Dain felt the invisible lacings of magic tracing back and forth among the three priests. The Reformed Church of the Circle was officially opposed to magic, yet these priests were highly trained in its use. What hypocrites, Dain thought angrily, to forbid the upland Mandrians to utilize proper magical safeguards against Nonkind raids, while the churchmen did as they pleased here safely south of the Charva River.

Well, as a test this was easy. He had learned this one when he was a young boy barely tall enough to peer over the top of Jorb's forge. Anyone who was going to work with fire needed to learn this simple trick to avoid getting seriously burned.

He reached out, but Sir Terent said quickly, "Not your sword hand!"

Dain nodded and stretched forth his other hand. The heat inside the box was intense enough to make him flinch, but he did not draw back.

The priest's mesmerizing yellow eyes captured Dain's gaze until he realized what the churchman was trying to do. Blinking, Dain shifted his eyes away and focused his mind on his task.

Ignore the pain withering my fingers. Think instead of cool ice from the mountain streams that freeze in winter. Become ice, so cold, so very cold. Become impervious to flame. Concentrating with all he had, Dain curled his fingers around one of the coals. The pain went elsewhere, and he kept it away, knowing that later there would be no burns at all.

Pleased, Dain started to withdraw his hand. As he did so, his gaze met the priest's.

The flash of satisfaction in the man's yellow eyes told Dain a trap was springing shut on him. This test was not about whether he could pick up a blazing coal with his bare hand, but whether he would do so unharmed and thus betray skills in magic.

Angered, he glared at the priest and let the ice in his thoughts go. Pain flared in his hand, so intense he thought he would pass out from it. He could feel his flesh burning, could hear a faint sizzle as the skin on his palm charred.

He drew out his hand, the live coal inside his clenched fingers, and the pain made him shudder. Without realizing what he was doing, he dropped to his knees as a hoarse, muffled cry of agony escaped his clenched jaws.

"Gods!" Sir Terent rushed forward to shake him by his shoulders. "Drop it! Drop it now!"

But Dain raised his streaming eyes to the priest, who was staring down at him with a scowl of disgust. "Is it enough?" he asked, gasping out the words.

"Sufficient," the priest murmured.

"Drop it!" the king commanded.

Dain tipped back his head in anguish and released the coal. It went rolling across the polished stone floor before the throne, smoking and leaving a black streak in its wake.

Shuddering, Dain cradled his burned hand against him and bent low, rocking himself from side to side in pain.

"Bring the ewer to him!" the priest commanded.

One of the men in livery obeyed.

"Sir knight, stand back," the priest said to Sir Terent. "This test is not finished."

"Your majesty, must the boy be maimed?" Sir Terent asked in appeal.

Silent and watchful, the king said nothing. Sir Terent was forced to withdraw as the servant knelt before Dain and proffered the ewer.

"Put your hand in the water," the priest said. "Cool your burn."

There was another trap waiting for him inside this water, Dain knew. Struggling to fend off his pain, he tried to think. Holy water would not harm him, but this was something else. His mind flashed to the priest's, but it held shut against him. His mind went to Sulein, and in the physician's fascinated thoughts, Dain found his answer.

The ewer held vitriol. If he plunged his hand into the liquid, his very skin would be burned off his bones.

Dain closed his eyes against another spasm of pain. The smell of his own burned flesh was sickening, but he refused to let it distract him. He dared not hesitate.

"Did you hear me?" the priest asked, bending lower. "Let this cool water soothe your burn. It has been blessed. Perhaps it may even heal you, *unless* you hold some taint."

Gazing into the man's eyes as though mesmerized, Dain whispered, "Thank you for your kindness," and reached out to slip his hand into the ewer.

It was his intention to knock the vessel aside, pretending clumsiness in his agony, but just as his fingers touched the ewer's lip, the king stepped forward.

"Stop!" he said. "I command it."

Dain froze where he was, trying not to look at the vitriol. His heart pounded in relief.

The priest almost hissed in frustration. "Your majesty," he said with forced courtesy, "the test is not yet complete."

But the king was drawing a silver vial from his own purse. Holding it up, he pulled out the stopper. "My personal holy water will soothe his wound. Turn over your hand, Dain."

Feeling a surge of gratitude, Dain obeyed.

But the priest did not withdraw. "Your majesty, he must

be tested for taint from both sides, from the fire and the water—"

"Is the water I hold not blessed?" the king countered. He held the vial out to the priest. "Take it and pour it on him yourself if you doubt me."

Turning pale, the priest bowed hastily and retreated. "Forgive me, your majesty."

The king gently clasped Dain's wrist, holding it while he dribbled cool water across the burned flesh and intoned a soft prayer. Dain could not keep from wincing as the first splash of water hit the burn.

Someone cried out, "Watch him! He is going to melt from it!"

Faint screams came from some of the ladies, but most of the courtiers crowded closer to watch.

Much to Dain's astonishment, after that initial discomfort, the majority of his pain began to fade. He was no convert. He had never finished his training in the ways of the religion of the Circle, but he felt a sense of ease, almost of peace, steal over him. The king's prayer was a true benediction, and as Dain watched, the worst blistering of his burn lessened visibly.

He stared, his mouth dropping open in surprise.

"There," the king said with a kindly smile, shaking out the last drop and replacing the stopper. "It looks less angry already."

Dain stared at his hand, and could not believe this small miracle. The fiery agony was gone, leaving only a tender sense of discomfort. His red flesh was turning almost a normal color, and some of the blisters had disappeared.

"A miracle," he whispered.

"Of course," the king said. "That is what faith is for."

"But I have not taken all the vows yet," Dain said. "I—"

"Perhaps this will turn your heart to complete belief," the king said. "Were you not already within the Circle in some part of yourself, this healing would not have taken place." He smiled at Dain, who was still kneeling there with his hand held up in amazement, then turned to send a steely look at the priests.

"The test," his majesty declared, "is over. This young man has proven his courage and his true heart. He holds no taint from his mixed blood. The final objections to his advancement are now silenced."

Bowing, the three priests retreated, as did the servant with the ewer.

"Remain kneeling," the king said to Dain, and drew his sword. It was old and well-polished by generations of reverent hands. A huge ruby flashed from its hilt as he raised it. "Dain of Thirst, you are hereby proclaimed Chevard of Thirst Hold, to inherit it in full, with all rights due your standing as son of Odfrey. This do I grant."

As he spoke, he touched Dain lightly on either shoulder with the flat of his blade.

There was a moment of silence. Dain was totally caught up in the significance of the king's proclamation, until he heard Sir Terent cough in warning.

Then he blinked, realizing the king was waiting for his oath of fealty. Dain's mind struggled to remember the words he'd been taught only minutes ago.

Instead, into his mind came a thought that was not his own: *You are now a chevard, Faldain, but never forget you are also a king.*

He swayed slightly and glanced around to see if the ghost-king had come to haunt him at this moment of triumph. He saw nothing but mortal faces around him.

His silence was lasting too long, he knew. Not wanting to offend, Dain fumbled hastily for the words he needed to say. "I, Dain," he began, and overheard Sir Terent mouthing the words behind him. But at the same time, he seemed to feel another presence enter him, unseen but strongly felt, a presence that gave him the words he sought. "As Chevard of Thirst, loyal freehold, do I kneel here to King Verence, sovereign and liege of Mandria. I give to him my oath of friendship and loyalty, pledging my heart and sword in alliance to his, as long as I do live."

Quiet fell across the audience chamber. Looking astonished, the king raised his brows.

Dain glanced swiftly around at the appalled faces, wondering what was wrong. Behind him, Sir Terent muttered, "You changed the words. You changed the words."

Still gripped by whatever unseen force had entered him, Dain didn't care. The words that Sir Terent had taught him would not come forth. They were wrong by the legal terms of Thirst's deed. Dain wondered if perhaps Lord Odfrey's spirit had not possessed him to keep him from inadvertently giving Thirst away. Yet he'd displeased the sovereign. King Verence's brow was knotted, and he looked stunned.

From the crowd, Dain once again felt a glimmer of a thought, too swift to catch or pinpoint. The enemy that lurked out there among the courtiers was pleased by his misstep, and Dain wondered if he had done more than just offend. Perhaps he'd thrown away everything he'd come for.

16

IN THE GENERAL hush which fell after Dain's amended oath, the king scowled at him. "Where in the name of Thod did you learn such a pledge?"

Dain opened his mouth, but he knew there was no explanation he could give. "I—I— Is it—"

"It's the ancient form, the same one Odfrey made to me," the king went on. Leaning down to Dain, he murmured harshly, "But in private, mind, not like this. How came you across it on your own? Perhaps you read it off the original charter of Thirst Hold."

"Your pardon, majesty," Dain said with a slight frown, "but Thirst Hold has no royal charter. It—"

From the corner of his eye he saw the chamberlain gesturing violently at him to be silent.

"Ah, of course," the king said. He regarded Dain somberly a moment longer, while Dain's heart thudded in his chest. "Thank you for the reminder. Here in lower Mandria we do not always remember the turbulent history of the uplands. Well! Your oath is not modern—"

"And is it legal?" Clune dared ask.

The king shot the old duc a scowl for daring to interrupt him. "Aye," he replied shortly.

Clune bowed and retreated.

The king's gaze returned to Dain, who tried to rise. "No, stay on your knees. You are proving to be an unpredictable young man, Dain of Thirst."

Dain bowed his head. "I beg the king's pardon."

"Why?" Abruptly the king laughed out loud. "Apparently you never do anything in the expected way. But as yet, nothing has proven you in the wrong. Odfrey chose you well for his purposes, it seems. Let us get on. Lord Dain, my newest chevard, you are young but already tried in the fields of battle. Who taught you arms?"

It took Dain a moment to realize he wasn't in trouble after all. A great rush of emotion surged through him. Lifting shining eyes to the king, he somehow found his voice: "Many of the knights at Thirst did instruct me, your majesty. But Sir Polquin, master of arms, taught me the most."

"The man did well," the king said. He gestured to a servant, who brought forth his sword. Tapping Dain on both shoulders, the king declared, "I knight you, here before this company of knights and lords, that you may undertake your duties as chevard without hindrance. Rise now, knighted and lorded. Your rewards are well-deserved."

Applause broke out, polite and restrained in some quarters, more enthusiastic in others. Dain got to his feet on a cloud of euphoria, still cradling his injured hand against his side. His head was spinning, and he hardly knew where he was.

The king, beaming with satisfaction, laughed aloud and reseated himself on his throne. "Take him away and see that his hand is treated. Then we will feast and make merry."

People rushed Dain as he backed away from the throne. Clapping Dain on the shoulder, his companions surrounded him on all sides. Sir Terent was blinking as though holding back tears.

Sir Polquin looked ready to burst with pride. "Knighted by his majesty," he said in awe. "Morde a day, I never thought I'd live to see you receive such an honor."

Thum was practically dancing, his grin splitting his face from ear to ear. "Well done, my friend. And well deserved."

Sulein, however, reached for Dain's injured hand. "The healing touch of kings is always helpful," he mumbled through his beard, "but a salve must go on, yes, and bandages, or it will not heal properly. You are fortunate not to be crippled for life, my lord."

"Gods," Sir Terent said with a sigh, mopping his brow. "I have aged a year or more this night. Let's get you away from this crowd."

But too many well-wishers surrounded Dain. As they were introduced, most seemed to be there simply to eye him at close range. They peered at his eyes and his ears, then hurried away as though they had scored a triumph. Those who congratulated him with the greatest enthusiasm did so with one eye turned in the king's direction, as though attempting only to curry royal favor.

Dain wanted nothing to do with such people. "Sulein," he said over the hubbub, "attend me now."

The physician bowed in compliance. With Sir Terent pushing a way for them through the crowd, Dain was able to escape to a quiet corner. A page appeared and conducted them to a private antechamber.

"Ah," Sulein said, glancing around at the small but exquisitely furnished room. "This is much more suitable."

With a sigh of relief, Dain sat down on a velvet-covered stool. It was quiet in here, and he bathed his emotions in the peace. So much had happened to him in such a short span of time. He needed this chance to recover his balance.

Sir Terent paced back and forth while Sulein's gentle fingers worked. Now and then Dain winced, but the pain was minimal compared with what it had been before. From one of his capacious pockets, the physician produced a salve in a minuscule jar. It smelled only of herbs and grease. Dain permitted him to smear it across his hand. Sir Terent took off his tunic and sacrificed a sleeve of his new linen shirt for a bandage.

Dain looked up at his protector in mute gratitude. He still marveled at being served by this large, rough-spoken man.

"Aye, you did well, m'lord," Sir Terent said, retreating in order to pull his tunic back on. He kept blinking with emotion. "Lord Odfrey would have been proud, if I may say it. As for that pledge—"

"I don't know how it came. . . ."

But Sir Terent was shaking his head and wiping his eyes. When he looked at Dain again, pride shone in his face. "The ancient oath, from when Thirst and the uplands were free. Thod have mercy, but I never thought to witness any man brave enough to say that to a lowlander king's face. That took courage, aye. Great courage."

"It did," Thum said quietly. "If only my father and grandfather could have been here to see it done."

Sir Polquin cleared his throat. "Brave, aye," he said gruffly, "but perhaps foolish as well. We'll have no talk of fomenting rebellions, if you please. Clune already has his hackles raised. The whole set of ministers will be fearful now of an uprising."

"Not from me," Dain promised. "It just came out."

"And no wonder, after those priests and their damned foolery," Sir Terent said angrily.

"Aye, a trap, that was!" Sir Polquin agreed.

"At least it's over," Dain said wearily. Tomorrow, perhaps he would feel angry at what the priests had tried to do to him. Tonight, he found that it did not matter. He had achieved his goal, and he wanted to savor that satisfaction. "Let us fret no more about it."

"There, that is finished." Sulein surveyed his handiwork with satisfaction. "Now you can return to the celebration."

Dain felt suddenly exhausted. "I think I would rather go to my room."

The men exchanged sharp glances.

"Are you ill, m'lord?" Sir Terent asked.

The alarm in his voice shamed Dain into thinking of the others. It was not right that he should deprive them of tonight's festivities just because he'd had more than he could assimilate. He knew they could not attend the feast and dancing without him. Sighing, he forced himself to straighten from his slump.

"No, I'm well," he said, smiling at Sir Terent. "It's just so much, so quickly."

" 'Quickly!' " Sir Terent said in surprise. "And after you've waited for it all this time? You're a wonder indeed, with the things you say. Uh, m'lord," he added hastily.

"If you're still in pain, I can mix a potion with wine," Sulein offered.

"Nay." Dain shook his head at once, as wary as ever of Sulein's concoctions. The man served ably, but Dain had never been able to trust him. "In truth, between the king's ministrations and yours, I cannot tell that my hand is burned, unless I flex it thus."

"Don't!" Sulein said in alarm.

Dain grinned at him and lowered his hand. He found that by hooking his thumb in his belt, he could keep his hand cradled unobtrusively.

Sir Terent was still frowning in visible worry. "If your lordship wishes to retire—"

Dain shook his head. "I was only jesting," he said, making his voice light. "Let's get back to the others. If I thought myself famished before, now I could eat the table."

Leading the way, he forced himself to smile as he returned to the audience hall. The loud hubbub of everyone's talking at once struck him unpleasantly, but he ignored that. Pushing his way through the milling crowd, Dain found himself waylaid by the chamberlain.

"Your lordship will sit at the king's table," the man announced. "Please come with me."

Dain hesitated and glanced at his companions.

Sulein bowed at once. "If I have your lordship's leave to seek my own place?"

"And I also, m'lord?" Sir Polquin said.

Dain nodded, realizing with disappointment that not even Thum would be allowed to sit with him.

"Come, Lord Dain," the chamberlain said, conducting him into the banqueting hall. Sir Terent followed close at his heels, and Dain was grateful for his protector's solid presence among so many strangers.

Long tables stretched the length of the banqueting hall. The king's table stood turned crosswise at the far end. Unlike the others, it was covered with a cloth of snowy linen. Huge candlesticks stood at either end of it. The king's tall-backed chair was positioned at the center, flanked by benches for his majesty's most honored guests.

Under the golden blaze of light, the feast itself was spread in astonishing bounty along the tables. Were it not for the divine smells of roasted fowl and pork wafting through the hall, Dain would not have believed that the fanciful creations were food. He saw sculptures of pastry next to tureens of bubbling stews. Loaves of bread baked in animal shapes were heaped in pyramids that served as centerpieces. Plates of colorful fruit turned out to be candy instead; the real fruit was gilded and spangled like jewels. A gigantic peacock, its brilliant feathers spread out to gleam in the candlelight, was in fact a pie containing live birds. One of them escaped as the servants were setting the peacock on the table. The pale dove flew about the room, followed by other escaping birds. The gathering crowd applauded, and Dain heard the king's laughter ring out from across the room.

Pages laden with wineskins hurried to fill huge goblets already on the tables. People rowed up, a few squabbling over who was to sit where. The chamberlain and his minions hurried here and there to soothe feelings and arbitrate these disputes.

Dain noticed that no one sat down and began eating. He did not understand why, but he guessed it had to do with Mandrian rules.

As though reading his mind, Sir Terent leaned forward and whispered in his ear, "Remember not to sit or eat until the king does."

Dain nodded at the reminder, though his stomach was growling and the smell of so much food made him feel wild. He'd eaten nothing in hours, and it had been a long, eventful day.

The guests for the king's table included the sour-faced Duc du Clune and Cardinal Noncire. Clune, wearing a sleeveless overrobe atop his tunic of embroidered silk, no longer looked like a scruffy escapee from a bandit attack. His gray hair was combed back from his brow, and his fierce brows jutted in a ledge over his eyes. He stared at Dain in open disapproval, and Dain dared not address him. The cardinal was a man Dain had heard much about, for during Gavril's stay as a foster at Thirst, he had mentioned his tutor frequently. Dain stared at this man who had educated the prince, taking in his massive girth, the jeweled rings on his fat fingers, the diamond-studded Circle hanging around his neck. Noncire had shaped and molded Gavril into what he was today; Dain flicked a contemptuous glance at the fat man, then bowed slightly to the duc.

Both men paused in their conversation, but stared at him coldly and gave him no greeting at all before resuming their talk.

Others noticed the insult. While they murmured and snick-

ered, Dain felt the pointed tips of his ears grow hot. He turned
away, understanding that he would probably always have
plenty of enemies, and shrugged it off. He looked at the food
still being placed on the already laden table and wished the
king would let them start eating.

"Hello."

Startled by the soft voice from behind him, Dain turned
and found himself gazing into a pair of tilted brown eyes
that made his heart lurch. It was the girl who had sat in the
king's box this afternoon. Close up, she dazzled him with lu-
minous pale skin and a face like a dream. Tonight her hair
was unbound and allowed to cascade over her shoulders and
down her back. There was so much of it. How softly it shone
in the candlelight, which turned the few glints of red in her
golden tresses to gentle fire. Longing to touch those silken
strands, Dain curled his fingers into a loose fist at his side
to control himself. She wore a little cap tied beneath her chin,
and ringlets and smaller curls escaped from the front to frame
her heart-shaped face in a most enchanting way. Her gown
was the hue of sand, and it glittered with thousands of tiny
pearls and crystal beads sewn in intricate patterns across her
long skirts. She was the most beautiful girl he had ever seen,
and when her clear-eyed gaze lowered from his, he was fascinated by the way her lashes swept her cheeks. She had
three pale freckles on her small, straight nose, almost hidden
by a dusting of powder. He hated the powder, for her beauty
was already so perfect it needed no artifice.

Belatedly he realized he was gawking at her like a serf
without manners. He blinked, struggling to find his wits and
his voice. "Hello," he said in response. "I—I—"

She smiled, revealing a dimple in one soft cheek, and curtsied to him.

Dain could not believe he was being curtsied to by a lady
as fine as this. He felt as though he were floating in a dream
where nothing was real. And yet, here he was, a lord, standing at the king's table, with the most beautiful lady in the
room smiling at him.

"It's so annoying," she said in a lilting voice. "We have no one to provide formal introductions. Would you be shocked if I threw aside protocol and introduced myself?"

"Only if I may do the same in return," he replied.

She smiled. "Your bravery is evident in everything you do, Lord Dain," she said, then laughed at her own words. "You need not introduce yourself after this evening's ceremony."

His face flamed. What a fool he was, trying to be gallant and only sounding stupid instead.

But she didn't seem to mind. "I am Lady Pheresa du Lindier," she said. A delicate tinge of pink touched her cheeks, as though her boldness embarrassed her.

Dain gulped and bowed hastily. Realization flooded him, and he could have groaned aloud for not having guessed her identity sooner. This was the daughter of the Duc du Lindier, as well as the king's niece, a lady promised already to Gavril and destined to be Queen of Mandria. She was far, far beyond his reach. He couldn't believe she even wanted to speak to him.

"Would it please you to converse with me while we wait for his majesty?" Lady Pheresa asked. "I hope you are not offended by my forwardness."

He blinked in surprise, amazed that she thought she could offend him in any way. "Nay, lady. I—I am grateful for your notice."

She studied him a moment, while he felt heat surge into his face. "You needn't be," she told him at last, apparently deciding to be frank. "I am not important here."

"Forgive me, lady, but you are. You're—"

"Let's not talk about that," she said firmly. She glanced away, but not before he saw moisture shimmer in her light brown eyes.

"You are engaged to—"

"No," she said, her voice soft but very clear. She lifted her gaze to his briefly, then dropped it again. The pink in her cheeks darkened. "I am not. So you may talk to me all you wish, *if* you wish."

Dain felt confused. Thum had told him the betrothal was completely settled, but it seemed his friend was wrong. Dain realized that to keep asking questions would only embarrass her more, and he didn't want to drive her away. "I am glad to talk to you," he said with a smile, trying to ease her distress. "After all, you are the only one willing to talk to me."

The faint crease between her brows cleared at once. She cast a swift glance around at the other people. "Aren't they horrid?" she asked, bending closer to speak in a whisper. "So puffed up with their own importance. They're snubbing you, because they do not approve of how the king has accepted you."

Dain grinned. "I'm used to disapproval."

"They disapprove of me as well," she confided, blushing again.

Dain was lost in fascination all over again. How could she blush like that? So lightly? So beautifully? He realized he knew almost nothing about maidens, but she seemed different from all the others. Not only was she beautiful, but kind, intelligent, and observant as well. Yet unlike the other females in the room, she was not surrounded by chattering friends. She seemed as alone as he was.

"Anyone who disapproves of you," he said, "is a fool."

"Hush! Not so loud," she protested, but her eyes shone with delight at his clumsy compliment. "You are kind to champion me, but—"

Trumpets sounded a flourish, and the buzz of conversations faltered. The king approached the table with a tall, slender lady on his arm. Pheresa whispered to him that the king's mistress was the Countess Lalieux, and that she was very powerful at court. Dain had already witnessed just how influential she was during the sword contest that afternoon.

"Why isn't she the queen?" he whispered back.

Pheresa's eyes widened in amazement. "Because she's married to the Count Lalieux, silly."

The chamberlain drifted over to them, his eyes grave with warning.

Pheresa pressed her fingers to her lips at once. "We must be quiet," she murmured, but her brown eyes were smiling.

General quiet fell over the hall as the king walked through the crowd with a defiant expression on his face. His mistress looked regal and haughty, but Dain couldn't stop staring, trying not to be shocked by what Pheresa had told him. Clearly his upbringing was far too conservative for the Mandrian court. He had a feeling he was going to be shocked often.

Beside him, Pheresa stiffened at the sight of the next couple walking behind his majesty. Dain shifted his gaze their way and saw nothing remarkable about them. The man was tall and handsome, his face lined with boredom and dissatisfaction. A jeweled order hung at his throat, marking him as a marechal, the Mandrian term for general. To Dain's critical eye, he no longer looked like the great warrior he must have once been to win such a high title. Like the king, he had softened in middle age. His body looked puffy beneath his costly raiments. His lady wife walked gracefully at his side, holding her head high. She was pale-haired and curvaceous, with a jaw and nose similar to the king's.

"My parents," Pheresa murmured. Her hands clutched together, and Dain sensed her sudden strain and worry. "Look, she is angry at his majesty. Oh, no. I feared this."

Unused to the courtier habit of gauging every moment by the mood of the monarch, Dain saw that the princess did indeed look annoyed. While the king seated his lady and took his own chair, Princess Dianthelle stuck her aristocratic nose in the air and veered away from the head table. Lindier turned to the king and made an apologetic little bow before following his wife. They sat at one of the lesser tables, throwing the entire order awry.

While the chamberlain flung up his hands and raced to deal with the problem, Dain looked at the king. His majesty's face could have been carved from stone. The countess patted his hand, and the king made a fist of it.

"Damne," Pheresa whispered, looking pale. "What am I to do?"

"What's amiss?" Dain asked her.

She looked away from her parents and frowned at him. Worry darkened her eyes. "They were to sit here next to the king, and I was to sit with them. It was all arranged. And now . . ."

"What does it matter?" Dain asked her. "Sit here anyway."

He wanted to say, "Sit here with me," but he did not quite dare.

She paid him no heed, instead looking in distress from her parents to the king. The other guests of the head table were finding their places now.

"Oh," Pheresa said softly, knotting her slender white fingers together. "Oh."

Dain did not understand why she was so upset, but he felt instantly protective. "Let me help you," he offered. "I will do anything you ask, if it will ease your distress."

She cast him a look of gratitude, but before she could answer, the chamberlain appeared at her side. "My lady, her highness your mother requests that you join her."

Pheresa drew in her breath audibly, but her spine stiffened. Dain saw a look of resolution cross her face. Lifting her chin, she said to the chamberlain, "Please convey my regrets to my mother. I am to be seated here, at the king's invitation."

A look of anticipation and delight glimmered in the chamberlain's eyes before he bowed and walked away to deliver her message.

Pheresa glanced at Dain and pointed to an empty place on the bench. "Will you assist me, my lord?"

Dain did so, reveling in the brief touch of her hand. Her full skirts rustled with mystery. He found himself standing there like a fool, his thoughts awash in the very sight and fragrance of her.

"Am I allowed to sit by you?" he asked her shyly.

The strain in her face vanished, to be replaced by relief and gratitude. "Please," she said modestly.

As Dain settled himself into the last place at the table, Sir Terent bent unobtrusively to his ear.

"She's intended for Prince Gavril," he whispered. "Have a care. The king is said to want it so."

Dain shot his protector a frown. "I know that," he whispered back, impatient with this interference. "But the prince is not here. I am."

A line of servants laden with trays of additional meats and other delectables entered. Music began to play from an unseen corner. Conversations resumed, and the king bent his head to drink from the cup the countess offered him.

Pheresa's parents glared at her, and she bent her fair head low in renewed distress. Dain realized she was trembling.

"Have something to eat," he suggested.

She lifted her head again, blinking back tears that shimmered briefly in her eyes. "Yes," she said as though to herself. "I must eat. I must not look concerned."

"There's been a quarrel. What of it?" Dain said without interest. "Let them work through it."

"You don't understand," Pheresa said softly to him under the general noise. She reached out and took a morsel of bread, chewing as though eating dust. "I— Oh, it is too complicated to explain."

"Then eat," Dain said, finding the roasted meats very tasty.

Pheresa ate like a bird, sampling only small bits of food before pushing them away. Dain watched her from the corner of his eye, wishing he could help her with her distress, but knowing he could not offer. Some of the courtiers were staring at her, possibly even laughing at her.

With a frown, Dain felt a new surge of protectiveness. "If you look so unhappy, these people are going to think I offend you," he said at last.

She looked around with a start. "What?"

Dain repeated his remark.

"No, you don't offend me," she said with a blink. "How could you?"

"I am an eld."

"Oh." She blushed and dropped her gaze so quickly he knew then that it had been on her mind. "Yes, but you do not seem strange," she told him. "I—I mean, in the ways we are taught as children. You look human and—"

"I am," Dain said. "Partly."

"Yes, of course."

She was looking troubled and distracted again. Dain pushed a dish of tasty minscels her way.

"These are delicious," he said. "Try one."

She took a serving, but after a single bite, she pushed it away. Dain could barely stand the waste. He noticed that most of the courtiers were eating the same way, sampling and picking their way through this excellent feast. Clearly none of them had ever gone hungry. Dain, well aware of how sharply the pinch of hunger could hurt, took care to eat his fill and left nothing on his trencher.

A muffled sound caught his attention. He glanced up to see Princess Dianthelle on her feet, leaving the banquet hall with a grand sweep of her crimson skirts. Lindier trailed after her, pretending indifference. Around them, the courtiers buzzed and craned their necks. The king, busy lipping a treat the countess was putting in his mouth, paid his departing relatives no attention.

But even Dain, new to the ways of court, understood that it was a grave insult to leave the hall without the king's permission. Had she thrown down a glove, the princess could not have made her challenge more clear.

Pheresa looked stricken. She gripped her goblet so hard her knuckles turned white. "How foolish," she muttered. "How unnecessary."

Dain leaned toward her. "What?"

"My mother's temper is too strong. She has forced a quarrel, and it will only make things worse." Pheresa flashed Dain a look that contained equal parts of distress and anger. "I cannot explain now. Please do not ask me."

He let her be, but he noticed that she sat straighter and made a better show of eating. It might have fooled those at the other tables who watched her with cruel, occasional smiles, but Dain knew she ate almost nothing. The servants who cleared her trencher knew it as well.

In the minds around him, Dain sensed no sympathy for her. Noncire's thoughts were closed, his thoughts unreadable as he ate and drank with steady concentration. The Duc du Clune, however, was smirking openly, and Dain longed to strike him for his cruelty.

When the banquet finally ended, the sedate music became more lively. Jesters and acrobats tumbled a performance, and the king went off to circle the hall with his mistress on his arm, stopping here and there to chat with his eager, fawning courtiers.

Dain stood awkwardly to one side while servants cleared the tables away for dancing. Lady Pheresa drifted off, her face pale and set. Dain saw some of the other ladies laughing at her. Though one skipped forward to take hold of Pheresa's arm and say something to her, the others all giggled. Pheresa smiled, but Dain could sense the hurt inside her.

Scowling, he started to go over to help her, but Clune blocked his path.

"Proved me wrong," he announced in his gruff way. "Never expected you to take Odfrey's title."

Dain frowned at the man. "It is what Lord Odfrey wished."

"Hmpf. Well, make your place at court if you can. Off on the wrong foot already with that pledge. Don't think you'll last long among the painted vipers. Better to go to your hold and fend off raiders at the border instead of capering about here."

"I think that would be best," Dain agreed.

Clune scowled at him. "And if you think you can bring the uplands to a rebellion, know this: I'll send every fight-

ing man I have against you, as will all the lords of lower
Mandria. What we've taken once, we keep."

Before Dain could reply, the duc walked away. Dain stared
after him, wishing he'd left the old man to fend for himself
in the woods that night.

Turning his head to speak to Sir Terent, Dain found himself confronted next by a thin, dark-faced man with a short,
pointed beard and furtive eyes. Dressed in yellow and shades
of brown, he seemed to appear out of nowhere and pressed
closer to Dain than necessary.

"You're the new favorite," he said. "Allow me to present
myself. I am the—"

Growling, Sir Terent thrust him back. "Move out of Lord
Dain's way."

"No need to unleash your brute, young lord," this stranger
said, straightening his clothes with an offended air. "I only
want to offer you superb bargains in court attire and acces-
sories. Every well-dressed young lordling should be an object of—"

"Are you a tailor?" Dain asked him in astonishment.

The man stopped his spiel and turned red in the face. "A
tailor?" he sputtered in horror. "Certainly *not*. You have even
less polish than I thought. When you acquire some, young
lord, you may wish to come to me for my excellent assistance, but I will *not* be available."

Sticking his nose in the air, he flounced off. Dain stared
at him and shrugged. "What was that creature?" he asked Sir
Terent.

"A flea," the protector said gruffly.

Feminine laughter caught Dain's attention. He turned
around to find Lady Pheresa smiling at him. Dain's heart
dipped in his chest. It was a moment before he could remember how to breathe.

"Forgive me for interrupting," she said while Dain bowed
low to her. "Will you escort me about the room?"

"Of course," Dain said. "Where are you going?"

"Nowhere," she told him with another chuckle. "We are

just going to circle about, the way others are doing. One must digest the feast before one dances."

"I do not dance," Dain said in some alarm.

"Then tomorrow you must engage a dancing master and learn the latest steps." Smiling, she moved away, and Dain matched his stride to her slow pace.

She walked with elegant, graceful posture. Glancing at her slender neck and proud chin, Dain saw beyond her smiles and the too-bright look in her eyes to the profound unhappiness inside her. She was too beautiful to be miserable. Dain could not understand why she had no friends here . . . except him. That, he had to admit, gave him pleasure.

"I hope your protector will not take my remarks amiss," she said after a few moments of silence, "but it is not seemly for you, my lord, to converse with him in public. To issue orders, yes, but nothing further."

"Why not?" Dain asked.

Her brows lifted. "You're a lord. He is your servant."

"He is my knight protector," Dain corrected her. "He would give his life for me."

"Of course. That is his sworn duty." She glanced away, catching the eye of someone, and gave the woman a stiff nod. "But if you don't want people to laugh at you and think you're provincial, then you must follow protocol."

Wondering what other etiquette disasters he would create that evening, Dain sighed. "More rules."

"Worry not. You'll soon learn the ways of court. During my first weeks here, I thought I would die of mortification. I did everything wrong, and the courtiers love nothing more than to laugh at the mistakes of others."

Glancing across the sea of faces, hearing laughter and chatter rising in a din against the background of music, Dain was aware of occasional waves of contempt or curiosity aimed at him. Acceptance probably would not come, he reflected, no matter if he followed every complicated rule perfectly.

"Have I offended you?" Pheresa asked softly.

Startled from his thoughts, Dain blinked at her. "Nay, I was thinking of all that there is to learn."

"Yes, a million things," she said. Her eyes smiled, crinkling enchantingly at the corners. "For one, you should not hesitate to dismiss the procurers. There are many of them, all annoying little creatures of no importance and little use."

"What is a procurer?" Dain asked.

"That man who approached you about a tailor. He is of insignificant rank, the younger son of a lord, who hangs about court because he is unwilling or unable to become a knight and go into some chevard's service. Instead, he is paid by various tailors to procure business for them."

"Ah. A peddler of wares."

Pheresa laughed. "Not exactly. Well, perhaps, yes. There are many like him. It is a way of putting coin in their pockets, and sometimes they can be of service. But find your own tailor and wine supplier in the town. You will pay less and do better."

Dain shook his head. "I will need neither. It's time I returned to Thirst and—"

"But you cannot go." Looking dismayed, Pheresa stopped in her tracks and stared at him. "You have only just come."

Dain felt a shiver pass through him. "Do you want me to stay?"

She dodged that question, however, by sweeping down her lashes. "The king will, I am sure. You cannot go yet. It is not seemly."

"More rules of protocol?" he asked gently, while inside he felt a part of him glow. She wanted him to stay. She liked him. In his company her spirits unfurled like a flower in the sunlight, and she grew more animated, even more lovely. "If you say I must stay, then I will linger a few more days."

She laughed. "What odd remarks you do make! You will stay as long as the king wills it. That is your duty, and it should be your pleasure."

He bowed. "I am commanded by you, lady."

Pleasure glowed in her eyes. She smiled at him, and the

dimple appeared in her cheek, but before they could talk further, the music changed and someone came to ask her to dance.

Moving to the edge of the floor, Dain stood with other spectators and watched as an intricate reel was performed. To his eyes, no other maiden was as beautiful as Pheresa. No one had her grace or presence. He did not understand why she was not popular.

Unless it was because she did not smile enough. When she was happy, her whole face and being seemed alight. But when she looked serious, as she did now while she jigged and skipped, her face grew pale and solemn. Dain stared at her and thought about learning to stand on his head or to perform other ridiculous tricks if they would make her laugh.

Someone's shoulder bumped him, and Dain turned his head to confront the one who jostled him. He found himself staring into the freckled, grinning face of Thum.

"Isn't this grand?" Thum asked over the music. "Look yon! The king is going to dance with his lady."

They watched a moment as his majesty performed the steps with the smiling countess, but Dain's eyes soon strayed to Lady Pheresa. She stood alone now, watching the dance. Her partner had left her, and no one else said a word to her.

Thum's elbow dug into his ribs. "Stop staring," he said. "She's not for you."

"She's unhappy," Dain said, never taking his eyes away from her.

"Probably because Prince Gavril is not here to pay her court." Thum shook his head. "On the morrow, he'll be through with his vigil and back to lead the dancing. Folks say he's excellent at it."

Watching the play of expressions on Pheresa's face, Dain didn't answer. He wanted very much to help her, but as yet he didn't know how.

"Dain!"

Startled, he blinked at his friend, who scowled back. "You'd better pay heed, my friend. She's destined elsewhere."

A plump maiden with raven-black curls and dark twinkling eyes swung around to smile at Thum. "Not if his highness doesn't choose her," she said breathlessly. "Don't you think Prince Gavril is handsome? He can choose anyone he wants for his bride. If he wanted her, wouldn't he have asked for a betrothal by now? Oh, I say a prayer every night that his eye will alight on me, or my sister." She giggled and blushed as she turned away.

Dain frowned. Now he understood why Pheresa was alone and unpopular. She'd been raised with the expectation that she would wed Prince Gavril, who'd both rejected and humiliated her. Although he'd long hated Gavril, Dain had never before considered him stupid. Not only was the lady beautiful beyond all compare, but she had courage as well. How else could she withstand the cruel jests and gossip at her expense? No one in the room was her equal.

And, he thought, *she is not going to belong to Gavril.*

Thum tugged at his sleeve. "No, Dain," he said with renewed urgency. "No."

But watching the lady of his dreams, Dain paid his friend no heed.

17

THE MEETING PLACE was a dim, dank room in the auxiliary buildings flanking the ruined cathedral north of the palace. Having missed his supper for the investiture fast, Gavril found the walk tiring and long. His feet made little sound on the soft dirt as he took a shortcut across a meadow. Overhead, clouds scudded across a thin moon. He found the solitary darkness unsettling. Tiny sounds startled him: the rustling of animals in the meadow grass, the soft call of a night bird seeking its prey, the sudden fierce singing of insects.

Several times he stopped in his tracks, listening to the night wrapped around him, while his hand clutched his dagger and his breath came short and fast.

He was not afraid, of course. Gavril knew himself to be no coward. But it was one thing to plan a clandestine meeting in a forbidden area, and a far different thing to actually carry it out, without companions or a protector or guards. He was unused to being alone, and he did not like it. He found himself wishing for the silent competence of Sir Los at his back, then angrily shoved such weakness away. Sir Los would have prevented him from coming here to meet the priests of the Sebein cult. And besides, Sir Los was dead, having failed him the one time it really mattered.

Gavril scowled in the darkness and looked ahead at the dark shape of the cathedral outlined against the night sky. No light shone from its windows. He listened, but heard nothing to mark the presence of even a single individual.

Alarm crawled up his spine. Would the priest meet him as agreed? Or was he walking into a trap? He'd been told never to do something like this, never to venture forth on his own to meet individuals not approved by the palace, never to go out without at least his protector at his side. Moreover, as outcasts, the members of the Sebein cult were hardly law-abiding citizens. Practitioners of the dark arts forbidden since the reformation, they might enslave him or hold him as a hostage or do any number of things to him.

Dry-mouthed, he swallowed with difficulty before squaring his shoulders and pushing on. Tanengard lay foremost in his thoughts. He *must* learn to control the sword. Next to the urgency of that, the risk he'd taken in coming here hardly mattered. Besides, he told himself, it would hardly further the cause of the Sebeins to harm him.

In a few minutes, he reached the stone steps of the cathedral. Only here, close up, did its exposed rafters from the missing roof show. Rubble littered the ground. His feet crunched across broken glass from the shattered windows. Although he had never been prey to wild imaginings, Gavril sensed something forlorn and eerie about the place that made him shiver.

Breathing hard, he clutched his Circle and muttered a prayer. He was one of the faithful; he could not be harmed here.

A shape stepped out from the shadows, making him start.

"So you have come," the man said.

Gavril had to draw in more than one breath to find his voice. "I have come," he replied.

"Alone?"

The priest's caution annoyed Gavril. After all, he had given his word. "Yes, yes, of course I am alone," he said pettishly. "It is exactly as we agreed."

"This way," the man said, gesturing. He walked off, his figure blending into the shadows.

Gavril followed him, now and then stumbling over fallen blocks of stone or pieces of timber that had fallen from the abandoned cathedral. Cardinal Noncire had periodically urged the king to order this structure torn down, but King Verence had always refused.

"Let it stand as a reminder of what we no longer believe," he would say. "Let it remind those who will not reform of what their fate can be."

I am not backsliding, Gavril told himself as he followed the Sebein into one of the buildings.

When the door to it was opened, light stabbed out briefly into the night. Gavril crossed the threshold, and another priest in dark robe and cowl hastily shut the door on his heels. Swallowing hard, Gavril glanced around at the poorly furnished room. Lit only by a single, wavering candle, it held a crudely made table and a collection of stools. The hearth lay cold on this summer night, its front heavily blackened from the past winter's fires. A large brass Circle hung on one wall. Small niches beneath it held objects that Gavril swiftly turned his gaze from.

He felt compressed by an immense weight. He could barely breathe, and his heart hammered violently inside his chest. His conscience was like something alive, twisting and writhing inside him. He should not be here. He knew that, knew it to the very depths of his soul, but although he could have opened the door and fled back out into the night, he remained there and stared at the two cowled figures, now standing shoulder-to-shoulder in front of him.

"How may we serve your highness?" one of them asked.

Gavril hesitated, then lifted his chin. "I wish instruction in some of the ancient arts."

"So your message said."

"Will you teach me?"

"Your highness is far too vague. What, specifically, do you wish to learn? Supposing we could even do as you ask—"

"Oh, come!" Gavril said impatiently, sweeping out his arm. "Let us not play such games. Of course you can. You're Sebeins. You have kept the ancient knowledge."

"The forbidden knowledge," the second man whispered.

Gavril glared at him. "Yes," he snapped. "Forbidden."

"Is your highness repudiating his beliefs in order to come to us?" the first man asked.

"No," Gavril said.

"Then I do not see how we can help you."

Gavril fumed. They were forcing him to tell them more than he wished to. He did not like the feeling of being cornered, of having less than the upper hand. But for

once, he was the suppliant. They did not have to cooperate with him. Nor had he means of forcing them to.
Even if he ran back to the palace and called out the guards,
these men would vanish like smoke. Beyond that, how
would he ever explain what he was doing here in the first
place? An uncomfortable image of having to stand before
the king, making long, impossible explanations, filled
Gavril's mind.

He found himself perspiring. It was too warm and close
in this low-ceilinged room.

"Very well," he said in annoyance, his words ending
the silence. "I have come across a sword, a special, extraordinary weapon. It is not fit for ordinary use. Its . . .
qualities need controlling. I want to learn how to be its
master."

The Sebeins exchanged glances. The taller of the two
stepped forward. "Did you bring this weapon?"

"Of course not," Gavril snapped. "I am supposed to
be at my vigil tonight. The sword is under guard, to be
given to me at dawn when I emerge."

"The one who guards it, is he capable of—"

"A mere servant, nothing more. He is under orders to
handle it by its scabbard only."

"Is it not against Mandrian law to own a magicked
sword, your highness?"

Gavril's mouth compressed itself into a hard line. He
shrugged. "What of that? The law does not apply to me."

The man bowed. "Does your highness know who forged
this blade of extraordinary powers?"

"Yes, a Netheran smith named Lander. He is bound to
Thirst Hold in the uplands."

"Not one of the famous smiths," the priest said thoughtfully. "From whence came the metal?"

"Nold. It was obtained from a dwarf in the Dark Forest. Beyond that, I have no further information."

"Was the sword made at your request?"

"No!"

"Pity. It would make things easier. How old is the weapon?"

Gavril frowned, growing impatient with these trivial questions. "I know not. Two months, perhaps less."

"Does the sword have a name?"

"Yes, it's—"

"Do not say it aloud!" the priest warned him with an upraised hand.

Gavril swallowed the word, and glanced apprehensively around the dimly lit room.

The priest lowered his hand slowly, letting out his breath in a sigh. "It is enough that you know it. Tell me, your highness, has its power been unleashed, or does it yet remain a virgin blade?"

Suddenly he was flooded by memories of that day on the bank of the Charva: the sunlight gleaming on the water, the grass verdant and green, the air soft and fragrant with the scents of summer—all shattered in an instant as the Nonkind monsters poured into this world from their own, bringing their stench and death with them. He remembered holding the reins tightly as his terrified horse tried to bolt. He'd been surrounded on all sides by the stalwart church soldiers holding drawn weapons. He remembered watching the battle as the monsters attacked and slew Lord Odfrey's courageous knights. Sir Damiend had passed orders to prepare his men for the onslaught that would next come at them. And all the while Gavril had sat there, unable to seize command as he had been born and bred to do, the very sight and smell of the monsters turning his bowels to water. He'd felt sick from his own fear, and it had taken all his willpower not to spew his vomit. Sitting there on his horse, he had not been able to shake off the remembrance of the shapeshifter's attack in Thirst Hold, of how its talons had raked him with agony, how he'd seen the crimson spurt of his own blood, listened to his own screams, felt the searing, fetid breath of the monster as its jaws opened for him. And so, shaking with terror as the Nonkind continued their attack at the Charva, he'd said nothing while Sir Damiend steadied his men and calculated whether they could gallop to safety.

Then there had come a blinding flash of light, as though lightning was striking from the cloudless sky. A voice had shouted over the din of battle, a voice speaking words in a language Gavril did not recognize. And through the clouds of dust churning over the battleground, Dain had come riding into view. Wearing no armor and wielding the sword that blazed with light, he'd fought off the monsters, slaying them and driving them back single-handedly. Dain alone, armed with Tanengard, had driven away the Nonkind forces.

As the battle ended, and the last fearsome shrieks of the monsters faded on the air, Gavril had felt so jealous of Dain it had been like a stab to his heart. *He* should have been the hero. *He* should have been the one vanquishing the foe. Instead, he had cowered like a child, consumed with fear, while Dain took all the glory. Moreover, it was unbearable that once again Dain should save his life. Gavril had never hated Dain more than he did at that moment. As soon as possible, he took possession of the magical sword, determined that Tanengard would make him the mightiest warrior Mandria had ever seen.

But today's defeat by Dain, in front of the court and his own father, despite the presence of Tanengard in his hand, had shaken Gavril to his core. It was inconceivable that he should wield the sword and *still* suffer defeat. That must never happen again.

"Your highness?" the priest said, breaking Gavril's thoughts. "Has the sword's power been used?"

"It has," Gavril said hoarsely.

"By you?"

"No. I want to learn how to invoke that power, how to control it. According to the legends, such swords sometimes serve only one hand. I want that hand to be mine."

The two priests exchanged another look. The one who
had been quiet now walked away and left by a small door
in the back of the room.

"Very well, your highness," the remaining priest said.
"Such a skill is relatively easy to learn, providing you
can release your fear."

"How dare you say I'm afraid!" Gavril said, reaching
for his dagger. "You insult me!"

"I speak the truth," the priest replied coolly. "Unhand
your weapon. We will help you. There remains only the
matter of price."

Gavril shrugged. "Name it."

The back door opened, and two individuals stepped
through. One of them was the second Sebein priest, carrying a small bronze cauldron. The other wore travel clothing of leather leggings, boots, and a tunic of undyed
linsey. He strode forward on very long, lean legs, and as
he entered the circle of wavering candlelight, there was
something both powerful and sinuous about him. The light
gleamed on his pitch-black hair, which was oiled to lie
smooth on his narrow skull. His eyes, staring boldly at
Gavril, were yellow, with strange, oblong pupils. He wore
a short, neatly trimmed beard as black as his hair, and
when he smiled he revealed a set of pointed fangs.

Gavril leaped back. "Morde a day!" he exclaimed before he could stop himself, and drew his dagger.

Halting, the Gantese laughed softly. "Do I alarm the
prince? Forgive." He bowed, but in mockery.

Gavril shifted his glare to the priest. "How dare you
bring this creature before me! Are you mad?"

"There is nothing to fear, your highness," the priest
replied soothingly. "Arvt has a certain matter to discuss
with you."

"I have nothing to discuss with him," Gavril declared,
backing toward the door. He kept his dagger pointed at
them, and found himself breathing hard and fast. This had

been a trap all along. He'd been a fool to come here. "All of you, keep away from me!"

The priest he'd talked to and the Gantese remained motionless. The other priest set up his cauldron in front of the hearth and began emptying the contents of several vials into it. Gavril eyed him with increasing alarm, fearing what he might be doing.

"Speak to Arvt, your highness. It is part of the price."

"What?"

"The price for your lesson. Hear what Arvt has to say."

"I will not listen," Gavril said. "You are traitors, and I—"

"Will you run to denounce us?" the priest asked quietly as Arvt began laughing again. "Will you tell the king why you came to us?"

"I'll tell him you kidnapped me and—"

"The lies are unnecessary," the priest broke in. "There is nothing to fear from Arvt. Hear his proposition."

"I won't!"

The priest folded his hands together as Arvt's laughter abruptly died. "Then go, your highness," the Sebein said. "We cannot help you."

Gavril backed his way to the door. Over by the hearth, the other priest muttered words that Gavril did not understand. But something about his tone made Gavril shiver. He knew he must escape this place before he was enspelled.

As he reached behind him for the latch, a light far stronger than the flickering candle could produce began to fill the room. From the depths of the little cauldron rose the image of a sword. It hung suspended in the air, spinning slowly.

Gavril recognized it at once. "Tanengard," he whispered.

He thought of its beauty and how perfectly it fitted his hand. He thought of all its power, power that would not obey him. His lust for the sword overcame him, and he let it. The moment of escape trickled away, untaken.

"Listen to Arvt," the Sebein said. "You have only to listen, and then we will arrange the lesson you seek. Now, your highness, is such a price too high?"

Gavril opened his mouth, only to shut it again without saying the words he meant to. The ambition inside his breast intensified. They had not demanded anything horrible, he told himself.

"Very well," he said reluctantly.

Arvt seized the opportunity like a vixlet pouncing on its prey. "The Chief Believer of Gant wishes to make treaty with Mandria. He has sent me here for that purpose. There are many years of enmity to overcome. This we know. But Gant hopes to be friend to Mandria."

"Mandria will never ally itself with Gant," Gavril said scornfully.

"Not even if it meant annexation of Klad grazing lands?"

Gavril's eyes narrowed. He turned his attention away from the revolving image of Tanengard and focused on Arvt. "Go on."

"Klad is barbaric land, broken among chieftains who are not united. Why should such savages claim valuable and fertile land, when it could be divided between Gant and Mandria?"

Gavril sucked in a deep breath. He had long had his eye on Klad, intending to conquer it as soon as he took the throne. But that, he knew, was years away. And in the meantime, his father had no interest in waging war.

"Your highness sees the possibilities," Arvt said.

"I do," Gavril admitted, eying the man with increased interest. "But I will not persuade my father to forge an alliance with you. Nor," he added hastily, "am I sure I want to. As you say, we have long been enemies with Gant."

"My land is unhappy place, filled with difficulty and

hardship," Arvt said smoothly. "We are terrorized by the Nonkind, which cannot be controlled."

"They do your bidding," Gavril said with scorn.

"Nay, your highness. It is not as you think. These creatures belong to the second world. There are many reasonable people in Gant who would see them and their handlers banished forever."

"Oh? I did not know of this."

"That is because no one ever hears our side," Arvt told him. "The Chief Believer wants to be friends with Mandria—even if it means inclusion of the Mandrian church to help us resist the monsters that plague us. There is much to be gained on both sides, if your highness is willing to help."

While Arvt spoke, the image of Tanengard kept spinning. Gavril tried to ignore that enticing lure, but he could feel the sword's pull.

Perspiring as he struggled to keep his wits, Gavril again forced his gaze back to Arvt. "Your proposal carries merit," he said carefully. "But I cannot promise what my father will—"

"Young prince, we in Gant live long. We know King Verence opposes change. You are future of Mandria. If you do not oppose us, then I know progress can be made."

Gavril's chest puffed out. "Yes," he said gravely. "When I become king, there will be many changes."

"Thank you, most excellent prince."

"Now," Gavril said to the Sebein. "I have listened. When does my first lesson begin?"

The crack of flesh hitting flesh resounded through the bedchamber. Pain burst through Pheresa's cheek, and her eye felt like it might explode. She went reeling back, tripped over a tasseled footstool, and fell sprawling on the floor.

Her mother's embroidered slippers moved over to stand

just inches from her throbbing face. Lying there, Pheresa struggled to hold back her tears.

"Get up," Princess Dianthelle said in a cold, furious voice. "Or I shall slap you again. You fool! How dare you embarrass your father and me before the entire court?"

Climbing unsteadily to her feet, Pheresa didn't bother to straighten her rumpled skirts. Her lip felt like it was swelling and her cheek still throbbed with fire. Tears burned her eyes, but again she fought them back. She forced herself to meet her mother's blazing eyes.

"I did nothing to you, Mama," she replied. "You chose to insult the king tonight. If he decides to punish you, you have only yourself to blame and—"

The princess slapped her again, sending her reeling back a second time. Pheresa caught herself against the bed, gasping and sobbing with pain.

"Now you add impertinence to your behavior. Such sauce! Is this all you have learned at court? You sully yourself by eating with that—that cow he keeps as mistress. You recognize her! Damne! You're a fool, Pheresa, a fool in every way."

"Mama—"

"Hush! I won't listen to your feeble excuses. I came here to beseech the king to take action on this matter, but he will not force the betrothal to happen. And *you*." Her mother's voice deepened with contempt. "You are a laughingstock. All this time, and you have accomplished nothing. Have you even tried to attract his highness?"

Pheresa opened her mouth to defend herself, but her mother raged on, not giving her a chance to speak.

"Making eyes at that freakish pagan before everyone. It sickened me so much I could not eat my dinner."

"He is not a freak," Pheresa said. "Dain is charming, and he is the king's new favorite."

"You should be that! You! Can you not charm even Verence, who melts at a smile? Thod's mercy, girl, I wonder if you have any of my blood in your veins."

"I have done my best, Mama—"

"Hah! What is that, I wonder? Look at you. Look at your gown. Out of style. No décolletage at all." She reached out and yanked at Pheresa's bodice, but the silk did not tear.

Gasping in alarm, Pheresa pulled away from her. "This is my best gown."

"I know—I paid for it. You were supposed to wear it at your betrothal ball. Instead, I see you parading around in it, and your maid says you have worn it several times. Bah! It is a rag now. Useless! And wasted."

"I had to wear it. I came here with my wardrobe unfinished, and you have not sent money for more."

"What do you need with more?" her mother asked scathingly, showing a complete lack of logic. "You have not managed to do anything with what you have."

She swooped upon Pheresa and snapped her long fingers under her daughter's nose. "When they laugh at you, girl, they laugh at me. They laugh at your father. I did not think I raised such a pudding as you."

"Gavril has been so busy, Mama," Pheresa said, hearing the defensiveness in her voice and hating it. "I have barely seen him, and there is never an opportunity to speak to him alone."

"If you had spent your time here at court making yourself into a fascination, so that everyone adored you and did nothing but talk of you, Gavril would have come to your side within an hour of his arrival," the princess said.

Pheresa frowned. "I have been busy keeping my reputation intact."

"No doubt. You look prudish as well as out of style."

"That is unfair!"

"I should never have listened to your father. His insistence that you be educated in a nuncery was a complete mistake. No doubt you would rather go back to the cloistered life."

"No!" Pheresa cried. "I have tried to conduct myself properly. You know what is required of me."

"I know that you have botched it. If Gavril has not claimed you by now, he never will," the princess said in a withering voice. "I have done my best to persuade my brother to interfere, but Verence will do nothing. Therefore, it is over. Finished. We are done here." She shrugged, then pointed her finger at Pheresa. "You have failed. There is no more to be said."

"I—"

But the princess stormed off and thrust open the door, where Pheresa's maid was hovering, obviously eavesdropping at the keyhole. "You!" she said imperiously. "Pack my daughter's belongings at once. She leaves the palace tonight."

"No!" Pheresa protested.

Her mother turned on her. "I tell you it is over. Your father is already starting negotiations to wed you to—"

Horror sweeping her as she realized her mother intended to drag her from the palace in total disgrace and humiliation, Pheresa interrupted, "I won't go."

"You will do as you are told." The princess thumped the shoulder of the gawking maid and gestured. "You, hurry up and start the packing."

The maid curtsied. "Yes, your highness. At once."

But as she scurried away to fetch the trunks, Pheresa shook her head and backed up until she was standing against the wall. "I will not leave the palace, Mama."

Princess Dianthelle sniffed. "This show of spirit comes at the wrong time. You do not impress me."

"I am staying here."

"You are finished here! Damne, girl, have you listened to nothing I've said?"

"There is tomorrow," Pheresa said. "The final ceremonies of state for Gavril's investiture. He could have chosen to simply let the king knight him, but instead he wanted the full religious—"

"Bah," the princess said in dismissal. "He is too pious for a young man of his years. One would think he wants to be a priest instead of king." She frowned at Pheresa while several emotions crossed her beautiful face. Dianthelle, a woman of great ability and intelligence, had never quite forgiven fate for giving her a younger brother who took the throne she wanted. She had then set all her hopes on Pheresa, determined that her daughter would one day reign as queen consort, at least. Now, she looked bitterly disappointed, so much so that Pheresa was tempted to run to her arms and comfort her.

But Pheresa was no longer a child, no longer anxious to please a mother who gave approval so rarely. She could not forgive her mother's tirade tonight, or the beating. Her own ambition was as strong as, if not stronger than, her mother's. She had no intention of throwing away all the weeks and months of loneliness and humiliation—not now, not like this.

"There has been no chance to grow acquainted," she said. "Gavril has been too occupied since his return. I am willing to wait—"

"It's futile."

"Nevertheless, I will wait."

Princess Dianthelle tossed her head. "Are you sure it's Gavril you wait for, or that freak of an eld?"

Pheresa's cheeks flamed hot, but she forced herself to face her mother's scorn. "You should not even have to ask."

"But I do, and what does *that* say? What? It says that you have botched everything. Your stubbornness accomplishes nothing and only makes us look like bigger fools. Come, Pheresa, have done with this rebellion. As a marechal, your father knows when to cut his losses and retreat from a battle he cannot win. You must do the same if our family is to retain any pride."

"I will not go," Pheresa said. The thought of leaving, defeated and destined to go to the hand of the first lord her father could persuade to accept her, was too awful to contemplate. Pheresa lifted her chin. "I am staying."

"To what purpose? What if you are wrong and I am right?" the princess asked her. "What will you do, linger here the rest of your days, a faded lady-in-waiting? You will waste yourself, waste all the good your father can accomplish with an alliance between our lands and that of your husband's—"

"I am staying at court."

"You dare defy me? I can have you beaten for such impertinence and drag you home all the same."

"And everyone will know it," Pheresa shot back defiantly.

"What of it? I am above opinion."

"Then you are above opinion on this matter as well," Pheresa pointed out. "Look at the logic of the situation and—"

"Logic, bah! I wash my hands of you. You are a fool, yes, and even worse, you are a pathetic one. You have already lost, but you insist on ruining yourself absolutely."

"The king likes me," Pheresa said. "If I am not betrothed to Gavril soon, his majesty can arrange another match for me. I'm sure I have only to ask him."

The princess sucked in a sharp breath and glared at her daughter. "So tonight's behavior was only a warning of more defiance to come. You would rather let Verence arrange your marriage than your own father?"

Pheresa flinched beneath her mother's scorn, but she did not surrender. "If I go home now, my father will throw me away on the first alliance he can arrange. No, thank you. I value myself more than that. As does the king."

The princess opened her mouth, but she said nothing. Her eyes narrowed to slits and her shapely mouth pinched white. In silence, she turned away and headed for the door with a furious rustle of her silk skirts.

Her personal page was standing there, gawking, and

did not move quickly enough. The princess swatted him, and the child jumped to pull open the tall door for her.

Pheresa could not bear it. She took a step after her mother. "Mama!" she cried out.

The princess paused on the threshold and glanced back. "You have made your choice," she said coldly. "So be it." She tossed a slim purse of coins on the floor. "Consider that your inheritance. There will be nothing else."

"Mama!"

But the princess swept out without looking back.

When Pheresa only stood there, frozen, her emotions in turmoil, the maid crept forward and picked up the money.

"My lady?" she said.

Outside, a few of the curious were loitering in the passageway. Pheresa glared at them. "Shut the door," she commanded. "Bolt it."

"Yes, my lady."

The maid shut the heavy door, and at last Pheresa allowed her emotions to overwhelm her. Sobbing into her hands, she ran for her bed and flung herself across it, weeping as though her heart would break.

PART THREE

18

THE OPEN FIELDS presented a shifting pattern of green and brown, and were bordered by silvery groves of olive trees and the dark, waxy foliage of clanyx. A trio of marlets, their white rumps flashing, raced through a small wood and broke into the open. The male, his twisted horns arching over his head, led the way, with his two does zigzagging at his heels.

Ducking a low-hanging branch, Dain spurred his mount through a thicket and burst into the open.

A shout from behind made him draw rein and glance back. King Verence came galloping up, his black steed wet and lathered. Nearly standing up in the stirrups of his red leather saddle, the king flashed Dain a smile and swept his hand forward.

"Let's away!" he shouted.

Dain's horse pranced under a short rein until the king thundered past them, then Dain let his animal run. He rode a striking chestnut of pure Saeletian bloodlines. The horse was bred for speed and endurance, with long legs, a slim, lean body, and an intelligence to match his noble heart. A gift from the king, the horse was named Soleil, for his golden mane and tail and the way sunlight struck sparks of gold from his dark coat. Dain loved the creature at first sight.

Soleil loved to run, loved to race. Now, he galloped after the marlets, bounding ahead with long ground-eating strides, his nose stretched eagerly forward.

Dain held him back a little, never letting him get too far in front of the king's horse, which was tiring.

They dipped along a slope, the horses rearing back on their powerful hindquarters and plunging down. A flash of white, and the marlets vanished into a thicket.

The king reined up. "Damne!" he shouted, red-faced and grinning. "They've gone to cover again."

But Dain's mind was running lightly with the quarry. "Nay, majesty," he said, and pointed. "They'll come out up there."

"I'll wager you they won't," the king said at once.

"Done."

No sooner did the words leave Dain's mouth than the marlets appeared where Dain had said they would.

The king uttered a good-natured groan and slapped him on the shoulder. "You have the best luck of any man I know. Someday, I shall learn not to bet with you. Come, away!"

He spurred his horse up the hill, and Dain followed. But as they crested the top, the king veered to the left. Dain and Soleil went to the right. The marlets darted and zigzagged, leaping stiff-legged across a rocky gully, then scrambled their way into a field of waist-high grain waving golden under the autumn sky. Tails up, white rumps flashing, they bounded away.

The king reined up. "Go, Dain! After them!"

But Dain pulled Soleil to a halt, fighting the big horse a moment until he accepted his master's wishes and settled down. Lowering his head, Soleil snorted at the ground and pawed his foot.

"Dain, why do you stop? That field will make glorious chasing. Look at the size of it. Let your horse run and overtake them if you can."

Dain wiped his hot face with his sleeve and shook his head. "Nay, majesty. Soleil has run enough today."

"Bah!" The king took off his velvet cap and fanned himself with it. "My horse is spent. But yours is fresh enough. Do not let politeness spoil the chase."

Dain had no intention of trampling through this field so near in readiness for harvest, nor did he intend to bring down the marlets. He took his thoughts from them, weary of their terror and instinctive desperation. "They gave us a fair chase, did they not, majesty?"

"Ah, now you're cajoling me." With a grin, the king shook his finger at Dain. "You are learning the courtiers' ways too fast. Grow too smooth-tongued, young Dain, and I'll take little pleasure in your company."

In the distance, a hunting horn sounded. Dain turned his head to listen. He and the king had broken off from the main hunting party, which Dain now judged to be half a league away, perhaps less. In this deceptive country of open fields, tiny hills, and unexpected gullies, distance was difficult to judge. Their protectors would be furious, but Dain and Verence were like young, naughty boys exhilarated by their momentary escape.

The king sighed and took a drink from the waterskin tied to his saddle. "Damne, that last gallop was a fine one, eh? I'll say this for you, young Dain: When we hunt together, I enjoy the best coursing I have ever known, yet I seldom come home with any game to show for it."

Dain grinned at him. "Your majesty has shot enough game to supply the entire palace for the winter. Let the sport be enough."

"I suppose that is the eldin view," the king replied, proffering his waterskin to Dain. In the early days of the hunt, it had been wine the king took with him. But Dain's abstinence had been noticed. Soon the king asked for water instead of wine. His disposition improved. His eyes and skin grew clear. His stamina strengthened, and he was a better shot for it. "Ah, Dain, sometimes I think your sympathy lies more with our quarry than with us."

Dain smiled and looked southward, where rows of vineyards followed the slope of the hillside. From this vantage point, he could gaze out at the sea, a shimmering expanse on the horizon that blended into the color of the sky. A white sail marked a ship, though whether it was coming to land or leaving could not be determined at this distance. The afternoon sun shone hot on his shoulders, but the breeze was mild, the air balmy. Far away in the wilds of Nold, the frosts would be turning the foliage gold and russet, animals would be growing denser fur or changing colors in preparation for the new season, and the air would hold a cool bite. Perhaps even the first light snows would have fallen.

Here, in this mellow, warm land, only the harvesting work told of the change of seasons. If he squinted, he could see two men wielding scythes at the far end of the field. They were only testing the grain, however. When they decided to harvest, an army of serfs would descend on this waving grain, with the women and children following them as gleaners.

The sound of the hunting horn came again.

"They've lost us," the king said with satisfaction.

"Time to go back," Dain said.

"Aye." The king sighed, looking pensive. He glanced at Dain, then away. "It's peaceful here, isn't it?"

"It's beautiful," Dain replied. "There is the land and sea in union. The ground is fertile. The rains are gentle. There is bounty rather than hardship."

"And no petitions, no audiences, no reports, no diplomats," the king added. He grimaced. "I hate to leave on the morrow."

"Your majesty can delay."

Temptation flashed in Verence's eyes, but he shook his head. "I've set back our return by almost a week as 'tis. Royal duties cannot be neglected for long. That is not how you keep a throne, young Dain." He smiled. "Or a hold."

With guilt Dain thought of Thirst Hold, still under the command of Sir Bosquecel, who waited for his return. For the past month, Dain had been writing laborious missives almost daily to his hold commander, informing him first of the king's granting of adoption and title, then mainly replying to Sir Bosquecel's reports and requests for orders.

Unlike lords of higher ranks, chevards were workers, overseers, and active protectors of the borders. They made countless decisions and judgments, from the matter of whether the water cisterns should be repaired before Aelintide to the fate of a runaway serf who had committed adultery with the wife of someone in the village. Dain could read Mandrian fluently now, but writing was still a skill he struggled to master. Recalling how Lord Odfrey used to fill a page of parchment with flowing script, Dain labored over one or two sentences, his cursive ill-formed and awkward.

Spending time with the king and his high-ranking attendants while away on this hunt, Dain had discovered how much he still lacked in knowledge and education. Their conversations referred often to history and philosophy largely unknown to him. Only if they talked of war and strategy did he feel at home. In so many ways he felt limited and unpolished, but he was learning fast.

During the first few days of this expedition, he'd learned how to mimic court manners. Next he'd tackled the complicated rules of protocol. He'd used his newly gained reading skills to wade through scrolls of philosophy and history late at night while the rest of the camp snored around him. He'd learned how to dress better, how to wear a cap with flair, and why doing so was important. He'd listened to the squires boasting about how to woo maidens. He'd dreamed of three pale freckles adorning a perfect nose and long, gleaming tresses of reddish-gold hair.

Still growing, he was now taller than the king and broader of shoulder than any except Lord Roberd. He looked less eld and more human as he matured into manhood. His jaw broadened, and the lines of his face grew more chiseled. His voice deepened again, and although Dain remained characteristically soft-spoken, he could—if sufficiently angered—make men quail with his voice's volume and sharpness.

He had named Thum his squire, and his friend took inordinate pride in seeing that Dain's saddle was cleaned and oiled, his weapons dry and polished. Sometimes Dain would awaken in the night with a start and not know where he was. All this would seem like a dream, and he would expect to find himself inside a burrow in the Dark Forest, dressed in rags of linsey, and his companions hungry and cold. But the past was far away now.

"Besides," the king said with another sigh, kicking his horse into an amble down the slope, "it is never wise to leave the Heir to the Realm unsupervised for long. I hear that in my absence his highness has commissioned a new wing to be built onto the palace. He will bankrupt the royal treasury, if given the chance."

Dain frowned. It was rare for the king to complain about the misdeeds of his much-indulged son. Usually Verence had only praise for Gavril's accomplishments.

"Surely his highness has enough judgment not to—"

"Of course," the king agreed, too quickly. He gave Dain a fleeting, insincere smile. "I was speaking in exaggerated terms. No doubt only the architects have been consulted."

"Savroix seems large enough to stay lost in for days," Dain remarked. "I have not seen half of the palace yet. Has anyone said why his highness thinks it needs to be bigger?"

The king grunted as he ducked beneath the delicate silver leaves of an ancient olive tree. Its massive, twisted girth supported a widespread canopy. Sunlight dappled through the leaves and spangled the king's face, bringing to life the mysterious colors of his eyes.

"I do not understand him these days," Verence complained. "This hunt was organized for his pleasure as well as my own, yet he said he could not leave Savroix after having just arrived home. Something else occupies him, I know not what. Do you think him too much in the company of priests and scholars? You have been with him more than I in the past year. Has he grown overly studious?"

Uneasy about being asked such questions, Dain frowned. "Nay," he said honestly. "His highness is not bookish. When he was at Thirst, he spent nearly every day outdoors, gone on horseback to hunt."

"Ah, he is hunted out, then." The king nodded. "If I had known it, I would have planned some other outing for us. Now that he is grown, this is the time to mold him, to begin his advanced training in statecraft. He and I have much to talk about, for it is not easy to be a king, even in a peaceful kingdom such as mine."

"Your word is law," Dain said. "You can do anything you please."

"That is the common man's view, Dain. As a chevard, surely by now you are learning differently."

Dain sighed. Yes, it was true. He had more responsibilities than he'd felt he could adequately cope with, and they were not one-tenth what the king handled.

"There is an even stronger reason to hasten my return than the wayward projects of my heir," Verence went on. "Muncel of Nether has sent me the offer of a new treaty between our countries. I thought my mind would clear on this hunting trip and I would return with a decision, but it has not been so."

Dain frowned, listening with attention as he steered Soleil along a row of carefully tended vines. Bunches of huge, heavy grapes in dusky hues of lavender and purple hung ready for picking. The fragrance of the ripening fruit filled the warm air with a heady sweetness while bees droned amidst the wildflowers growing in the tall grass.

"Is this treaty so wrong, then?" Dain asked.

The king cast him a sharp look. "It does not seem so. I have read its terms a dozen times. Yet when Muncel first took his throne, the treaty we had was more than adequate. I mistrust his reasons for wanting a new agreement now, when Gant is so restless on his other border."

"I've heard the Gantese are often in Nether," Dain replied.

"It is rumored that he has formed an alliance with Gant. That is intolerable to me. His diplomats give me no straight answer on the matter." The king slammed his fist on the pommel of his red saddle. "I will not be linked to Gant, not even indirectly."

Dain found a break in the row of vines and turned his horse through it. The king followed him. It was always thus: They rode as far away from the others as they could, then it was left entirely up to Dain to figure out their way back.

"If you distrust this king," Dain replied carefully, aware that Verence wanted to think aloud, not receive advice from his newest chevard, "then do not treat with him."

"Mandria and Nether have been allied for nearly a hundred years," Verence replied. "It has served both our countries well. We have both prospered. There has been no need for war between us, not even when my father was subjugating the uplands once and for all.

"Ah, Dain, I was not on my throne long following the death of my father when King Tobeszijian was crowned. We met soon thereafter at the Nether-Mandrian border to renew terms. Thod's bones, but it was cold that day. A snowy wind tried to tear the roof off our lodgings. Servants carried endless supplies of firewood to keep the hearth warm. I thought my fingers would snap off from being so frozen. And although I wore furs and every layer of clothing I could pull on, nothing warmed me. Nothing. It's a damnable place, the uplands in winter."

Dain grinned, knowing the cold all too well. "Aye, majesty, it does turn bitter when winter comes on."

"And the rain . . . morde! When it was not snowing, it was drizzling and pouring, and if there was no snow or rain, then there was sleet." The king's frown deepened in memory. "But Tobeszijian, like all Netherans, must have been born with ice in his veins. He strode in, that first day of our meeting, clad in a cloak of splendid pale lyng fur, and frost hanging on his eyebrows from the ride. He was an enormous man, taller than you, Dain, and as broad in the shoulder, with black hair and eyes as blue as the sky. He looked at me while the chamberlains and ministers were still bowing and bleating their ceremonial drivel, and he asked me to come out and hunt with him."

The king laughed aloud. "We coursed a stag for the rest of the afternoon. My ministers were furious, and I thought I would die of the cold. It took me hours of sitting near the fire to thaw out that night—that, and plenty of mulled wine. But, damne, the man could hunt. Now there was a king. We were both glorious in those days, young and in our prime, utterly fearless. We formed a friendship in an instant. I never met a more decent or honorable man. His word was inviolate. We forged a treaty fair to both our realms. And when we shook hands across our signatures, we did so without deceit. To this day, I have kept those terms."

Dain listened to his account in fascination. He thought of the vision, of the ghost-king who had appeared to him twice. *My father,* he thought, and shivered. "King Tobeszijian was lost, though."

"Aye," Verence said sadly. "It's a strange legend of deceit and betrayal, the downfall of a good man with too many enemies who beleaguered him. He was betrayed by his own half-brother, this Muncel who now sits on the throne. Or at least I believe so; there is no clear proof of the matter. Nether was once a land of honorable and valiant men. Now it festers with pestilence, failing crops, corruption, and foul misdeeds. The serfs are starving, and most of the nobles who were loyal to Tobezijian are dead or exiled."

"What happened to the royal family?" Dain asked softly.

Verence cast him a sharp look. "The queen died, taken by a sudden illness. Yet she was of pure eld blood, and they do not suffer fevers."

Dain thought of Jorb, who used to contract miserable colds in the winter, sneezing and coughing in his bed while Thia nursed him with herbal teas. He thought of how Jorb used to curse them for being eldin and thus immune to such maladies as he suffered.

"Then," he asked carefully, "was the queen murdered?"

"Probably by poison." Verence cleared his throat. "And what I tell you is not for chattering about with your friends, young Dain. 'Tis unseemly to talk publicly about the untimely deaths of monarchs."

"No, majesty," Dain said at once. "I won't discuss it."

"There were two children," Verence continued. "Very young, a girl and a boy. They disappeared with their father into thin air, right there in Grov Cathedral, before the entire assembly. It is said that Tobeszijian appeared in a flash of magic, riding a foul darsteed with his babes perched on the front of his saddle. He stole the Chalice of Eternal Life from the service and vanished with it, never to be seen again. It must have been fearsome magic he used that day."

Dain listened, enrapt. As the king talked, he could envision it all, for he had seen Nonkind burst from the second world in just such a way. This account of the deeds of Tobeszijian made him, for the first time, seem real to Dain, a man of flesh and blood rather than a ghost.

"And the legend says he remains lost in the second world?" Dain asked. "He is not hiding somewhere instead, in exile?"

"Never!" Verence declared. "Tobeszijian was no coward. He would never abandon his realm to the evil which has overtaken it. Had he died, his bones would have been found. No, he is forever lost within the spells he cast that day. He is said to have used much magic, so much—he and his queen—that the people turned against him in favor of reformation."

"What sorts of magic?" Dain asked in curiosity. "Besides commanding darsteeds and being able to travel within the second world?"

Even there, riding alone in the golden autumn sunshine with not another soul nearby, the king hesitated and glanced

around before replying, "Many of the greatest warriors of
Nether have carried magicked swords."

"Aye," Dain said, nodding. He thought, *And now your
son carries one too. Do you know that, majesty?* But he
dared not say it aloud. "They are the best defense against
Nonkind."

"No, Dain. They are not," the king said sternly and with
a sudden frown. "Let not a churchman hear you say that. It
is faith that defends a man, faith that strengthens his arm."

Blinking, Dain could not help but wonder how many battles with actual Nonkind the king himself had fought. Perhaps none at all, he decided, for him to make such a foolish
statement. Dain remembered Gavril's brandishing his Circle
at the shapeshifter that night in Thirst Hall, but it had been
god-steel and salt that had saved the prince's life. Later, on
the banks of the Charva, it had been the magic forces in
Tanengard that saved the prince. Why could these Mandrians not accept what was demonstrated to them over and
over?

"We digress," Verence said into the silence. "Tobeszijian
was not of the reformed faith, and not only did he carry a
magicked sword, but it is said his armor was magicked as
well. And he wore a ring of tremendous powers."

"A ring, majesty?"

"Aye. I myself saw it on his finger. Cast of eldin silver,
with runes carved on the band and a large, smooth, milky
stone in the setting."

Dain stared at Verence, and his mouth went dry. He knew
that ring. He had seen it in Sulein's strongbox. The physician had asked him to translate the runes, and when Dain
had spoken the word aloud, the very walls had trembled
around them. Dain felt cold to his marrow. How was it that
Sulein came to have his father's ring of power? How was
it that Dain had come to Thirst, the one place in all the world
where the ring could be found?

He felt suddenly dizzy, with little spots dancing before

his eyes, and realized he had stopped breathing. He blinked and sucked in a deep breath, forcing his lungs to work.

Staring into the distance, Verence seemed unaware of Dain's reaction. "It is one thing," he said thoughtfully, his gaze still far away, "to gossip about spells and talismen with potent powers, but—"

"What," Dain asked hoarsely, "did the ring do?"

The king shrugged. "In the legends, the ring and the Chalice of Eternal Life were given to Solder First by the gods—"

"Solder?" Dain whispered in shock. That was the word spelled out by the runes. He half-expected the ground to rumble beneath his horse's hooves when he said it, but nothing happened.

"Aye," Verence said impatiently. "Solder, first king of Nether. With the power of his ring and the Chalice, he united the tribes of Nether into a country and made himself king over all. But enough of this kind of talk. Old legends do nothing but pull wayward minds into further weakness. Tobeszijian, a man of tremendous abilities, put too much store in his magical possessions and spellcraft. Ultimately they led to his downfall, for he is now lost forever. It is a great pity, but he should have heeded the reforms."

Dain felt renewed shock. "Does your majesty mean that what happened was his own fault?"

"Of course. He clung to the old ways and would not heed the fact that reform was needed. Religion must grow and change with our further understanding and enlightenment. By rejecting the teachings of Tomias, King Tobeszijian doomed himself and his family."

"But it was this Muncel who betrayed him—"

Verence raised his hand and gave Dain a gentle but unyielding smile. "Do not defend him. We of Mandria have forsworn the old ways of magic, taking it out of the Church of the Circle. We live safer that way, and better."

Dain frowned, ignoring the latter remarks as he struggled to assimilate so much new information. His emotions were reeling. He wanted to turn Soleil around and go galloping back across the fields until he rode the wind itself. Were these legends true? They had to be, for Verence had known Tobeszijian. He had seen the ring.

Dain reached deep inside himself, seeking some scrap of memory that would prove to himself that he was in fact Tobeszijian's son. He had no recollection of his mother, this Queen Nereisse who had died of poison. His earliest memories were of Thia, holding him after bad dreams woke him in the night. She had sung to him her nonsense words until the dreams of dancing, headless men and black mist flowing across the floor to get him were all banished from his mind. Nor, try as he might, did he remember his father. He had no memory of riding through a cathedral on a darsteed, and surely such things would have forever branded themselves in his mind had they actually happened to him.

Wistfully, he plucked at Soleil's mane with his fingers and sighed.

The king reined up inside a clanyx grove that cast dense, cool shade. His blue and green eyes stared intently at Dain. "You are Tobeszijian's son, of course."

Startled, Dain lifted his head and met the king's stare. He sucked in a sharp breath, but he could not speak. The air—the very world—seemed to have frozen around him.

The king's gaze went on boring into him as though it could see to his very soul. "Yes, his son, without doubt . . . Faldain?"

Dain gulped. His heart was thudding. He wanted to believe it with all his being. "I—I have been told so," he managed to say.

"You sound unsure."

In sudden shame, Dain dropped his gaze. "I am unsure, majesty."

"You are a young man of the right age. You appear mysteriously one day to Lord Odfrey from nowhere. You are three-quarters eld and one-quarter human, and you seek refuge in Mandria because your sister and foster family are all dead. Am I correct?"

Astonished that the king had remembered these details, no doubt reported to him by Lord Odfrey a year ago, Dain could only nod.

"You quickly exhibit abilities far above your apparent station in life. It is obvious from your face, hands, and stature that you are no serf, but instead a boy of the best breeding. You know the ways of the ancient religion, the forbidden ways. You are as unafraid of the Nonkind as any *sorcerel* from Nether who has been trained to go into battle. You come to my court, and you wear king's glass set in the finest eldin silver. But you do not call it king's glass. Nay, you use the Netheran term of bard crystal. But the true confirmation comes from the setting itself, which has the private rune of Tobeszijian's family name stamped on it."

Gasping in surprise, Dain reached inside his tunic and drew out his pendant. The bard crystal lay warm on his palm. Even in the shade of the grove, it seemed to catch the sunlight and glitter with inner fire. He could hear its faint song as he turned it over and squinted at the tiny markings on the setting. He hadn't even recognized them as runes. They were not dwarf marks, which were what he knew.

"Faldain," the king said sternly, "what was your sister's name?"

"Thia," Dain replied, his voice hoarse and unsteady.

Verence tipped back his head and closed his eyes, muttering something beneath his breath. When he returned his gaze to Dain it was as intense as before. "Dain and Thia," he said. "Faldain and Thiatereika, the missing children of King Tobeszijian and Queen Nereisse. You are his image reborn, you know. I saw it the moment you walked into my audience hall that first night. You have not his height, but you walk like him. You carry yourself like him. As unpolished and unlettered as you were that night, you exhibited a presence no ordinary young man could. That test of the priests confirmed to me—no, I did not request it—but it confirmed to me that you were no apparition, shapeshifter, or false claimant."

He paused and cleared his throat, while Dain went on staring at him, not daring to interrupt.

"I expected you to declare yourself in front of my court. You did not. Instead you gave me that ancient oath of alliance, which proves that beneath your shy facade lies a mind like a steel trap. Many that night thought you brazen, but I understood why you swore no fealty. A king cannot serve another king. Knowing that, I gave you lenience and took no offense."

Dain swallowed hard. "Majesty," he whispered, but Verence held up his hand for silence.

"Why do you think I whisked you away from court so quickly? To utilize your hunting skills? Nay, I have been watching you this month, watching you while I've kept you from the hands of Netheran exiles and others who will foment trouble."

"I—"

"You are playing a dangerous game indeed, coming among us in this disguise of yours. If you think pretending to be a barbarian keeps you safe, throw the notion away."

"But it isn't—"

Verence's gaze pinned Dain. "A disguise," he repeated firmly. "No doubt it has guarded you well from Muncel's agents while you lived in the uplands. But you cannot hide forever, especially not in lower Mandria. Why did you come here if not to declare yourself? Why seek the lesser title of chevard before my court? Are you simply a coward, or is it some convoluted strategy that guides your actions?"

The criticism stung, and Dain flushed.

"Only recently, in a vision, was I told of my identity," he said with difficulty. "I have not entirely believed it. I have had no proof to offer men." He frowned. "How can I ask anyone to accept this, when I myself am not sure?"

"But *I* am sure," Verence told him. "I knew your father.

Anyone who did would recognize you for his son. You resemble him unmistakably."

Emotion choked Dain's throat. He found himself clutching his reins too tightly, and ease his hold. "And did he wear a breastplate of hammered gold, majesty?"

"Yes. I have one myself. It is the right of kings, you know."

"I—I didn't know," Dain whispered. "And his darsteed—you say he rode one like a Nonkind warrior?"

"It is the strange tradition of Netheran monarchs," Verence told him. "A darsteed is captured in some manner, perhaps by a *sorcerel*. By spellcraft the creature is forced to submit. They are savage, dangerous, unwholesome beasts, but when the king is astride one, custom has it that his enemies are often too terrified to fight."

"Aye," Dain agreed wryly. "I can believe that."

"And you, Faldain. What of you? Have you this mysterious ability to master a darsteed if you need to?"

Dain blinked, but he knew already the answer to that question. "Aye," he said.

His simple, honest, confident answer made Verence turn pale. Dain saw him swallow.

"Great Thod," Verence said softly. "I believe you could. That is the proof you can offer. No one but the rightful king would dare."

"Doesn't Muncel ride a darsteed?"

"Nay, lad. He does not."

They stared at each other in long silence. Dain's thoughts were spinning so rapidly he could not keep up with them all. He didn't know whether to shout in gladness or wheel Soleil around and run. *It's true! It's true!* his thoughts kept saying, and yet he still had trouble believing it. He was a king, but he still felt like Dain of the forest. How, he wondered, were kings supposed to feel inside? Arrogant and conceited, like Gavril? Tremendously assured, like Verence?

"Muncel wears not the Ring of Solder," Verence said now. "He carries not the sword of his father. The Chalice of Eternal Life is not his to guard. But he sits on the throne, keeping Nether tight in his fist, because no rightful claimant has ever stepped forward to challenge him."

Dain hardly knew what to say. "The vision—my father—told me to find the Chalice of Eternal Life and return it to Nether as proof of my claim. Without it, the land cannot prosper."

Verence looked solemn indeed. "That is a noble quest, and if your father—reaching to you from wherever he is lost—has ordered it, then you should obey. Since its disappearance, Nether has suffered much."

"If my father took the Chalice and hid it for safekeeping from his enemies," Dain said slowly, "why then does he ask me to search for it? Why not tell me where it is? I do not understand the meaning of such a quest. I could spend my life searching across the world and never find it."

"Are you saying you mistrust your vision?" the king asked him. "Do you think it false?"

"I know not. It helped me the first time. I sense no lie in it, but I was told that I know where the Chalice is, and I swear to you, majesty, that I do not."

"Are you sure, Faldain?"

"Of course I'm sure! To find it would be the most glorious act in the world. You say I look like Tobeszijian, majesty, but I have no memory of him. When I see him in my visions, he is a stranger to me. Would I not remember something of my past?"

"That, I cannot say."

"Majesty, what would you advise me to do?"

"One king does not advise another," Verence snapped.

Dain bowed his head. "Right now, I am not a king. I am merely your chevard, and I have—"

"When do you intend to claim your birthright?"

"I . . ."

"Come, come. I know you are neither hesitant nor as modest as you pretend to be. On this hunting trip, I have watched you master our customs. While I admire your steely patience in biding your time and letting my nobles grow more accustomed to having an eld in their midst, I realize you will not wait much longer. No doubt when we return to court you will begin seeking support. You will need an army to reclaim your throne. You will need money and backers. Your exiles have proud names but little else; few of them escaped with their wealth intact. Which means you must seek help from Mandria."

The king gestured. "Several times you and I have been alone like this, yet you have said nothing. Why not? What do you intend, by wasting these opportunities to woo me and my lords?"

Dain's eyes widened. "Would I have your support if I asked for it?"

"No."

Such bluntness took Dain aback. He wondered why the king had brought up the notion of support if he meant to withhold it.

"Well?" Verence demanded. "Have you no answer for me?"

"Must I answer your majesty now?" Dain asked, trying to gain himself some time. "I have just become your chevard—"

"Yes, my chevard," Verence snapped. "But for how long? When will you abandon Thirst Hold for your throne? Or do you mean to abandon it?"

"Thirst is mine."

They glared at each other, and Dain suddenly saw into the king's mind. "You think I will seize the uplands. Conquered though they are, the old unrest is still alive. You think I will use that to pull them into my cause as I use Thirst for a base to attack Muncel's armies, and if I succeed in winning my crown I will then try to annex all of Mandria north of the Charva."

Snarling a curse, the king reached for his sword.

Dain held out his hand in a peaceful gesture. "Majesty!" he said sharply. "Why would I betray you like that?"

Verence glared at him. "Why would you not?"

"Your majesty has shown me nothing but kindness since I came to court. I would not repay you with betrayal. On that, you have my word and my oath, not as the son of Tobeszijian, but as the adopted son of Lord Odfrey, who was your friend. Odfrey trusted me. He was the first human to treat me well, to show me that not all men are cruel to those of my kind."

"You are human too, Faldain."

"Not enough," Dain said. "Not enough for genuine acceptance. Mandrians take one look at my eyes, my ears, and they make up their minds against me. They assume I am a pagan or that I will cast spells on them. I am to be hated, feared, and reviled. Education and fine clothes, even a title, do not protect me much."

Verence did not stop frowning, but his grip slackened on his sword hilt. "You play this part well, but it will not do."

"I speak with truth."

"Perhaps," Verence said. "But sometimes kings must lie to get what they need. You need an army. As Chevard of Thirst, you have acquired a small one already."

"Aye," Dain said. "I have. But I swear to you my intent is not to divide Mandria."

Doubt remained in Verence's eyes. Within his short-clipped gray beard, his mouth remained a tight line. "I have another concern, Faldain. My son has spoken often against you. It is plain that there will never be friendship between you. Am I correct in this?"

Dain frowned, but he met the king's gaze without guile. "Your majesty is correct."

Verence winced. "And when I die, and my son succeeds me, he will be King of Mandria. If you are King of Nether, will there be war between you?"

Dain's eyes widened. He had not looked that far ahead. But he felt exasperated with Verence for trying to control the future. "I do not know, majesty. It could happen."

"I detest war, Faldain. Mandria has prospered because my

father quelled the final uplands rebellion and kept the peace.
I have committed my life to preserving that peace. As much
as I admired Tobeszijian, I do not intend to involve my realm
in Nether's present difficulties. Civil war there has been
waged for many years now. The kingdom is bankrupt, the
people starving. I would not see the same thing happen to
Mandria. If you want your throne, you must go into that
maelstrom alone, without my backing."

"And if I raise my army elsewhere?" Dain asked. "Away
from upper Mandria? Would I have your support then?"

"I would still lose Thirst, and it is very important to me,"
Verence said.

Dain frowned. "You truly do not want me to seek my
throne, do you?"

Verence stared at him without replying.

"Why ask me these questions?" Dain asked in frustration. "Why confirm the identity I had only suspected? Why
do that, if you are against me?"

"I am not against you," Verence replied. "Look at the
matter as a whole. Look at it!"

Dain stared at him in bewilderment. "I don't understand."

"Evidently. Would it be to my realm's advantage to have
you on the throne instead of Muncel? I do not know. You
tell me."

Realizing he was being given a lesson in statecraft, Dain
struggled to respond. "I—I—Your majesty suspects Muncel
of having a secret alliance with Gant. This is abhorrent to
you."

Verence nodded. "A good start. Go on."

"Were I ruling Nether, there would be no such alliance
with the Believers."

"How do you know?" Verence asked him sharply.

"Majesty?"

"How can you make such a confident pronouncement?
You could find Nether bound to treaties and agreements that
cannot be broken."

"They could be broken," Dain said grimly.

"Would you rouse your wretched kingdom to war? Against Gant? In the past, Nether could defeat that vile land and hold its inhuman forces at bay. Now? I doubt it."

"We would fight," Dain said. "I will not ally myself with Nonkind."

"What if you had no choice? What if you found your treasury depleted, with no funds to pay an army? What if you found that army in disarray, with the auxiliary forces comprised of Gantese?"

"Is your majesty trying to encourage me or discourage me?" Dain countered.

"Neither," Verence retorted. "I am trying to make you think. Young men your age are filled with bravado. War and conquest seem the obvious solutions. Gavril himself is eager to take on Klad, for the glory of Mandria. But youth seldom understands that glory consists of fat coffers, secure borders, and happy serfs. War means death, deprivation, and the risk of defeat. People suffer when there is war, Faldain. I want you to understand that. If you seek to recover your throne, you will start a war among your people. Do not be naive and think all Netherans will welcome you home. Those who have prospered under Muncel will be your enemies. Those who are exiled have nothing to give you except old legends and talk."

"Majesty, I—"

"Not only will you fight Netherans, but you say you will fight Gant. And when Gavril takes the throne here, will you also fight Mandria?"

"No, I—"

"Stop," Verence said quickly. "Make no assurances about a future you do not as yet have. I find resentment and hurt in your eyes, Faldain, but I speak harshly to you today out of kindness."

Dain scowled and looked away. His body felt like wood. His hands were knotted into fists around his reins.

"Muncel is despicable and weak," Verence said. "Were I a warmonger, I would have attacked Nether and annexed it to my realm. But despite what Muncel has done to his own people, he has given Mandria no trouble. It is to my advantage to let it remain that way. Even a new treaty with Nether is better than nothing. If I reject his request for additional trade agreements, I fear he will allow his starving people to raid the uplands. Raiding can lead to ideas of conquest. That must not be allowed."

"I understand, majesty," Dain said quietly.

Verence looked at him. "I hope so. Now, with all that said, let us consider Thirst Hold. It is a key fortress that guards the Nold border. If you cannot or will not serve there as chevard, loyal and faithful to me, then I must choose someone else."

There it was at last, the threat that was the nexus of this entire discussion. Alarm stiffened Dain's spine. Was the king asking him to renounce his new title? He stared hard at Verence, but the king's face was stone.

"I do not understand," Dain said. "Thirst is mine."

"Not entirely. I remain sovereign over it."

"But it belongs to—"

"You have read the original deeds," the king interrupted him. "But what you've failed to consider is that the last rebellion ended in defeat. That invalidated the original deeds, and new warrants were issued. As sovereign, I can renounce your title and declare you traitor. Then Thirst lands rightfully revert to me."

Dain's frown deepened. "I do not want to fight you, majesty."

"Nor do I wish to fight you," Verence replied. "But were I to, consider the fact that my army outnumbers yours considerably. If we besieged you, you would find the outcome hopeless."

"Majesty, I—I—"

From nearby came the sound of a hunting horn and galloping hooves. Verence frowned. "This is our last opportunity to speak in true privacy," he said. "Everything we have discussed today is for our ears alone. But I would have this settled with you before I return to Savroix."

"But I—"

"Well? I will be frank with you, Faldain. Your worthiness shines from you. I have been most impressed with your qualities, and I want you as my man. You can be of inestimable use to me if you remain my chevard."

Dain's emotions were threatening to overtake him. The king's praise would have swelled his head, were it not for all the rest that had been said.

"If you intend to seek your kingdom," Verence said, "tell me now and I shall divest you of your rank of chevard."

Dain grew hot with resentment. It was unfair for the king to insist that he decide his entire future so quickly, with such scant warning. "Must I say at this moment?" he asked.

"How long would you delay?" the king replied harshly. "Two choices for your future lie before you. When we return, you will meet Prince Spirin and the young Count Renylkin, two exiles whom I have welcomed to my court. Let them champion you. Lead them and the other Netheran refugees back to your blighted land, where Muncel will defeat you. Or, remain a chevard and keep Thirst secure for me. Remain loyal to me, and I will see that you are rewarded generously. I can increase your land, your serfs. I can award you the title of baron. Your wealth will multiply. You can go far with me. In fact, when we return to Savroix you have my permission to choose a bride from among the maids at court."

"Marry?" Dain gasped, goggling at the thought. Indeed, the king caught him off guard at every turn.

"Of course," Verence said with a grin, clapping him on the shoulder. "You're a fine, strapping lad. It's time you wed and settled down. We believe in early marriages here in Mandria. It makes for much happiness."

Dain could not speak. His mind was spinning.

As Verence's smile broadened, the thunderous sound of approaching horsemen made Dain look in that direction.

The horn blared over the barking dogs, and someone stood up in his stirrups to wave. "Good king, we have found you!" he shouted.

Ignoring the hunting party coming straight for them, the king went on staring at Dain. "Yes, a wife," he said. "Choose her well and quickly. Enjoy the prosperity I can guarantee you. Or throw everything away on a gamble you cannot win. Your choice lies before you, Faldain. Make it now."

The ruthlessness in his tone warned Dain that the king would carry out this threat to strip away his title, his new wealth, the chance to woo Pheresa . . . everything that had come to matter. Dain gazed at the ears of his fine horse and frowned. He did not want to return to being a beggar in rags.

Am I a coward? he asked himself, but there was no time to sort out his feelings or his desires. Time was running out.

"Well?" the king demanded.

"I remain chevard," Dain muttered.

A grin brightened the king's face, and he laughed aloud. "Excellent! You are more sensible than I expected. Well chosen, my boy. You won't regret this. On that, you have my word. Lord Odfrey himself would be pleased."

Feeling as though he'd made the mistake of a lifetime, Dain bowed his head. "Yes, majesty. Thank you."

"Ah, and they're upon us," Verence said.

Dogs and riders reached the grove, plunging to a halt on all sides. Laughing, the men chattered rapidly while the dust they'd stirred up clouded everyone. The dogs, pink tongues lolling, milled around between the horses' legs, yapping with excitement and leaping at the king's stirrups.

Laughing, the king petted the animals, then straightened in his red saddle. Taking a ring from his finger, he handed it to Dain. "Here. I believe I must pay for my lost wager on the marlets, Dain."

Their eyes met. It was not "Faldain" before these others, he noted, but simply "Dain." His heart felt sore at what he'd thrown away. Yet it had only been a dream, he reminded himself, never reality. King Verence was right: Claiming his throne would have been a hopeless gamble. Then again, taking what was sure was the dwarf way, the way Dain had been raised. He wished he didn't feel as though a rock sat on his chest.

"Take the ring," Verence said.

Dain frowned. He'd sold his kingdom for a ruby, it seemed. He didn't want the trinket. "Our wagers have always been for sport, majesty, never for real."

"I know, but today I feel generous. Take it."

Everyone was staring with avid curiosity. Self-conscious, Dain reddened, then took the ring.

Verence chuckled and glanced around at his men. "He always wins when we wager which way the accursed animals will run. Who has a full waterskin remaining? Mine is dry."

"No water, sire, but I do have wine," a man offered.

Verence hesitated only marginally. "Well, why not?" he said gaily. "The hunting is over. Let us go back to camp and celebrate our last night here beneath the stars."

Whistling to his dogs, Verence wheeled his black horse around, laughing at what his protector said to him in chastisement, and spurred the horse away.

Dain held a fretting Soleil back as they all galloped after the king. Only Sir Terent, looking hot and disapproving, remained with Dain.

"You are one as bad as the other, m'lord," he said. "I have a mind to start—"

"Don't scold me," Dain replied absently. "I need to think."

"Well, put that fancy ring on your finger before you drop it in the dust," Sir Terent said.

Starting from his thoughts, Dain looked down at the heavy band of gold and its handsome ruby setting. It was a generous gift indeed, worthy of a king. Dain slid it on his finger and found the weight a shackle.

Sir Terent grunted with admiration. "Now you look like a lord."

Dain resisted the urge to hurl the ring into the bushes.

Instead, he cantered atop a vantage point, where at last he drew rein. There, with the sinking sun turning the water into molten copper and the sea breeze whipping his hair back from his face, Dain faced what had just happened.

For all his surface geniality, the King of Mandria possessed a mind as ruthless, sharp, and manipulative as any of the plotters and intriguers in his court. Letting Dain think that today was going to be just another adventure in coursing game, Verence had sprung his trap with wily cleverness. He had by turns astonished, angered, and shocked Dain, seeking to keep him off guard and pressured. He had boxed Dain in, forcing him to make a rapid choice while sweetening the rewards with first the offer of a bride of Dain's choosing and then this magnificent ring. Dain saw how he'd been outmaneuvered. His lack of confidence and belief in his true identity had been his weakness.

Yet was he wrong to do as Lord Odfrey had wanted? He'd kept his promise to the dying man, and Dain knew he could run Thirst Hold ably for the rest of his life. Why not be happy and accept it?

His conscience refused, however, to lie easy. He could not help but remember the torment in Tobeszijian's ghostly eyes. The guilt. Tobeszijian had preserved the sacred artifacts of Nether from his murderous half-brother, but he had not saved his people. Even among the dwarves, Muncel's atrocities had been talked about for years. Dain grimaced. The mess in Nether had been his father's doing. Why should it now be his responsibility? After all, he'd been abandoned by Tobeszijian too.

For a moment, he saw Thia in his mind's eye. With her blond tresses stirring and writhing on her shoulders, she was slim, regal, and imperious. Were she still alive, she would not have hesitated to throw Verence's gifts back in his face and called for war. The hopelessness of its outcome would not have daunted her.

Moved, his eyes burning, Dain reached inside his tunic

and clutched his bard crystal. "Dear sister," he whispered, "I need you now."

But Thia was not with him. She would never again be with him, never guide him or tell him what to do. He was a man now, a man with his own choices to make and his own life to lead. His heart called out to her spirit, but he heard in reply only the haunting cry of a seabird, wheeling in the air, while the waves crashed endlessly on the rocks below.

19

THE KING'S RETURN to Savroix was met by exuberant fanfare, fluttering pennants, and cheering crowds. They rode through the town while people leaned out of windows and thronged the paved streets. Riding among the king's large party of companions and servants, Dain listened to the cheering and gazed out at the happy, admiring faces. King Verence truly was loved by his subjects. Waving and smiling, the king motioned for a squire to ride alongside him and hold aloft a basin filled with coins. Scooping up handfuls of money, Verence tossed it into the crowd.

With eager whoops, people fought and scrambled for the coins that rained down on their shoulders and bounced over the cobbles. Trumpets sounded from the walls of the city, and Verence exited the massive gates with a final wave.

But even more crowds lined the broad avenue leading from the town to the palace. As the king's party rode by, additional folks came running, prosperous merchants and serfs alike. Children in rags ran alongside the horses, yelling and waving their hands.

Halfway up the road, a cheery piping of reedoes and flutes met them. Musicians in the king's colors parted on either side of the road, loudly playing his favorite melodies.

Looking delighted by this surprise, Verence laughed and spurred his horse ahead with the eagerness of a boy. "Home!" he shouted.

It seemed the entire palace had turned out, servants and courtiers alike, to welcome their monarch back. The Countess Lalieux stood on the balcony overlooking the steps. Attired in a stunning gown of emerald-green cloth woven with threads of gold, the king's mistress shimmered with every movement, and she blew his majesty bold kisses.

Laughing, he saluted her in return. Then a look of surprise crossed his face. "Where is the prince?"

While the cheering died down, servants conferred hastily. The king's brow grew thunderous. He beckoned to a page. "Inform Lady Lalieux that I shall join her later."

The page bowed and hurried away.

"Well?" the king shouted, picking up the flagon of wine that was brought to him. "I have traveled a hard road today, and I expect my son to be here to greet my return." He drank deep, then slung the dregs on the pavement like splatters of blood. "What is your answer, damne! Someone must know what is meant by this insult."

A steward of the palace began stammering a vague reply, but he was interrupted by a broad figure in spotless white robes who was slowly descending the steps to the courtyard.

"May I speak, your majesty?" asked the soft, velvety tones of Cardinal Noncire.

"Ah, Cardinal," the king said. "Of course *you* will satisfy this little mystery. You have always been able to keep my son on your leash."

Noncire's small black eyes sharpened, but his expression never changed. "His highness had every intention of being here to welcome your majesty's return. In fact, he has planned a surprise."

"Has he?" Verence said coldly.

Farther back in the king's party, Dain shifted impatiently in his saddle. He didn't understand why Verence refused to dismount so the rest of them could. Coated with dust and so parched his tongue was sticking to the roof of his mouth, Dain wanted only to go indoors and find a pail of water to drink and another to bathe in. With those comforts satisfied, he intended to seek out Lady Pheresa and Sulein, in whichever order.

But the cardinal, like most priests of his religion, was proving to be long-winded and officious. Silently, Dain urged him to get on with it.

"Your majesty must remember that his highness is still a young man, with a young man's passions for new endeavors. I believe you will find him in the Field of Salt."

Several people gasped, and Dain saw Verence turn pale. The king stared only for a few moments before he clenched his jaw tight and wheeled his reluctant horse around. His gaze swept the men.

"Lord Roberd," he snapped. "Lord Dain. Accompany me."

Dain swallowed a groan, but knew he dared not show his reluctance. The king seldom lost his temper, but when he did it was unpleasant for all concerned.

Beside him, though Thum looked apprehensive, he gathered his reins, ready to stay at Dain's side.

Dain shot Thum a quick glance. He knew that Gavril had once threatened Thum's family and might do so again if Thum witnessed whatever was about to happen between royal father and son.

Quickly he said, "See to our quarters, if we still have any. Find Sulein, and tell him I want to see him as soon as the king dismisses me."

Thum looked as though he'd been given a reprieve. "Aye," he said in a grateful voice. "I'll make sure that all is ready for your return."

Dain kicked Soleil forward to fall in behind the king's protector. Lord Roberd, his own protector swinging in alongside Sir Terent, rode next to Dain.

As they rode away, leaving behind a crowd gone quiet, Dain glanced at Lord Roberd, but the champion's face remained impassive. Although dust coated the man's black tunic and cap, he seemed tireless as he kicked his mount to a trot.

They crossed the fine gardens, where the horses' hooves cut up the meticulous lawn, but the king did not seem to care.

A trio of servants on ladders, busy shearing dense green shrubbery into fanciful shapes, paused in their work and bowed precariously to the king as he rode past them. He acknowledged them not.

Dain glanced over his shoulder at the multistoried palace rising above him. Its many windows, evidence of the king's tremendous wealth, glittered as they reflected the afternoon sun. Was Pheresa in one of those rooms? Dain wondered. Did she see him riding by? Would she care if she did?

During the journey back to Savroix, Dain had decided not to ask for her hand the first moment he saw her. She might not share his feelings. After all, she knew not who he really was. Perhaps she would be insulted by an offer of marriage from an eld of no proven background and lineage, an eld only recently made a lord.

But she likes me, Dain argued to himself. That had to count for something. If he could make her like him even more, if he could convince her to love him, would she then not smile on him with favor?

Deep in these thoughts, Dain barely noticed as they passed long beds of golden flowers interspersed with blue. Grown leggy and windblown, many of the flowers had fallen over and lay trailing their petals extravagantly on the lawns.

The riders passed through a gap in the shrubbery, and Dain found himself in an open field. The gardeners had cut a broad swath of grass as a transitional boundary between the gardens and the field itself. Along the horizon, the King's Wood rimmed the far side of this field. It teemed with game preserved exclusively for Verence's personal hunting whenever he could not leave his court. Scents of the forest mingled with that of the sun-kissed wild grass waving in the breeze. In the distance stood the stone tower of a ruined cathedral, its roof long since fallen in and its rafters exposed like bleached bones.

Dain's keen ears heard the faint clang of distant swordplay; his nostrils picked up the acrid scent of magic. Instantly alert, he looked ahead. "Thod's bones," he muttered, then frowned in unease. "Your majesty!" he called out. "Have a care!"

The king ignored him, but his majesty's protector glanced back at Dain in quick attention. Dain gripped his dagger hilt in warning and frowned. Sir Odeil, a grizzled veteran whose scarred jaw and throat told of his battle experience, nodded and spurred his horse closer to the king's.

Sir Terent rode up beside Dain, his eyes troubled. "What's amiss?" he asked softly.

"Spellcasting," Dain murmured back.

Sir Terent's eyes widened. He mouthed a curse and set his hand on his sword hilt.

On Dain's other side, Lord Roberd was staring. Dain said nothing to the man. He'd given enough warning; already some of his initial alarm was fading. Whatever spell was being woven in the churchyard, it was not a strong one. Perhaps it would have been wiser not to say anything, but the presence of a spell here at Savroix had startled him.

His gaze strayed ahead and narrowed on the two distant figures circling each other in the weedy churchyard. Only one of them was armed, but Dain knew that lithe, cat-quick form all too well.

"Gavril," he said under his breath, knowing it was Tanengard the prince was wielding. "You fool. You *fool*."

"Eh?" Lord Roberd asked, frowning at him. "What did you say?"

"Nothing, my lord," Dain replied quickly.

Whatever the prince had in mind, Dain knew, he was learning the wrong spell. Although weak, this spell's power came from a tainted source. As a human, especially one of his intense religious beliefs, Gavril had no business toying with something like that. It could hurt him; or more likely, it could hurt those around him.

"Raise it higher. Higher."

Semi-crouched with Tanengard's heavy weight trembling in his grasp, Gavril kept his eyes closed and his teeth gritted. Sweat poured down his naked chest, and he heaved in another breath as he strained to hold the shaky spell he'd managed to weave.

"Work *with* it. Feel its power flow through you," the Sebein priest murmured encouragingly. "Don't control it. Merge with it."

Gavril struggled to obey. With his eyes closed against all distractions, it was easier to concentrate. He kept the five points of reference clear within his mind, and felt the abrasive, raw power of the magicked sword swirl through his consciousness. It carried lust and fury and the hunger for war.

Soon, he promised it. *Soon, I'll take you to war. Serve me!*

Become me, the sword replied inside him.

It had never spoken to him before. Amazed and exhilarated, Gavril felt the blade lift of its own accord. His heart lurched, and he grinned. "Look!" he cried. "Look at it! I have it! I have it!"

"Concentrate," the Sebein told him. After all these days of working together, Gavril still had not learned the man's name. "Do not speak. Stay with its force, and be what it wants you to be."

But the sword lifted yet higher in Gavril's hands and swung itself around to the south like a pointing compass.

Startled, Gavril opened his eyes, and saw the tip of Tanengard pointed directly at the king.

The transition was too sudden. He stared, caught off guard by this completely unexpected sight of his father, who rode up travel-stained and dusty on his black stallion, his face like a black cloud. Gavril blinked, not trusting his eyes. How had his majesty come to be here? Gavril had not heard him or his party approach. The king might have appeared from thin air.

Gavril blinked, his wits still entangled in the spell, which was fading from him rapidly. He smelled it burning in the air, as strong as the guilt ablaze in his heart.

Gasping, he tried to choke out a greeting for his father. He knew he must bow, must think of some swift explanation. But Tanengard seemed frozen in the air. It still pointed at the king . . . no, at someone behind his majesty.

Gavril tilted his head to one side, and saw the pagan Dain astride a beautiful chestnut horse of such exquisite lines it could only have been a gift from the king's own stables. Dain, grown manly, fashionable, and formidable in recent weeks. Dain, no longer a stripling without letters or resources. Dain, who had saved Gavril's life from the shapeshifter, who had defeated Gavril in front of everyone at the tourney, who could effortlessly command the sword Gavril now held.

Tanengard still wanted to serve the eld. It quivered now in Gavril's hands like a dog kept from its master. Cursing to himself, Gavril struggled to lower the weapon. He was horrified at being caught this way. It looked as though he had brandished his sword at the king. Had his father's guards been present, Gavril would likely be lying flat on the ground at this moment with someone's weapon tip at his throat. As it was, Sir Odeil, knight protector to his majesty, looked murderous and ready to spring from his saddle.

"Father!" Gavril said, his face aflame. He tried again to lower Tanengard, without success. Exasperated, and not knowing what else to do, he took his hands off it completely and stepped back. He thought it would hang suspended there in midair. But as soon as his touch left it, the treacherous sword fell to the ground.

The king's face turned red with a combination of amazement, disappointment, and outrage. Clearly he thought Gavril had swung at him, then thrown down his sword in surrender.

There was no way to explain without confessing the truth, and Gavril choked on doing that. He refused to condemn himself. Would the king order him tried for heresy? Rarely did Gavril feel alarmed, but there was a dreadful, hollow feeling in the pit of his stomach.

Not knowing what to say, Gavril bowed. With his head lowered, he glanced around for Sebein, but the priest had vanished from sight.

An awful silence hung over the scene. Gavril, unable to remain bowed like a servant about to be whipped, slowly straightened and forced himself to meet his father's eyes.

"Sire," he whispered. His voice sounded hoarse and strangled, and he stopped, swallowing hard. The king still said nothing. Gavril recalled old lessons in Noncire's study. To act guilty was to be considered guilty. Drawing a deep breath, he forced a smile to his lips. "Father, welcome home!" he said brightly. "Forgive me for not being at the palace to greet you. I fear I lost track of the time."

The king dismounted stiffly, tossing his reins to Lord Roberd. Clapping his gloved hands together in a small cloud of dust, Verence walked forward slowly until he stood in front of Gavril. His stony expression did not change.

"You look road-weary indeed, sire," Gavril said. "How far did you come, this last leg?"

The king ignored his attempt at chatter and kicked Tanengard lightly with his toe. "This sword you use instead of my own, which was offered to you as a gift—how did you come by it?"

"I—" Gavril thought quickly. "Why, I picked it up after the battle by the Charva. One of the men must have dropped it. I found it perfect for my hand, and so I kept it."

"It seems a bit ornate for a common knight to carry," the

king observed. He bent down to pick it up by its hilt, and both Gavril and Dain moved as though to stop him. Ignoring them, the king turned Tanengard over in his hands to examine its golden ivy carvings and rosettes.

Gavril glared at Dain, still in his saddle, and thought, *You jealous fool. You want it for yourself. You hate it that I took it from you.*

Dain was frowning. His gaze was on the king, who swung Tanengard experimentally back and forth, hefting its balance.

"A fine-looking blade indeed, with these carvings. It is new." The king ran his fingertip along the rosettes carved into the steel, and shuddered. "Yes, I can see the attraction," he continued, his voice calm and conversational now. "It's a sword worthy in looks for a prince . . . or a king."

Dismay pierced Gavril's heart. Surely his father was not going to claim Tanengard for himself. That would be too cruel. The king owned everything. Why could he not be content to let Gavril keep this one possession of value for his own?

"Sire," he said in protest. "Please."

The king shot Gavril a sharp look, and too late Gavril saw the trap that Verence had laid for him.

"So you fear I will take it from you," Verence said softly. "You stand here in dread, lest I keep it for myself. And although that is my complete right as your sovereign, still you protest. Have you forgotten yourself so completely?"

Gavril stared at him. He had never been scolded this sharply by his father before. The king's reprimands were usually mild ones, accompanied by long lectures that left Gavril yawning. But today Verence was furious, and Gavril did not understand why.

"Why do you stare at me this way?" the king demanded. "So lost, so blank, so unrepentant? What has become of you, Gavril? Have you destroyed your soul completely, that you stand here on this unhallowed ground, in a place foul, a place I have forbidden anyone to go near?"

"Father," Gavril said reasonably, "it's just an old churchyard. The place has been abandoned for years—"

"Do not take me for a fool!" Verence bellowed, and Gavril flinched. "You know these stones remain impregnated with the old spells. It is not safe here for anyone weak in the true faith. That you—"

"Ah, Father, but I am not weak," Gavril said with his old assurance. "My piety is—"

"I question your piety!" Verence shouted. "Who was that man here with you?"

Gavril's smile faded. He had been hoping the king hadn't seen the Sebein. "Sire?"

"Will you add lying to your list of offenses?" the king demanded. "Who was he?"

Gavril shrugged. "A man, a swordsman hired to teach me techniques used in other lands. No doubt he's a ruffian of some sort. I wouldn't be surprised if he's wanted for various crimes, but he was willing to do this work for me. Coming out here was the only way to get privacy."

"And where is your protector?" the king asked.

"I can defend myself against one man. I did not need protection."

Doubt flickered in the king's gaze. There was enough truth in Gavril's words to give them some credibility. Gavril's confidence returned.

"Father, please forgive me. I did not mean to displease you." He held out his hand in supplication.

But Verence's brows knotted together, and he moved Tanengard aside as though he believed Gavril was reaching for it. Sorrowful disappointment filled his green and blue eyes. "You must think I am a fool," he said softly.

Astonished, Gavril blinked. "Sire?"

"This is a magicked sword!" Verence roared. Turning livid, he held it aloft in a fist that shook with rage. "Do you think you can prance about court with such a weapon and have no one—least of all myself—recognize what it is?"

Discovery. Feeling sickened by the thought of his disgrace, Gavril put out both hands in appeal. "Father, have mercy. It is a tool that can be used for good—"

"It is evil!" the king shouted. "Evil! Look what it has done to you. You crave to hold it in your hands again the way an addict craves his opiates. My son, have a care for your immortal soul."

Shame overtook Gavril. Tears burned in his eyes, and he looked away from his father's wrath to hide his emotions. The king spoke the truth; he *was* like a man crazed. He could think of little lately save the sword and how to master it. Yet he was pious and strong in his faithfulness to the teachings of the church. He could not be suborned so easily. Even meeting the Sebeins in secret was not a sign that he was in danger of losing his soul.

"Majesty," Dain said, his quiet voice breaking the momentary silence, "take care you do not hold the sword too long. Do not let it overtake you."

"Thod above!" the king said in distaste. He stared at Tanengard with a grimace. "This is a weapon that could lead a man into the greatest folly, perhaps even to turn against *me*."

"No, Father!" Gavril said in anguish. "I would never do that."

Eyes hard with suspicion, Verence stared at him. "Would you not? And what of your plans to add a new wing to the palace? A wing built for the pleasure of Lalieux?"

Gavril felt as though he'd been poleaxed. How did the king know about *that*? "Sire," he gasped. "I—"

"She is *my* mistress," Verence said, his voice harsh with jealousy. "Her pleasure is none of your concern."

"But—but you misunderstand," Gavril said hastily, feeling as though the ground was crumbling beneath his feet. The countess was a fascinating, intelligent woman. He had happily spent time conversing with her whenever she permitted him to visit her little circle of ladies. "I merely sought to abate her loneliness during your absence. The building was proposed for her amusement only. I did not—"

"You have also been busy seeking to be named marechal of my armies," the king continued. "When we discussed this, I told you I did not wish you in such a position."

"Father, I could—"

"You went to my nobles behind my back! You think yourself above me!"

"No, Father. I would never do anything that displeased you—"

"But, Gavril," the king interrupted angrily, "you already have. During my absence you have walked perilously close to both heresy and treason. I believe it is all because of this accursed sword."

"No," Gavril whispered, staring at his father in horror. He reached out. "Please forgive me. I will put Tanengard away, lock it away, and I will not use it until I face the forces of darkness."

"What?!"

"Father, you don't understand. In the uplands, where the Nonkind roam and attack, there is need of weapons such as these. When men of other lands use them they do not become tainted. I swear to you that I will put Tanengard away and use it only if I cross the Charva to—to defeat the enemies of Mandria."

The king's eyes narrowed. "You mean, when you cross the Charva to attack Klad."

"No!"

"I know your ambitions. You want conquest, my son. You are content with nothing I have offered you. You are greedy and ambitious." The king shook his head. "Do you honestly expect me to believe these feeble assurances you offer? This sword will fester you and corrupt you further. No matter what you claim, I do not think you can withstand its temptations."

"I can. I can," Gavril said desperately. He took a step forward. "Please, sire, have mercy. I know your heart is kind and just."

Verence's face twisted with pain. "Mercy? Aye, that will I grant you."

Holding Tanengard, he strode over to the church and climbed its crumbling steps.

Gavril watched his father without comprehension, but Dain suddenly jumped off his horse.

"Majesty!" he called out in alarm, "do not—"

Ignoring him, the king swung the sword with all his might. "I will break this blade and drain its magic, that it may never harm another!" he shouted as he struck the cornerstone of the church.

The clang of steel against stone was loud, but it was the tremendous flash of light and the clap of thunder that made Gavril cringe back, eyes squinted and hands clapped over his ears. Faintly he heard the others cry out in startlement. The king screamed and reeled back.

"Majesty!" Dain shouted. Shoving Gavril out of his way, he ran to Verence as the king staggered backward down the steps. Unbroken, Tanengard dropped from the king's slack fingers and bounced, end over end, to lie shining in the dirt.

Verence's eyes were wide and empty. His face was slack, as though all the intelligence had been drained from him. Gavril stared at his father in horror.

Dain reached for the king's arm as Sir Odeil came charging up. The king shuddered in Dain's grasp, then his vacant eyes rolled back in his head and he crumpled to the ground.

20

DAIN CAUGHT THE king as he fell, but the older man's weight propelled them both to the ground. Even through Verence's clothing, Dain could feel the power Tanengard had unleashed against him rampaging through his body. Despite Dain's attempts to hold him, the king stiffened and began to convulse. Foam ran from a corner of his mouth, and he sounded like he was choking.

By then the others were crowding around, all except Gavril, who stood apart in frozen horror.

"Get his tongue," Sir Terent said to Sir Odeil.

Nodding, the man pried open the king's clenched jaws and thrust a stick between them. Lord Roberd moved Dain aside and used his greater bulk to hold the king down.

The convulsions seemed to go on forever before they abruptly stopped. Then, white-faced, the king lay sprawled on his back, his closed eyes sunk deep in his head.

In silence, they all slowly straightened and stared at him.

Lord Roberd wiped his perspiring face with an unsteady hand. "What in Thod's name happened?"

"The king is ill," Gavril said in a shrill voice. "He is ill! That is all that's happened!"

The men ignored him.

Dain said, "When he sought to destroy the sword, it unleashed its power against him. The spells it carries shouldn't have harmed him, for he is not of the Nonkind, but they are powerful. He had no defenses against them."

"Is he dead?" Sir Odeil asked.

Dain shook his head. "Nay."

"His heart beats much too fast," Sir Odeil said worriedly, pressing his hand to the king's throat. "Perhaps he should be bled, to release the terrible humors that have entered him."

"He should be seen by the court physician," Lord Roberd said in a sharp voice. "Let us carry him back—"

"And have the court see his majesty struck unconscious, perhaps dying?" Sir Odeil said. "'Tis unseemly! The court will panic."

"Wait," Dain interrupted them, then quickly added before they could argue, "Move back from him. Let me try something."

Gavril hurried up and shoved Dain back. "Don't touch him! You intend to do him some harm while he lies helpless. Sir Odeil, keep this eld creature away from his majesty!"

Immediately Sir Odeil rose and drew his sword, but it was in Gavril's face that he put the tip of his blade, not Dain's. Gavril's blue eyes widened in shock, then growing rage.

"How dare you raise your blade to me!" he said, his voice cracking. "I'll see that you're broken for this. You—"

Sir Odeil's scarred face grew fierce. "Hear this, highness," he said, and his flat voice held no respect. "We five witnessed what transpired between you and his majesty. And here and now we do swear to keep silent on it all, until his majesty releases us to speak. But you, highness, not this chevard, are the danger to his majesty, with your proven heresy."

"Dain is an *eld*, you fool!" Gavril said furiously. "He will cast a spell on the king. He will—"

"Be silent," Sir Odeil said with contempt.

Gavril gasped in disbelief, but obeyed.

Sir Odeil gave Dain a nod. "Do whatever you feel is best, my lord."

The men moved Gavril back, leaving Dain alone with the king. Kneeling beside his majesty, Dain pulled off Verence's gloves and folded his hands across his stomach. He put one hand atop the king's and his other hand on Verence's face. Closing his eyes, he let his thoughts skim the king's mind.

Gavril shouted something, and there were sounds of a brief scuffle, but Dain ignored these distractions. He wished, with all his heart, that Thia were here. She'd been the one with gifts for healing. Her touch alone could have roused Verence from the dark place where his mind had gone.

Dain searched the king's chaotic thoughts, but he felt no taint within them. Instead he found fear and anger so strong it burned against Dain's senses. And sadness beneath it all, sadness born of crushing disappointment in Gavril, layers of it, as though Gavril had failed many times to please his father. Jealousy too, of the son who had youth and a full life ahead of him, jealousy of the son who would one day succeed the father. Guilt, for actions left undone, for wrongs unrighted, for self-indulgence. On and on, through the complexities that were the king, Dain searched until he found a bright small nugget of Tanengard's twisted power, shining within the king's mind.

Dain had no training in this sort of thing. All that he knew came to him naturally. But he began to weave in his thoughts an eldin song. With his eyes still closed, he hummed it and heard the sword's resonance hum back. Dain thought of mountains, strong and bold against the sky. And he sang of them. He sang of rock and its treasure ore deep in the dark stone cavities. He sang of power and strength that withstood the ravages of the elements, the mining of the dwarves, the carving away of the mountains little by little over the eons. He sang of stone and dirt, and dirt and stone. He sang until Tanengard stopped humming and the small portion of its power faded from the king's mind.

Falling silent, Dain took his hand from Verence's face. He paused, then began a new song. The sword responded eagerly and savagely at first, but little by little, it grew less strident. The tormented humming and restlessness inside the blade became calm. He promised it that no mortal would destroy it, and Tanengard accepted his song.

Dain's voice fell silent once more. When he opened his eyes the sun was going down and the air felt cool on his shoulders. The others huddled together, staring at him in wonder and fear.

Somehow Dain withstood his sudden, overwhelming feelings of fatigue, and said, "One of you must take the sword and put it in safekeeping. Lock it away where no one may handle it without due care."

"No!" Gavril protested. "It belongs to me. I shall say what's to be done with it."

Lord Roberd stepped forward, ignoring the prince. His eyes, grave and a little apprehensive, met Dain's. "I will take this duty," he announced. He continued forward, but his stride became hesitant.

"Do not fear it now," Dain told him. "I have made its powers sleep. It will not harm you."

Nodding, Lord Roberd bent to pick it up.

Gavril shoved him away and lifted Tanengard, only to drop it with a sharp cry. "What have you done to it?" he demanded, charging Dain. Sir Terent blocked his path, holding him back. "What have you done to it?" Gavril shouted.

Dain looked at him with pity, while the others stared. After a moment, Gavril glanced around at them all and seemed to realize what he was doing. He backed up, his face white, little flecks of spittle at the corners of his mouth. He said nothing else.

Lord Roberd shot the prince a look of contempt before he approached the sword again.

"Take heed," Dain said in warning. "Do not handle it more than you must. Do not touch the blade with bare flesh, or it will come awake again."

Lord Roberd pulled on his gloves with a grim air. He picked up Tanengard by its hilt and held it at his side with the point nearly touching the ground. "Your highness, where is its scabbard?"

"Over there," Gavril said, pointing.

While Lord Roberd looked among the shadows at the base of the church for the scabbard, the king stirred.

Dain swung his attention back to Verence while the others gathered closer.

"Give him air," Dain said in warning. "He must wake up of his own volition. Do not call out his name."

Nodding, they remained silent, their faces tense with worry.

The king stirred again, groaning, then his eyes flickered open. Dain saw fear flash in their depths, followed by puzzlement. Sitting up, the king looked around. "Odeil?" he asked, his voice weak and quavery.

Sir Odeil knelt at once before him. "I'm here, majesty."

"What happened?" the king asked, pressing the heel of his hand to his forehead as though it ached.

"Sire, you—"

"No," the king interrupted. "Don't tell me. I remember now. Where is that accursed sword?"

"Lord Roberd has it," Dain said soothingly. "He will put it in safekeeping."

"No! It's not safe!" the king said in alarm. "It must be destroyed."

"Nay, majesty," Dain said gently. "Not here and now. You cannot break a magicked sword . . . as I believe your majesty has now learned."

Verence dropped his head in his hands and groaned. "What did it do to me?"

"It defended itself, majesty," Dain said gently. "Better to put it under lock and key for a time until—"

"Give it to Noncire," the king said.

Dain frowned, not sure that was wise, but Lord Roberd bowed. "It shall be done at once, your majesty."

The king looked up. "Take care with it, Roberd. I would not have it harm you."

Lord Roberd smiled at his monarch. "I appreciate your majesty's concern. Lord Dain, however, has worked some wonderment on it, and he says its power is contained for now."

The king's gaze went to Dain, and he frowned. Dain wondered if he would now have to stand trial with Gavril for heresy, but the king said nothing.

"The guards will come looking for us if we stay out after dark," Sir Odeil said in warning. "We've sworn, your majesty, not to speak of this without your leave. None of us will break our oaths."

The king glanced around at all of them and nodded as though his head still ached. "Thank you. Sir Odeil, help me up."

The protector obeyed and kept a steadying arm around the king once Verence was on his feet. His wits seemed to be intact, but he was deathly pale. He took a few unsteady steps, then groaned and bent over to be sick on the ground.

Odeil held him, murmuring softly, and wiped the king's mouth when he finally straightened.

As Dain watched in concern, Sir Terent edged closer to him. "Will he recover, m'lord?"

"Aye. He'll be well again, but he was hit mortally hard. He won't feel himself for a while."

"Damnation on Lander for making such a weapon," Sir Terent cursed.

Guilt curled through Dain. "And on me, for helping him bring the metal home, for taking the sword when he asked me to bring it here. I should have—"

Sir Terent gripped Dain's shoulder as though to silence such confessions. "It was not your fault," he said. "You meant to throw it into the Charva, where it could have harmed no one. Blame yourself for nothing else, m'lord."

The king chose to ride back to his palace rather than be carried. He had to be helped into the saddle, however, and once he was up there he sat hunched over like an old man. "Gavril," he said.

Looking much subdued, the prince went to him at once.

"Walk by my stirrup," the king commanded. "Let us go home."

"Yes, sire," Gavril said. He gripped his father's stirrup in his right hand, his golden head bowed in the rosy light of sunset. But as he and the king started off, Gavril glanced back at Dain with a look of pure hatred.

Dain frowned, and understood that the truce that had existed between them was now at an end. Gavril would be better off without Tanengard, but he would never admit it. And Dain knew all too well how patient and devious Gavril could be in planning revenge. Whatever the prince did against him would be cruel indeed, and certainly deadly.

For seven days, the king remained secluded. While the court speculated worriedly about his illness, the king confined himself mostly to his own apartments and seldom appeared.

When he did grace a function, he looked pale and haggard, and rarely stayed longer than a few minutes.

The Hunting Ball, traditionally held each autumn, was postponed until his majesty's health improved. Delegates from Nether, waiting to discuss the new treaty, were obliged to kick their heels with no hope of being granted an audience. The king saw no one, no matter how pressing the business.

"King Muncel could take this delay as an insult. Perhaps King Verence does not want a treaty between our realms," the Nether ambassador said huffily.

It did not matter what he said. There was no audience.

During his illness, the king received only his mistress, his son, and his spiritual adviser. It was reported that his appetite was poor. He refused almost everything except toasted cheese and wine. And although his majesty grew thinner, and his barley-colored hair turned visibly gray, he finally laughed aloud one day at the antics of the countess's pet monkey. From that point on, he mended quickly. And soon the word was passed through the palace: The ball would be held at the end of the week.

Dain was not idle during these days. The very night they escorted a shaken Verence back to the palace, Dain found himself taken to his new apartments in the central portion of Savroix. Very grand they were, very stylish, courtesy of his standing in the king's favor. When he walked in, marveling at the luxury and opulence, Dain found Sulein waiting for him as he'd requested.

"Ah, thank you," Dain said to Thum. "I wish to talk to Master Sulein alone."

Thum nodded. Although he was clearly agog to discuss all that had happened, he shooed out the servant Lyias, who was so proud of their new quarters that he wanted to take Dain on a tour of everything. Sir Terent removed himself to the far side of the study and busied himself in polishing his dagger blade. Dain circled through his apartment quickly, noting that he now possessed a study, a bedchamber, and a dressing room large enough to hold Sir Terent's cot. The furnishings were worthy enough for a prince, but Dain barely gave anything more than a cursory glance.

In his new study, he gestured for Sulein to be seated.

The physician, clad in brown robes edged in monkey fur and wearing his red, conical cap, clasped his long, chemical-stained fingers loosely in front of his stomach and sat down on one of the stools near a desk of beautifully carved wood.

Dain hesitated a moment, then walked around it and seated himself in the tall-backed chair. During the journey back from the south, he had considered many ways to approach this matter with the physician, none of which he was sure would work.

Now, he abandoned all his tactics and simply stared at Sulein. "I want the Ring of Solder," he said.

The physician's swarthy face turned pale above his frowzy beard. One of his long-fingered hands strayed up to touch his chest, then he spread out both hands before Dain. The rings which glittered on his fingers were none that Dain recognized.

"As you can see, I do not have the ring."

"Where is it?" Dain asked harshly.

Sulein shrugged. "At Thirst. Presumably you have discovered some estimate of its worth. If you have, then you know it is not for taking on long, perilous journeys."

"It is not for leaving behind either."

Sulein smiled and tilted his head to one side. His dark eyes gleamed with anticipation, and perhaps a challenge. "Ah, so at last you begin to value these possessions. And how did you decide that you wanted this ring, my lord?"

Dain had sparred frequently with the physician in the past. Now, although Sir Terent was in the room, Dain saw no reason to dissemble. Lifting his chin, he said, "As you have long suspected, I, not Muncel, am the rightful king of Nether. The Ring of Solder belongs to me."

Sir Terent nearly dropped his dagger. While he stared at

Dain with his mouth open, Sulein laughed and lifted his hands aloft to the heavens. Uttering something in his native tongue, he brought his gaze down to meet Dain's.

"At last it begins," he said eagerly. "What has convinced you, my lord? What proof have you been given?"

"The ring is part of my inheritance," Dain said, ignoring these questions. "I would know how you came to have it."

"Ah, who can trace the mysterious journey of an artifact lost from its previous owner?" Sulein replied, laying his forefinger against his beaky nose. "I bought it from a peddler many, many years ago. I did not know for certain what it was at first, but I realized it was an object of antiquity and importance. When you read the runes to me, I knew instantly what it was and what it could do."

"You didn't tell me."

"No, you were concerned only with petty matters then," Sulein said.

"You must send to Thirst immediately," Dain said, "and have your strongbox brought here. I want the ring."

Sulein shook his head and made a tsking noise of regret. "Alas, alas," he said. "It is not that simple."

"Of course it is."

"No, young lord. It is not."

Dain scowled. "What game do you play with me?"

Sulein beamed at him, dark eyes shining. "No games, young lord. All I seek is to remain important to you."

"I can have your strongbox sent here without your permission," Dain said.

"Can you indeed? I wonder."

Dain stared at him, trying to curb his rising impatience, without much success. He thought of Sulein's tower at Thirst, and how the door to it was probably spell-locked in the physician's absence. He thought of Sulein's ambitions and mysterious purposes. Suspicions curled through his mind, but he did not act on them as yet.

Instead, he tried a different tack. "Tell me what the ring's powers are."

Sulein crossed his arms. "They are great indeed."

Dain frowned at him and made an impatient gesture. "Sulein, you may think yourself clever, toying with me in this manner, but if I order you searched I think we shall find the ring concealed on your person."

Sulein continued to smile, but a faint quiver at the corners of his eyes confirmed Dain's suspicions. "Violence," Sulein replied with smooth bravado. "The resort of the uneducated."

Dain ignored that gibe. "You claim your ambition is to rise in favor at the Netheran court, when the rightful king once again sits on the throne. If that is true, why do you hesitate to assist me? Why do you keep my property from me?"

"I do not *keep* it from you," Sulein corrected him. "I guard it for safekeeping until you are able to control it."

Anger sharpened Dain's voice. "And are you its master now? What makes you presume—"

"Dain, I am not your enemy," Sulein broke in, rising to his feet. "Never have I been your enemy. You persist in distrusting me, but indeed I am your friend and ally."

Dain held out his hand. "Then give me the ring."

Sulein spread out his fingers. "If you can discern which is the ring you seek, take it from my hand."

Angered, Dain glared at him, but Sulein met his eyes with a confident smile, challenging Dain to see through the disguise he had wrought.

Dain did not want to play this game, but he realized he had little choice.

"One moment," Sulein said, and snapped his fingers in Sir Terent's direction.

Dain looked that way and saw Sir Terent standing frozen by the window with a blank expression on his face. Astonished, Dain glanced from his protector back to the physician. "What did you do to him?"

"Are our secrets for such as him?" Sulein countered. "He

is merely suspended for a few moments while we finish our discussion."

Dain smelled no use of magic, yet the hair on the back of his neck was prickling. Frowning slightly, he glanced at Sir Terent again. If the palace guards grew suspicious that any magic was being used, Dain and Sulein would both find themselves in prison.

"You should take care with your spells," Dain said.

"You should trust me more and Sir Terent less."

"He is loyal."

"Loyal or not, he is a Mandrian. They cannot go where we would tread." Sulein spread out his fingers again. "Now. Let your eldin powers serve you. Which is the ring you seek? Choose carefully, young lord, for the one you choose will be the only one I shall give to you."

Dain frowned and stared at the three rings gleaming on the fingers of Sulein's left hand. His right hand was bare of ornamentation, yet he held it out as well. Dain suspected the trick to this game might well be that Sulein was wearing the Ring of Solder concealed beneath his clothing. Stifling his impatience, he tried to concentrate.

Fatigue made it difficult to focus his thoughts. He was exasperated and annoyed, but after a few moments he succeeded in calming his mind. He stared at the rings carefully until he sensed the spell overlying them. The disguise was woven with amazing skill. The rings themselves provided no information. His senses could not choose from among them.

Disappointed, he frowned and leaned back. If the ring he sought was among them, it should emit a power of its own. He should be able to feel its resonance.

"Quickly," Sulein muttered. "I cannot hold the spell on Sir Terent much longer."

Dain felt a waver in the physician's concentration. He stared at the man's lean hands and pointed at a wide band of embossed gold on his middle finger. "That one."

Sulein laughed with satisfaction. "A handsome choice,

young lord. Not as handsome as the ruby you already wear, but it will make a good companion."

He took off the gold band and held it out to Dain.

Furious with disappointment, Dain struck it from Sulein's hand and sent the gold ring flying. "Which one is it?" he demanded.

"None of these, young lord. Perhaps your eldin gifts are not as clever as I thought. Hmm?" Smiling broadly, Sulein held up his right hand, clenched it, and turned it over in a quick gesture. There on his finger appeared the ring of heavy silver with the milky stone. The fine rings on Sulein's other hand shimmered momentarily and became only dull, cheap ornaments of brass.

Dain stared, realizing how thoroughly he'd been tricked.

Sulein laughed again. "How disappointed you look. But you see, young lord, I bought this ring with good coin. I cannot give it away."

"It doesn't belong to you," Dain said through his teeth.

"But it does. Your name is not inscribed on the band in these rune carvings. You cannot prove ownership, especially when I possess it. Had you seen through its disguise, then I might have felt compelled to surrender it to you. But we have made our bargain, and you didn't choose it."

Dain's eyes narrowed. He stared coldly at the gloating physician. "What do you want for it?"

"Ah! Now that is the first sensible thing you have said tonight." Sulein scratched his beard. "What do I want? Ah, indeed, a delightful question that opens doors to all kinds of possibilities."

His greed was suddenly revealed in his face, naked and intense. He smiled at Dain, while his dark eyes remained calculating and sharp. "If possession of this ring will grant you your kingdom, surely it must be worth a great deal. How large is the Netheran treasury?"

Contempt rose in Dain. Sulein would forever cling to him, sucking at his resources like a leech.

"The treasury, I am told, is bankrupt."

"Pity. Then you will have to acquire funds elsewhere. From Prince Spirin, perhaps? He and I have already discussed your future. What is your favor with King Verence worth?"

"Little," Dain snapped. "He will not support me."

Sulein's bright smile faded. "Are you saying you have spent a month in his majesty's company and accomplished nothing? Have you not built on your advantages? Have you acquired nothing for yourself—no lands, no additional titles, no sinecures?"

Dain's shame was like acid in his throat. If only Sulein knew what he'd really acquired . . . and given away. He reached for his dagger. "Enough of this. Your greed is unmatched—"

Lifting his hands, Sulein backed away so hastily he knocked over his stool. "The stakes are high . . . majesty."

Dain paused, sucking in a sharp breath.

"It has a pleasant sound to it, does it not?" Sulein said softly, never taking his eyes off Dain. "You have seen at close hand how it is to be king. You want that, don't you?"

Dain blinked, throwing off the spell Sulein was using to cloud his mind. "What I want is my father's ring."

"Then you must pay for it."

"How much?"

Sulein shrugged. "Is this the night to decide such a weighty matter? Why not wait until the throne is yours before we decide on payments and rewards?"

There would be no throne, no rewards. All Dain wanted was the ring. Getting it out of the hands of someone as unscrupulous as Sulein was the least he could do for Tobeszijian. "Why not put everything on the table and make our deal now?" Dain countered.

"You bargain like a dwarf rather than a lord," Sulein complained.

Dain bared his teeth and sprang at Sulein. Before the startled physician could back away from him, Dain was gripping the front of his robes, twisting them while he pressed his dagger point to Sulein's throat. He forced the physician against the wall.

"You try my patience," Dain said through gritted teeth. "Off with it, before I slice through your finger."

"Take it by force, and have it you will not," Sulein said quickly. Fear flashed in his eyes, but he had not lost his courage. He glared at Dain defiantly, lifting his chin to ease the dagger point from his flesh. "I can disappear with it, quicker than thought, and nevermore will you find me."

Dain glared at him furiously. "A bluff."

"No! It is the power of this ring. How else did King Tobeszijian escape his enemies? How else did he cross and recross this world, hiding first the Chalice of Eternal Life and then you? Three times can a man travel thus on the power of Solder's ring. Back away from me now, and give me what I ask for, or I swear to you on all my ancestors that I will vanish and take this ring to King Muncel. He will pay my price, if you do not."

Dain said nothing. Anger roared in his ears, filling him with such heat he thought he might burst into ashes. After a moment, he managed to master himself enough to back away from Sulein. He sheathed his dagger with an unsteady hand and stood there, glowering at the floor for a long while, before at last he forced up his gaze.

"For the last time, I ask your price."

Triumph filled Sulein's eyes. He stepped away from the wall. "A position as your court astrologer and chief adviser."

Dain's eyes narrowed, but he said nothing.

Sulein smiled. "My own palace and servants."

Dain waited.

Sulein rubbed his hands together. "One-third of your wealth, not only taken from whatever lies within the treasury at the time of your coronation, but also one-third from your revenues thereafter, for my lifetime."

The request was outrageous. Dain had not expected Sulein to be *this* greedy. He frowned in an effort to hide his shock, and realized that Sulein could have asked for half. Still, the price would not be paid.

"Well?" Sulein asked him. "Think as long and hard as you wish, but there's no way around this bargain. Of course, if you want time to decide, then I shall—"

"No," Dain said abruptly. "I agree."

This time it was Sulein's eyes that widened in shock. He stared at Dain as though he could not believe the bargain was struck. "You swear this?" he asked hoarsely.

"I do. When I sit on my throne, you will have your price." Dain held out his hand. "Now give me the ring."

Sulein's laughter rang out loudly enough to wake Sir Terent from his spell. While the protector was sneezing and rubbing his face in confusion, Sulein shook his head. His eyes danced ruthlessly. "No, no, no, young lord," he said. "And have you vanish to parts unknown without me? No."

Dain had thought he'd made his face as impassive as a stone carving. Could Sulein sense the truth hidden inside him? "I have given my word."

"Yes, indeed, and your word I do accept," Sulein told him. "But I shall keep the ring safely under my guard for you. That way, you will not forget to take me along whenever you leave for the north."

"Eh?" Sir Terent said, blinking and yawning. "What's that, m'lord? Are we leaving for Thirst?"

Seething, Dain managed to tear his gaze away from the triumphant physician. He wanted to wipe that smirk off Sulein's face, but he did not doubt that Sulein would make good his threat to disappear if Dain pressed him too hard.

"M'lord?" Sir Terent asked again. "Are we leaving for Thirst?"

"Not just yet," Dain managed to say. His fists were clenched at his side, and anger was a flame inside him. It was all he could do to make his voice sound normal. "We must wait for the king's leave before we can go."

"But we'll go soon, do you think?" Sir Terent asked wistfully. Homesickness was plain to hear in his voice. "Before the snows fall too heavy?"

"Aye, perhaps," Dain said.

With a mocking bow, Sulein took his leave. "If there is any other way in which I can serve you, young lord, you have only to summon me. Perhaps, when Prince Spirin calls on you, I may be present?"

Dain nodded curtly, and the physician walked out with a beaming smile.

As the door closed behind him, Dain walked over to a small table to pick up an ornate ewer. He turned it over in his hands, but did not really see it. He wanted to throttle Sulein. By tomorrow, when he refused to meet with Prince Spirin, Sulein would guess the truth. Then there would be no chance of getting the ring away from him. He might even carry out his threat of selling it to King Muncel.

Dain sighed and flexed his tense shoulders. He felt like a failure, and the physician's taunts did not help.

There must be some way to trick him out of the ring, Dain thought. Somehow, he had to find a way.

"M'lord?" Sir Terent asked, still rubbing his face and looking confused. "Did I hear you tell Sulein you're the King of Nether?"

"No!" Dain said sharply. He set the ewer down with a bang. "I'm king of nothing, Sir Terent. It was only a jest."

Stripped to the waist, Gavril knelt in the palace chapel before the altar. A snowy cloth embroidered with circles of gold thread glittered in the candlelight. Despite the coolness of the air, he was sweating profusely. Blood dripped down his back from the cuts he'd inflicted with the knotted whip. Clutching it, he bowed his golden head and struggled against his inner demons of fury and fear.

On either side of the aisle behind him, priests stood chanting prayers for his soul. Wine-colored smoke from the swinging braziers filled the air with clouds of incense. Bishops

and cardinals gathered behind the altar in a semicircle of
censure.

When the chanting stopped, Noncire stepped forward. His
white slippers made no sound on the stones. As he halted
before Gavril, his robes swished around his ankles.

"Has your highness found penitence?" he asked.

This was the third time he'd asked the question. Twice
before Gavril had answered with a truthful no; twice before
Noncire had ordered him to flagellate himself again.

Now, Gavril crouched lower, awash with pain and misery, his face wet with tears and self-loathing.

"Your highness?" Noncire repeated. "Have you found
penitence?"

No mercy could be heard in that soft voice. Gavril knew
this could go on for hours, as long as he exhibited strength
and honesty. All he felt in his heart was raging agony at
being parted from Tanengard. He did not repent of his actions. He felt sorry for having been caught, nothing more.

Knowing that he *was* at fault, that he had indeed sinned
most grievously, Gavril wanted to be penitent. He knew there
must be something seriously wrong if he could not renounce
the hold this strange sword had taken over his senses. With
all his heart, he wanted to discuss this problem with Noncire, the way they once had discussed everything. But the
cardinal had withdrawn his sympathy and friendship to judge
Gavril. Tonight, he showed no more mercy than he had during the previous days of Gavril's ordeal . . . during the enforced fasting and the appearance before the church tribunal
for questioning about his alleged heresy. There were always
multiple sides to any issue; this at least had been what Noncire taught him before. Now, however, it seemed that the
church knew no mercy. It considered nothing but its strictest
rules. It permitted no leeway, no reinterpretations.

And for the first time in his life, as his back and shoulders burned with self-inflicted pain, Gavril questioned the
authority of the church that he'd previously embraced with
such fervor. Its rules were for lesser men, not him. The

church, he felt, should suspend its rules long enough to let him explain his reasons. But instead, he had been summarily judged and ordered to make penance for the safety of his immortal soul.

As a result, tonight he abased himself like a lowly serf. He cried out and wept in his pain and misery. And the churchmen watched, standing there in their silk robes, holding their Circles of gold and jewels in plump white hands. Their eyes held no compassion, no mercy whatsoever. Not even for him, not even after all his efforts to serve the church, to find the Chalice for the church's glory.

Gavril's emotions hardened into a knot of resentment inside his throat. It threatened to choke him.

Noncire took a step closer. "Your highness must answer. Have you at last found true penitence?"

Slowly, Gavril straightened his spine. Would he be rewarded for honesty? Would the truth bring mercy and forgiveness? No, it would not. They would only go on punishing and punishing. He knew that worse things—such as hot tongs and the Boot—awaited him once the flagellation was over.

"If your highness does not answer, then resume the punishment," Noncire said.

Gavril felt himself go cold inside. He lifted his head, and his dark blue eyes were swimming with tears. "I have found penitence," he lied. "I beg for the mercy of Tomias the Reformer."

The chanting resumed.

Noncire emitted a gusty sigh and smiled very briefly. He rested his plump hand on Gavril's head. "Mercy is given. Put down the scourging whip and drink this cup of bitterness."

The cup was brought to Gavril. He drank the nasty, soured wine it contained, choking a little. After that, they prayed over him and raised him from his knees. His wounds were attended, and clean garments were brought to cover him.

Noncire praised his brave piety in returning to the correct path. "All men who are worthy," the cardinal said, "go through a crisis of faith. You have survived yours, and you will be the stronger for it."

Gavril's gaze flickered to him, then away. The prince's heart was stone inside his breast. He heard the cardinal's words with shrill inner laughter and contempt. If only Noncire realized that Gavril's faith had just died inside him. If only the man knew that he had driven the final wedge between Gavril and all he had believed in before.

The prince was escorted back to his apartments, and the word was officially released to the king the next day. All was forgiven in the eyes of Tomias.

Relieved, the king sent a letter to Gavril, but the prince set the parchment down unread. He thought of how his father had found him in the churchyard at his dark lessons. He thought of Dain, risen so high in the king's estimation, higher perhaps now than Gavril himself. He thought of Tanengard, its powers silenced by that meddling pagan, still under Dain's command and not his own.

And his anger hardened into a hatred deeper than anything he had ever felt before. Dain had long ago ceased to be merely a nuisance. Now, with this betrayal, he had put Gavril in grave jeopardy. No doubt it had been Dain who'd learned of Gavril's secret lessons, Dain who'd whispered word of them to the king, Dain who'd led the king to the churchyard and that awful moment of discovery. Gavril could not forget the painful disillusionment that had flashed across his father's face. Until then, he had always felt secure in his father's unquestioning love for him. But Dain had tainted that as well. He had exposed Gavril, had made Verence see the truth about his son, and Gavril could not forgive him for that.

For a few days Gavril bided his time, until the opportunity came to speak in private with Arvt, the Gantese agent.

"Your highness sent for me. I come," Arvt said, bowing low from the shadows, while Gavril stood on the palace ramparts and pretended to gaze out across the landscape toward the sea. "How may I serve?"

Gavril never looked at the man. His emotions were icy cold inside him. "There's little time to arrange this. I will bring suspicion to myself if I elude my protector for more than a moment. You know the chevard, Lord Dain?"

"Ah, the king's favorite," Arvt said.

It was like having a shard of ice driven into his heart. Gavril shuddered. "Him. I want him removed. Use whatever methods you prefer, but make it quick."

"'Removed,'" Arvt said, his strange accent rolling over the word. "You mean killed?"

"Yes, killed!" Gavril snapped. He slammed a clenched fist down atop the stone crenellation. "I want him dead!"

"It can be easily done," Arvt said with another bow. "But the price will be—"

"Name it. Anything." Gavril spun on his heel so fast his cloak flared out behind him. He could hear his protector calling his name. Gritting his teeth, Gavril started down the steps. "I'm here!" he called out, then shot Arvt a glare. "Get it done quickly, and I'll pay the price."

"Will the king's ball be soon enough, highness?" Arvt whispered after him.

Gavril kept going down the steps without replying, but inside he smiled with cold satisfaction.

21

THE NIGHT OF the ball, the palace blazed with lights, music, and excitement. For days, servants had been working feverishly to prepare for the festivities. Now, the state galleries had been transformed, with swags of fruit entwined with

gold, russet, and dark green ribbons hanging over every doorway. Animal hides lay on the polished floors. Long brown-
and-blue-speckled feathers plucked from the tails of goursen,
the plump and stupid birds of the southern meadows, stood
fanned decoratively in baskets and drinking horns. Shallow
copper pans held ploven eggs, considered a rare delicacy
and available only in the autumn. Their pale hues of green
and soft blue were enhanced by the polished copper gleam
of the vessels. Crocks of mead, smelling richly of fermented
honey, stood open on tables next to long-handled dippers.
Baskets of fresh-picked apples, pears, and quince stood about
in bounty. There were even rushes strewn across the floor
of one gallery, imitating the cruder life of upland holds.

Walking into this rustic setting that contrasted so completely with the magnificent tapestries and paintings on the
walls, plus the gilded woodwork and plaster boiseries, Dain
felt as though he had slipped sideways through time and
space into a far different world. Beside him, Thum was staring with a grin of appreciation.

Tonight they both wore doublets of dark Thirst green.
Dain's crest was embroidered on his, and a new pin of
worked gold held his cloak folded back fashionably over his
right shoulder. He was nervous and excited as he walked
about through the decorated rooms, marveling at all he saw.
The crowd was slowly gathering as more courtiers appeared
for the evening's festivities. Some wore outlandish hunting
costumes, complete with embroidered quivers of gold-
fletched arrows, and carried tiny bows carved from ebony
strung with gold cords.

Outside in the gathering darkness of eventide, a storm
was brewing. Clouds had brought nightfall early, and now
and then Dain heard a muted rumble of thunder. The very
air seemed charged with expectancy, and it made him more
restless than ever.

That afternoon, he had gone out to the gardens and picked
an enormous armful of the blue and yellow flowers. Recalling Thia's deft way with arrangements, Dain had tried

to imitate what his sister would have done with such fragrant beauty. From an arbor in the shrubbery, he pulled down a vine covered with white, sweet-smelling blooms and used this to tie the flowers into an enormous bouquet, wrapping their long stems with the ends of the vine, then tucking in a few delicate racemes of something pink for contrast.

Carrying his bouquet into the palace and ignoring the stares of those he encountered, Dain handed the flowers to a diminutive page who then, staggering beneath the fragrant burden, went off to give the tribute to Lady Pheresa.

Now, he waited nervously for her appearance, hoping his gift had pleased her.

The Duc du Clune was announced, with his two daughters. Thum eyed the ladies appreciatively. "The younger one is fair, don't you think?" he asked Dain. "Her name is Roxina."

Dain glanced unwillingly in that direction. He remembered Elnine and Roxina from the night when they'd sought refuge in his camp. Their faces were pretty enough, and Roxina was the more buxom of the two sisters, but Dain considered them both foolish and spoiled, with affected manners and too much conceit. Still, if Thum sought an evening's flirtation, Dain had no intention of discouraging him.

"Roxina," he said with a nod as the lady simpered at an acquaintance and fluttered her silk scarves. "Very pretty."

Thum grinned and rocked back and forth on his toes. "Aye," he said in satisfaction. "And nicer than her shrew of a sister."

"You've spoken to her?" Dain asked in startlement.

Thum nodded, acting extremely casual. "You're not the only one with romance on your mind," he said. "May I have your leave?"

Dain nodded, and Thum sauntered off in Lady Roxina's direction. A little surprised, Dain glanced over his shoulder at Sir Terent. "Knew you about this?"

Sir Terent seemed amused. "Aye, m'lord. I heard that

young Thum cut quite a swath among the ladies while we were gone with the king."

"Did he now." Admiration for his friend made Dain smile. "And is he serious about this lady?"

Sir Terent shrugged. "No more serious than a young man can be while he courts three different ladies in three different weeks."

"Oh." Dain opened his mouth to ask another question, but at that moment the Countess Lalieux arrived with her entourage, to much fanfare and applause from the courtiers.

The lady looked magnificent in a gown of quilted silk edged with fur. Her tilted eyes swept the assembly, and she seemed a little put out to have arrived before the king. The young women in her entourage came chattering in behind her, and Pheresa walked gracefully among their number.

Seeing her, Dain's heart stopped. He forgot everything else as he watched her enter the room. Her new gown was constructed in the latest court fashion. She wore vivid blue trimmed with the merest touch of white ermine at the bodice, as was her royal right. Long sleeves also edged in ermine ended in long points over her hands. The neckline of the dress was cut lower than usual, showing off the lady's lovely figure and flattering the graceful slenderness of her throat. She wore her long tresses braided and looped at the back of her head, and not until she turned to speak to someone did Dain glimpse the white-flowered vine woven among her braids. In her left hand she carried one of the yellow flowers he'd picked for her.

The rock inside his chest lifted, and he felt suddenly as though he could fly. Everything was worth it, for her.

Sir Terent grabbed his arm. "Have a care, m'lord. It's fire you play with—"

Ignoring him, Dain pulled free and pushed his way through the crowd toward her.

Clad in a new doublet of pleated dark blue silk, with a velvet-lined cloak swinging from his shoulders and his jeweled dagger glittering at his waist, Gavril strode impatiently into the king's apartments past the bowing servants. Halting in the center of the room, he glanced around, a frown marring his handsome young face.

Sir Odeil, the king's protector, appeared and bowed low. "Come this way, your highness."

"I'm late," Gavril complained. "I—"

"The king is expecting you," Sir Odeil said firmly.

Gavril compressed his lips and swept past the man to enter his father's bedchamber with more inner trepidation than he wanted to admit. The royal bedchamber was as large as one of the galleries, for in the mornings it had to hold the courtiers in favor as well as the gentlemen of waiting, each with their own specific duties in assisting the king to dress for the day. In the center of the room stood the immense bed, with its canopy of gilded wood and purple plumes. Velvet hangings were tied to the massive posts with tasseled cords. The royal coat of arms hung over the bed, and the coverlet was priceless silk, also embroidered with the king's crest. Railings of wood stretched out across the room on either side of the bed. Someday, Gavril told himself, those railings would hold back the crowds of the curious when King Verence lay on his deathbed. It was believed by the common folk that the breath of a dying king could bestow great fortune. *Yes,* Gavril thought, *one day they will come to see you die, and I will be king thereafter.*

But tonight, by the light of the flaming candles, his majesty was very much alive and standing before a reflecting glass as his valet fussed over the final details of his attire. Magnificent in gold cloth and rubies, his crown on his head, the king had already dismissed his gentlemen of waiting and was making a final selection of the jewels he would wear.

"His highness, Prince Gavril," Sir Odeil announced.

The king turned away from the mirror at once and held out his hand in greeting. "My boy."

In the past he would have advanced halfway across the

room to meet Gavril, treating him almost as an equal. Now, however, he stood where he was and let Gavril come to him.

It was subtle behavior, but the implications were a slap of reproach. Aware that he was still not completely forgiven for his transgressions, Gavril burned with resentment. How long did the king intend to punish him? Even the church had pronounced forgiveness. That should be enough to satisfy anyone.

In retaliation, Gavril slowed his pace as he approached his father, making the king wait. At last, however, they stood facing each other. Gavril bowed deeply.

Verence's green and blue eyes regarded him somberly. The king had lost weight since his recent illness. Dark circles still smudged the skin beneath his eyes. His light hair had turned noticeably gray.

Good, Gavril thought spitefully. *Hurry and age. That is what you deserve for trying to destroy Tanengard.*

"All of you may go," the king said to his minions. He glanced at Sir Odeil and nodded, and even the protector left the room.

Gavril raised his brows and hooked his thumbs arrogantly in his belt. "Well, sire? We are delaying the start of the ball."

"What of it?" the king replied. "There is something we must discuss."

Gavril decided to stop needling his father. "I am at your majesty's disposal."

"Another letter has come to me from Lindier."

Gavril's interest perked up. He hoped the marechal would join the faction who believed they should conquer Klad. "How does my uncle?"

"He is angry, Gavril, and frustrated. As, I will admit, am I."

Shrugging, Gavril turned away. He understood now why he'd been summoned. It was going to be another lecture about his betrothal.

"Don't you think you have insulted Pheresa long enough?"

Gavril glanced up sharply. "It is not my intention to insult her."

"You've ignored her since your return to court."

"What of that? Really, Father, I have been much occupied—"

"Better that we do not discuss your 'occupations,'" the king said grimly.

Flushing, Gavril bit his lip and fell silent.

The king began to pace back and forth in front of him. "You know your duty. What have you against the girl? If she were squint-eyed and toothless, I would understand, but Pheresa has no flaws, no blemishes."

"I have nothing against her," Gavril replied. "Except her eagerness. She's bold, don't you think, sire? Why did she come here like this, as though assured I would choose her? Why didn't she wait at home for me to pay my court?"

The king laughed. "Is that all this is? A misunderstanding of etiquette? I invited her here, my boy. I wanted to become acquainted with her myself, see that she acquired some court polish. She's pretty, well-behaved, intelligent, and sensible. Her nuncery education has made her modest. My sister did an excellent job in raising her."

"No doubt, sire." Gavril sighed. Of course the king would champion this girl. He would say he invited her, but Gavril knew his aunt well. She must have pushed for the invitation that permitted her daughter to come to court. Therefore, it was just as Gavril thought: Pheresa was too bold. Had she been otherwise, she would have insisted on staying home. "But there are many maidens in this realm who have been excellently raised."

"And still you have no interest in Pheresa or anyone else." The king frowned. "Is there something wrong with you?"

"Nay!" Gavril protested, his face reddening. "It's just . . . I wanted to choose my own—"

"Well, you've had a month or more to look about the court and choose someone else, but as far as I can discover you've failed to do even that." The king shook his finger at

Gavril. "It's your duty to marry early and well. You must prove your ability to produce heirs."

"I shall," Gavril said. "In time, I intend to—"

"Now, Gavril, now! Pheresa is a suitable candidate. The people expect you to choose her. Every day that you do not brings gossip and slander against her. She does not deserve that. Had you found another maid to fill your eyes, it would be different, but you have not. Damne, here's her father writing to tell me that he has another suitor for her hand and dowry. While you've dallied, she may well have taken a fancy to some other young man here at court. She's winsome enough to have her pick of suitors. Dain of Thirst, for one."

"Dain!" Gavril said in disgust. "I hardly believe that."

"Then it would appear you're as heedless of gossip as you are of your intended."

"She wouldn't choose a pagan! He's nothing, a mongrel of no background whatsoever."

Looking delighted, the king watched Gavril sputter. "Aha, so there is a spark of interest after all. I thought as much, despite your airs of indifference."

"My cousin could do better than Dain of Thirst."

"Think you so? The young man has rough manners, but he learns quickly. He's charmed and flattered her. Which is more than I can say of you."

Gavril scowled, unable to believe she would waste her attention on someone as contemptible as Dain. Had she no discernment at all?

"From what I've observed of the girl, she is eminently suitable to be Princess of the Realm," the king announced. "Before she gets away, I am making your decision for you. Pheresa will be your bride."

"Father—"

"The matter is settled," the king said brusquely, and gestured. "Go to the ball, my son, and court the girl."

"But, Father—"

"After the way you've ignored her, she may reject you, but by Thod you'll ask her. Tonight!"

"Father—"

"Let me hear no argument, Gavril. My mind is set. You'll propose, and that's an end to it. Come morning, I want to be awakened with the news of a betrothal."

Gavril hated being coerced into this. "May I not gain her acquaintance first?"

"Why should you? You've known her since childhood."

"I did not like her when we were children."

"Then learn to like her now!" the king shouted. "Damne, what ails you? She's here, available, and ambitious to be queen."

"Too ambitious, perhaps," Gavril murmured. He didn't want a clever, perceptive wife, one possibly both intelligent and resourceful. She might become more popular at court than he, and the thought of that was unbearable.

The king was staring at him angrily. "Do you refuse my direct command?"

"No, sire. I just—"

"The discussion is over. You know my wishes. That is all."

With a final glare, the king swung away. Gavril had no choice but to bow to his father's back and depart. His face was on fire, and his pride smarted from having been dismissed like a servant.

Seething, Gavril left the king's apartments. Once again, Dain had appeared at the root of his troubles. How dare that despicable worm of a serf-born pagan dare to even lift his eyes to her? This is what came of allowing the riffraff acceptance at court. It was bad enough that Dain had been made a chevard, with all the privileges thereof, but now he thought himself as good as a prince. Well, tonight he would learn different.

Gavril headed for the ball, where already he could hear music playing. A cold, cruel smile played on his lips. Tonight, if Arvt did as he promised, would be Dain's last.

• • •

Jostled by the crowd of people eager to fawn over the king's mistress, Pheresa moved away from the others and walked over to admire the tables of refreshments. Orange gourds carved into bowls held aromatic delicacies, and the bread loaves were warm from the oven and freshly sliced. She was hungry, for since receiving Prince Gavril's tribute of flowers this afternoon she'd been too excited to eat. Smiling to herself, she twirled the spray of yellow blossoms in her fingers. Her heart was beating a rapid dance of its own in eager anticipation. It had taken all her patience and fortitude to wait, but at last his highness was paying her court. She'd been so astonished this afternoon when the page came running in to give her the enormous bundle of yellow and blue flowers tied with moon vine. She'd recognized them at once, for they came from the prince's garden and were his personal colors.

How the other maidens had gathered around her, oohing and admiring this bountiful tribute that had come so unexpectedly. There were so many flowers, the vases could not hold them all. Their fragrance had overwhelmed her small room, and she'd left many of them lying atop her bed, to scent it for her slumbers later tonight. It was a lavish, princely gift, and it made up for how Gavril had neglected her.

She smiled to herself, not caring tonight if others observed her happiness. Gavril had not written a note to her, or perhaps he had and the page had lost it. She did not care. He would come and find her. Tonight, her patience knew no bounds.

"Good eventide, my lady," said a familiar voice.

Pheresa glanced up and found Dain standing before her. She smiled in gladness to see her friend. As he stood there, looking tall and handsome in his own exotic, foreign way, she saw the kindness in his pale gray eyes and realized she'd missed his company.

"Hello," she said. "This is the first time I've seen you since your return. Welcome back to Savroix."

"Thank you. A journey of any distance is sweetened by the welcome home of dear friends."

Her brows lifted in surprise. He'd acquired some polish since he left. This new assurance and suavity impressed her a great deal. Twinkling, she gave him her hand and was impressed yet again when he bowed smoothly over it. He might have been born a lord, she thought.

"You are very kind, Lord Dain," she said. "Do you think the king will appear tonight? I am famished, but we may not eat until he arrives to open the ball."

Dain glanced around. Despite his new manners, he'd retained his natural alertness and erect bearing. When he looked across the room, it was with an eagle gaze. He seemed to see so much more than any of the rest of them could discern. She had the feeling that were danger ever to strike, it would be Dain who would react first, who would know exactly what to do. Being with him made her feel safe.

"I think I hear his majesty coming now," Dain said.

Pheresa frowned. All she could hear was music and the babble of voices, but moments later trumpets sounded and the heralds came sweeping into the room to announce the king.

She stared at Dain in amazement. "Your ears are very keen, my lord."

He smiled, his taut lean face bronzed from the southern sun. "Sometimes a blessing, my lady. Sometimes not. You look beautiful tonight."

Pleased by the compliment, she swept her hand across the lovely lines of her blue skirt. She had chosen this color as a reply to Gavril's tribute, but now she wondered if he was even coming.

Then, as the crush of people surrounding the king moved aside, she saw the prince standing across the room. All the blood seemed to leave her head, and she was suddenly faint and unable to breathe.

"My lady?" Dain asked in concern, stepping closer to her. "Are you well?"

She struggled to regain her composure. "I—yes, of course."

"Will you dance with me then?"

Surprise made her laugh. "Have you learned the steps?"

"Of course. You said I would need to, and I have obeyed my lady's commands." Grinning, Dain bowed to her.

With a smile, Pheresa curtsied and put her slender hand in his. "I am pleased to accept this dance."

Dain proved to be an excellent dancer, and as she became aware of the admiration of other couples, Pheresa's own high spirits carried her, smiling and happy, lightly through the *spinnade* with twinkling feet before she ducked beneath the clasped hands of the others and took her place at the end of the line. In a moment, Dain joined her. His gray eyes were smiling, and his black hair curled slightly on his brow. When his hand grasped hers to lead her through the second part, she marveled at the strength of his fingers. His hands were slender and well-shaped, speaking of his noble blood, however mysterious his origins. He never stopped smiling at her, and the blood swirled in her head until she felt giddy. He had never been this charming before. He seemed to have lost all his shyness. In its place was an assurance that made him seem older and much more mature. But, as suave and appealing as he'd become, Pheresa found herself missing the old shy, unsure, gawky Dain she had befriended during his first days at court.

The dance ended with a flourish, and Pheresa was spun unexpectedly against Dain's chest. She laughed. He released her at once, laughing in return, then his gaze sobered.

"Would you like some fresh air?"

She carried her grandmother's fan and used it with pretty little turns of her wrist. "I would rather have something to eat."

Dain escorted her to the tables and stood by while she sampled the treats there. Again she looked for Gavril, and saw him with a cluster of his friends.

The prince's gaze, however, was on her. She smiled at

him, thrilled to know she had his attention. He frowned and
turned his head away.

Her spirits came tumbling down. She stared at the spiced
apple in her hands while her vision blurred with tears. Was
he angry because she was talking to Dain?

Then Pheresa's own anger, deep-rooted and born of many
such humiliating occasions, came surging up inside her. Stiff-
ening, she lifted her head. Let the prince be angry. He had
no right to dictate her actions. Compressing her mouth, she
threw down the yellow flower she'd been holding all evening.

Dain bent and picked it up. "Does this no longer please
you, my lady?"

She did not want it. She loathed it. But she accepted it
back with her face aflame.

"I do want some fresh air, please," she said softly.

He tucked her hand in the crook of his arm and escorted
her out through the open doors to the dimly lit balcony overlooking some of the gardens. She could hear the faint splash-
ing of a fountain. The air smelled fragrant, soft, and clean
after the perfumed, overheated rooms inside.

Gripping the stone balustrade, she inhaled deeply and
vowed to herself that never again would she let Gavril do
this to her. She must destroy her infatuation with him. She
must swallow her pride and ask the king for permission to
leave court. He'd been a kind uncle to her. He would surely
agree to arrange a different marriage at her request. She'd
lost her gamble, and whatever game Gavril sought to play
with her was at an end. She would no longer let herself be
an object for his cruelty.

"Pheresa," Dain said softly from the shadows. "Thank
you for wearing my flowers tonight. I hope this means that
you carry some affection in your heart for—"

"What?" she said abruptly. "What flowers?"

"These." He took the yellow bloom from her fingers and
lifted it to his nostrils, then his hand stole up and gently caressed her hair. "And these. I have never given flowers to a

lady before. I wasn't sure—I didn't know if you would like them."

Astonishment filled her, driving away her other thoughts. She turned around to face him. "Are you saying you—it was *you* who sent these to me?"

"But of course," he replied in puzzlement. "I thought you knew."

She drew in a ragged breath, her mind reeling. "No. I— I didn't. Dain, where did you get them?"

"I picked them from one of the gardens. They are at the end of their season, and it seemed a shame to let them go to waste."

Appalled, she knew not what to say. "Did anyone see you?"

"I don't know." He took a step closer to her in the darkness and pressed his lips to her hair. "What does it matter, as long as they pleased you?"

"But—but—it's forbidden to pick them. They belong to—"

He laughed softly. "Another rule broken. My dearest, I would break them all for you."

Her mind spun rapidly. No wonder Dain had been so at ease, so full of smiles and compliments this evening. He had mistaken her happiness. By wearing his tribute, she had given him all the wrong ideas.

"My lord," she said quickly. "Please don't."

He was kissing her hair again, his lips moving tenderly down to her ear.

She stiffened and stepped away from him.

"Do I frighten you?" he asked.

Something was wrong with her lungs. She could not believe this evening had gone so completely wrong. She wanted to weep, and yet she had to explain. "No," she managed at last, her voice unsteady. "I—you mustn't touch me that way."

"I'm sorry," he said, but his voice held no apology. "Pheresa, I love you. From the first time I saw you I have been consumed by your beauty and grace. You are—"

"Stop!" she cried, trying to turn away from him. She wanted to flee, and yet his words touched a yearning emptiness inside her. If only it could be Gavril saying these compliments to her. "You mustn't. I am not—"

He caught her hand and held it against his chest. "Are you not free?" he asked. "There is no betrothal. You are not bound to Gavril. Or am I mistaken in this?"

Tears stung her eyes. She was grateful for the darkness that hid her bitter shame. "No," she said, her voice choked. "You are correct."

"Then let me declare my love for you," he said eagerly, lifting her hand to his lips. Their caress seemed to burn her fingers, and she trembled in his grasp. "I ask for your hand, my lady. I have been given the king's permission to marry whom I choose, and for me there can be no other than you."

"Oh, Dain," she whispered.

Her emotions careened inside her. He was so sweet, so tender, and yet she found herself astonished by his boldness. How had she let things go this far? How had she been so blind to Dain's growing infatuation with her? Had she been too friendly? Had she led him into believing her affections were the same as his? By wearing his flowers tonight, she had certainly given him every reason to think so.

But he was no one, really. King's favorite or not, he held only a minor rank, and that through dispensation rather than actual birthright.

Dain cleared his throat, breaking the silence. "Of course I cannot offer you a—a kingdom," he said. "I am not Gavril, but only a second choice. Perhaps less than that."

"Dain, please," she said quickly, but he put his fingers against her lips to silence her.

"Thirst Hold is plain and modest compared to all this. It's not a palace at all. But it's a decent place. And what I cannot give to you in riches, I would give to you with my heart."

"Dain," she said, touched to the core by his words, "please say nothing else. Please."

He obeyed her, standing there patiently with his hand still gripping hers.

She marveled at him and his big, simple heart. Under his new sophisticated manners, he was still an impossible boy who did not know or understand his place here.

And yet, she could not fault him for his honest declaration. He loved her. She doubted it not at all, and despite his rough edges, there was something undeniably appealing about him. Pheresa, with no better offer before her, found Dain's tempting. After all, had she not just made up her mind to seek marriage with someone other than Gavril, who did not, would not ever, want her? And here was this pagan boy who loved her, who'd risked punishment to give her flowers, who did not know that she was as far above him as the stars above the ground. Yes, she was tempted. Her heart held such churning anger and resentment at Gavril that she almost told Dain yes out of spite.

But just in time, she held her tongue. Sighing, she leaned her head against Dain's powerful chest. His arms encircled her, and he too sighed, with happiness, while she struggled not to weep.

She did not want to hurt him, but she could not accept his offer, not even to punish Gavril. Oh, the prince would hate it if she married Dain. She knew how little the two liked each other. Gavril clearly had never forgiven Dain for beating him in the tourney, especially after Gavril had made such a spectacle of himself beforehand.

Well, she knew now that she didn't love Gavril. Dain had showed her what love should be. She could feel his happiness as he held her close. It made her own misery and confusion that much more acute. For she loved neither of them, not like this, not with Dain's simple honesty. And for the first time she understood that the depths of her ambition to be queen went far deeper than she'd ever realized. Gavril had been hurting only her pride, not her heart. She wanted to rule Mandria someday, and Gavril was her only means of doing so.

And not even to be cherished by Dain, not even perhaps to be happy, was she willing to surrender the chance to rule.

"We will be happy," Dain promised her. "I cannot give you much now, but one day, when I have—"

"No," she whispered, sliding her hand up to his cheek. "No. I am sorry."

He started to speak, but she withdrew from his embrace.

"Pheresa?" It was Gavril's voice that called to her in the darkness.

Startled, she and Dain both turned.

"Would you dance with me, my lady cousin?" Gavril asked her.

Dain drew in a sharp breath as though he would protest. Pheresa gripped his arm in warning, and he stayed silent.

Relieved, she struggled with her emotions a moment longer, then walked forward. *So it has worked at last,* she thought. *The attentions of his rival have finally stirred him to notice me.*

Gavril stood there in the doorway. Light spilled across his blue-clad shoulder and illuminated half of his face. This was the moment she'd dreamed of and waited for, when her handsome cousin would offer his arm to her and ask her to dance with him. She went to him, waiting for joy to fill her heart, but even when he took her hand she felt only numbness.

"Dearest cousin, I believe we have some matters to discuss," Gavril said with a glance at Dain.

Pheresa heard Dain walk up behind her. Her heart leaped in alarm, but he stopped and came no closer. Sighing, she gave Gavril a slight curtsy and allowed him to lead her back to the ball.

The candlelight blazed around her, hurting her eyes. Despite the overpowering heat in the room, she felt cold to the marrow. She had scarcely a coherent thought in her brain.

Across the room, the king sat on his throne, with the countess beside him. He smiled at Pheresa and saluted her with his cup. She gave him a stiff, wooden smile in return as Gavril led her to the dancing.

It was a slow madrigal the musicians played. Together, she and Gavril joined the line of dancers, taking up the stately and dignified steps of a *gliande*. Pheresa could hear the whispering that ran across the room at the sight of her and Gavril in each other's company at long last. Her cheeks felt hot, but defiance flashed in her eyes. *Let them talk,* she thought. She no longer cared.

"You look lovely tonight, cousin," Gavril said.

Even had it not come on the heels of Dain's compliments, this remark would have sounded wooden and insincere. A few hours ago Pheresa would have smiled modestly and said something agreeable, but not now.

She flashed him a look of scorn. "Thank you. I cannot compare to your highness in looks or fashion, but I do contrive to be my best."

He frowned, clearly taken aback. "Forgive me. How have I offended you?"

"How have you not?" she replied sweetly as she circled beneath his upraised arm, spun, and faced him once more in the line of dancers.

Red tinged his face. "You have grown a tart tongue, my lady. Is your personality as shrewish as your manner?"

With a start she realized how dreadfully she was behaving. She clamped self-control on herself and bit her lip for a moment. "No," she replied at last, her voice completely different. "I am no shrew, your highness. I am merely angry and seeking to pick a quarrel."

His brows shot up, and he began to look intrigued. "Oh? For what reason? Was my asking you to dance an offense?"

"No."

"Then I interrupted your private conversation."

"Yes, it was an interruption," she said in cool tones.

Annoyance flickered in his dark blue eyes. "Shall I return you to where I found you?"

"No. I am content with your company now."

"My lady, I do not understand you at all. Your mood is very strange tonight."

"How would you know that?" she replied, meeting his eyes. "Perhaps this is my normal mood."

He smiled a little. "No. I have seen you elsewhere, standing quietly with that simper on your face, looking meek and well-bred. Tonight, your eyes flash with spirit. You are very different."

"Is that to my advantage or detriment?" she asked. "Tell me," she went on before he could reply, "have all the other ladies begun to bore you?"

"In what way?"

"Well, you have finally chosen to dance with me, your simpering cousin. I wondered if your highness could find no amusement elsewhere."

"You have the sting of a little scorpion," he told her, frowning.

"It seems I do. I quite surprise myself tonight."

Abruptly the prince stopped dancing. He held out his hand, and when she placed hers in it, he led her away.

More murmurs and speculation followed them, but Pheresa delighted in it. She could see Gavril's ears and the back of his neck turning pink. She hoped he felt embarrassment tonight. Yet at the same time, she was appalled by her own behavior. It was as though she had climbed aboard a runaway wagon that she could not stop, and at any moment she expected to come crashing to harm.

Gavril led her over to an empty corner far in the back of the room and faced her with a glare. "Whatever has put you into this mood, my lady, it is less than charming. I have—"

"You asked if you interrupted something out there on the balcony," she broke in. "Yes, you did. Marriage was being proposed to me."

He stared, his mouth slightly open, and seemed unable to reply.

Pheresa had the sensation of having burned her bridges.

Clasping her hands together in front of her, she went on, "I do not know why your highness has chosen at last to speak to me. You have ignored me for so long, I fear I have quite lost my composure. But then, I am not used to receiving unexpected proposals on balconies."

Anger filled Gavril's face. His eyes shifted away from her and he glared across the room. "That miserable cur," he muttered. "I'll have him whipped for daring to offend you."

"Please don't," she said curtly. "I was not offended by the offer, and you would only make me more an object for harmful gossip than you already have."

Unwillingly, Gavril returned his gaze to her. "Do you dare reprimand me, my lady?"

"Were you not a prince, I would do so," she replied.

" 'Twas you who chose to come here to court, displaying yourself like a prize ware."

Anger fired her cheeks. For a moment she was too incensed to speak. "How dare you!" she uttered at last. "Is *that* what you think of me?"

"It is precisely what I think of you."

Her eyes flashed, and her chin lifted. She wished she wore a dagger so that she could run him through. "How arrogant and judgmental you are. Knowing only a part of the whole, you can still make up your mind."

"What is there to doubt?" he asked with a sneer. "I see your behavior. Before I even returned from my fostering, you had already ensconced yourself here like some strumpet—"

"I had no choice," she said furiously. "The king summoned me. Would you have had me refuse his majesty's express command? You may be permitted to rebel, sir, but I am not!"

Gavril frowned, saying nothing.

She glared at him. "What assumptions you make! If you wish to see a strumpet, look about you. Look at Sofia de Briard, married but still not respectable. Look at the majority of the ladies who wait on the king's mistress. See how they dress? See how they flirt and throw themselves at men? I have had to live here in this court without even the protection of a betrothal. I have witnessed scandalous behavior and wild licentiousness. I have been shocked again and again. Because I am only a simple maid, with a nuncery upbringing, I am considered contemptible. Did you ever think about my position here, in a court like this, without a queen to keep moral order, with greed, caprice, and vicious gossip at every turn?"

Gavril's frown had grown thoughtful, but he shrugged. "You did not have to join Lalieux's circle."

"No," she said bitterly. "I did not. I could have gone on sitting in my room, night after night, hiding there. I could have read my two volumes of poetry by candlelight, bitterly alone, while the music played here and people laughed and talked to each other. I could have hidden, as I did while there were two royal mistresses in the palace and every occasion such as this was a battleground. But when Lalieux became the sole favorite here at court, it became an offense to the king to snub her." Pheresa sighed. "One must survive political intrigue, even of the feminine sort, your highness. It does not compare to your level of statecraft between kingdoms, but it can be just as dangerous."

"I see."

"Besides, when your highness returned to court," she said with a bitter little smile, "I was obliged to appear, was I not?"

He looked uncomfortable, even possibly apologetic. "You have explained yourself very clearly. You are intelligent and articulate for a maiden. But so composed have you always appeared that I thought you in no need of rescue. You are very poised and assured in public. There was no evidence that you felt humiliated."

She wanted to cry over this stupid misunderstanding. Her training and deportment had helped her endure life at court, but it seemed it had also cost her dearly. She made a little gesture of frustration. "I am of royal blood, your highness," she said. "I do not know how to display histrionics in public, but my feelings are as easily hurt as anyone's."

"I see that now," he said.

She drew in a breath and looked away from him. Across the room, a tall, broad-shouldered figure caught her eye. It was Dain, watching them.

Gavril turned and saw whom she was looking at. His face darkened. "I'm glad I did interrupt his proposal. He should be whipped for it."

"You would not do so," she said in quick defense of Dain. "Your highness speaks in jest, I'm sure."

Gavril frowned. "You are, of course, too sensible to have accepted him."

Her chin lifted. "Why does your highness say that?"

"Because it's absurd! He should be cleaning stables, not—"

"Regarding his worthiness, I will dare to disagree with your highness," she said with spirit. "His proposal was not absurd."

"You are *my* intended."

"And you have not betrothed me. Am I not technically free to choose elsewhere? I am older than most highborn maidens when they marry. If your highness has rejected me, then I must see to my future. I will not linger at court as a rejected spinster."

He frowned, looking taken aback. "Why do you keep saying I have rejected you?"

"Haven't you?"

"Thod's mercy, but you *are* bold," he said in displeasure.

She lifted her hands. "I know. You want a maiden who will flatter you and gaze up at you with adoring eyes. Before I learned not to care, I would have done that, your highness. I would have done anything to please you." Tears suddenly choked her voice, and she had to turn away. She was furious with herself for losing her self-control.

He stepped closer to her. "Pheresa."

She could not look at him. A tear slipped down her cheek, and she slapped it angrily away.

When Gavril touched her elbow, she flinched. He released her at once, but circled around to stand in front of her. "Pheresa," he said again in wonder, "have I made you cry?"

She could feel the whole room staring. Her emotions overwhelmed her, and she could no longer endure being watched. "Please," she murmured desperately, "give me leave to go. I—I am unwell."

"Of course," he said at once. "But I will escort you."

"No," she began, but he ignored her protest.

Taking her arm, he led her out of the room and along a short hallway to a tall window. They stepped outside onto a tiny balcony. A flight of torchlit steps led down from it, but Gavril stopped and stood beside her while she buried her face in her hands and battled not to weep.

Her mother had taught her that although they had to be used wisely and sparingly, tears were a woman's best weapon. Pheresa despised such advice. She feared that weeping would only drive Gavril further away.

"I'm sorry," she whispered, knowing she was destroying the chance fate had finally awarded her. "I'm sorry."

Gavril's hand touched her shoulder. His fingers felt very warm on her skin. "Do not apologize. I understand how upset he has made you. He is shameless. He understands no boundary, while my father thinks it amusing to let him do as he pleases."

Puzzled, Pheresa lifted her damp face and stared at Gavril through the gloom. It took her a moment to realize he was again talking about Dain. "Your highness, he didn't—"

"This insult to you is his worst action yet," Gavril went on, unheeding. "But have no fear. He shan't be around much longer to pester anyone."

"I know he must return soon to Thirst." As she spoke, she thought of all Dain had said about his hold. His pride in it had rung in his voice as he described it for her. "He made it sound appealing. So quiet and ordinary."

"It's an appalling mud hole—freezing in the winter, with scarcely a civilized amenity to it," Gavril said with loathing.

Someone shrieked with laughter inside. Pheresa frowned at this first sign of the ball's growing more lively and riotous. "Perhaps a mud hole, with decency and goodness in it, would be preferable to the civilized amenities of drunken orgies."

"Pheresa, tell me you are not seriously considering going there," Gavril said in astonishment. "How can you?"

She was annoyed that he would believe it of her, and yet for the first time she felt a little sense of power over Gavril. It was thrilling to think she might have piqued his jealousy at least. At the same time, an undercurrent of self-disgust ran through her. So she was her mother's daughter, despite all her intentions. For here she was, with the means at last to leverage Gavril into a proposal, and she intended to use it.

"How can I not consider Thirst?" she replied coolly, feeling her pulse beat hard in her throat. "I have no better offer."

"Ah," Gavril murmured, and took her hand. "Perhaps you do."

In the overheated ballroom, Dain's head was buzzing. He had gone this evening from high expectancy, to exhilaration, to despair. Even now, as he watched Pheresa walking away from him with Gavril, he still found himself unable to believe that she'd turned him down. He'd been holding her in his arms, holding her with such tenderness and passion. His senses had reeled from the fragrance and softness of her. While he was working up his courage to kiss her, suddenly she was gone, pulling away from him and going to Gavril instead.

Someone jostled him in the crowd, but Dain paid no attention. He watched her dance with Gavril, so beautiful, her eyes flashing as she spoke to the prince. Dain felt himself on fire, yet his head was cold and numb, as though it had been cut off and was now floating above his body. He did not know what to do. He had thrown away a kingdom for her, and she did not want him.

Again he was bumped into, and a man said, "I beg your lordship's pardon. It's very hot in here, eh?"

"Aye," Dain said absently. He barely looked at the fellow, who was no one he recognized.

"Have some wine. You look as though you need it. Good stuff, eh?"

The man was holding two cups. He offered one to Dain, who realized how thirsty he was.

Taking it, Dain gave the man a little nod of thanks and lifted the cup in salute. "To your kindness, sir."

Laughing, the man returned the gesture and shouldered his way on through the crowd. Dain scowled at the dark wine in the cup. Its bouquet was ripe and heavy, assaulting his nostrils. He was no wine drinker, even at this court where the stuff flowed like water at all times, but right now, he thought, perhaps it would be wise to drink until the hurt spreading through him was dulled and lifeless.

It had never occurred to him that her smiles and friendly chatter hid an indifferent heart. He believed her feelings matched his own, and he had let himself weave such a tremendous fantasy for himself that now, now it hurt more than he could stand.

Sighing, he watched them leave the dancing and go to talk on the far side of the room. He told himself to go outside, to get away and stop watching her break his heart, but his feet seemed rooted in place. If the prince made her happy, then Dain could force himself to accept it, but she was shaking her head and frowning at Gavril. She averted her face, and the prince moved closer to her.

Dain growled to himself and lifted the cup to his lips. The heavy smell of the wine repulsed him enough to hesitate. *Drink deep,* he told himself.

She started crying, and Gavril escorted her out of the room.

Without tasting the wine, Dain lowered the cup and rushed
after them.

It was difficult for him to push through the crowd. Some
of the courtiers were now well-flushed with drink and beginning to laugh and carouse tipsily. Sir Terent stood by the
refreshment table across the room. He saw Dain leaving, but
he was hampered from following by the crush of people.

That suited Dain well. He did not need his protector in
the way, preventing him from doing the foolish things he
intended to do. Gavril was going to make Pheresa desperately unhappy, and Dain refused to let it happen. She was
only trying to do her duty, but she was too fine to be shack-
led to the prince for the rest of her life. She deserved better, and Dain was not going to let her be coerced into
something she did not really want. Besides, if he could not
make her love him, what was he going to do?

Still carrying his cup, Dain was bumped into by a woman,
and half of his wine sloshed over his sleeve, soaking it to
the skin. He shook droplets of liquid from his hand and
started to lick his fingers dry, but there was no time. Instead,
he hurried on to the door, wiping his hand on the front of
his doublet as he went.

Outside the ballroom, the air was cooler and the noise
level dropped. Blinking in relief, Dain glanced around and
heard the low murmur of voices in the distance. He hurried
along a short hallway and saw them, standing outdoors on
a small balcony.

Gavril was holding her hand, but Pheresa was trying to
pull free. Instead of releasing her, the prince stepped closer
and encircled her waist with his arm. He kissed her lips, and
Dain lost his head.

"Unhand her!" he shouted.

Behind him, Sir Terent called out, "M'lord, wait!"

Dain paid no heed. Setting his wine cup down on the
balustrade, he confronted Gavril, who by now had stepped
away from Pheresa. She gasped and pressed her hands to
her cheeks.

In the torchlight, Gavril's blue eyes flashed with anger. "How dare you interrupt me."

"You are annoying the lady," Dain said.

"Dain, please don't!" she said, but he heard only the wretchedness in her voice, not her words.

"You whelp," Gavril sneered, reaching for his dagger. "It's time you were taught your place. Guards—"

Dain tackled him before he could shout for help, and together the two of them went sprawling at Pheresa's feet.

Crying out, she jumped back. Gavril's flailing fist caught Dain in the jaw, and his head rang momentarily from the blow. Dain hit him back, and the prince cursed savagely before thrusting Dain away and scrambling to his feet.

Again the prince reached for his dagger, but Dain gripped his ankles and pulled his feet out from under him. Gavril landed hard, and as he lay there, momentarily winded, Dain gripped him by the front of his fancy doublet and jerked him upright.

Gavril's fist connected with his jaw, and Dain's head snapped back. With the world reeling around him, Dain stumbled backward across the short balcony to the top of the steps. He teetered there, but caught his balance and did not fall.

Cursing, Gavril rushed at Dain with his dagger drawn. Dain drew his own dagger and tried to shift his back to the wall for protection. Gavril thrust hard with his dagger, and as Dain blocked the blow with his own dagger blade, he lost his balance and went tumbling down the steps. By quick instinct, he grabbed hold of Gavril's doublet with his free hand and pulled the prince down with him.

It was a jolting, wild, painful tumble. Dain felt the jar of every step as he rolled head over heels with a cursing Gavril entangled with him. When he landed, all the air was knocked from his lungs, and he could only lie there, wheezing and half-stunned, with Gavril lying on top of him.

Slowly, hurting all over, Dain rolled the prince off and staggered to his feet. He had dropped his dagger in the fall.

Looking around for it, he saw it lying on one of the steps halfway up.

Pheresa stood on the balcony, a vision in blue, the torch-light sparking red highlights in her blonde hair. Pressing her hands to her mouth, she stared down at them.

"Dain!" she cried out. "Please stop."

Out of breath and sorely shaken, he lifted his hand in a salute, but before Dain could answer her Gavril regained his feet and attacked him from behind. Instinctively, he tried to twist around, and felt Gavril's knife blade slice along his ribs. Fire burned in the cut, making him grunt. Watching them, Pheresa screamed.

Gavril was cursing viciously. He thrust again, but Dain caught his wrist in time and strained to hold him. Gavril's lips drew back in a snarl, and sheer hatred blazed in his eyes.

"You'll die tonight," he said. "I have sworn it. This time you've gone too far."

Dain didn't care. Any punishment was worth it, if it meant ridding the world—ridding Pheresa—of this arrogant, cruel brute. Still straining to hold Gavril's knife hand, he struck the prince in the face with his other fist.

Gavril's head snapped back. Dain hit him again, and then there were shouts and the sound of running feet. Strong hands gripped Dain and pulled him back from Gavril.

The prince glared at Dain and twisted his dagger to nick Dain's wrist as they were separated.

Wincing, Dain clamped his hand upon his bleeding wrist and struggled to catch his breath while the guards pummeled him and marched him up the steps.

The king was standing at the top, with Pheresa behind him. The torchlight glittered on Verence's crown and rubies. He looked furious, with his mouth compressed to a tight line and his brow furrowed. Curious people were crowding onto the balcony, only to be pushed back by palace guards.

Sir Terent fought his way through and came running

halfway down the steps, only to be motioned back by Dain's captors.

"M'lord!" he said in despair, looking with horror from Dain to Gavril's puffy, bleeding face. "Great mercy of Thod, what have you done?"

The king glared at Sir Terent and gestured at one of his guards. "Remove this man."

The guards shoved Sir Terent away, and Dain was brought up to the balcony to face the king and Lady Pheresa.

His gaze went at once to her. She had turned as white as the ermine trim on her gown. Her brown eyes were huge in her face, and she was breathing hard with distress.

"You fool," she said in despair. Tears shone on her face. "You poor, idiot fool."

Dain didn't understand. "He was making you cry."

Fresh tears slipped down her cheeks, but before she could reply Gavril came staggering up the steps, flanked by two supportive guards. His blond hair was standing on end, his doublet was wrinkled and torn, and his blue eyes blazed with rage.

"Order his death, sire!" he shouted, pointing at Dain with his bloody dagger. "He attacked me, aye, and would have killed me had I not defended myself." Gavril gestured at the steps behind him. "There lies his weapon in proof."

Hard-eyed, the king moved his hand. One of the guards picked up Dain's dagger and brought it to the king. "There is no blood on his blade," Verence said in relief. "Thod be thanked."

"Aye, Thod's grace and my skill in fighting are all that saved me," Gavril said, partially out of breath. "I could have broken my neck being thrown down those steps."

"Gavril, how can you lie so?" Pheresa demanded. Still pale, she was struggling for breath, and waving her hands aimlessly about. She turned to the king. "Sire, it was not as—"

"Who began this fight?" the king asked angrily.

Gavril ignored his father and turned his rage on

Pheresa. "How dare you accuse me of lying! Have you lost your wits, or did it please you to see us fighting over you like—"

"No, it did not please me!" she retorted with equal fury. "Never have I been more mortified. You might have been two mongrels attacking each other in the dirt." Her angry gaze swept over to include Dain. "This is not the way men of honor behave. Both of you are horrible, horrible! I—"

Choking, she coughed and turned away.

Dain tried to go to her, but his captors held him fast. "Help her. She's going to swoon," he said.

One of the guards caught her as she sank down. Still coughing, she could not seem to catch her breath.

Swearing, the king glanced around and saw the wine cup that Dain had set on the balustrade moments before. He picked it up and held it to her lips. "Drink this, child."

Gasping, she did so, and her coughing eased. The king touched her face gently in concern before turning back to Gavril and Dain with a scowl.

"Your behavior is unfit for any lady's eyes," he said sternly. "Both of you—"

Pheresa shuddered and loosed a little cry of distress. Dain saw her face twist in sudden pain.

"Help her!" he said in alarm, trying again to pull free of his captors. "She is ill."

The king turned, but by then Pheresa was moaning with pain. Her face turned a strange color, and her eyes grew glassy. Her body jerked in the hold of the guard supporting her, then she doubled over and fainted.

The king stared. "What in the name of—"

"Poison!" Gavril said, looking as horrified as Dain felt. "What was in the wine? Where did it come from?"

The king looked at the cup in his hand with revulsion and started to throw it away.

"No, sire!" Dain shouted. "Let a physician test its contents. But send for help immediately while she still breathes."

Commotion broke out. The guards pushed the courtiers

away, and Pheresa was carried into a small chamber and laid on a bench. Her skin had turned the gray hue of death, and she was breathing hard, with short, rasping breaths.

"Let me attend her," Dain pleaded desperately. "At least until the physician comes."

"Father, do not allow him near her," Gavril protested. "He could do her more harm."

The king looked at his son, but then gestured at Dain's guards. "Release him."

Still gripping his bleeding wrist, which was dripping through his fingers, Dain went to her side and knelt there.

"He is too filthy!" Gavril protested. "Keep him away from her."

The king instead issued a command, and one of the guards tore a strip of cloth and bound up Dain's wrist. His pale blood soaked through it quickly, but Dain paid no heed. Ignoring everything except Pheresa, he gripped one of her hands in his.

She was burning hot and still gasping for breath. He could feel the poison in her veins. It was strangely slow-acting, for it had not killed her yet, but Dain felt more gratitude than puzzlement. He closed his eyes, trying to draw some of the poison into himself, but he lacked the skill.

Frustrated, he opened his eyes and stared at her in anguish. "It's no common poison. I don't know how to save her."

A stricken look filled Verence's eyes. He lifted the back of his hand to his mouth and began to pace back and forth.

Gavril stood in silence a moment, then scowled and pointed at Dain. "You did this to her," he said. "It was your cup. You brought it to kill her."

Dain rose to his feet in astonishment. The movement made him dizzy, and he blinked hard to fight off his weakness.

By then the king was staring at his son. "What accusation is this?"

"Have him questioned," Gavril said harshly. "He has tried to murder my betrothed—"

"That's a lie!" Dain shouted.

At that moment the doors burst open and Cardinal Noncire, followed by a trio of priests and two court physicians, entered the room. One of the latter went to Pheresa and bent over her.

Seconds later he straightened and made the swift sign of the Circle. He murmured into the cardinal's ear, and the men exchanged somber looks.

"What is it?" the king asked. "What can be done?"

"All must clear the room," Noncire said. "If she is to be saved at all costs, majesty?"

Verence frowned and seemed to hesitate, but Gavril stepped forward. "Yes, yes, at all costs. How can you even ask such a thing? Noncire, if there's any way to preserve her life, do it! She is to be my wife."

The king met the eyes of the cardinal and nodded. Noncire bowed. "By your command," he said. "All must leave. Quickly, before it's too late."

Dain wanted to protest. He distrusted these men, for they were the same priests who'd tested him that night before King Verence. But he was given no chance to speak. The guards pushed him out of the room in the wake of Verence and Gavril, and no sooner did he cross the threshold than the doors were slammed behind him.

He turned back, frowning at the carved panels. His keen ears could already make out the strange words the priests were chanting softly. Hairs prickled on the back of his neck, and he caught the burned whiff of magic. His mouth went dry. They were casting a spell over her.

"What are they going to do?" Gavril asked in the corridor.

"Whatever they can," the king said grimly. "Come away."

Eyes wide with astonishment, Dain turned to him. What hypocrisy was this? To preach against and condemn the use of magic, to torture Gavril for having tried to learn the weakest of spells, and yet to order its use now. Dain had not expected to find such contradictions in the king. "Your majesty," he said.

The king's gaze flicked to him, and Verence nodded grimly as though to confirm Dain's suspicions. "By my command only can it be done," he said. "And only in a true emergency, such as this, will I command it. Now, both of you come with me. We will get to the bottom of this."

22

BY THE TIME they reached the king's study, a spacious room with a wall of leaded windows overlooking the central courtyard of the palace, the chamberlain and some of the ministers were waiting. A harried servant bustled about, trying to light candles. The room was shadowy and cool, with a long wooden table in its center.

The chamberlain stepped forward with a bow. "Your majesty," he said in a hushed voice of profound shock. "May I express our deepest sympathies regarding the serious illness of your lady niece."

Clune also came forward, his old face looking tired and haggard. "Not plague, is it?" he demanded. "Don't want my daughters exposed to plague. Be a panic if it is."

The king glared at him impatiently. "It is poison."

General consternation broke out among the others while the chamberlain lifted his hands ineffectually for silence.

The king glanced at his master of arms. "Remove these men."

"But, your majesty, please," the chamberlain protested. "Affairs of state must be—"

"Everything must wait," the king told him. "Until we know if she will live or die, there is nothing to be done. She—" His voice grew hoarse and cracked. He stopped, frowning, and cleared his throat. "She is betrothed to his highness. You may announce that. You may also ask the people for their prayers on her behalf."

The chamberlain bowed and backed himself out, while the ministers did likewise.

As soon as the guards had shut the doors, Gavril flung himself in a chair and demanded that the servant who was building a fire in the hearth stop what he was doing and bring him wine. Drinking deeply, he pointed at Dain. "The pagan must be put in the dungeons, sire, without delay. He attacked me, and he must pay the price."

Blinking against the dizzying little dots that kept swimming in front of his vision, Dain opened his mouth to speak in his defense, but no words came out. He closed his eyes for a second, and opened them again to find that he'd sunk to his knees before the king.

Pacing back and forth, Verence gestured impatiently at Dain. "No need to beg. I am not ready to execute you . . . yet."

"Sire, you are too merciful. He is both a liar and an assassin."

"Gavril, please hush these wild accusations," the king said, and rubbed his face. "'Tis I who gave her the stuff to drink. Damne! I feel the guilt of that most strongly."

"The poison was in my cup," Dain said in a thin voice. "It was meant for me."

Gavril leaned forward in his chair. "And did you drink any of it?"

Dain met his gaze, feeling Gavril's hatred wash over him with such violence he swayed on his knees.

The king stopped pacing and frowned at Dain. "Did you?" The color drained from his face, and before Sir Odeil could stop him he hastened over to grip Dain's shoulder. "Great

Thod, it was half-empty when I picked it up. No, no, my boy, not you as well."

Dain tried to tell him he had not drunk the poison, but his voice failed him again. Through a strange roaring in his ears, he heard the king issuing orders. The fire was blazing now on the hearth, casting its orange light across Dain's face and body, but he could not feel its warmth. He was very, very cold. And then he knew nothing.

He dreamed that he stood in a gloomy cave, a place of dank, bone-chilling coldness. Ice glistened on the stone walls where water had seeped through the rock and frozen. His feet and hands were numb. When he looked down at himself, he wore a shroud of white linen and his feet were bare. Wondering if he was dead, he shivered and looked ahead to the source of pale clear light that illuminated the cave. He saw the Chalice of Eternal Life shining from a niche carved into the wall. Light emanated from it, and as Dain drew closer, he felt himself bathed in its radiant purity.

Awed, he knelt before it and traced a ring about himself in the dirt. He had no salt, no ash rods, no candles with which to make the proper rituals. All he could do was worship with his heart.

"Faldain."

Turning around, he faced King Tobeszijian. Ghostly pale, almost transparent in places, the lost king wore his gold breastplate and mail. His great sword hung at his side. Dain rose to his feet before this vision of the man who had been his father. Aside from his pallor, Tobeszijian still looked young and vigorous. An invisible wind stirred his black hair back from his stern, forbidding face. His eyes, pale blue and fierce, blazed into Dain's.

"Father," Dain whispered.

The vision glared at him a moment, then held out his gauntleted hand.

A rush of emotions choked Dain's throat. He went forward and knelt, then reached out to grasp his father's fingers, but his hands passed through the vision and touched only air.

Pain pierced Dain's heart. He wanted so much to grasp his father's hand, to feel this man just once, to know he was indeed real.

"You cannot touch me, Faldain," Tobeszijian said, his deep voice booming within the cave. "We exist in different worlds."

"But am I not dead too, Father?"

Tobeszijian's fierce gaze shifted past Dain to the Chalice. "Do you remember this place, my son?"

Dain glanced about and slowly rose to his feet. "No."

"I brought you here when you were a toddling babe. Remember the cave, Faldain. You must remember the cave."

"Father, I—I have failed you," Dain admitted in a choked voice. "I made a terrible choice, a mistake."

"Nether needs its true king. It is being consumed by darkness. Take the Chalice home, my son."

Hope grew inside Dain. He looked at the sacred vessel, shining its pure light, and wondered if he dared touch it.

"Were I not threatened by Verence with war—"

"Verence is not your enemy."

"Then when I have the means to gather an army—"

"You are king!" Tobeszijian boomed, making Dain jump. "The army will come to you."

"How—"

"Find your faith," Tobeszijian said, his gaze far away. "Do not shirk your duties as I did. For all eternity, I must pay for my sins. Go to Nether, my son, and cleanse it. Be the king I failed to be. Go to Nether."

"But I—"

"Eldin poison is strong, Faldain. 'Tis how your mother died. Beware your enemies, for they gather close."

The vision of Tobeszijian was fading. Alarmed, for he had dozens of questions still to ask, Dain stepped toward it. "Father, wait! I—"

"The Ring of Solder you have found. It will help you in

your hour of greatest need. But beware its terrible powers. Use it only for the sake of the Chalice." Tobeszijian drew his sword, a mighty weapon that flashed with power inside the murky cave. "On Mirengard, swear this."

Tobeszijian extended the sword, hilt-first. Dain reached out, and to his surprise his fingers brushed the jeweled hilt and found it solid. He gripped it hard. Icy cold it was, so cold his hands seemed to freeze, and yet sparks of its power stung him with a strange sense of exhilaration. "I do swear to use the ring only for the sake of Chalice," he said.

"Never for your personal gain," Tobeszijian said.

"Never for my personal gain," Dain repeated.

The sword faded from within his grip. Tobeszijian himself wavered, as though he would vanish.

"Wait!" Dain called. "How do I—"

"Beware the one who will betray you last."

"Who—"

"Beware," Tobeszijian whispered, and was gone.

Dain awakened with a start to find a cloth pressed across his face. Disoriented, believing himself being smothered, he struggled to fight off his attacker.

A set of strong hands gripped his wrists, bringing a sharp flare of pain to his forearm. But the cloth was taken away, leaving only the unpleasant smell of herbs on his skin. It was dark where he lay. The sole illumination came from a meager fire. Shapes and shadows moved about him, all mysterious. Afraid, Dain struggled again, but his strength evaporated like water poured onto sand, and he was pushed down.

"Hold him," a voice spoke in irritation. "This is the third time he's fought off the infusion. If he will not take it, I cannot be responsible."

"Poison," Dain said fiercely, turning his face away.

"He must stay quiet. Keep him from thrashing, Sir Polquin."

"Damne, man, I'm trying."

Dain frowned. Was Sir Polquin here? Then he must be

safe. He stopped his weak struggles, wishing the light were stronger. "Why is it so dark?" he asked. "I do not like this dark."

Someone apart from the others groaned in despair. "Merciful Thod, do not let him die."

Dain tried to tell them to make the fire bigger, for he was perishing of cold, but the darkness swallowed him again.

Several times thereafter he dreamed and awoke, dreamed and awoke, until present friends and those of his past blended together and he knew not where he was, or with whom. Sometimes Lord Odfrey sat beside him. Sometimes it was Thia's voice he heard. Singing in her pure, clear voice, she smiled at him tenderly with her sister's love and kissed his cheek. "Be brave, my little brother," she whispered. "There is much for you to do."

He smiled back, glad to see her again. "I've missed you. Where—"

But then Jorb's voice, gruff and cursing in the dwarf tongue, called him, scolding all the while about the work Dain had left undone. Angrily, Dain started to shout back.

"Be still," a sweet and unfamiliar voice said to him.

Dain turned his head away and saw a vision floating over his bed. He shivered, thinking it was Tobeszijian returning to him, but instead there was only a golden light and a presence without form or face. He heard song more beautiful than anything Thia had ever sung to him, the notes pouring over him like healing waters.

Lying back, he felt himself relaxing and growing warm. Dim memories floated through his mind, memories of when he was small and helpless, memories of being comforted against her warmth and love, memories of the songs she used to sing to him in a voice soft and lovely. Those songs had been of life and strength and growing and love. Now, she sang to him of life and strength and healing.

Smiling, and feeling safe with her nearby, he slept.

• • •

"You're awake!" Thum stared at Dain with his hazel-green eyes wide. The bundle he held fell to the floor. "Sulein!" he called. "Master Sulein!"

"I don't want him," Dain said with a frown. He was lying in bed with his head and shoulders propped high on soft pillows. Sunlight streamed in through a window, and a hearty fire crackled and hissed busily on the hearth. Confused, he thought of his dream and looked beneath the covers, but the Chalice was not in bed with him. Ah, of course, he thought, it could not be that easy. Still, disappointment sharpened his voice. "Is it morning already? Have I missed breakfast?"

"Aye," Thum said, with a catch in his voice. "You've missed several. Oh, Dain, it's good to see you better. I thought you would die."

Dain frowned in puzzlement. "Why? I took a scratch from Gavril's dagger, nothing more."

"Nothing more!" Thum echoed in astonishment. "Why, you—"

"Here, here, what is all this noise?" Sulein said, hurrying into the room. Clad in his long brown robes and missing his hat, he shooed Thum back and smiled down at Dain. "So you are awake at last. This is good. Thum, go and tell the others, but do not let them all come crowding inside. I wish to make an examination first."

"Yes, Master Sulein." Sounding breathless, Thum gave Dain a grin and hurried out.

Sulein peered into Dain's eyes, listened to his breathing, and changed the bandages of his wounds. His hands were gentle and skilled, and for once Dain felt grateful for the man's care.

"Lady Pheresa," he said, wincing, "is she—"

"Fret not," Sulein said. "She lives, and that is enough. You must rest and regain your strength."

"From two dagger cuts?" Dain said in scorn. "You make too much of them. I—" He started to sit upright, and found himself too weak to do it. Alarmed, he frowned at the physician. "What ails me?"

Sulein finished tying off the bandage on Dain's ribs and rearranged his sleeping robe. Pulling the covers back up to Dain's chest, he paused and met Dain's eyes. His own dark ones were very serious. "Your majesty nearly bled to death. The wrist gave us much trouble in stopping the bleeding, and your dark clothing concealed your other wound until it was almost too late. You must learn to tell your companions of your injuries. I realize it is the eldin way to seek no help for hurts and ailments, but this you must overcome."

Dain frowned, staring at the heavy bandage encircling his forearm.

"In addition, it was believed at first that you had also taken the poison. The cup was half empty before the lady drank from it."

"No," Dain said impatiently. "I spilled it in the crowd."

"Ah, yes. A simple explanation for what has been a great puzzlement. The king was determined to put you in the care of his own physicians, which would never do." Sulein raised his brows at Dain. "Would it, your majesty?"

"Stop calling me that," Dain said in irritation. "No, it would not do. Thank you for your help, Sulein. It seems I owe you much."

The physician smiled and inclined his head in acknowledgment before rubbing his hands briskly together. "Not as much as soon you will owe me."

Dain ignored the remark. "It's eldin poison."

"I know."

"How?"

Sulein smiled modestly. "I tested the stains on your sleeve and found the dose a lethal one. You are fortunate you did not drink it."

"But Pheresa . . . she's not eldin. It shouldn't affect her the same."

"It has not," Sulein replied. "The poison is acting very slowly on her system, which is fortunate, because the court physicians are fools and took far too long to discern the problem." He frowned. "They would not permit me to be of assistance, though I have had more experience in such exotic illnesses than they."

Dain sat up, wincing and holding his side.

Sulein gripped his shoulders and shook his head. "You must not get up. You are too weak."

"But this is ridiculous," Dain said in frustration. "She's the one who needs tending, not I! She—"

"They are taking good care of her now," Sulein said. "Do not fret."

"But is she all right? Is she recovering?"

"Lie down. Please."

Dain saw that Sulein was not going to answer his questions until he cooperated. Sighing, he allowed himself to sink back onto his pillows.

"Good. Now, it would be wise if you rested a while—"

"Sulein, tell me!"

"If you insist. She is very ill." Sulein held up his hand to forestall Dain's questions. "The action of the poison has been halted, yes, yes. But the lady cannot stay indefinitely in such a state of suspension. A cure must be found for her."

"What kind of cure?" Dain whispered, feeling cold to his marrow.

"Rest now. You are tired."

Dain glared at him. "What kind of cure? Why will you not tell me all?"

Sulein sighed and spread out his hands in a shrug. "What cure exists for eldin poison? Perhaps the eld folk know. I do not. The physicians here do not. The inevitable has been delayed for a few weeks at the most. It is a respite for her, yes. But the priests here are far too optimistic about her chances of recovery. They think she has much time, but it is not so. If something is not done very, very soon, the lady will die."

Grief jolted Dain. "No!" he whispered.

Sulein placed his hand on his heart and bowed. "I am very sorry."

•   •   •

By evening, Dain was able to eat his supper of broth and bread without assistance. As the tray was cleared away, Thum came in with an eager face, carrying a gaming board.

"They say you're feeling better. I thought you might like a game of tables."

Dain agreed without much interest, and Thum set up the pieces on his bed.

"It's marvelous news, Dain—um, I mean, your majesty. I never dreamed that you were really a king. If you could have seen Sir Terent's face . . . A feather would have knocked him over."

Deep within his own thoughts and worry, Dain finally began to pay attention to Thum's chatter. "What are you saying?"

Thum froze with a playing piece in his hand. His freckled face turned red, and he gulped. "Your majesty, if I've said something I shouldn't, I beg your pardon."

"Aye, you have!" Dain shoved the pieces off the bed so that they went flying in all directions. "What is Sulein doing, telling you such—"

"Stop!" Thum said, preventing him from getting up. "You must stay in bed. You're too weak."

Dain shoved Thum's hands away, then winced and gripped the side of the bed to keep himself from falling over. A wave of weakness washed through his legs, making them tremble. Clenching his fists, he tried to will some strength into his body. "Damne," he whispered.

Thum ran to the door. "Sir Terent!" he called. "Help me."

The protector came bursting into Dain's bedchamber, his face red with alarm. He was in time to catch Dain as he attempted to stand.

"Nay, sire," he said, his strong arms steadying Dain. "Your knees won't hold you yet. Better lie back now. Easy. We don't want those wounds to reopen."

Furious and too weak to do anything about it, Dain was forced back into bed. He lay there with his eyes half-closed, shivering and wretched. "I must get up," he said. "I have things to do."

"They'll wait, majesty."

"Stop calling me that!" Dain snapped. He glared at both Thum and Sir Terent. "Sulein . . . Whatever he has told you, it's—"

"'Tis King Verence who announced your true identity, sire." Sir Terent gave Dain a proud, if crooked, smile. "Aye, I always had a feeling you were made for great things. But you being a king . . . well, now, I never dreamed of that."

"Verence told you," Dain said blankly. He frowned. "But why?"

"It's true, isn't it?" Thum said with excitement. "Morde a day, what a secret to have. And us banging about, cursing and roughing with you, without any idea."

"Aye," Sir Terent said. "You've shown the patience of Tomias, sire, putting up with all of us as you have. 'Course, had we known, we wouldn't have—"

"You weren't supposed to know," Dain said, draping his arm across his eyes. "Why did the king tell you this?"

"He told everyone," Thum said. "The whole court knows, and you should see the talk. The ambassadors from Nether have been pestering us for days, trying to gain audience with you."

"Thod's bones!" Dain cried in exasperation. "Whatever for?"

"But, Dain—I mean, your majesty—if you're the rightful king of Nether, then why wouldn't they want to see you?"

Dain opened his mouth, then closed it again. This was too tangled for explanation, and he remained confused about Verence's motives. "I am exposed to my enemies now, and in small position to protect myself."

"Aye," Sir Terent said, nodding. "'Tis what the king himself said. This attempt on your life has all to do with that. A pity about the lady getting harmed by it."

"I don't understand," Dain said. "Why would he tell?

What had he to gain? Why insist that I—ah, this makes no sense at all."

Thum and Sir Terent exchanged worried glances. Edging closer, Thum gripped Dain's shoulder. "Don't fret yourself now. You're to rest, and we've upset you too much."

Dain glared at him. "Tell me the whole of it. Tell me all that you know."

Frowning, Thum stubbornly said nothing.

"Then I won't rest," Dain threatened. "I'll get out of this bed somehow, and I'll—"

"Morde a day, as hard to handle as ever," Sir Terent said with a sigh. "He'll do what he says, Thum lad. He'll fret himself to tatters."

Thum rolled his eyes, but gave in. "Well, it's this way. The prince was making all kinds of accusations against you. We didn't know the truth of what happened, not being there, but others saw you fighting him. You know the penalties against it. You've been through that before."

"Gavril made her cry," Dain said grimly. "I would attack him again, with no regret for the punishment afterward."

"But would you let yourself be executed for it?" Thum asked.

Dain scowled, pleating the covers with his fingers. All he knew was the rage in his heart at seeing Pheresa made so unhappy.

"The king saved your life," Thum said. "In telling who you really are, he made it clear that you rank higher than Gavril. As such, it is Gavril who must apologize to you for provoking the fight."

Understanding dawned inside Dain. He marveled at King Verence's goodness in saving him. It would have been easy for the king to remain silent and leave Dain to his doom. Now the secret was out, and political fortunes would have to change, no matter how much Verence might want to keep them the same.

Thum laughed. "Aye, the prince must beg your pardon. I'd pay coin to witness that."

"I don't want his apology," Dain said in anger. "If he'd let Pheresa be, none of this would have happened. She'd be safe."

"That can't be helped now," Sir Terent said in a gentle voice. "Ease yourself, for what happened is done. There's no going back and undoing it."

"Think of this," Thum said in concern. "What if you hadn't rushed out there and fought the prince? What if you'd drunk the poison as you were meant to? You'd—you'd be dead now."

A chill passed through Dain as he thought of it. Someone had known his secret all along. He thought of how Verence had said anyone who knew King Tobeszijian would recognize Dain as his son. Believing he could remain incognito at the Mandrian court was futile. The Netheran assassin had lost no time. And undoubtedly another attempt would be made soon, and another, and another.

Anger drove out his momentary self-pity. It was no good keeping secrets and living a life of caution. He might as well be bold and accept his destiny. Verence had been wrong to try to keep him from it, and Dain had been even more at fault for trying to comply with the king's wishes.

Gazing up at his friends, Dain thought of how good and loyal they were. He was grateful to have them with him. Choking up, he gripped Sir Terent's hand. "Thank you for good service, my friend. I'm not—I can't be your chevard and a king too."

"Now there, sire. No need to sort it all out just now," Sir Terent said hoarsely, his eyes shining bright. "Why, I'll follow you no matter what title you wear. Aye, and so will all our knights at Thirst. Have no fear of that."

Sharp regret made Dain smile crookedly. "I gave Verence my word I would not take Thirst into Nether's battles."

"Bless you, sire, but you haven't asked your men. 'Tis to you, their chevard, that they make their pledge, not to his majesty."

A lump filled Dain's throat. He could not speak.

"When do we ride?" Thum asked excitedly. "Your own kingdom! Dain, it's like a minstrel's tale, only better. Why, the—"

"I'm king of nothing while my uncle holds the throne."

"That won't be for long," Thum boasted, smacking his fist into his palm. "When your people hear you're on the march, they'll rise up against their tyrant."

Dain thought of what his father had told him in the dream, and his heartbeat quickened. "Aye," he said softly. "I must go there, and soon."

"You'll fight no war during winter," Sir Terent said in a practical voice. "Come spring, you'll have supplies and men gathered—"

"No," Dain said. "We are going there now."

Thum's eyes widened, and Sir Terent's cheeks bulged.

"Nay," the protector said sharply. "Rushing in afore you're ready . . . why, 'tis folly."

"I go there now not to fight," Dain said, "but to save Lady Pheresa."

"How?"

"The eld folk are best found in Nether," Dain said. "They will know the cure for this poison. And also . . . the Chalice may be hidden there. If it can be found . . . if she can drink from it . . . she will be cured."

Sir Terent sighed. "You might as well wish for the stars to come down to your hand as have hope of finding where it's hidden."

"Nay!" Thum said with fervor. His green eyes blazed at Dain. "The legends say that Tobeszijian hid the Chalice in some special place. And if you're his son, then you were with him when he did this. You *know* where the Chalice is!"

"Indeed you must!" Gavril's voice said, breaking into their conversation.

Startled, Dain lifted his head and tried to sit up, only to be gently held in place by Sir Terent's hand on his shoulder.

Accompanied only by his silent protector, Gavril walked

into the room with an arrogant swing of his cloak. He held his gloves in one hand, and his cap was tilted rakishly on his blond hair. His dark blue eyes, steely and hostile in contrast to his smile, held Dain's.

"May I enter?" he asked, giving Dain a mocking little bow. "Or is your . . . majesty too ill as yet to receive guests?"

"He's ill," Sir Terent said gruffly, and stepped forward as though to keep Gavril from coming closer.

With a smile, the prince positioned himself at the foot of Dain's bed. "King Faldain," he said. "Well, well, well. You *are* a source of eternal surprises. And now it seems that you know where the Chalice is, and have known it all along."

"I haven't said that," Dain replied.

"There are many things you haven't said, King of Secrets. One might believe it discourteous to live incognito for so long, especially among one's peers. However, we will discuss that later. At present, I am here to ask your pardon for wounding you so grievously." Gavril's smile grew forced. "Although you did attack me without provocation, my response was . . . excessive. There." He lifted his chin as resentment flashed in his eyes. "I have said it, and said it prettily. Don't you agree? Have I your pardon?"

"Yes."

Gavril inclined his head. "Thank you."

He turned to go, but Dain leaned forward. "Wait. Lady Pheresa must go to Nether, if she is to get well."

"Oh, must she? Why is that, when our priests and physicians think she should stay where she is?"

"She will die here," Dain said in concern. "I have heard she is safe for the moment, but that the poison will continue to work inside her."

Gavril's fist tightened on his gloves, and his false smile vanished altogether. "She is hardly safe. Come and see her. Come and see what they've done to her."

Dain pushed off the bedcovers, but Sir Terent again held him in place. "Not now," he said firmly. "Your majesty is not well enough."

"But—"

"When you can, then," Gavril said angrily. His gaze went to Dain and flicked away. He seemed anxious to hear about how Dain could help, yet unwilling to listen. "Come to her, when you can, and see what has been wrought because of you."

Two days later, when Sulein finally, reluctantly allowed Dain to leave his bed, he walked through the palace, flanked by Sir Terent and Sir Polquin. His progress was a slow one, for the courtiers came flocking out of curiosity. Dain found it strange to see them bowing and curtsying to him. The exiled nobles of Nether clung to him with sobs of great emotion. Gravely, his manner stiff and rather shy, he nodded in return but paused to speak to no one. Those who tried to insist were held back by Sir Terent.

"Please, m'lords, let him pass. He goes to the chapel. Let him pass."

"Ah, your prayers, majesty," one of the Netherans said in a heavily accented voice. He spoke further in Netheran, but Dain did not understand.

The chamberlain came to Dain's rescue, pushing his way through the crowd of exiles trying to kiss Dain's feet. "Clear the way for his majesty," the man boomed. "Prince Spirin, bid your people let him pass."

Slowly, they parted before Dain. Many were elderly, their withered and lined faces weeping openly with such joy and renewed hope it made him pity them. They acted like he had saved their country already. Their hands, reaching out to touch him as he walked past, felt like ghostly fingers plucking at his cloak. Their voices, thin and foreign, called out, "Faldain! Faldain!"

Escaping at last, Dain crossed the courtyard to the small chapel where Lady Pheresa rested. It was a bleak, cloudy day, gusty with a damp wind that blew under the eaves of the palace and tossed leaves across the courtyard and walkways.

Where guards stood outside the chapel door, dozens of

flowers and tokens from well-wishers littered the ground. A
servant in Verence's livery waited there.

He bowed to Dain. "It is good to see your majesty in
better health. Come inside. The king and his highness are
here to pay their daily visit. I am to take you in at once."

Dain's legs were weak with exhaustion, and as he wrapped
himself tighter inside his cloak to ward off the cold wind,
he resisted the temptation to rest on one of the benches.
Now was not the time to think about himself. He had been
wracking his brain for solutions, trying to unlock the puz-
zle of Tobeszijian's words, and he wanted to lay his plan
before King Verence.

"Are you ready to enter, majesty?" the servant asked.

Nodding in silence, Dain ignored Sir Terent's sharp look
of concern.

They walked into the dim, incense-laden interior of the
chapel. It was all carving and gilt, the dark woods absorbing most of the light from flickering candles.

At first the numerous men inside the chapel confused
Dain, but then he realized these were not courtiers. Lady
Pheresa lay on her back with her pale slender hands crossed
over her midriff. Still clad in the blue dress with ermine
trim, she looked asleep inside an encasement of glass. Her
beauty, if anything, seemed more radiant than ever, yet there
was something unnatural about her stillness. For one horrified moment Dain thought her dead, yet just then her eyes
opened, fluttered, and closed.

Horrified to see her like this, he drew in a shaky breath.

In a semicircle around her stood thirteen priests, silent
and motionless. Their cowled heads were bowed. Dain felt
a powerful force exerting itself from each of the men. The
skin on his arms crawled, and his heart began to beat faster.

At first he thought it a holding spell, but then he realized
it was something else, something far different. Not really
magic at all, but instead a field of faith woven and rewo-
ven around her, keeping her from death, but unable to bring
her wholly back to life.

Verence and Gavril were at the foot of her encasement. The king's head was bowed in prayer. Gavril, however, stood gazing at Pheresa, with one clenched fist resting atop the glass.

The servant escorting Dain and his companions paused a moment in respect, then cleared his throat softly.

A priest in white robes came from the shadows to intercept them. However, as soon as he saw Dain, he bowed low and retreated without further protest.

Dain walked slowly forward, and by the time he entered the candlelight which shone upon her, Verence had straightened and turned around to face him.

"Faldain," he said in greeting. His eyes held grief, and his voice was deep with emotion. "It is good to see you well and whole again."

Dain inclined his head. "Your majesty's concern honors me."

Gavril swung around impatiently. "Let us be done with these useless courtesies. Dain says he has a plan to save her, sire. Let him tell it to you."

Verence frowned, and his gaze penetrated even deeper into Dain. "What is being done here comes at great personal and spiritual cost to these thirteen men." He gestured at the priests. "That it took this many to arrest the poison's progress indicates its potency." His frown deepened. "It would have killed you in an instant."

"Aye," Dain agreed. Never again would he be able to eat or drink without wondering if death waited in his next mouthful. "I must take her to Nether."

"No," Verence said.

Gavril gripped his father's arm. "Listen to what he has to say."

"No!" Pulling free, the king gestured refusal. "I will permit no such undertaking. We discussed this before, Faldain."

"Aye, but the circumstances were different then," Dain said. "I go not for myself but for the lady."

"Come, come. You may possibly believe that, but I do

not. This is folly, and you are asking me to permit you to ride into Nether at the head of a Mandrian army."

"Oh, Tomias above!" Gavril interrupted. "What does this matter? If he can help Pheresa, let him."

"Since it is eldin poison," Dain said to the king, "the eld folk will know how to stop it. And they are best found in Nether."

"I shall send word to them."

Dain shook his head. "They cannot be reached that way. Also, why would any of the eld folk come to this land which accepts them not?"

The king sighed. "Your enemies have already struck at you here. How will you survive in Nether?"

"She matters now," Dain said. "Send word to Muncel, asking his leave for the lady and her companions to travel through his realm. Say nothing about me. Officially I will stay here under your majesty's protection. But *unofficially* I shall go as a guide to find my mother's people."

"How can you refuse?" Gavril demanded. "She is my betrothed. I will go with her to protect her safety."

The king looked from one to the other of them with worry furrowing his brow. "I like this not," he said. "There is too much danger."

"Father, you have only to finish the terms of the new treaty," Gavril said impatiently. "Then Nether will be again our ally, and what better way to seal the agreement than by allowing me to take my bride on this quest?"

"And if Nether turns in treachery?" Verence asked. "I could lose you and Pheresa both."

Gavril shrugged. "She is lost already if she remains here. Dain has said so."

The king looked sharply at him. "Is this true? Noncire assures me that she can be supported for years—"

"And what kind of life is this?" Gavril asked, tapping the glass with his knuckles. "Can she be wife to me? Can she be companion and consort? I would rather have her dead than lie here like this forever!"

The king gripped his shoulder, and father and son bowed their heads in mutual anguish.

Dain watched them, his own suffering and love for the lady hidden in his heart. It felt odd to be in agreement with Gavril. Hearing his announcements of love and concern for the lady drove splinters of jealousy through Dain's entrails, but he forced himself to ignore them. Although she did not love him, he could not turn his back on her now.

"She has only a few months like this, majesty," he said quietly. "Weeks perhaps. Not years. This kind of spell is unfamiliar to me—"

"It isn't a spell," the king said sharply.

Dain shrugged. "Whatever it is, it is weak, and will not hold."

"The priests have assured me—"

"Majesty," Dain dared interrupt, "the source of this poison is darkness, not some plant extract. It has been brewed from malice and evil. Your priests cannot hold it indefinitely. They have not the strength."

The king swung his gaze to Gavril, who said, "These objections only delay us. He thinks he can find the Chalice there. If he can, it will cure her. We must take the chance. I am willing, as is Dain. Let us go."

The king stared at Dain for a long while, then glanced at Pheresa. "I do not believe this quest has a chance of success, certainly not with winter coming. Nether is a cold and dangerous land, rife with Nonkind and Thod knows what. The guardian priests can keep her alive until spring. Wait that long. You cannot go to the far north now."

"The only certainty we have is her death if we remain here," Dain told him. "The autumn snows will not be deep. If our journey is swift and meets with success, we may be able to evade the worst of winter."

"Thod! Do you have an answer for every objection?"

Dain made no answer as the king paced back and forth. Finally his majesty threw up his hands. "Very well. But, Faldain, it is my son who will be in command. You must conceal yourself. I fear you will be taken if your presence becomes known."

"Agreed," Dain said. He glanced at Gavril, but the prince's frowning gaze remained on Pheresa. Dain looked back at the king. "All care must be taken with the pretense that I remain here. My recent illness is a perfect ruse. The chamberlain has only to announce that I continue to be unwell, that I am recovering less quickly than was hoped and must stay confined to my apartments."

"You have been seen by many today, hale enough to come here."

Dain smiled. "I am about to suffer a relapse."

"Ah. Clever." The king smiled back, but only briefly. "I can play my part, sending queries to your servants every day about your health. But in truth, Faldain, are you indeed recovered enough for such a journey as this?"

"We must go slowly for her sake," Dain said. "That will serve me as well."

"We'll go by boat," Gavril announced. "As far as the Charva can take us. Then we'll load the lady on a wagon and journey overland with all care."

The king looked at his eager son. "And you, Gavril? Can you put aside your enmity for Faldain during this journey? Can the two of you stay together, allies for this purpose, without quarreling or fighting each other with the intent of harm?"

"If he can lead us to the Chalice, and cure her," Gavril said, "I shall endure his company gladly."

The king's gaze shifted to Dain, who replied, "I give your majesty my word of honor."

"Mind this well, Faldain. The army I send is not for your purposes."

Dain bowed in silence, but inside he was thinking of what his father had told him in the dream: *Be king, and the army will come to you.* Rubbing his arms under his cloak, he shivered.

Verence was still talking: "You will also take personal

guards, priests, these guardians of her life, and my own physicians. If Nonkind attack you—"

"I'll be able to defend us with Tanengard," Gavril said with shining eyes.

"No!"

"Father, it is the best means of ensuring our safety. Dain will agree."

"I forbid it," Verence said. "Not even to save Pheresa will I allow you to condemn your soul."

"But Dain has silenced its powers," Gavril said. "It cannot harm me now. Its powers will awaken only against Nonkind. Would you have us slain when we could be protected?"

The king shook his head. "This is the gravest folly. I retract my permission. You will not go, Gavril. It is far too dangerous. I will not risk your life in that barbarous place."

"I am going!" Gavril shouted. "I must go! It is my duty."

"Gavril—"

"No! Am I to turn my back on her, when she needs me most?" Gavril demanded. "Could any subject respect me after that? Could *she*? No, Father, I must do this." Pursing his mouth in frustration, he gestured at Dain. "Let *him* carry Tanengard if you do not trust me. He can make it slay Nonkind. Its powers do not endanger his soul."

"I will guard the sword, majesty," the soft, velvety tones of Noncire announced.

Dain turned and saw the fat cardinal approaching from the shadowy front of the chapel. With distrust, Dain wondered if he'd been hiding there all this time, listening to them.

"I feel it my duty to accompany these young people on their quest," Noncire said. "Someone of authority must minister to the guardians. My guidance will strengthen them all."

The king raised his brows. "Are you saying you approve of this foolhardy quest, cardinal?"

"It is dangerous, with much risk, but surely Tomias would approve a quest to recover the lost Chalice. In seeking to save the lady's life, both these young men show their valor and worthiness."

Gavril clapped his hands. "Then it's settled. We're going at first light."

Verence winced. "Hardly that quickly. It will take time to—"

"Father, every minute shortens her life. Let the dispatch riders go ahead. We can meet our army at Tuisons, where we'll leave the boats. Church soldiers are my recommendation. You don't want to weaken the holds by drawing on their forces for this purpose."

"It seems you have everything planned," the king said helplessly. "What if Nether refuses my request for your passage?"

"Then let them turn us back at their border, at their peril," Gavril said darkly.

Verence turned to Dain, who was frowning. "And you, Faldain? You have grown silent. What have you to say about these arrangements?"

Dain cared little how Gavril organized their party. He knew all too well that the prince would seize the first opportunity he could to betray Dain to the Netherans. All Gavril wanted was the Chalice. Even Pheresa's recovery meant little to him next to the chance to get his hands on the sacred vessel. But Dain had been warned by Tobeszijian, and he would remain on his guard. There was only one last detail to mention.

Meeting the king's gaze, Dain said quietly, "Several days ago, I made you a promise that I would take no Thirst knights across the border."

Behind him, both Sir Terent and Sir Polquin stirred. The king noticed, although he did not shift his gaze from Dain. "Yes?"

"These men," Dain continued, "wish to accompany me. I will not take them without your leave."

The king was silent a long while, but the light of respect filled his eyes. "Do you mean to return to Mandria?"

"My path lies elsewhere," Dain replied. "I thought I could change that, but I must follow my destiny."

Verence nodded. "My leave is given. These men may serve you as they wish, wherever you go."

As Sir Terent and Sir Polquin bowed, the king extended his hand to Dain. "Thod speed you on this journey. It is not what I wanted for any of you, but fate has decreed otherwise. That you would think of this maiden's life first, before your own throne, speaks highly of your character. I wish you well in all that you do. Furthermore, I do herewith release you from all the promises and oaths I have asked of you in the past. Go with Thod, Faldain. Seize your throne with both hands, if you can."

Choking, Dain bowed low. "My father told me you would be ever a friend," he said, his eyes brimming with gratitude. "I thank your majesty for all you have done and taught me."

The king's eyes grew moist. Compressing his mouth, he nodded curtly.

Gavril stepped forward. "Now then, Dain. Whatever preparations you need to make, see that you get them done quickly and in secret. We'll leave at dawn."

He still spoke to Dain as a master would to his servant. And although others frowned at his tone, Dain made no objection.

Instead, he walked over to where Pheresa lay sleeping in her spell, neither of this world now, nor of the next. Her lashes lay in a dark ring upon her cheeks. Her rosy lips were parted slightly, and her breath misted on the glass.

He pressed his hand against the cold surface of the encasement and closed his eyes a moment. Whatever lay ahead, he would do all he could to save her. That, he vowed from the depths of his heart.

After a moment he straightened, blinking against a little wave of dizziness, and strode out of the chapel. Dusk had fallen outside in the courtyard, and the wind blew sharp and cold. His nostrils drew in the scents, and already he seemed to find the north calling to him. Calling him homeward.